THE LOVES OF RUBY DEE

"Beautiful and touching . . . A wonderfully crafted and thoroughly heartwarming tale . . . This is a book guaranteed to touch your heart."
Romantic Times

"A superb story . . . one that will stay with you, in your heart and in your mind, for a long time to come."
Rendezvous

"Ruby Dee is so sweet, so loving, so wise that you know she'll get it right in the end, and you'll stay with her all the way."
Detroit Free Press

LOVE IN A SMALL TOWN

"A must read for all women."
Rendezvous

"*Love in a Small Town* reminds us all that there can be more love wrapped up in a tire change and a quart of oil than in a whole bushel of long-stemmed roses . . . Come along for the ride. It's a wonderful trip."
The Romance Reader (on-line)

Other Avon Contemporary Romances by
Curtiss Ann Matlock

LOVE IN A SMALL TOWN
THE LOVES OF RUBY DEE

CURTISS ANN MATLOCK

IF WISHES WERE HORSES

AVON BOOKS ◆ NEW YORK

This is a work of fiction. Names, characters, places, and incidents either are the product of the author's imagination or are used fictitiously. Any resemblance to actual events, locales, organizations, or persons, living or dead, is entirely coincidental and beyond the intent of either the author or the publisher.

AVON BOOKS
A division of
The Hearst Corporation
1350 Avenue of the Americas
New York, New York 10019

Copyright © 1998 by Curtiss Ann Matlock
Inside cover author photo by James D. Matlock
Published by arrangement with the author
Visit our website at http://www.AvonBooks.com
Library of Congress Catalog Card Number: 97-94314
ISBN: 0-380-79344-X

First Avon Books Printing: March 1998

AVON TRADEMARK REG. U.S. PAT. OFF. AND IN OTHER COUNTRIES, MARCA REGISTRADA, HECHO EN U.S.A.

Printed in the U.S.A.

WCD   10   9   8   7   6   5   4   3   2   1

Never, ever give up. A little money helps, but what really gets you through is to never, under any circumstances, face the facts.

Ruth Gordon

I

The Wish Chasers

One

Etta spent the three days following her husband's death in the guest-room bed with the covers pulled over her head, blocking out light and sound and trying desperately to block out thought. It was not so much her husband dying in another woman's bed that had sent her into shock, but his dying at all. Roy had been only thirty-five years old, and while he had been in many a woman's bed, he had never died on her before.

A weak heart, the doctor said, one of those strange flukes, like the Pettijohn boy who had dropped dead of a blood clot in the brain as he was throwing the winning hoop shot during the season playoffs. Etta found this image further disturbing.

She kept lapsing into self-blame, thinking that she should have seen signs of Roy's weakening heart. Lately there had been several afternoons when he looked pale, went to bed and slept for a day, but he always awakened and reached for her, saying, "Come here and make me feel like a man." A man who made love as Roy Rivers did surely could not have too bad a heart. (Latrice said it was this prowess that kept him alive until it killed him.)

Even now, after all, Etta could not stop herself from lowering the patchwork quilt and listening, expecting to hear the front door open and Roy's voice call out like he always did, no matter how many days he'd been away or whom he'd been with, "Darlin', I'm home!" And she'd go, and there he'd be, hat in his hand, fair hair falling over his forehead, his lips grinning that sheepish grin, while his green eyes pleaded with such a fearful, desperate need that never failed to melt her angry heart.

Roy's voice did not call out, although a number of other voices did, voices coming to get their due. The saying was, "You can't take it with you," but it began to appear that Roy had done just that. At least he was gone, and everything appeared to be going right with him.

A man from the Oklahoma City auto dealer came and repossessed the new gleaming white Cadillac, for which Roy still owed the first payment. A woman from the electric company called, saying their electricity was in danger of being shut off and hadn't they had the notice. Lot Jones, the John Deere tractor dealer, came and took the brand new humongous Deere Roy had bought last fall, and then Harry Flagg showed up to take away the remaining horses.

Harry arrived early on the morning of the funeral. Etta had at last gotten out of bed, pretty much poked and prodded out by Latrice, and was in the bathroom, dreaming of coffee and returning to bed.

Naked, holding a towel to her breast, she hurriedly wiped a circle on the steamy window and peered out to see Harry's big black two-ton truck pulling a wooden stock trailer, easing over the potholes. Harry's arm encased in an old army coat sleeve hung out the window, as was his habit.

Etta stared for a long moment at Harry's truck. *No . . . no . . . no!*

Tossing aside the towel, she snatched up her flowered satin robe. Opening the door before she even began slipping into the robe, she ran from the moist warmth of the bathroom into the crisp coolness of the hallway. Because she was in too much of a hurry to tie the robe, it went flying out behind her she raced, bare feet pounding down the cold oak stairs and through the rooms to the back door. She did not race smoothly, as she was nearly six months pregnant and somewhat unbalanced by her growing belly.

In the kitchen Latrice had the radio volume turned up, listening to "*The Morning Hour of Prayer*, brought to you by Bright and White Grocery and Wayman's House of Furniture."

When Etta burst through the swinging door, Latrice whirled from the counter, eyes wide and mouth popping open. Etta took no time to speak. She tugged on her old brown cowboy boots setting at the back door, hopping and stuffing and opening the door at the same time, while Latrice cried, "Cover yourself!"

Etta tied the robe but it slipped, and she clutched the folds of it around her body while trying to hold her belly, too, as she went racing out across the yard beneath the tall, winter-bare elms. The first fresh air she'd had in three days seared her lungs. Without socks, her feet slid around inside the stiff boots.

"What are you doin', Harry?" she cried breathlessly.

"I'm afraid I've come for my stock, Etta. Like I told Latrice yesterday. I figured she told you." He cast her a quick, somewhat shocked glance and then averted his gaze and headed on toward the barn. He was a big man with a long stride. Etta went beside him like a panting little puppy.

"I'll get the money, Harry."

She shook from emotion and from it being only thirty-five degrees. The satin was like ice on her skin. She gripped the folds tightly with her fists and pressed her elbows against her sides and gazed up at the giant man. Harry's head, with his closely shaved flat-top, resembled an egg with two pinpoints of eyes almost lost in the flesh. His head swiveled, and he gave her another quick perusal, and she saw his pity and discomfort. She thought that she had to play on that.

"I'll pay you, I promise I will. I just need a little time to get things straight . . . see exactly what I have. I really haven't been up to that, Harry."

After a moment, frowning, he said, "I know you'd pay me if you could, Etta, but where are you gonna get that kind of money?"

Her heart thumped in her chest. "I don't know right now, but I'm sure I can get it. I'm going to go over the assets with Leon tomorrow or the next day." She reached up to brush her hair from her eyes. Seeing Harry's eyes widen and realizing her robe was hanging open dangerously, she clutched it together again. "Right now I'm a little busy, you know. The funeral is in a couple of hours."

Harry did have the decency to look a bit embarrassed about coming before the funeral. But he still said, "I need my money, Etta. I got business problems of my own, and Roy should have paid me six months ago. As it is, I heard he went and sold a top mare out of here three weeks ago. That's one hell of a mess. Now, I got the papers showing the lien on this stock, and I got a buyer lined up waitin' for 'em. There's nothin' else I can do, Etta."

Turning from her, he motioned to his two Mexican hands, who were hanging back by the big truck and staring at Etta, Mrs. Roy J. Rivers, clearly naked and pregnant beneath the thin robe. At Harry's command, they turned their attention to the stables.

Etta clumped beside Harry, who was once more picking up his pace as he entered the barn. "Roy isn't even in the ground yet, Harry. I tell you I'll get the money. If nothin' else, I have jewelry I can sell."

"Roy leave you with that much jewelry?" he asked absently, his attention on checking the horse stalls, peering over the thick wooden walls.

"I've got these." Etta held up her wedding rings, hoping to shame him, although it occurred to her the rings wouldn't come up to being worth what was owed Harry, who barely spared a glance at them.

She said, "I'll raise the money, Harry. Just give me some time." She thought she might cry . . . thought maybe it would help. But tears would not come. She had not yet been able to cry over Roy, either.

Harry shook his head. "You'd better hang on to those rings, Etta. You might be wantin' to think about what you're gonna be livin' on."

"I'll make out, Harry. I just don't want to lose these horses. I can't . . ."

Harry's small eyes came down and rested on her for a moment. The deep pity of his expression fell all over Etta and about burned her clean away. She felt herself shrinking into her cold robe.

"Let it go, Etta. You don't need these horses anyway. They ain't worth the ten thousand, but I'll let them settle the debt and we'll be even."

"I didn't borrow the money from you, Harry."

He slanted her a glance but didn't stop.

Etta fell to begging in earnest. "Harry, that mare and filly are my own. I pulled that filly and spent three nights with her."

The bay filly—Missy Bee—nickered at Etta as she was led past. Etta stretched out her hand and felt her heart going out her fingertips.

"Roy's name is on the papers as sole owner, Etta. I'm sorry."

Etta slowly followed the men out of the barn. She stood clutching her robe and pressing her elbows into her sides, watching as the men continued to empty the stalls and load the trailer. One gelding, three mares, and a yearling filly, the last of the horses from a stable that echoed of fine yesterdays, a few of them anyway.

As they were loaded into the trailer, the horses whinnied and knocked around on the rough plank flooring. All the commotion brought the three-year-old in the corral behind Etta rushing up to the fence and calling excitedly to his companions.

"I guess I'll leave that red gelding," Harry said, coming over to her after he'd slammed the tailgate closed. "He'd just be more trouble than he's worth to haul."

He took a deep breath, looked out at the horse, then back at Etta. "I'm real sorry, Etta . . . but I need the money, too."

Etta thought maybe she should say something like, "It's okay, Harry." He did have a family to think about, and he seemed to expect her to say something. She tried, she really did, but there suddenly seemed no words inside her. Nothing but a profound emptiness. All she managed to do was look at him very sorrowfully and then at Missy Bee nosing a crack in the wooden tailgate.

Harry walked away and got in the truck, slammed the door. Etta watched that rear gate shake and listened to the horses whinnying plaintively as the trailer rattled and creaked out of the yard and down the drive to the highway.

Left behind, the red gelding ran up and down the corral fence, calling out, frantic now, a heartrending sound that echoed in the cold air beneath the tall, leafless trees.

Etta turned and went to the fence, put a hand up to stroke his neck, murmuring, "Little Gus . . ." For an instant she put her face to his neck and his thick winter hair, inhaling the horse scent of him that she had always loved. Then, quivering, the horse jerked from her and ran to the corner, straining and looking off in the direction of the now disappeared trailer, as if he could still see and hear what Etta could not. She gazed at him, at his flying mane and tail and the burst of early morning sun glinting on his raggedy sorrel coat. Tears choked in her throat but wouldn't come out her eyes.

"Damn you for dyin', Roy Rivers," she said through clenched teeth.

"Leave that horse and get yourself in here," Latrice said from the back porch. "Come on, honey. There's nothin' more to be done out here. You'll just catch your death, and then I'll have to bury you both."

Drawn along by Latrice's command—Latrice did have a commanding way of speaking—Etta started for the house. The rising sun cast soft golden rays over it all—long and thick and solid, gray stucco on the bottom and brown shingles on the top, and colored glass in the staircase window. The porch at back wrapped around the side and stood there waiting to give shelter. Etta had always adored the house, but found it hard to look at in this moment. She found it a difficult reminder of her disappointments.

When she was almost to the porch, she caught the faint,

familiar aroma that caused her stomach to turn over. Pausing with her foot on the first step, she glanced at Latrice. Latrice looked back.

"Where is it?" Etta demanded.

She looked around Latrice's body and spied the black cord snaking out the kitchen window. It ran around the corner. Etta stalked past Latrice, peered around the corner, and beheld the offensive sight of the electric percolator sitting on the porch floor. She stared at the chrome pot, and then she flounced around and marched past Latrice and on into the house, letting the screened door bang. In the kitchen, the radio announcer was booming from the radio: "Now brothers and sisters, let's join in a hymn and dedicate it to the generous folks at Bright and White Grocery and Wayman's House of Furniture."

Latrice kept the radio loud so as not to miss one precious word of the daily sermon while she moved about the house. Latrice was devoted but mainly she didn't want to miss a chance to correct the preacher, an opportunity that seemed to come her way daily. Latrice had read and knew the Bible backwards and forwards, as she had most of Shakespeare, the Constitution, and much of William Faulkner, until his last novels, which she deemed unworthy. All of this literary intake made Latrice very hard to argue with; she could attack with some big, confusing words.

Etta, retying the belt of her robe, crossed the kitchen and banged through the swinging door into the dining room, passed the table that was loaded with funeral food—covered dishes, pies and cakes and breads that wouldn't spoil— and over to lift the lid on the big galvanized cooler sent over by the owner of the bottling plant—Drew Pierce, who'd been about Roy's best friend, both of them kind hearts and fast-living heartbreak men.

Etta plunged her hand down into the watery ice, pulled out a bottle of Royal Crown Cola, snapped the lid off on the opener, then hurried on through the living room, feeling her stomach coming up in her throat. She didn't realize she still wore her old boots until she caught the left one on a step and stumbled. She shook the boots off right there and left them on the stair, and raced on upward, bare feet smacking on the oak flooring, clutching the bottle of cola with one hand and her belly with the other. She raced down the hall, the entire time thinking that she absolutely would not throw up.

As she passed her and Roy's bedroom, she veered to the far side away from it, keeping her eyes straight ahead so as to not look in the doorway which Latrice made certain stayed wide open. Floating up after her from the living room came the chimes of the New Haven mantel clock—Roy's mother's beloved clock, calling out quarter past the hour and seeming to call it out as a threat, too.

Hearing it, Etta had the really wild and strange urge to go knock that clock flying and scream, *Who's gonna wind your mother's clock now, Roy?*

The clock would go for ten or twelve days on one winding, but Roy had wound it every Monday morning because that had been how his mother had done it. Roy doing that one thing so reliably seemed the strangest thing. Roy was not a reliable sort of man, which was not to say that he was never reliable but more saying don't count on him to be.

Then, sinking down on the side of the bed, pressing her arm tight over her midsection and a hand tight over her mouth, Etta rocked back and forth and thought: Roy *was* no longer and had become *had been*.

Two

In that moment, if anyone had asked Etta what she wanted most in the entire world, she would have said, "Coffee!"

She would have screamed it. She had lost her husband and was little by little losing all she possessed, and here she sat thinking she would just about kill for a cup of coffee. That struck her as obscene, if not on the verge of insanity.

Oh, Lordy, she thought, wiping the cool, moist RC bottle across her forehead.

Here she was, six months pregnant and still suffering morning sickness until noon. The mere aroma of coffee at dawn would send her rushing for the bathroom. The sound of her retching had so unnerved Roy that he took to driving down to Obie's cottage to enjoy his morning coffee. The fancy obstetrician prescribed a new wonder drug, but it didn't work. The obstetrician said it was all in Etta's mind, and she told him that it was there and in her stomach, too, and if he wanted to find out to please come over one morning and she would throw up last night's supper on him.

Latrice's footsteps broke into Etta's thoughts. Latrice wore thick, lace-up shoes with heels you could hear coming. She was a big woman, not fat, simply substantial with big bones and an hourglass shape, and she walked as if intent on planting her mark in the world.

She entered the room. "Here's some hot cola syrup, honey, and a piece of jelly bread." These were Latrice's anti-nausea potions. They did not cure but they did a sight more than the fancy doctor's medicine. These foods stayed down.

Twenty years ago Latrice had been a midwife, learning her skill as an assistant to her own mother. She had delivered babies, Negro, white, Indian, and a mixture, many of whom had been turned away from real doctors because of their race or inability to pay. Times changed and a worship of hospitals flourished, curtailing Latrice's practice, a fact she considered an outrageous waste of her talent.

Etta lifted the cold bottle of RC for Latrice's viewing.

"Give me that." Latrice snatched the bottle away. "You shouldn't be havin' cold stuff on your stomach."

"Well, you made yourself coffee," Etta accused, vaguely realizing the two statements did not at all relate.

"Yes, I did. I felt the need of sustenance. Now, here . . . drink this cola while it is hot so it will calm your stomach."

"It isn't coffee."

Etta had the urge to throw the cup across the room and was somewhat shocked at herself, for she had never done such a thing. Momentarily intrigued by the prospect, she wondered what such a burst of emotion would feel like. The next instant she thought about having to clean up the mess and simply felt too tired for it.

"Apparently," she said, casting Latrice a dark look from beneath her lashes, "I am quite alone in my sufferin'."

"No, you aren't, honey . . . we're all sufferin' right along with you, believe me," Latrice said smartly. Then she noticed Etta's hand shaking and guilt pricked her. Her mood was stretched thin; her quickly gulped cup of coffee had only made her crave more.

Sucking in a deep breath, Latrice lifted her shoulders and straightened her spine, pushing up her black lace–covered bosom. Beneath her floral cotton apron, she already wore her favorite black crape funeral dress, which she counted on to give her the proper attitude. She thought the best thing to do was to get Etta into her funeral clothes.

"Come on, honey. Let's get a look at you in this pretty dress," she said, pulling from the chiffarobe the black wool flannel dress Maisie Nation had whipped up in a day's time, there not being a single black dress in town to fit a skinny pregnant woman.

Latrice believed in funerals as much as she believed in regularly eating garlic paste. Funerals made people remember the good things such as fine china and high respect, and the value of being alive to enjoy both. And if asked, Latrice would openly admit to a certain enjoyment of funerals. There was the enjoyment of dressing and visiting and giving forth of emotion and most especially watching others give forth of emotion. She herself had been known to think: *Oh, I could use me a good funeral.* Although she was having to put up with a lot for Roy J. Rivers's funeral and felt she was not getting a sufficient return.

"It's a funeral dress," Etta said, looking dourly at the dress. She wasn't happy with the idea of getting dressed at all, much less in black. She had always looked ghastly in black.

Etta had always considered blue her best color. Blue had been Roy's favorite color for her, too. "Blue brings out your eyes, Precious." His pet name for her was Precious. Or it had been, she thought.

"That doesn't mean it isn't pretty," Latrice said. "Oh, law, you don't have any stockin's down here."

"Oh . . . no," Etta said vaguely. "I guess they're back in my dresser." She noticed Latrice giving her a look. Not only was Latrice very tall and very dark but she could put forth a look that could move mountains and make sinners repent.

Etta, however, had known Latrice all her life and simply reached over and took up the jelly bread.

Latrice went from the room, saying, "You are goin' to have to go back into that bedroom sooner or later, and it'd be a lot better sooner so that I wouldn't have to keep goin' back and forth."

Etta felt her insides shift around. With shaking hands, she tore a piece off the bread, putting it into her mouth while she listened to Latrice's firm footsteps go down the hallway to the front bedroom.

Since the morning Sheriff Atkins had come to tell her Roy was dead, Etta had refused to enter their bedroom. She panicked every time she thought about it.

Considering Latrice's statement as she finished off the cup of warm cola and wished it were coffee, she couldn't see any reason that she would ever have to go into the bedroom. She could have the entire room emptied without ever having to enter it, or even look into it. She pictured the scene: men carrying the big bed with the pineapple-topped posts out the door and off into a moving van. She would give it to the poorest family in town—the poorest woman with the most children and a boldly philandering husband—she thought, suddenly warming to the plan. It made her happy to picture a poor, worn woman lying in her magnificent bed, and with all the fine cotton percale sheets and thick chenille coverlets and down-filled pillows, too.

Then she imagined the door to the bedroom boarded right over so she never had to enter or look into the room again. At first she saw a man hammering a nail into the board, but then she herself was hammering the nails in, pounding with the hammer, again and again.

"I hope none of these have runners," Latrice said when she came back through the door.

"Why?" Etta asked, licking her fingers.

"Well, it's a bit hard for a woman to look dignified with a runner in her stockin'."

Etta looked at her and blinked. She had not fully left behind Latrice's earlier comment about having to return to the bedroom.

"No . . . I mean why do I ever have to go back into that bedroom? I don't see the truth in that statement."

Latrice put her hand to her hip. "Well, it *is* your bedroom. You spent all that time and money tearin' out the wall to make it bigger and bought that fancy new mahogany bedroom set from Dallas. And all of your things are in there," she added.

"Pretty soon all of my things will be in this guest room," Etta said, "and this bedroom set is perfectly acceptable. I'll give away the mahogany bed to a poor lady." She looked around. "We will have to make new draperies, though. It is too bright in here first thing in the mornin'."

Latrice murmured, "If you ask me, we may turn out to be the poor people." Then she fixed Etta with one of those looks. "It is plain foolishness avoidin' that room. It isn't as if Mr. Roy died in there."

The next instant, realizing her error, she shut her mouth tight.

"I know perfectly well where my husband died, thank you."

Etta felt a heat, like a flame, burn up from her chest and fill her brain. She blinked, thought she might cry, and flopped her hand over the nightstand, looking for the handkerchief Latrice had put there. Latrice had put handkerchiefs all around, to be ready for use, although thus far Etta had not been able to have more than blurred vision.

"Oh, honey, you go ahead and cry." Latrice sat and gathered Etta against her full bosom. "You need to cry it all out . . . let those tears wash away the hurt."

Etta inhaled the warm, sweet scent of Latrice, of talcum powder and rosewater so familiar since childhood. She held on to Latrice's stout body and felt emotion seething and roaring, but it simply wouldn't pour forth.

"Well, I can't!" She pushed away and jumped to her feet. "I can't cry, damn it. Why can't I cry?"

Even in her distress she realized she had sworn, and Latrice had such a fit when she swore, and oh, Lord, what did it matter? Stalking across the room, she caught sight of her image in the mirror as she passed. The sight of herself, swollen belly and colorless face drawn tight, was startling. *Who was that woman? Who had she become?*

She whipped around and tossed at Latrice, "Well, say it. You certainly said it enough before—it was a great mistake for me to marry Roy Rivers."

Latrice looked patiently calm. "A time for every season. This is a season of mournin', and nothin' else matters right now."

Etta, shaking her head, reached out and gripped the turned footboard. "Nothing else matters? Well, I don't know what I'm doin'—mournin' or cussin'. How does that sound? It's real hard to mourn a husband who went and died in another woman's bed."

Latrice said, "Honey, you just have to get through it."

"Well, that is not much of a suggestion," Etta said. She stared at Latrice, who looked pained and a little at a loss. Etta wasn't accustomed to Latrice being at a loss. Usually Latrice had the perfect answer for everything—or at least she could appear to have the perfect answer.

"Well, I cannot go through all this today," Etta said. "No. Everyone will be lookin' at me and whisperin'. Half of them will be sayin' they knew it would never work out with me and Roy Rivers from the beginnin'. That Roy married down, and it all told out because I could not satisfy him."

"Now, that's not true. Plenty of people, like sweet Miss Heloise, have been on your side all along . . . and those that aren't, well honey, just like ornery dogs, if you face people and show no fear, they are gonna slump away and let you be."

"Oh, no, they won't," Etta said emphatically. Now that she was talking hard truth, she was no longer teary. "I'm not sayin' people are all that bright, but most of them can think a little ahead of dogs. Oh, you better bet people are gonna chew on this for a long time"—she pressed a hand on her belly—"and someday somebody will tell the whole story to my child—in a nice way and for her own good, of course."

"I imagine that might happen," Latrice conceded. She appeared momentarily flustered, which added to Etta's own upset. "But I think there's enough on our plate today without worryin' over tomorrow."

"You make a good point," Etta said. "There is enough on our plate today, so I don't see the need to add to it by goin' to the funeral. I simply don't need to put myself through it.'' Her gaze lit on the bed, ''I'm goin' back to bed, and you can just tell people I'm too sick to come out.''

Throwing herself across the bed, she fell back on the thick feather pillows and dropped her arm over her forehead in a dramatic gesture that somehow soothed. She felt she had come upon the answer at last. She simply would not go. She would stay in this bed. They could all come and take everything around her, but she would stay in this bed. She would possibly stay in this bed for the rest of her life, an idea that seemed at once perfectly strange and perfectly logical.

''You know you can't do that.''

Latrice's voice cut into Etta's spinning thoughts. She refused them and talking entirely. She was in bed. She was not conversing.

Latrice said, ''You cannot continue to claim bein' sick and not go into the hospital. You got out of visitation yesterday evening with that, but it won't wash windows today.''

Etta pulled a pillow over her head and tight around her ears. She began humming and forced into her mind the picture of the red flying horse from the gasoline sign. She imagined herself flying away on him.

Latrice grabbed the pillow and the two of them grappled with clawed fingers and heavy breaths. Latrice won because she was twice the size of Etta. Etta pressed her hands over her ears, squeezed her eyes closed, and hummed louder, feeling herself spinning and spinning in a desperate wind.

Then Latrice was right in Etta's face, the sheer force of her causing Etta's eyes to pop open.

''No, I am not goin'. I will *not* see Roy dead!'' Etta yelled, coming up to her knees.

''You will,'' Latrice said, her eyes dark, hot pools. ''You have to, honey. If you turn from this now, you will always be turnin'. That is the way your mother went. Is that what you want for yourself? *For your child?*''

Etta, staring into Latrice's eyes and hearing the cracking of emotion in her voice, went rigid.

Latrice said with a soft, even tone, "Mr. Roy, bless his soul, has done enough to disgrace himself and you. The only way you can turn that around is to show honor. You have to do that for your child, and for yourself."

The words *your child* echoed in Etta's mind and in her heart, and she thought of Roy, and of her mother, and of the dear baby in her womb. Pressing her hand to her belly, she got off the bed and got dressed because she knew the truth in all Latrice said. She had had her little hissy fit and felt a bit better because of it.

Getting dressed turned out to be not so difficult a task, after all, with Latrice helping to shove Etta's clothes on. "Turn around and let me fasten your bra. Yes, you have to wear panties, it's cold out there. Here's two matchin' stockin's . . . oh, here, let me do it."

Etta's feet were almost too swollen to fit into her black patent leather heels.

"How can my legs be so skinny and my feet get fat?" Etta said, struggling to get the shoe on her foot.

"It's all that Co-Cola you've been drinkin'."

"Well, I can't drink hardly anything else—and I don't know how it can be the cola. I keep peein' it all out."

"Salt," Latrice said, jamming on the other shoe. She would not allow Etta to wear her black dressy sandals instead, as she pronounced them too flashy.

Then Etta was standing before the mirror, and Latrice was saying of the dress, "It looks right nice."

"It looks like a tow sack died black."

Latrice made a scolding sound and brought out the string of pearls Roy had given Etta as a present on their wedding day. The pearls did help the dress.

"I look a lot like Mama," Etta said in a small voice.

At that moment, she saw the stark resemblance to her mother's exotic elegant looks. Roy had always said Etta drew him with her elegance. "You have the kind of class that's born in, Precious," he'd say so very proudly.

Latrice said, "Here . . . let me comb your hair."

Etta sat on the vanity stool and closed her eyes, enjoying the sensuous tugs on her scalp, and felt a child again, took refuge in the feeling. Latrice hummed "May the Good Lord Bless and Keep You," with a blues tone.

Etta fingered the pearls, felt their cool smoothness, saw Roy's eager joy when he had given them to her. She recalled his smile, his frown, him sleeping, him eating, all of the pictures coming over her in quick waves, making an ache in her chest that hurt so badly she felt she could very well die right there. A lump in her throat, she quickly twisted, looking up at Latrice and trying to hold on.

"Oh, Lord, Latrice . . . I just keep wishin' things had been different. I think if I had not lost the baby right at first, or if I could have gotten pregnant again right away, we would have made it. Roy really wanted a child. I know that would have made a difference."

She wished she hadn't said some things that she had to him, either. Wished she had not let other things go unsaid. Wished for a second chance with all she had learned. Wished to turn back the clock, and herself.

"Regrets and guilt are natural to grievin'," Latrice said.

Etta, still fingering the pearls, gazed again into the mirror. "Remember what Mama used to say? If wishes were horses, we'd all ride. Remember her sayin' that? I'd say, 'Mama, I wish I could have red cowgirl boots,' or 'I wish we could have an indoor toilet,' or 'I wish Santa Claus would bring me my own pinto pony,' and she'd say, 'Honey, if wishes were horses, we'd all ride.' "

She recalled her mother's faraway eyes and flat, hopeless tone of voice that cut through Etta's heart and made her feel guilty for every want she'd ever had.

"Miz Ria had some clear thoughts sometimes," Latrice said quietly, and then added, "It was just that they didn't much tend to run together."

Etta sighed, feeling the tense pain ebb. "No, they didn't." She gazed into the mirror, thought bleakly of her mother, and of how all of life seemed made up of wishes strung together.

Latrice was bringing the black hat with the sweeping brim when the doorbell rang. "That'll be Maveen, I expect," she said with a heavy sigh. The mention of Miz Ria,

whom Latrice had both loved and hated, had brought her
down, and she wasn't thrilled with the idea of Maveen coming to attend the house during the funeral, either. Maveen
was a young second cousin who in the past had jumped at
the chance to come to the Rivers home to help with heavy
cleaning in order to get a look at the house and its fine
contents. She was exceedingly clumsy and broke something
every time she came.

"Well, I'd best go get Maveen busy . . . try to keep her
from breakin' anything." She laid the hat on the edge of
the bed and glanced at her watch. "Mr. Alvin will be here
with the limo in about twenty minutes. Don't forget the
hat," she added firmly before she left.

Listening to her heels strike the hallway, Etta thought
that Latrice would be bossing her when both of them were
rocking on the front porch of the old-folks home. It was a
comforting thought. She knew quite starkly in that moment
that she could go on living without Roy, but she did not
think she could live without Latrice. Roy had known this,
and it had hurt him.

Lifting the lid on the crystal face powder container, she
dusted her face and then dotted on a bit of rouge and carefully applied lipstick. Studying the results, she thought she
looked like a peaked woman with red dots on her cheeks.
Perhaps she should not expect anything better, being a recently widowed pregnant woman who kept vomiting.

Rising, she slipped into the coat Latrice had laid on the
bed. It was a black wool tent style that was popular at the
moment. Heloise Gardner had sent it over from the Style
Shop. Since marrying Roy and coming up in the world,
Etta had gone to buying her clothes there. She settled the
black hat with its sweeping brim and volumes of veiling
over her head. It was also from Heloise's shop. She adjusted the veiling down over her face, and then stared at
her image in the mirror.

The image was shadowy through the layers of tulle. She
was a stranger, elegant, mysterious. Etta gave several poses
to the mirror, experimenting, and thinking that Roy would
be tickled.

Latrice yelled from the foot of the stairs, "Time's marchin' on!"

"I'm comin'."

Taking a deep breath, she picked up the small black patent leather purse Latrice had left for her on the bed and started down the hallway.

Feeling compelled, she stopped at the open doorway of her and Roy's room. Heart beating fast, she put her hand to the door frame and looked inside. The scent of Roy—of his expensive cologne and Camel cigarettes and lemon drop candies he loved—came to her.

Then she saw him, over by the window, blond hair rumpled, wearing his brown sport coat, with his hands tucked easily into his trouser pockets.

He whistled low. "Darlin', you look like one of those women out of that *Vogue* magazine." Roy had always been free with compliments.

Etta stared. He appeared so real, as if she could touch him, grinning that sensuous, touching grin, the one that could make a woman take leave of her senses and be glad to do so. Oh, never let it be said that Roy Rivers had only been a taker. He had always given, as well.

His voice came to her again, "Ah, Etta . . . I still love you . . . forgive me . . . I need you, Precious," and his green eyes were as desperate and pleading as they ever had been.

Seeing them so clearly, Etta's breath stopped in her throat.

It had all been so complicated between them, something she could never put into words and something most people could never begin to understand. Roy had loved her, and knowing this had held Etta to him. His attentions to other women had had nothing to do with his love of her. She had made a vow to be his wife, until death do them part, and she hadn't been able to step over that vow. She had not been able to turn her back on him, because she had come to understand him so well, and to know his need of her went as deep and thorough as blood, and that he most assuredly would have gone crazy and died had she left him. She had held on and kept trying to save him, until she was on the brink of dying herself. And she had loved him.

"I can't help you anymore, Roy," Etta said flatly to his image that was beginning to fade, his hand stretching toward her. "You've just gone too far this time, honey."

Before the image was completely gone, she turned away and went down the stairs.

Three

Mr. Alvin Leedy himself, the eldest of the three brothers who owned the Leedy Funeral Home, had brought the limousine and stood holding the door open. Etta went carefully down the brick stairs. She was experiencing a growing light-headedness. It was a disconcerting sensation of suffocation, and also of being in a dream, where all objects possessed a gray aura. It vaguely occurred to her that the layers of black veiling could be contributing to these sensations, but she wasn't about to lift the veil, as she felt more and more comforted, hidden, by it all the time. It was the closest she could get to being in the bed with the covers over her head.

She slid into the backseat. The limousine was warm and smelled musty, closed like a closet, or a coffin. She rolled down the window, hard and fast.

Latrice, with several heavy breaths, slipped into the seat beside her, glanced quickly around, and made a sound of approval. Etta turned her face to the window, trying to catch the air. It poured in as the limousine took off fast enough to press them back into the seat, cruising over the gravel driveway like it was hardtop, tossing up a good puff of white dust behind.

Etta had never in her life ridden in a limousine. She felt

as if she were caught in a surreal dream and would at any
moment wake up and turn over and there would be Roy,
his head on the pillow that was scrunched the way he liked
to make it, his green eyes eating her up and his hand slipping onto her breast in the manner of a man intent on
having his way. But then he would say, "Are you gonna
go get me some breakfast?" like a little cajoling boy, and
she would have to laugh.

She clung to these good pictures. The others, the hours
of waiting and looking for Roy to come home, the anger
and hurt when he finally did, smelling of another woman's
perfume, passed across her mind, but she pushed them
aside. Pull the veil, close her eyes, do not see because she
could not bear the hurt right now.

Just then the limousine came to a stop, hard and jarring,
causing Etta to put one hand out to catch herself. Latrice
let out a "My land!"

A light blue pickup truck, a recent model but well used,
with a wooden rack in the back for hauling stock, was
stopped right in the entry from the highway. The driver—
a cowboy sort wearing a dark hat—stared at them through
a dirty windshield, and Mr. Leedy, Etta, and Latrice stared
back. Then the driver of the pickup leaned out his window
and hollered something that didn't quite reach them in the
backseat of the limousine.

"Who is that?" Latrice asked Etta in an aggravated
voice.

"I don't *know*."

Latrice stared at her, and Etta turned her head to gaze
out the window, stubbornly willing herself out that window
and back to the house and into bed with the covers over
her head.

The limousine did not move. Mr. Leedy appeared to have
taken the view that his was the bigger and grander vehicle
and wasn't about to budge.

Etta felt Latrice lean forward. "Mr. Leedy," she said,
"it would probably be easier for us to back up than for the
pickup to do so. And it seems the gentleman wants to speak
to us."

Mr. Alvin nodded and said, "Yes'm, Miss Latrice," probably before he realized.

Etta felt the limousine jerk as it was thrown into reverse. She breathed deeply, and the veiling tickled her face. Then the pickup was pulling alongside. Mr. Leedy rolled down his window, so now both windows on that side were down and the wind was whipping in, cold and sharp.

The driver of the pickup again leaned out his window and touched the brim of his hat. Right there in front of her face, Etta had to look at him, although she knew he could not clearly see her through the veiling over her face. He looked familiar. He looked like a thousand other drifter cowboy types Etta had seen in her life, and she saw the battered saddle hanging over the top of the wooden slats of the stock rack in the back of his truck as the damning proof.

"Good mornin', sir . . . ladies," he said, peering curiously at Etta for a second before swinging his gaze and grin back to Mr. Leedy. "I'm lookin' for Mr. Roy Rivers. Is this his place?"

His breezy manner and easy drawl went clear through Etta. He's from Texas, she thought, suddenly finding that a high offense. His dark hair lit by sunshine, the life of him there framed in that truck window was suddenly intolerable to her, as was his speaking Roy's name. Roy who was dead, and if this man didn't know that, he should have.

Mr. Leedy had already started to speak when Etta said, "I'm sorry, but Roy Rivers is dead." The stranger's startled eyes returned to her, but she looked forward and said smartly, "Please go on, Mr. Leedy. We're goin' to be late."

"Yes, ma'am."

Mr. Leedy was a man set to please. Immediately the limousine started forward, pressing Etta and Latrice back in their seats again and leaving the Texan and his pickup behind in a cloud of dust. Mr. Leedy rolled up his window, but Etta insisted on leaving hers down.

"I can't breathe," she said and then sank back into silence and the dark veiling as she would into a dark hole had anyone shown her the courtesy of allowing her to do so.

Etta thought silence was the best way to go. If she held on to silence, she wouldn't scream at Mr. Leedy for driving like an idiot and making her stomach want to come inside out. She wouldn't say aloud that the funeral home had a mildewy smell, and that Mrs. Leedy just had to redo Roy's hair and get that perfectness out of it. Keeping silent, she wouldn't ask for a comb to do it herself. She furtively used her fingers.

Then she slapped his cold face.

Latrice grabbed her hand, pulled it down, and led her over to sit down. Etta stared at the coffin, thinking that no breath, no life force came from the body. That was not Roy lying there on that satin.

She looked at those around her and wanted to say, "Well, y'all can go home now. Roy isn't here. He's over at Corinne Salyer's . . . or he's down at Beetle's playin' pool . . . or he's back in his bed, waitin' for me to bring him a cup of coffee," which of course would have given everyone a good start. She felt herself coming to pieces, about like a red rose whose velvet petals were drying black and falling one by one.

People came up to her. "My condolences, Miz Rivers." Or "Fine man . . . we'll miss him." Or "I'm sorry for your loss."

Etta thought that when a person died, he immediately assumed an exalted position. It was true that Roy had aggravated people all the time with his antics, yet they had still loved him. A person could not help but love Roy.

Heloise Gardner, owner of the Style Shop and also Roy's distant cousin, actually said this when she came over and hugged Etta. "That man could be the devil, but a body couldn't help but love him." And then she started crying and seemed to go to pieces, elegantly, but to pieces just the same, before Etta's eyes. Watching Heloise fumble unsuccessfully for a handkerchief, Etta passed over her own and put her arm around the older woman and helped her to sit down. She was halfway down the aisle to the door after she'd done that, and she might have continued on out and away from the entire business, except Latrice captured her and escorted her back to the front pew.

When Pastor Johnson spoke the funeral service, Etta heard only the first sentence before she took note of his tone and wished she had seen to getting someone else to preach the service. Roy had more than once compared the pastor's voice to the engine on an oil well pump—steady but with annoying backfires. Roy had made a point of avoiding Pastor Johnson in life, and he likely wouldn't come to hear the pastor now in death. In her mind she stood up in front of everyone and said that Obie Lee, the tall Negro man who slipped into the back row, ought to give the eulogy, because he had known and fished with Roy for a lifetime, and Roy often commented that he could listen to Obie tell stories for hours. She was in fact preparing to rise when Latrice's hand called her back to her senses.

Then people were filing past Roy's casket. Etta saw Roy's Aunt Alice—his mother's sister—was one of the first. As she passed Etta, she gazed down from above the mink fur wrapped around her shoulders. Her face was powdery white and her eyes icy. Then, leaning heavily on her husband Edward's arm, she walked to the casket and began sobbing over Roy's face.

Etta sprang to her feet and crossed to the casket. Alice straightened and went at her. "You should have saved him. He counted on you to do that."

Etta, hands clenched and fury tangled on her tongue, said, "There's only so much a wife can do for the man his mother made."

Alice looked like she was about to spring on Etta, but Edward grabbed her and led her away.

"Do not make a scene now," Latrice said, putting her arm around Etta. "It won't help anyone."

Etta looked at Roy, then headed for the door at an amazing rate. Mr. Leedy reached for her, but she did not slow down, and Latrice and Mr. Leedy had to hurry to catch up with her as she went out into the bright sun and took a good, deep breath. Mr. Leedy hurried on his skinny legs to

the limousine and whipped open the door, gesturing for Etta
and Latrice to enter.

Etta settled again on the musty backseat, and Latrice
slipped in beside her with several grunts and a "My land."
Mr. Leedy edged the limousine up to the stoplight, and Etta
twisted around to look out the rear window at the procession of cars falling in behind. A second limousine nosed at
the one in which Etta and Latrice rode—it bore Alice and
Edward Boatwright; they were direct kin, and Edward was
also director of the First Citizens Bank. Then Leon Thibodeaux, the Rivers's family lawyer, and his wife, Betsy,
lined up in their stately black Cadillac, and Heloise behind
the wheel of her peculiar-looking Crosley, wearing an enormous flamboyant hat, then Beetle Monroe, who owned the
roadhouse, in some sort of big, chunky car. The line kept
coming out from the chapel. Etta found the number of people who had come somewhat surprising and very gratifying.
She hoped Roy knew this.

Mr. Leedy started off across the intersection, and Etta's
eye fell on a familiar truck. Why, it was the pickup truck
of the Texas cowboy who had appeared only hours before
in her own driveway. It was parked at the curb, and the
cowboy stood outside the driver's door, holding his hat
politely pressed over his chest.

Etta had the confusing sense of a dream again. She noticed the sun glinted on his dark hair . . . and that he stood
at an odd angle. She wondered what the cowboy had been
to Roy. Wondered what Roy had owed him, for she had
no doubt this was the case.

Then he passed from her sight, swallowed up by city
buildings that blurred past as the limousine continued
smoothly through town, past the street where Corinne Salyer lived, the very corner Roy would have turned the night
he had dropped dead. Etta craned her neck and caught a
glimpse of the big magnolia in the Salyer front lawn.

*Would it have been different if I had confronted them
both together? Would that have made a difference?* Of
course it was easy to ask these questions now, when she
could see the road ahead. It was living life and not being

able to see the future that was the tricky thing.

Then they were flying down the blacktopped highway to the cemetery. As Etta got out of the car and was led up to the grave, she saw a woman standing far off beside a dark sedan. Corinne Salyer, daring to come, standing there in black. Not close enough for Etta to truly see her face, but Etta knew it was her.

Latrice whispered, "Don't look at her," and her fingers dug into Etta's wrist.

The people gathered in two groups, one large around the waiting hole in the ground, and a second, smaller group of several Negroes. One thing about Roy, he had been color-blind, after his mother had died anyway. Of course Latrice was color-blind, too, and she stood straight and tall beside Etta, her comforting arm around Etta's shoulders. The sun was bright in a cloudless sky and the breeze high. Roy was buried on the Methodist side of the cemetery, in the big Rivers family plot, next to his brother, Robert, who had drowned at age ten, and at the foot of his mother, which somehow seemed fitting.

Beside Leon, his wife, Betsy, broke out in great noisy sobs, the effect much like a cherry bomb thrown into a church service.

Etta and Latrice looked at each other. Looking again at Betsy's broken face, seeing a number of people cast curious glances and watching Leon poke his wife with some anger and then put his arm around her, Etta thought of Roy.

From the shelter of her veiling, she looked at different women's faces, wondering frankly which of them, if any, had enjoyed flirtations with her husband. She began to shake with what others surely took as crying but what was actually rueful laughter at the situation.

"Always laugh at every opportunity," Roy would say. He had liked to laugh, but more, he had liked to make others laugh. Especially women. His charm was not something he could help, either, any more than he could help breathing. Until now.

The funeral broke up, and people melted away. Miss Heloise stopped to press her moist, paper-thin cheek against

Etta's and said, "He was the last of the Riverses . . . except for that child you're carryin'. Thank God for that baby."

Etta heard her words with something of surprise. In her distraught state, she tended to forget the child. She put a hand to her belly, holding it, caressing it.

The funeral adjourned to the Rivers house. That was how Etta thought of it—an adjournment. She sat ensconced in the big wingback chair, watching the mourners who came to pay their respects. She watched everyone through the heavy veiling of the sweeping hat. Latrice positioned herself in a straight-backed chair at Etta's side, and those who came to speak condolence to Etta gave Latrice furtive glances, as if asking permission to approach.

Alice Boatwright was the exception. She saw Latrice, but pretended otherwise. Almost immediately upon entering, she came to Etta and said, "Roy was my nephew, my sister's child. This was my sister's house. Lord knows she hated it, but it was hers, and I'd like to speak to you about what we are goin' to do about her things."

Latrice leaned forward. "Miz Etta is not available for interviews."

Alice started in surprise, and then frowned. "You forget your place, Latrice. You always have."

The two had a staring match, and Latrice won, of course. Alice was not frightened of Latrice, but neither was she a fool. Ignoring Latrice, she said to Etta, "I shall call upon you tomorrow, and we can get things straight."

Latrice had the last word. "I suggest you telephone first. Miss Etta is carryin' Mr. Roy's child and needs to rest."

Alice turned away and went about the room, as if inspecting it.

"She is markin' the things she wants," Latrice whispered to Etta without moving her lips.

"She is Roy's mother's sister. She's entitled to those things that were Cynthia's."

"Those things belong to the child, the grandmother's grandchild."

"Are you so certain it is a girl I'm carryin'?"

"Yes."

They spoke to each other in whispers, like a game, two sticking together.

The house filled with people who gradually grew relaxed and jovial as they ate and drank and settled into pleasant reminiscing, forgetting the cause of that reminiscing. Etta saw a number of men slip out the door, one after another, to smoke on the porch or to partake of a nip from a bottle in their car or coat. Drew Pierce, who had sent over the cooler full of soft drinks from the bottling company, passed out bottles of the cola and sweetened a number from the pint bottle in his coat pocket. Heloise began helping Maveen serve at the dining room table. China and silverware clinked and snatches of conversation seemed to bounce around the air over Etta's head.

"Remember what happened at Robert's funeral? Cynthia liked to have shot Carterroy. Roy managed to get the gun . . ."

"Carterroy wasn't above runnin' bootleg, I can tell you . . ."

"After what happened with Robert, Cynthia wouldn't let up on Roy. She kept him . . ."

"Have y'all seen Alice and Edward's new color television? Big son-of-a-gun . . ."

Etta remembered how Roy used to say his family provided entertainment for everyone. She used to tell him that his family provided for the upper-class people of the county, and that hers had provided for the lower.

She ran her gaze around the room, from mouth to mouth, watching the lips move but not hearing anything. Or rather hearing what sounded like one big noise. There were a number of strange mouths, those of people she didn't even know but whom seemed to know the house and Roy.

And then her gaze lit on a familiar face. *Mercy!* It was the Texas cowboy from the blue pickup truck.

Etta's eyes followed him. She thought to call Latrice's attention to the man, but remembered that Latrice didn't know who he was, either. He was bareheaded and close enough for her to see his hair was neatly trimmed but thick and wavy on top, an unruly strand brushing his forehead, which had a faint tan line across it. He wore a coat and string tie at the neck of a white shirt. He carried two plates of food, balancing them carefully as he weaved between people, nodding and saying excuse me, to the front door and out of it.

Etta stared at the door for some seconds and saw him duck back inside and shut it. He was gone.

A crash coming from the dining room jerked Etta's attention that way. Maveen had dropped something. Latrice swore beneath her breath and got up to go see what it was. Thus abandoned, Etta sat there feeling a strange panic of vulnerability slip up into her breast. She saw Betsy Thibodeaux heading toward her.

Etta rose and said, "Excuse me," to no one in particular and hurried up the stairs to the bathroom, where she slammed shut the door and leaned against it. Then she fought her way from beneath the layers of veiling, jerked off her hat, and ran to the toilet to throw up. To no avail, as she had not eaten enough to throw up.

She looked in the mirror. Her face was white as paste. She put a damp rag to her face and began to feel better after a few minutes. She sat on the edge of the tub and removed her shoes and rubbed her crushed feet. She thought briefly of running cool water over them, gave up the idea and thought instead to return to bed and cover up her head.

Coming out of the bathroom, she stood in the hallway, listening to the murmur of voices below and gazing at the opened doorway of the bedroom she had shared with Roy. The afternoon sun poured through the doorway, illuminating dust motes.

Footsteps approaching up the stairs caused her to dart quickly into the room and close the door behind her.

Roy isn't here, she told herself, even as her gaze roamed the room looking for him—over the bed in which they had lain and in which he had taken her to heaven, to the chair where he would pile his clothes, to the dresser where their wedding picture sat. His scent came strongly, wrapping around her. The cologne he used to order from New York, of all places.

Etta went to the tall bureau, opened the top drawer, and swept Roy's brush and comb, assorted keys and coins, a folded handkerchief, and several lemon drops into it and closed it with a hard thud that matched the hard beating of her heart.

She spun around, her gaze running over the room and stopping on Roy's brown sport coat hung neatly on his valet chair.

"I sure never meant it to end up like this, Etta."

At the sound of the voice, Etta looked over and saw Roy again, staring at her from the corner, that subtle desperation on his face.

"I get crazy sometimes, Precious, but I've never stopped loving you."

He had said all that to her that night he had gone to Corinne's, that night he died. For the first time that night, Etta had thought to leave him. She had actually spoken of it to Latrice.

She said to his image now. "If you had stayed here, Roy, you might have at least died in your own bed."

He looked pained. And then he began to fade, while she heard him saying, "Etta . . . Etta, don't be angry at me."

Then he was gone, and the corner was just a corner.

Etta strode across the room, grabbed the coat from the valet chair and the shoes she spied beneath it. Jerking open the mirrored door of the corner chiffarobe, she tossed the things inside in a heap beneath the neatly hanging garments, slammed the door closed and leaned back against it, as if the things inside might try to pop out.

After a long minute she turned, opened the door again, and drew out the balled-up coat. She arranged the shoes neatly next to the others and shook out the coat. Change rattled in the pocket. Sticking her hand inside, Etta's fingers closed around not only change but a palm-sized metal object.

She drew it out—a goldtone lady's compact, with the initials C.S. engraved upon it. The compact felt cool on her palm. Her gaze traced the swirling designs and the C and the S. Then, tossing the brown coat to the floor, she marched to the window, threw it up, and drew back her arm.

She stopped, imagining the compact landing in the dried winter weeds and lying there, sinking into the orange sandy dirt and rusting, forever ignored and forgotten. Just as her hurt had been all these years.

No.

Wrapping the compact in her tight fist, she closed the window and left the room. Realizing she was barefoot, she stopped to retrieve her shoes from the bathroom floor. At the guest room she slipped into her coat Latrice had laid across the bed. Then she tiptoed down the back stairs that came out in the kitchen pantry.

She was caught up now by fury long pressed down into deep recesses where it had grown like yeast in volume and strength until it no longer intended to be restrained.

Four

When he saw the gal, Johnny Bellah was out in the corral with the red horse, studying its feet. In Johnny's opinion, the most important part of a horse was its feet. Lots of poor horses had been sold by being shown in tall grass. Johnny had pulled that trick a time or two himself. He didn't feel guilty about it. If a fellow was stupid enough not to look at a horse's feet, then he deserved to get took.

The young gelding appeared born of an even temperament and had obviously been handled. Once Johnny got him hemmed up into a corner, he allowed Johnny to pick up first one foot and then the other. He was a little squatty son-of-a-gun, rangy and not at all much to look at, but Johnny still had to look at him anyway, so there he was, bending over, the high breeze tugging at his hat, when the horse stiffened.

Johnny looked over to see the gal on the back porch and thought: *Well now.*

The woman—Roy Rivers's widow, he knew now and recognized by her dress and coat—hung on to the porch post and put on her shoes. The action seemed a mite odd. Then she lit out across the yard, coming toward him. It was his first sight of her hair, shiny honey curls blowing in the breeze. The wind caught her coat, and Johnny saw with something of a start that she was pregnant.

It struck him as quite tawdry, a man dying in a lover's bed and leaving at home a pregnant wife. He had overheard comments made at the funeral—obviously he hadn't quite caught it all—but being a man who didn't care to indulge in gossip, he hadn't discussed the subject. He figured there was a lot he didn't know, a lot even those people doing the talking didn't know. Besides, Roy Rivers's business had been his own.

Johnny remembered then that he was standing in Roy Rivers's corral, and he felt a little embarrassed. It was possibly a rude move on his part, taking the liberty of going into a corral and messing with a horse not his own.

The gal wasn't coming toward him, however; she hadn't even seen him at all. She was heading for the old Ford sitting beside the barn. The horse brushed past Johnny and stuck a curious head over the fence, but the gal paid him no mind. She got into the Ford and tried to start it up. Johnny was surprised when it cranked, for about fifteen seconds, sluggishly with its last dying breaths. Then it went completely dead, which Johnny didn't think should come as any great surprise. Weeds were growing up around its tires; that Ford was old and couldn't have been driven since last summer.

Johnny, reticent about calling attention to himself, watched the gal get out of the car and struggle to get the hood up. He couldn't leave her to do such stuff, of course, so he went toward her, his bum knee protesting since he'd been standing a bit long.

"May I help you, ma'am?" he asked while still inside the corral. He thought it best to to alert her to his presence before approaching closely. As it was, she spun around, her hand pressed over her heart.

It was Johnny's first good look at her face that had before been thoroughly covered by veiling. He saw eyes big and blue, the bluest, most beautiful eyes he had ever seen. Eyes a man could fall into.

Then he realized she was staring at him, and that he had

been staring at her in a most impolite manner.

He shifted his gaze, saying, "Uh . . . I let myself be forward and took a look at the colt. I didn't mean any harm." He gestured at the car. "Could I be of assistance, ma'am?"

"Oh . . . yes, please." She drew her gaze from him and motioned toward the car. "I thought maybe if we could clean the battery cables, it might start."

Johnny had high doubts about the car ever starting, but he slipped through the fence to open the hook just the same. He cast quick glances at the gal as he did so, and noticed she cast him a couple of curious looks, too, in the manner of a man and woman who are strangers, yet suddenly thrown close together.

"Would you have a pocket knife?" she asked, even as she impatiently started right in trying to loosen the cables from the battery terminal by hand.

"Sure . . . let me pry them up for you."

The gal gave way for him, but as he worked on the corroded cables, she stood close, giving advice as to how he could loosen them. She had that sweet smell about her, like women do. While the dark bowels of the engine were full in his face, he kept thinking of her blue eyes.

He got the cables and the terminals clean and put back together. "I'll be the first to admit I don't know a lot about engines, ma'am, but I don't hold out a lot of hope for this to help much."

She only glanced at him, went around, slipped into the seat, and tried the key again.

The starter still didn't turn over, didn't even give out so much as a click. Johnny felt a little at a loss at not having helped her. He might not know about engines, but he had noticed in the past that a person could feel death in mechanical things just like living things. This car felt dead. He looked through the windshield at the gal, wondering about her and Roy Rivers.

She got out from behind the wheel and slammed the door hard. Pushing back the honey-brown hair the breeze was whipping into her blue eyes, she said, "Could I borrow your truck?"

The request startled him.

He gazed at her, wondering why she wouldn't ask someone in the house—a friend or relative? And she looked to be in something of a state. He didn't think she needed to be driving his truck in a state.

"Well now, ma'am . . . I'm livin' in that truck right now," he answered, rubbing the back of his neck. He didn't want to be impolite by refusing outright.

"I don't want to take it from you," she said, her voice having an impatient edge. "I only need to go up to Chickasha for a bit. Maybe an hour."

Johnny thought that he had just eaten a fine meal out of her house. He considered as he looked over at the red colt that was nibbling what weeds he could reach beneath the bottom rail.

"I guess I could drive you. It has a tricky clutch." He truly doubted she could handle the clutch. She might lose control.

She looked a little relieved, but without bothering with a thank-you, the gal turned and went on ahead of him to his pickup. Johnny followed, his bum knee slowing him down. He never liked to hurry with it; the way he gimped along made him feel awkward and like a worrisome old man when he hurried. When he got behind the wheel, he saw she had pushed aside stuff in the seat and slung her feet over his bundles in the floorboard. She slumped down, hiding.

Johnny glanced at the house, then down at her. She looked a bit uncomfortable. He was a little uncomfortable.

"Will you just go on," she said.

"Yes, ma'am." He looked out the windshield and started the truck.

Once they were headed along the road, she sat up. He told her she could roll the window up, if she wanted, but she shook her head and let the wind bat her hair about her face.

She looked very young. A girl, Johnny thought, but with a woman's eyes. His gaze slipped down to her belly. She had pulled her coat closed, and he might not have thought her pregnant, if he hadn't already seen. And he had seen. He wondered about Roy Rivers running around on such a woman. It was funny how a man soaked up gossip, despite not wanting to pay it heed.

He saw her glance down at the seat between them—at the fancy china plates and the silver fork that belonged in her dining room.

"I didn't have a chance to take the plates back inside," he explained. Then, not wanting her to think he was just any old freeloader, he added, "I wanted to pay my respects, but it was a little crowded in there, so I came on outside."

Somehow, his explanation came out sounding as if he had been totally intent on the food, which was the truth of it. He figured Roy Rivers owed him enough to give him a meal.

"I didn't think you were stealin' two plates and a fork," the gal said. "What did my husband owe you?"

Johnny was taken by surprise, and it was a second before he said, "Eight hundred dollars."

"Well, I don't have it," she said, turning her face away, and tucking her hair behind her ear.

Johnny didn't know what to say. Talking about money in this particular mourning moment seemed in poor taste. But the gal seemed like she was just going to let it all go at that—that her saying she didn't have it should serve. Johnny did not think that Roy Rivers's dying changed the fact money was owed him. He expected the Rivers estate to pay up. Johnny needed that money.

The funeral meal was the most substantial Johnny'd had in almost a week, the amount of time he had been sinking ever onward to flat broke. Today he had begun to consider what he would pawn—his last remaining army medal, or one of the two silver belt buckles he had left. He had a nice bit left, but it wouldn't bring much. Maybe his hand-made snakeskin boots. He thought a time or two about his saddle, but he didn't think he was that far down yet. He had eight dollars left and a full belly. Surely things were looking up.

"You can turn left here at the grocery store," the gal

said, startling him out of his thoughts. "That way's a little shorter."

Johnny put on brakes and made the turn, causing his tires to squeal. He continued to think hard about what was appropriate to say to the gal. He felt something should be forthcoming on his part, and it would be best that it lead into the subject of the eight hundred dollars he was owed.

Finally he came out with, "I'm sorry about your husband, Missus Rivers. He was as fine a man as any I have ever worked for." He thought she might ask him about the work he had done.

The gal cast him a sideways glance through her wind-blown hair and didn't say anything at all, which gave Johnny the impression that he might as well refrain from speech altogether. The remaining twenty-minute drive seemed awfully long.

When they got to Chickasha, she directed him through the streets and then to turn down an alleyway behind some swank houses with careful lawns and tall elms and maples, pretty much leafless but heavy-budded.

Johnny had the swift thought that maybe she was going to rob someone. Maybe she was going to kill someone. He didn't know why his mind had the tendency to run in such directions. He had always been a man possessed of a great imagination.

She told him to stop at a clapboard garage, the sort that looked like it had once had a chauffeur's apartment up-stairs, but it wasn't used anymore. There was a brick walk leading across a neat backyard to a big white house.

"Wait here for me, okay?" she said and hopped out.

"Yes, ma'am," he said, tamping down his irritation at her high-handed manner. In Johnny's opinion irritation generally served no purpose except to ruin a good mood. He didn't like poor moods, and he felt he needed to make allowance for the gal, being recently widowed and pregnant.

She didn't hear his sarcasm anyway, didn't even cast him a backward glance, intent as she was on going to the house. As she rounded the hood, he looked at her hand that was stuffed into the pocket of her coat. Concern nipped at him again. He sure hoped she didn't have a gun in there. He would then be an accessory.

Johnny watched until she was hidden by the corner of the garage. Then he took off his hat and raked his fingers through his hair, wondering what he had gotten into. *Why* he had gotten into it, the way he seemed to get into a lot of predicaments in his life. Predicaments just seemed to trail after him. Thinking this made his mood dip low.

He rubbed his aching knee and thought about driving off, but he couldn't let go of his eight hundred dollars that easily. Besides, he had nowhere to go. He'd seen a roadhouse on the way into town, but like as not it wouldn't open until nearer dark. Thinking about the roadhouse, though, made him think of the bottle of Jim Beam in his glove box, and he drew it out and took a couple of swigs.

Thoughts passed across his mind—his money, and the red horse at the Rivers place, and the big barn with the hand's room he'd seen inside it. And the gal's blue eyes.

He had told the gal he would wait for her, and he generally tried to follow through with his word.

He drank a few more swigs from the whiskey to ease the aching in his knee. Then he turned on the radio. Music usually lifted him up. Ol' Hank singing "Kawliga" came out of the round speaker, and Johnny immediately felt a little better. As he rolled himself a smoke, he patted his boot to the rhythm. Then he dug behind his seat and found the current book he was reading, *The Foxes of Harrow*, by Frank Yerby. The binding was a little warped from where it had been thoroughly soaked sometime before he came upon it at the Salvation Army store. He forced the book open straight and propped it on the steering wheel to read, while he waited for Roy Rivers's widow.

Etta felt herself carried along by the one fervent thought, and that was telling Corinne Salyer a thing or two. She had in times past imagined herself doing so, but what she had perceived as good sense and refinement had held her back. Also uncertainty of consequences.

Well, Roy was dead now. Etta didn't think consequences

could get any worse than that. She intended to have the satisfaction she had long forgone with Corinne. She wanted satisfaction even more than she wanted coffee.

The maid was surprised to see her at the back door, of course. Etta drew herself up and said, ''Would you please tell Miss Corinne that Missus Rivers is here to see her.'' She wished she had worn her hat. It gave her courage.

The maid said, ''I'm sorry, Missus Rivers, but Miss Corinne ain't here.''

The maid and Etta stared at each other, and then Etta said, ''I'll wait.''

She was prepared to sit in a chair in the hallway, but the maid said, ''I'll show you to the study.''

Following behind the woman, Etta glanced around. She had been in this house a number of times with Roy, but she always felt then and still felt now like the poor white trash walking through the big shot's big house. She felt that way because that's exactly how things were, she thought, and told herself to breathe. It would definitely be in poor taste to pass out from lack of oxygen and sprawl across the rose-patterned runner.

The maid politely told her to make herself comfortable and then closed the door. Etta, pressing her arms ever tighter to her sides, slowly, hesitantly moved into the room.

She had caught a couple of glimpses of this room in the past, when they came for dinner parties, as Roy would disappear into here to talk with Wilford Salyer and other men, leaving Etta alone with Corinne and her mother Amy and other women with whom she had had nothing at all in common. Mostly she had remained shyly quiet, and mostly they had rudely ignored her. This had been hurtful at first, but gradually Etta had realized their rudeness and had grown confident that she could by her presence annoy them. It had become something of a game, one she had never mentioned to Roy. These people were his friends. His people, she thought of them.

The room was fairly small, with quite a bit crammed into it. There were two floor-to-ceiling shelves of books and a desk, a fancy little drink cart, and leather chairs, and beside one of these was a standing ashtray and a small, well-used table. A wadded-up newspaper was shoved in the corner of the cushion of this chair.

Etta sat down in the chair without the newspaper, then got up and walked around, then sat down again and shook her arms loose from her sides. Her spirit had begun to sink. She popped to her feet again, reminding herself that she had a few things to say to Corinne Salyer, things she should have said long ago.

So, what did she intend to say to Corinne, her husband's lover?

It struck Etta sudden and hard that she really had no idea of what she intended to say. In the fervent picture in her mind she had given forth witty and cutting truths that ripped the pride right off the woman, making her grow smaller and dimmer, while Etta grew bigger and shinier. But she had not actually heard any of these witty and cutting truths.

Oh, dear.

Etta closed her eyes, and thought of yelling at the woman: *Slut, tramp, you ruined my life and my child's life . . . Did he die in the middle of it?* The image of her husband pumping atop Corinne made her eyes pop open and her mouth go dry.

She abruptly decided she would leave . . . through the garden door. That was the best solution, most especially as she had suddenly realized that she had to go to the bathroom. This was not good. How could she be strong and confident, and tell Corinne whatever it was she needed to tell her, when her bladder was about to burst?

Just then she realized her fingers played with the compact in her pocket. She pulled it out and gazed at it.

She would leave it on the desk, she thought. Leave it like a calling card of sorts, and let Corinne wonder about her coming and leaving it. That seemed a viable alternative to staying—a rather romantic, mysterious act. Corinne would wonder. And if she wanted to know more, she would have to come to Etta. It was not perfect, not much at all, but Etta thought it would do.

Just as she was about to bring the compact out of her pocket, however, as if all of fate conspired to heap coals upon her head, the door creaked and swung open and Corinne appeared, standing there in the opening like an unpleasant vision.

Etta felt herself shrivel. She wrestled the feeling, pulling herself back and facing the woman squarely, making herself stand as tall as she could. Corinne was a full head taller than Etta and five years older and had been to the Oklahoma College of Women while Etta was still going to the two-room rural schoolhouse along Elm Creek.

Corinne carefully closed the door and said, "You wanted to see me?"

For a moment she was in deep shadow where Etta couldn't clearly see her face. Then she was coming forward across the floor in a slim-skirted black dress that shushed with every step. She floated, Etta saw—and none too steadily—right on past Etta in a whiff of expensive fragrance and glory and on to the shiny drink cart.

"Didn't Mary offer to fix you a drink? That was inhospitable of her. What may I fix you? We have some excellent brandy." She turned and smiled crookedly. "I'm sure drinks will help us over this awkward conversation."

Etta was struck hard. Corinne's black curly hair was windblown and her mascara was smeared, and someone must have hit her hand while she was putting on her lipstick, a bright cherry-red color that looked tacky as hell. Etta's spirits rose with the observations.

"I'm not drinking these days," she said very coolly. The satisfaction she felt in pointing out her pregnancy rode high and fast and echoed, "Ha!" inside her for a glorious moment.

"Oh, that's right . . ." Corinne turned back to the cart, dropping ice in a glass. "You're with child, aren't you."

Etta watched Corinne splash liquor into two glasses, no matter what had been said. She began to feel her quest for satisfaction was slipping away. Anything Etta had to say would likely bounce right off the woman's alcohol-swollen skin.

"We should toast the little Rivers that Roy left behind," Corinne said, languidly turning and bringing up both glasses, extending one toward Etta.

Etta's arm slashed the air. Her hand connected with the cool glass and sent it flying through the air and against the edge of the desk, hitting with a thud and spewing its contents over half the room.

Etta stared at the dribbles of liquor moving down the desk.

Corinne said, "You really are a little rowdy. I suppose that's what your kind of trash comes from, though."

The woman's words were slurred, pitiful. Etta gathered her fractured wits and said, "I just came here to return somethin' that belongs to you." She stepped to the desk and placed the compact there, beside the blotter, where it gleamed against the glossy walnut.

"I found that in Roy's coat. I thought it should be returned to the woman to whom it belongs. I guess it's yours because of the initials, although I imagine it could belong to someone else, Roy bein' Roy."

Etta felt a great relief, thankfulness at having control of herself, while she watched whatever control Corinne had ever possessed evaporate. She snatched up the compact, saying desperately, "It's *mine*."

Watching the woman, Etta felt as if her blood drained out her toes. It came to her with stark clarity that her mission had been futile from the start. There wasn't anything to take from this woman. Corinne Salyer had nothing left to take.

Despair falling all over her, Etta pivoted and started for the door.

But then Corinne said, "You caused it all. It never would have happened, if not for you."

Etta looked around to see Corinne, her face jutting out, the big crimson-painted mouth wide and bitter as her voice rose.

"You took him from me first. Roy was supposed to marry *me*." She jabbed her chest with a finger. "Everyone knew it. His mother and my mother even had notes for the wedding plans. Oh, Roy was wild, but he would eventually want to settle down and have a family. All men do, and when he was ready, it was *me* he was going to marry. But then his mother died, and he met you. You. The pretty little thing. You were the one to turn his head. You were younger and exciting—different, I suppose, from the class he was used to. Different from his mother, that's for sure.''

For an instant there, when Corinne was saying *me*, jabbing her chest, and talking about how Roy was to marry her, Etta felt pity so profound she wanted to cry. But then as Corinne continued on, getting haughty, Etta's pity slipped over into disgust.

''You are pathetic,'' Etta said.

Corinne didn't appear to hear Etta at all. She began to cry and sort of wail. ''I kept hopin' he'd leave you and come to me. But then I knew he never would—not when you managed to get pregnant. Oh, no, he wasn't gonna leave you then.'' She tossed back her head. ''You want me to say it? I loved him, and he was crazy for you, but I could not quit lovin' him.''

''Crazy for me and every woman in the human race,'' Etta said. She really wished she could stick to her emotions during this discourse—either pity or disgust. As it was she realized the confrontation was pointless, had been from the start.

Corinne was withering again. ''It's all over town. Before people could only suspect and make a few jokes, but now everybody knows. Oh, it's okay to have affairs, but get caught and everything changes. Daddy wants to send me away. All my mama ever wanted was for me to marry Roy . . .''

Etta could not believe she was standing there listening, watching Corinne grope for a chair, fall into it, and go on and on, with her mascara running down her elegant face. Etta stood transfixed with the sight, as she might while watching someone stabbing herself over and over.

''Do you know, he even would mention you to me. He would tell me something you did or said that he found so delightful that he couldn't help but tell. You,'' she added with a wave of her hand, as if Etta was not much, while she sobbed morosely. Corinne's head flopped so far down that Etta could see her crown and several gray hairs there among the glossy dark ones. Seeing that for some reason made a sadness wash over her in a great wave, so heavy that she felt herself being tugged under.

Turning, following what seemed to be the voice of common sense—which sounded like Latrice saying, "Get ahold of yourself"—Etta went to the door. When she opened it, the maid, who had obviously been pressing her ear to the door, jerked back in startled surprise.

Etta said, "I think you had better get Miss Salyer up to her room and maybe call the doctor."

The maid stared at her for a moment and then hurried past into the room.

With quick footsteps, Etta went down the hallway to the door at the back, out it and down the steps and along the walk. She saw the cowboy had waited, and until that moment it didn't occur to her that he might not have. He was napping, his head back and his face hidden beneath his dust- and sweat-stained hat. When she opened the passenger door, he shot up, sending his hat and a book in the air, and looked around, blinking.

Etta got up into the seat, slammed the door closed, and said, "I'm ready to go."

She felt the cowboy stare at her. She looked downward and twisted her wedding rings, seeing the broken woman inside the house and Roy lying in his coffin. She saw him naked, his penis white and shriveled.

The cowboy said, "Well now . . . yes, ma'am." He started up and headed the truck down the alley.

Etta braced her arm against the door, realizing then that she had to go to the bathroom really badly. Her situation was not helped at all by the cowboy seeming to hit every bump. When he came out on the street, she directed him toward the main road out of town, and when she saw the red flying horse on the Mobil sign, she said, "Pull in here!"

Five

Responding immediately to the gal's urgent tone of voice and hand jabbing the air—he was already highly concerned with her pasty coloring—Johnny immediately jerked the steering wheel to the right and pulled swiftly into the gas station. The truck hadn't come to a full stop before the gal was swinging out the door and hit the ground running.

Johnny didn't think she should be running like that. He watched her disappear around the corner of the building and worried that maybe he should go after her. Uncertainty and a natural aversion to intimacy held him in his seat. He was, after all, a total stranger to her and couldn't quite throw himself into chasing after her to the ladies' room.

Taking in a deep breath, he cut the engine. His heart was beating fast, having been startled awake like he had been. He had always been a deep sleeper, and being faced with the sight of the woman who appeared on the verge of flying to pieces and made to drive on down the road, only to be yelled at to stop, had served to jar him hard as a wild bronc.

A teenage boy came over and asked, "Fill 'er up, mister?"

Only then did Johnny realize he had automatically pulled up beside the pumps. He shook his head. "You might wash my windows, I guess. I'm just waitin' for the lady."

"We don't wash windows, 'less you buy gas," the boy said, which really annoyed Johnny. He considered it inhospitable behavior.

"I guess you don't wash these windows, then."

"Okay, but you don't need to block the pumps for payin' customers."

"I don't see a line just buzzin' in here," Johnny said and sat where he was.

After a minute he pulled the whiskey out of the glove box, slammed the door, twice as it bounced back open, sat back, and took several bracing swallows, thinking as he did so that his contact with pregnant women was really limited; he wasn't at all certain of what was normal. Mrs. Rivers had looked to be more in a state than ever. He sure hoped she was okay. He felt he was in some way responsible for her welfare, since he had been driving her around in his pickup.

A car, a brand spanking new red and white Ford, driving in on the opposite side of the pumps drew his attention from his worries. He noticed the car and then he noticed the yellow-haired gal driving. She had ruby-red lips that smiled at him the minute she put her window down. Women tended to like Johnny, and while he could be shy, when one smiled at him like this one did now, he took it easy.

"Afternoon, ma'am," he said and gave her his most charming grin.

"Good afternoon," she said politely, but her eyes were sparkling and saying things Johnny imagined to be something on the order of: *Yessir, I'd like to get my arms around you*, and he was making his eyes say about the same thing while the little pipsqueak boy came over and filled her tank.

Just then the passenger door of his truck opened, and Mrs. Rivers was back, getting into the truck. Johnny felt a little embarrassed, because he saw the blond jerk her head forward and roll up her window. All thoughts of her vanished, however, as he studied Mrs. Rivers. She appeared to have regained at least some control of herself. Her coloring

was a lot better. She looked wrung out, but not about to
fly to pieces anymore.

Slipping the whiskey bottle down onto the seat, Johnny
started the engine and set his mind to forming a way to
discuss the money he was owed. The best course seemed
to be to ease up on it by getting a general conversation
going. After all, he had always been good with talking to
women.

He started by suggesting she roll up the window, since
it was getting awfully chilly with evening coming on, and
didn't that sky to the north look like it could bring in rain?
They really needed rain, the grassfires being so bad lately.

She rolled up the window without saying anything, obviously not getting the idea of conversation at all.

He tried again, remarking that Chickasha appeared a
pleasant town and that this was his first visit to it. "I guess
you could say Fort Worth is my hometown," he said, "but
I spend most of my time out in the country. All over Texas
and in Oklahoma some, too. I train and sell horses."

The gal continued to look out the passenger window, or
down at her hands in her lap, turning her wedding ring set
around and around. It was a fancy set, with a cluster of
diamonds raised up. It looked a little big for her finger. It
looked well worth Johnny's eight hundred dollars.

"I met your husband down in Fort Worth," he said,
beginning to get a little irritated. "I sold a couple of horses
for him at the stock show."

"You missed the turn," she said.

"What?"

"You missed the shortcut. It's okay . . . you can catch
the road up here a couple of miles."

Johnny lost his train of thought then about his money
and began to worry that he would end up driving all over
the county in trying to get the gal home. He asked her what
highway he was looking for and peered for signs. When he
came to the highway and turned, he felt relieved and once
more began to think of how to broach the subject of his
money. By then he was getting pretty frustrated with the
entire situation.

Then she suddenly said, "Could you turn in up here?" in an anxious tone of voice.

"What? Here?"

She was pointing at the cemetery, and Johnny quickly pulled in. Then he stopped the truck and looked at her.

She bit her bottom lip. "If you wouldn't mind . . . I'd like to see my husband's grave without all the other people around."

Johnny took a deep breath, shifted down, and headed along the narrow lane. He had not joined the procession to the cemetery, but he instinctively headed for the fresh grave with the flowers piled on it. A lot of flowers, he thought as he pulled to a stop on the gravel and cinder lane. He looked at them and recalled when his mother had been buried. So many years ago that it no longer hurt, but it made him sad to remember because the only flowers had been those he'd brought and those of a good friend.

Before he could get around the hood to open the door for her, Mrs. Rivers was out of the truck. She headed up the slope to her husband's grave. Johnny leaned on the front fender and rolled himself a cigarette. As he stuck it in his mouth, he watched the gal. Then feeling awkward, as if he needed to give her privacy, he half-turned and looked at the clouds growing in the northwest. The wind was on the rise, and evening was coming early as the clouds darkened and blocked out the setting sun. The spring storm he'd noticed growing earlier was gathering steam.

When he looked back at Roy Rivers's grave, the gal had gone down on her knees. He could hear her crying. He figured it was a natural thing, but the crying still perturbed him. The next instant, Mrs. Rivers was up and yelling things and kicking and throwing the flowers every which a-way.

Shocked, Johnny watched for long seconds, torn between thinking it was none of his business and concern that she might hurt herself. Concern won out, and he hurried up the hill to the grave.

"Missus Rivers?"

She was sobbing and yelling something about her husband having been too good to have thrown his life away like he did, no matter what his mother had told him. Johnny winced, uncomfortable with hearing private matters.

Then she was looking right at Johnny, with tears streaming out of her beautiful blue eyes.

"He threw it all away—himself and me, and for what?" she demanded. "God, that woman is pitiful. All the time I kept thinkin' I could save him . . . I did everything I knew to do, but you can't save someone who doesn't want to be saved. And I just let him take me, too. I just couldn't let go."

Johnny stared at her. The north wind was blowing her hair and tugging at Johnny's starched shirt.

"Well now, ma'am, I guess I don't have an answer for you—except that there is a storm comin'. I think we should get out of it."

"Are you like that?" she asked him. "Are all y'all men like that—so stupid as to throw yourselves away on trashy women and gamblin' and craziness?"

"Well now . . . I can't answer for all men," Johnny said uncertainly, caught in a predicament he didn't understand one bit. "I guess men are people, and people can be confused."

"Oh, good Lord, I'm carryin' on a ridiculous conversation with a handsome heartbreak cowboy."

Johnny watched her shake her head. He gathered his breath and said, "Ma'am, we need to get you home."

At that the gal covered her face and went to sobbing for all she was worth. Johnny bent and took hold of her arm and pulled her to her feet.

"Come on. I may be a man, but I'm all you got right this minute."

She kept her head averted from him as he put an arm around her and led her back to his truck and got her up into the seat. As he slammed the door closed, she leaned forward into her hands.

Johnny went around and slipped behind the wheel. He put his hand on the key to start the truck, paused, and looked over at the gal. She was mumbling something he couldn't understand. He had the awful thought that such hard crying could shake the baby loose. He felt he had to get her to stop crying.

"Ma'am . . . Missus Rivers." When he shifted his rear, he felt the whiskey bottle. He took it up, and threw his hat out of the way on the dash, and slipped closer to the gal. "Here . . . take a bit of this." He uncapped the bottle of Jim Beam and put it in front of her face, hoping to give her a whiff, but she kept her hands firmly over her face, giving forth sobs that set Johnny's nerves twanging.

At last he put a tentative hand on her shoulder. "Ease up, gal, before you shake yourself to pieces."

Then, somehow, he had her in his arms and was patting her back and stroking her silky hair and murmuring soothing things he really had no idea of. "Easy now, easy . . . slow up . . . here now."

She felt so small and fragile. He tried to hold her together until she could hold herself together, and people didn't have to know each other to do that. In his lifetime he'd held a lot of horses and a few women and even a couple of men during his army days. His mother had taught him; she'd held a lot of people in her life. She had always maintained that being held was the most important need of the human race, which was why she could make money at it.

Roy Rivers's wife gripped Johnny's shirt and soaked it with her tears. Her shoulders were bony and shaking beneath his arms. Gradually her warmth and fragrance came to him, too. Her hair was soft as silk, drawing his hand. He stroked her hair, again and again, and felt vaguely like he should not be feeling things he was feeling but not denying he felt what he did.

Her sobs slacked up, and he felt her become aware of her position. She pushed away.

"Please," she said in a ragged whisper, "I'd like to go home."

Johnny thought that a fine idea and started the truck. Unfortunately he had to go around and back past Roy Rivers's grave. The gal looked out the window, saw the grave, and started crying again.

Totally at a loss and ever more fearful her violent sobs might tear loose the baby right there in the cab of his pickup, which was already overcrowded, Johnny pressed the accelerator and headed along at a good clip for her house. He sure hoped he would not take a wrong turn and was extremely relieved when he saw the driveway of the Rivers farm up ahead.

When he pulled in front of the house, he saw the yard was now empty of cars. By instinct, he kept going to the back door, where he'd seen the gal appear earlier that day. As he came to a stop, a tall Negro woman came out of the house.

Hopping from the truck, Johnny cast her way, "I got Missus Rivers. She's pretty upset."

He went around to open the passenger door. The Negro woman came pushing around him and started pulling the gal out, saying, "Come here, honey. Law, I figured you'd gone to her. Didn't you know it wasn't gonna do you no good? I thought you knew that," welcoming and scolding all in a melodious, soothing tone. The two women, the younger one leaning on the older, went across the brown grass and up the cracked steps and disappeared into the house, leaving Johnny standing there in the empty yard with the sharp evening hovering over him.

He stared at the closed door a full minute, at the red print curtains showing through the glass. Then he went around and got back behind the wheel of his truck. He leaned forward to turn the key and stopped, setting back.

He didn't know where he was going to go.

He had eight dollars, and it was too late to try to pawn something. The eight dollars would buy him either gas or a meal or a room, but not all three. And he was about to run out of whiskey, he thought, as he took up the bottle.

While he considered his predicament, dark clouds rolled overhead and wind buffeted the truck. He listened to the tree branches knocking together overhead and watched the mane and tail of the red horse blow as the horse pranced in the fast fading light. Then he happened to look down and see the china plates still sitting on the seat.

The silver fork had slipped down in the crack, prongs upward, and he had to fish it out.

Gathering the dishes and fork, he got out of the truck and went up to the back door. His knee hurt considerably, echoing the coming damp and cold. He knocked and listened to the muffled music from a radio inside while he waited. He noticed that the house trim could use a coat of paint. Thinking about the money Roy Rivers owed him, he felt a little sick.

There came the sound of heavy footsteps, and the door opened. The tall, handsome Negro woman stood there.

"May I help you?" she asked through the screen door.

"Yes, ma'am. I'd like to return these."

She opened the screen and snatched the dishes out of his hands. "Thank you."

"Uh . . . ma'am," he said quickly, as she was pulling back behind the door, "I'd like to know if someone could settle up a bill Roy Rivers owed me. I have it right here in his own handwritin'." He quickly produced it from his jacket pocket and held it up at the screen. "I would not intrude on a day like today, ma'am, but I need the money."

The woman glanced at the paper and said, "Well, I guess you have Roy Rivers's signature, but he is dead." She started to shut the door, then stopped. "There's a room and a bed in the barn, if you'd like to use it. I thank you for bringin' Miz Etta home . . . although it would have been better if you had not taken her off."

She shut the door.

Johnny leaned a hand on the door frame for about sixty seconds in which he considered smacking the glass out of the door.

The urge passed, and with a defeated sigh, he turned and went back to his pickup and started the engine. Raindrops hit the windshield. He began to turn the pickup to leave, thinking to go find a roadhouse and give over his last dollars to the constant tugging of demon liquor, when his gaze fell on the wide entry to the barn. As if drawn by a force, he drove the truck toward it and just as he pulled into the barn's gapping darkness, the rain came down outside in full force. He got out of the pickup, helping his knee along. It was aching considerably now.

He smelled the familiar scent of cold dampness seeping into the wood and manure and earth, sweet smells to him. He walked over and peered into the small sleeping room. He entered and pulled the string on the single light bulb hanging from the ceiling. That the light came on surprised him. Glancing around, he saw the narrow bunk with a dirty, lumpy mattress, wooden crate beside it, old three-drawer chest against the wall, and a mass of bottles and tins atop it. Vet medicines—and among them a half-filled bottle of whiskey.

Well now . . .

He tugged off the light, returned to his truck, and spread his bedroll in the back. He knew where the dirt in his truck came from and preferred it to the dirty mattress. The whiskey eased the pain of his bad knee and lack of money considerably.

Etta stood in her filmy white cotton gown, in the room lit only by the hall light, and gazed through the sheer window curtains. Through lingering tears she couldn't seem to stop and the curtains and the raindrops on the glass, she saw the cowboy standing in the barn entrance, in the glow of the pole lamp. Pushing aside the sheers, she got closer to the window. The man remained in the doorway, leaning against the side of it, smoking a cigarette.

Latrice's footsteps sounded from the hall and entered the room. She said, "Here, honey. I've brought you some hot Co-Cola and a bit of cream of wheat. It'll help you sleep."

Etta, still looking out the window, said, "That cowboy is still out there . . . he's in the barn."

"Yes, I saw that. He needs a place to stay." Latrice turned on the bedside lamp, and its reflection made seeing outside more difficult.

"Roy owed him money," Etta said, turning from the window as Latrice pressed the hot cola at her. "I was very rude to him. I didn't even ask his name, and he drove me to town and everything."

"We would have been better off if he hadn't done that," Latrice said, her lips forming a disapproving line. "You do not need to be runnin' around, making a spectacle of yourself. Roy Rivers managed enough of that, embarrassin' us. You don't need to do more."

"Embarrassin' us? Is that what you're worried about?"

Latrice gazed at her. "Roy Rivers is dead. We have to go on livin'. Goin' to talk with that woman doesn't do nothin' but keep stirrin' everything up."

"God forbid we stir anythin' up," Etta said, the anger coming swiftly from where it had been ready to spring. "Let it lie . . . and that's all it's been, big lies to each other and to ourselves."

"Just forget it," Latrice said. "There is nothin' you can do about it, so it doesn't matter now."

"It does matter! How I feel matters. That I'm so furious and the one person I should be screamin' at is dead matters. That I cannot mourn my husband matters to me, whether or not it makes any sense. That I threw away all these years married to him matters. Can't change any of it, but it damn well matters. My *feelings* matter!"

She was practically yelling and shaking so badly that Latrice took the cup from her hand.

"Get ahold of yourself," Latrice said.

"Oh, I'm sure that will help a lot—to get hold of myself. Well maybe if I hadn't been trying so hard to hold on to myself and be perfect for everyone for all these years, I might have let go of a losin' proposition. And I suppose I *do* have hold of myself, because if I didn't, I'd be out there diggin' Roy up and kickin' his butt all over the damn cemetery!"

Latrice stared at her with a pained expression.

"I'm sorry," Etta said, shaking her head and turning away. She felt so sorry for her entire life.

Latrice said, "Come on, I'll help you to bed."

"Don't." Etta pulled away. "You can't fix this for me, Latrice. You've always tried to fix things for me, but this time you just can't. Please leave me. I need to be alone."

*   *   *

Outside the door, Latrice hovered, listening. She was afraid to leave Etta alone. This was the first time that Etta had ever turned away from her, and she didn't know how to react.

Not seeing anything else to do, however, Latrice went downstairs and made a gin and tonic from Roy Rivers's liquor cabinet, took it into the kitchen and sat in her rocker, drinking and praying to God for Etta and damning Roy Rivers to hell, and because of this having to pray for her own soul.

From the first moment she had laid eyes on Roy Rivers, Latrice had done all she could to dissuade Etta from falling into his arms. She had dug in her heels and fought, the same way a woman fights wrinkles and age spots, knowing perfectly well all the time that the war will not be won.

Oh, men had always flitted around Etta, and Latrice had had to be very vigilant. Etta had been so hungry for love and tenderhearted and pretty that she had been an accident just waiting to happen. From the time she reached fourteen, she had all the time been bringing home any male who looked hang-dogged at her. They came after her like panting puppies, and Etta fell in love with them all.

Thankfully, however, Etta had been possessed of enough sense not to fall in bed with them—and she'd had Latrice to be vigilant, too.

But then Etta had met Roy Rivers. Roy Rivers had not been the first in Etta's heart, but he had been the first to get into her pants. That boy had been able to charm the bees right away from their honey.

Latrice had refused to go to the wedding, and when the two had returned from their honeymoon (in Las Vegas, of course, where Roy Rivers could gamble his heart out), she had stubbornly held off coming over to the Rivers house for an entire month. She knew she was going to break down and go eventually, and she even began to haul home boxes in preparation for packing the things in the little white cracker box of a cottage she and Etta had shared, just the two of them since Etta's mother had died and her daddy had run off. But she was holding out until Etta summoned her, which she knew Etta would do sooner or later.

When Etta had called, it had been in a distressed state, crying because she had miscarried the child she had held in her womb even as she married. Upon hearing that news, and the total despair in Etta's voice, Latrice had summoned her cousin Freddy the cabdriver and headed for the Rivers farm. Passing by a grocery, she'd had Freddy stop so that she could shop for supper that evening. She figured she might as well carve her place into the situation immediately. Besides, she knew good and well Etta had not had a decent meal since her wedding day, because Etta was a poor cook.

In the Rivers's big shiny kitchen (which she instantly coveted but would not admit) with Etta safe and secure in the rocking chair, Latrice whipped up the meal—lean ham slices and collards and new potatoes and cornbread, with sweetened peaches and milk for desert.

Watching him ladle big scoops of butter onto his bread and insist on cream for his peaches, even in the face of his wife who could barely eat, Latrice saw the truth of it all in his florid face and smooth grin—Roy Rivers wanted Etta, and he intended to have her in the way of a grasping man who has always gone after and gotten his exact desire and will. Latrice was ashamed that she had failed in her duty to protect Etta and educate her against such men as this.

Over after-supper coffee, Roy Rivers said to her, "You know you have to come here to live, Latrice." He used his smoothest voice and smile as he struck a match to light up a cigar. "I'll give you your own room and an allowance."

"I want my own bathroom, too," she said, figuring she might as well make the best of this situation.

"I'll have it built," he said.

Later he turned it into a brag, getting a kick out of telling people, "My wife came with her own nanny."

Roy Rivers had tried to charm Latrice, and when that hadn't worked, he had tried to buy her goodwill with perfume, a new Westinghouse clothes washer and dryer, and a radio powerful enough to pick up, on good nights, Chicago to the north and the Border to the south, just for her, because he knew that in alienating her he ran the risk of displeasing Etta, and also because Roy Rivers really had trouble with a person not liking him.

In his way, Latrice had to concede, he had been as needy as Etta. She supposed she at times had felt sorry for him, but that was before he had died and left them in such a bind.

Latrice came awake to discover that morning was approaching and that she had slept all night in her rocker. She was stiff as a starched sheet and highly annoyed because sleeping in a chair seemed something that old people did, and she was not old—only forty-one.

After lighting the oven to take the chill off the kitchen, she plugged in the percolator out on the back porch. Glancing at the barn, she saw the cowboy's pickup still showing in the entrance. She gazed at it for a long minute. She had an uneasy feeling about the cowboy. It seemed odd the way Roy died and then the cowboy had appeared. Seemed a portent of some kind. One thing Latrice knew, nothing in life was coincidence.

While the coffee perked, she went into the tiny bathroom built off her bedroom, bathed, and dressed in a long-sleeved navy-blue shirtwaist and arranged her hair in an artful wave above her forehead, securing the rest in a roll at the back of her neck. Strands of gray had begun to show in her glossy dark hair at her temples. High cheekbones, a family trait, gave her face an ageless quality. Her mother had been handsome even as she died at thirty-eight from cancer eating her away. Latrice knew herself to be an attractive woman. Many a man had told her so and had wanted her. It was her choice not to have any of them. Having been sorely disappointed by the death of her fiancé, she guarded her heart and her freedom. Being tied to Etta was enough.

Latrice had always thought when Etta was well settled, she might then look around and chose a man. But that time had certainly not come with Roy Rivers. And the years got away.

She went out onto the porch to pour her cup of coffee.

The fresh morning air was damp and crisp. There came the sound of Obie Lee's old pickup truck chugging down the lane from his house through the woods, backfiring like it always did. Obie Lee, a widower of some six years, worked forty acres of the Rivers land on shares and worked around the farm for cash money.

Latrice stood there and watched the battered truck stop at the barn. Obie, all six and half feet of him, unfolded himself from behind the wheel, flashed her a bright grin, and started straight for her. Obie Lee was in love with her.

"Mornin', Miss Latrice . . . mighty fine day, ain't it." His lazy tone of voice could annoy Latrice no end.

"There's not enough of it to tell yet," she replied.

"Guess I'm anticipatin'," he said. "I brought my thermos and thought I might fill it—your coffee bein' so much better than mine." He gazed up at her from the ground, his eyes like a red-bone pup's, all warm and friendly and hopeful.

She said, "It's here, I guess." She felt sorry for being so sharp with him, yet irritated that he could be so pliable that he never let her sharpness bother him.

"And I thank you," he said, opening his thermos. "How's Miz Etta doin'?" he asked, his expression getting serious.

"She's not awake yet, but when she does get awake, I imagine she'll be havin' a hard time."

Obie nodded and said, "I imagine."

Latrice thought that he might as well not have said anything at all, although she bit her tongue on this observation. She knew she was in a bad mood and being overly critical. He cast her another hopeful look—trying to wrangle an invitation to breakfast, she knew.

She said, "I have things to do," and went back into the house.

At the door she sipped her coffee and watched Obie walk back to his truck, slumped over as if she had shot him.

Each morning she felt a silly expectancy in her chest, for

what she didn't know, but she would look for Obie, and he would come with his own hopefulness, and whatever it was she expected from him, he never did, because then he would go away, and she would feel disappointed.

Six

When Johnny got himself awake enough to sit up, he saw a man off to the right, hefting a feed bag onto each shoulder and toting them past the pickup. The man was one tall drink of water Negro, a lean pole topped by a blue ball cap.

"'Mornin'," the man said to Johnny, as if he saw a stranger wake up in the back of a pickup truck in this very barn every day.

"Mornin'," Johnny returned with equal politeness.

Realizing he was scratching his head, he stopped, not wanting the man to think he might have bugs. He knew he looked pretty poorly. He watched the tall man continue out and dump the sacks of feed in the back of his own truck.

Despite wanting to do better, Johnny sank back against his saddle. His head was pounding like a jackhammer. The tall man came three more times for feed sacks, while Johnny tried to get his head to quiet down. He listened to the red horse's hooves gallop around in the corral, listened to the morning birds, listened to the tall man drive off in his truck. It gave a few good pops, which didn't help Johnny's head.

Suddenly he realized he smelled coffee. He thought he had to be dreaming, but he sat up again and saw a steaming enamel cup sitting on the edge of the tailgate. He had not heard the tall man's footsteps, but he knew it had been him that had brought the coffee.

Johnny eased gingerly to the tailgate, dragging his boots along, stuck them on, and reached for the cup. He curled both hands around it, savoring the warmth and the aroma of the dark brew before tasting it. It was strong enough to open his eyes wide. Coffee warming and easing his pounding head, he sat and gazed at the house out across the yard. It looked silent.

After he drank the last drop, Johnny went and snaked the hose connected to the outside spigot into the barn, secured it over the partition of a stall, and took himself a shower. He cursed a couple of times, splashing on the icy well water and watching goose bumps grow and parts of him shrivel in the cold water and air.

Johnny had always been particular about keeping clean. He felt it came from his mother being somewhat of a fanatic about keeping him clean as a boy. He had been raised around a lot of women early on, his mother being a whore in a house in Fort Worth. All the women there had mothered him. They'd wanted so much for him, as mothers tend to do for their sons, and they had insisted he always be exceptionally presentable.

Even when down on his luck, Johnny always managed to find a way to wash himself, but sometimes washing his clothes was a bit more difficult. It did seem, though, that things always turned around for him just when all his clothes got dirty. He found either a job or a woman. As he slipped into his last clean shirt, he figured things were due to turn his way that very day.

Once more dressed and warmed by a flannel-lined denim jacket, shaved with cold water, teeth brushed and hair neatly combed, he made himself a cigarette and went out to the corrals. The gelding was running in the large one, head proud and tail flowing, as some horses were given to doing when the morning sun broke over the horizon.

Standing very still so as to not draw attention, Johnny watched the horse, watched his movements—the way he stretched his legs when running and the way he tucked his rear when he stopped short and turned. Johnny's interest sharpened. When moving like that the gelding took on an amazing beauty, didn't seem like the same horse at all.

Then the horse stopped and turned his head to Johnny. Once more seeming a little disjointed, he ambled over to the fence where Johnny stood and stuck his head over, sniffing at Johnny's coat pocket containing the tobacco pouch.

"Well now, you little son-of-a-buck, you like tobacco, do ya?" Johnny took out some tobacco and fed it to him. A lot of horses liked tobacco.

Johnny was standing there at the fence when the tall Negro man returned in his pickup, the black truck chugging and popping up the pasture road that curved from around some trees. Johnny had halfway been waiting for him—or for some indication what to do next.

The tall man stopped his truck in front of the barn, got out, and said good morning again. "Well, you look like you might just live now."

"Thanks to you. It was touch and go, I admit. Whiskey provided comfort last night and near death this mornin'."

"Figured. I've been there a time or two. I emptied my thermos while I was feedin' the cattle, but there's a percolator sittin' over there on the porch, and Miss Latrice likely has made fresh. She usually does."

He took the lid to his thermos and Johnny's cup over to the back porch and returned with both steaming. He was perhaps past fifty. It was hard to tell. He wore a tattered baseball cap with a big gold M on it, and he was sort of like a clothed skeleton walking, all his bones attached by strings. The hand that held out Johnny's cup of coffee was large and strong and callused.

"Okay . . . I have to know. Why do these people make their coffee on the back porch?" Johnny asked.

"On account of Miz Etta bein' pregnant. The poor gal cain't stand the smell of coffee. She been awful sick right along with the baby."

"Oh."

Johnny ducked his head and took a drink of the coffee. He felt a bit peculiar at the mention of Mrs. Rivers, and the word *pregnant* always made him feel uncomfortable. It was an intimate, private thing. He felt foolishly like he'd been intimate with the gal, after carting her over to town on the sly and then having her bawling against his chest.

Suddenly grinning, he stuck out his hand to the tall man. "I'm Johnny Bellah."

"Obie Lee," the tall man said, taking Johnny's hand in a firm shake.

"Obie . . . well, good to meet you, sir."

The tall man's eyebrow went up at the formal address, and Johnny felt a little silly and self-conscious. Still, he'd been raised to be polite. They drank their coffee in companionable silence for a few minutes, leaning on the fence and watching the sun rise to light the day.

"Didn't I see you round at the funeral yesterday?" Obie asked, surveying Johnny curiously.

Johnny nodded. "I dropped in to speak to Roy Rivers. I didn't know he had passed on."

"It was kind of sudden," the man nodded, respectfully as one did when speaking of the dead. "A lot of folks put out by Mr. Roy dyin' like that. Lot of folks sayin' a lot of things . . . but Mr. Roy was like most of us, filled with bad and good. He knew how to fish up a storm and how to make playin' poker better than playin' a woman. You know Mr. Roy well?"

"Well enough to know he did play good poker. I got an IOU from playin' with him, and I was aimin' to get it cashed in."

Obie shook his head, chuckling, "I got a few of those myself, and I don't imagine I'll hold my breath till I see the money."

"I was afraid of that."

"How much he stick you for?"

"Eight hundred."

Obie whistled low. "You didn't look that foolish to me, son."

"Well, I'm supposin' you knew Roy Rivers a lot better than I did, and you say you got a few, so how much smarter than me does that make you?"

The dark man grinned. "All of my notes together don't come to twenty dollars, and I never counted on seein' the money. That's what makes me different." He cocked his head. "How come you took an IOU like that from a fella you didn't hardly know?"

"I knew him," Johnny defended himself. "I handled sellin' a few of his horses, and he paid me right on the spot. How was I to know he would be gone from the hotel when I went to collect on my IOU?"

"Well," Obie drawled, "if it's a comfort to you, I'll put forth that Mr. Roy probably did have your money back at the hotel, only when he got there, he probably went ahead and spent it. He meant to pay you, but he just managed to get in that position with a lot of folks, and whoever got to him first was who got their money."

"Yeah, well, I guess I might have known that goin' in, but I was half-drunk and had a redhead on my knee. He invited me play poker with the big boys over in a back room at the stockyards. It didn't really dawn on me till later that of all those big boys, I was the only one givin' out cash money."

The tall man shook his head in commiseration, took off his ball cap, and turned it in his hand, gazing at it.

"You play ball?" Johnny asked, nodding toward the cap.

"Oh, yeah." He gave a shy smile and a nod. "While back—Negro Leagues, you know."

"No kiddin'? I've seen some of those games. What team—hey, the Monarchs?"

"Yep, Kansas City Monarchs. Outfielder and first baseman." The man shook his head. "Long time back, but I like to wear the hat, you know. I played till I was nearin' forty, almost twenty years."

"Well, I bet I saw you play. Probably more than once. You probably could have spit at me a couple of times, 'cause I liked to get right down front." He thought about how he must have seen the old man play, and then here he was, meeting him. "Funny world sometimes, idn't it?"

"You said it," the tall man allowed.

"I was in rodeo myself," Johnny said. "All-round cowboy three times . . . long time ago, too,'' he said. ''You ever go to many rodeos?'' His gaze fell to the man's dark hands, and he felt a little foolish for the question. The races did not mix as readily at rodeos.

The older man's teeth gleamed and he drawled, ''Guess I was always either pickin' cotton or pitchin' baseballs.''

Johnny nodded and averted his gaze. It lit on the red horse that was nosing at stubs of grass now. ''You work around here then?'' he asked.

''Yeah, a bit.''

''What's the story on this colt? He's about three, idn't he?''

''Three back first of March, I guess. He was born runty as could be, had his legs all folded up, and then his mama died. Didn't look like the critter had much of a chance, and Mr. Roy wanted to shoot him on the spot.'' He slipped his hat back on and tugged at the brim. ''Mr. Roy had a deep soft spot in him when it came to anythin' sufferin'. He didn't care that the colt weren't worth nothin', but he could not stand sufferin'. Ever' fish Mr. Roy ever caught and intended to keep, he killed right away. He said to me, 'Nothin' on earth should have to go 'round sickly and hurtin', Obie.' Mr. Roy'd been pretty sickly as a boy.

''Anyway, he went to get his gun, but Miz Etta, she throwed a fit and said to give it a chance, and that it wouldn't hurt it to struggle for a few days. She set out to hand-feed it and tend it. I found a plow horse could give it milk, and Miz Etta and me got the colt to suck off her, and that mare took him fine. In three days that colt was jumpin' around, his legs gettin' straight. Those scars you see there, that's from when he got tangled up in the bo'b wire fence out yonder last year. He was a good mess again, and there were plenty of people would have put him down directly, but Miz Etta got Miss Latrice to tell her what to do, and she worked him over again. She ain't one for givin' up, Miz Etta.''

''What's his breedin'?'' Johnny asked.

Obie shrugged. ''I don't know much about that. Miz Etta knows about stuff like that. She was raised up with horses.''

"He seems sound. Does Missus Rivers think he is?"

"Well, I guess she hopes he is, but ain't nobody been on him. Mr. Roy, he tried twice and got throwed pretty good twice and called that quits. He just wasn't interested. Miz Etta would have rode him, but 'bout that time she found out she was pregnant and couldn't get on him."

Johnny had slipped through the fence and was running a hand along the horse's back. The animal quivered and twisted to sniff for the tobacco in Johnny's pocket. "I might take this colt in exchange for my IOU. Do think Missus Rivers might do that?"

Obie squinted an eye at him. "I don't suppose I could say 'bout that."

Johnny looked at the horse. He knew he'd never get anywhere near eight hundred dollars for him. He might possibly be able to talk the horse up to two hundred dollars, and he was good at talking up interest in a horse. Still, anything he might get out of the animal would be better than nothing.

He really wouldn't want to sell the colt, though. He'd rather keep it and see what it could do first. He was always curious to know what a horse could do, and what he could do with a horse. If he could get it to win a race or show some talent for cutting a cow, he could boost the price. Maybe this colt would be one who could naturally be used for roping first time out.

A long time ago, when he was thirteen and thrown out on his own because of his mother's death, he had come across a horse that had never been trained but could do anything right off that you set him to doing. A miracle, and that's what he'd named the animal, Miracle. Johnny had been able to keep himself fed by renting the horse to cowboys at rodeos. Like this one, Miracle hadn't been much for looks, and maybe that was why he felt drawn to this red one now.

Johnny knew very well that he wasn't in a position to increase the horse's value at the moment, though. With no money to tide him, no place to put his hat, much less to work on a horse, all his ideas were pretty much pie-in-the-

sky ones. That knowledge did not stop his mind from twist-
ing around trying to make a plan just the same.

"You feelin' pretty hungry?" Obie asked.

Johnny glanced over to see the tall man looking at the
house, at the Negro woman who had come out on the porch
and was vigorously shaking a rug.

"My backbone's pressin' my stomach," Johnny said.

Obie was already walking. "Well, come on. Maybe Miss
Latrice's of a mind by now to give us some breakfast."

As he approached the porch, Obie Lee jerked his hat off,
hoping as always to please Miss Latrice. He never was
certain, however, if anything he did pleased her. She
seemed put out with him at least half the time. Try as he
might, he could not figure out exactly why. He felt he was
a fool to keep longing after her, but he couldn't seem to
help himself. Feeling the way he did about her had come
on him slowly, about like a wild grape vine growing over
a tree until it had a stranglehold. He'd spent four lonely
years mourning his wife's passing, and then one day he
woke up to see Miss Latrice living up the hill from him.

He said now, "Miss Latrice, I thought you might could
use some company for breakfast."

She looked at him, her black-as-night eyes seeming to
see him for the first time. "I guess you just got hungry,"
she said.

"Yes'm, and you're the best cook in the county, so I'd
be foolish not to try to get breakfast."

He thought he saw a flare of warm amusement in her
dark eyes.

She said, "I suppose I could make you some breakfast."
Her eyes traveled beyond him, to Johnny Bellah. "You're
one to make yourself to home."

Johnny was smart enough to answer, "Yes, ma'am.
Thank you."

She studied him, looking a little deflated, Obie thought.
Fearing their breakfast might evaporate, he quickly said, "I
imagine Johnny could sure use one of your good meals,
Miss Latrice."

She gave out a "Humph," then tossed aside the rug,

saying, "You men remember to wipe your boots. " She opened the kitchen door and held it for them to file through, like schoolboys. "Miz Etta came down a little earlier feelin' poorly and went to my bed, so please keep your voices down."

Obie looked at the closed bedroom door, a little intrigued by the idea of Miz Etta sleeping in Miss Latrice's big feather bed. He often thought of Miss Latrice in there, dark and big and sinkin' into the feathers.

One thing he liked about Miss Latrice was that she was tall; he liked a tall woman. He had caught several glimpses of Miss Latrice's big fancy brass bed and feather mattress and had entertained a few fantasies of himself in it with her. He eased himself down into a chair at the table and watched her dress strain over her full breasts and her hips with each of her movements. His hand itched to rest on her hip.

Miss Latrice served up a fine meal, and Johnny and Obie ate every last crumb of it. Over an hour and a half passed by, taking Johnny's initial optimism that perhaps Mrs. Rivers would appear with it. Hoping she would come, he lingered over coffee and complimented Miss Latrice again and again for the meal, but then Obie Lee was rising, and Johnny had to, too.

He said just before going out the door, "Ma'am, do you suppose I might speak to Missus Rivers about her husband's IOU?"

"Not today," Miss Latrice said. "And even when you get your chance, you'll be standin' in line."

Obie spoke up on his behalf. "Johnny was thinkin' that Miz Etta might would trade Little Gus for the IOU. He'd be willin' to do that."

"I'll tell her when she's feelin' up to it," the woman said, "but I wouldn't hold out hope. She's fond of that horse."

She held the door open for them to leave, appearing to sweep them right out. In the yard, Johnny paused, looked back and watched Obie Lee linger before stepping off the porch.

"You enjoy more in there than the food," Johnny said, amused at the expression on the older man's face.

Obie adjusted his ball cap. "Yes . . . I may have a few years on me, but I ain't blind . . . or dead."

Johnny smiled, shoving his hands in his pockets.

"Where you headed now?" Obie asked.

Johnny sighed and looked over at his truck. "Well now, I guess you could direct me to the nearest sale barn. I might be able to pick up a bit of work. Usually somebody around there needs help this time of year."

"You ride with that leg?"

Johnny looked downward, rubbed his leg. "I can still ride, and I train these days. Just can't do the rodeo no more."

Obie nodded, tugged at the bill of his cap and gave the directions to the sale barn. "Today's sale day, I believe, so you're in luck."

"Oh, I'm usually pretty lucky . . . blessed actually. Thanks for the coffee . . . and stuff."

He stuck out his hand, and Obie Lee took it in a firm shake. Their eyes met, and Johnny saw something in the older man's. Each man recognized a friend, and then each shifted his eyes away in the manner of men.

"Bye!" Johnny called, giving a wave as he turned his truck and drove off down the lane beneath the row of elms. He looked in his rearview mirror. Obie Lee was already out of sight. All he saw was the house, and no one watching him go.

He found the sale barn with little effort, and as it turned out, right there in front of his face, the horse of one of the fellows pushing in cattle got agitated (Johnny did not think the rider helped because he was jerking on the horse's face with a vengeance) and both horse and rider went down, and the rider got his leg broke. Johnny was the only one to get hold of the horse and calm it, and the next thing he knew he had the fellow's job for the day and an offer of it for the rest of the week, which he took.

That night, when he went looking for a bottle of whiskey, the manager at the local roadhouse offered him a bottle and ten dollars to go over to Highway 81 and meet a truck bringing a load of booze from Texas and cart it back in his pickup truck.

Johnny had sense enough to ask, "What happened to your regular fella? Did he land in jail?"

"Nah. He's sick. Nothin' to this. No one much cares one way or the other."

Johnny was thinking about how much he wanted a drink of whiskey. Seemed like an easy deal.

"This'll be waitin' for you, cowboy," the man said, tucking a ten-dollar bill under a bottle of Jack Daniels on the shelf beneath the counter.

Johnny did the job that night, and two nights later the manager asked him to make a run up to Minco to pick up some home brew. The money was welcome, but between the day and night jobs, Johnny lost a lot of sleep. He had no idea why he kept doing it. He was no saint and had been known to have a wild spell now and again which landed him overnight in a jail cell, but quite possibly this was the first time he had knowingly gone against the law.

Still he continued, working cattle and mending fence by day and hauling bootleg around by night, making deliveries to private homes on the nights he didn't meet a delivery truck. There were no other jobs waiting for him elsewhere. No home for him to go to, and no one at all in the world looking anxiously out a window for him. He began to feel a forgotten soul.

Seven 🌹

The days immediately following the funeral, Etta spent as much time as possible away from the house—the scene of her failure and perplexity, and where Roy kept calling out to her. Awakening well before the sun, she would dress in a long-sleeved thermal shirt that stretched tight around her bulging middle, a dark plaid flannel shirt, and baggy overalls. These were clothes she had saved in a cardboard suitcase secreted away in the attic, her own clothes, worn during the myriad of menial jobs before she became Mrs. Roy Rivers.

"Where in sweet mercy did you get those clothes?" Latrice asked in high surprise when Etta at last got dressed that first day. "I thought they were long gone."

"Well, they weren't."

Latrice raised her eyebrow. Etta turned away, pushed through the screen door, and raced out to hail Obie Lee chugging passed in his old truck.

That day, and the rest of the week, Etta spent much time with Obie, checking the cattle and doctoring them. He was thoughtful not to make conversation, and he seemed totally comfortable with her silence. If he was uncomfortable when tears welled in her eyes, he didn't reveal it.

When there was no work with the cattle, Etta would walk

the rutted farm tracks beneath the wide blue sky and then return to work and groom Little Gus for hours on end. Being with the animals gave her a measure of peace, and she tried to wear herself out so that she could not think, an effort that proved impossible. Memories and regrets nagged at her, demanding understanding, or simply acknowledgment.

People had said that Etta Marie Kreger had married Roy Rivers for all she could get. This had been true. She had wanted it all: love and companionship, a lovely home and the ability to buy lovely things, and freedom from the constant struggle just to stay alive. It was interesting to note that people did not say that Roy married her for all he could get, which he had. His wants went along the same lines, if from a slightly different point of view. Etta had never yet known anyone who did not want at least some part of love, companionship, and a comfortable life. And to Etta's mind, only fools and no-counts did not seek to better their lives. Certainly anyone with any sense, who had grown up as Etta had, would have wanted to change her life.

Etta's life before Roy had consisted of a succession of rickety shanties in small, dusty towns around west Arkansas and south Oklahoma, and two parents who scarcely knew she existed. Her father was quite frequently absent, and her mother was even more frequently crazy.

Oddly enough, the one concrete thing Etta and Roy had in common was their lack of responsible mothers. Roy had said his mother had been "off the beam" since the death of her favorite son, his older brother. Etta had never known a time when her mother had not been lost in a melancholy madness.

The doctors—and by the time Etta's mother had seen doctors she was nearly middle-aged and sent to a state home for evaluation—had attributed her mother's mental instability to physical changes during her first pregnancy, which had not gone well, and the child had died at birth. Etta's father had said this was when he had first noticed his wife beginning to behave strangely and that it had gotten worse after the second child, who had also died at birth.

Jory Kreger apparently never considered that his leaving his wife alone for months at a time, to worry about how she was going to live without any money or the man she loved, much less bear the babies he filled her with, while he was off rodeoing or training horses, always chasing the best horse that ever lived, might have contributed to her unbalanced state of mind. Etta thought that losing two babies at full-term births would tend to make a woman act strange and should have a little bearing.

Latrice, too, scoffed at the doctors' theories. "Miz Ria just had too much intelligence and too much poverty. Her mind was sat on is what happened."

It had been true that Wysteria Harlinger Kreger—a name Etta thought might contribute to craziness—had graduated with the highest honors of anyone ever in her rural Arkansas high school and received scholarships to several universities, which would have enabled her to pull herself up from the sharecropping farm society into which she had been born, when her wits deserted her for one week in May, and she ran away with a blue-eyed cowboy who possessed nothing but a good horse and strong hands. Then along came babies, only two of which had lived—Etta and an older brother, Kyle. With each pregnancy, Wysteria Kreger's senses further deteriorated.

While growing up Etta had to endure hearing the neighbors gossip about her mother. This is how she learned about her mother trying to abort Etta herself.

"Is it true?" she asked Latrice. She was six.

Latrice gazed at her for a long moment, then took her hand, sat her down, and told her the truth of everything. "Your mama cannot help it," she said, "no more than Mr. Ruggles can help smackin' his gums or Missus Yoley can help talkin' to her dead husband all night long. Your mama doesn't know what she's doin'. She doesn't mean anything against you by it. She is angry at herself, not at you."

"She's crazy, and everyone talks about it. They hate us."

"No, they don't. They like Miz Wysteria because she smiles and is so pretty and gives them somethin' to talk about other than their own pitiful troubles. People always talk. You have to ignore it. There's nothin' else to be done about it. Live with it, is all.'' Then she touched Etta's cheek. "I love you, baby.''

Etta looked at her. "I love you, too, Latrice, but I wish Mama loved me.''

She had also wished to have a family like other girls she knew or like ones she read about in books: mother, father, sisters and brothers, all eating supper and talking around a table at night. She would run home from school and try to draw her mother out of her madness. "Mama, look at the drawing I made for you in school today. I love you, Mama.''

Sometimes her mother would reach for her and say, "I love you, too, sweetheart,'' in the most beautiful voice, and Etta's heart would soar with hope of a mother like she saw in the Shirley Temple picture shows. Shirley always ended up living happily ever after with a lovely family in a lovely white cottage with a rose-covered picket fence.

Only time and again Etta was disappointed when her mother lost touch with reality. Inch by inch her hope for a storybook childhood, or even a passably normal one, died.

Her mother began spending all afternoon and evening at the movie theater, where she was content and totally occupied. Then, when Latrice brought her home, she would either repeat, word for word, the dialogue of the actors that day, or she would retreat into silence before her vanity mirror, where she would do her hair and makeup, trying her best to look like Carole Lombard. She had in fact resembled the actress to a remarkable degree, and she had also died in an unexpected accident, although not on an airplane but in an automobile in which she had absconded from the parking lot of a Bright and White Grocery, driven erratically down First Street, and ran into a tree. She had just seen a movie in which the character had stolen a car.

Etta was thirteen when her mother died. Right after the funeral, older brother Kyle went away into the army, setting his sights to see the world. Etta went to see him off at the bus station. It was an awkward time for each of them because they barely knew each other.

"Goodbye, brother," she said, wanting to kiss him but not seeing any invitation to do so.

"Goodbye, kid," And he swung up into the metal stairs, was away with one wave.

As she stared at the rear windows of the departing bus, Etta wondered if she would ever see her brother again. She had not. Kyle saw Germany and Turkey before he ended up dying of a particularly virulent case of food poisoning.

Etta's father, Jory Kreger, went off as he always had. Etta was so used to him going away for big blocks of time that she maintained she didn't even miss him for a month after her mother's death. That particular time he was gone for four months, returning as usual with a new horse and several buddies he expected Etta and Latrice to cook for. He would pay Latrice when he was home, if he had money.

When Etta was sixteen her father went off supposedly to a horse sale and never returned. Not too many months later, in January, Etta received word from authorities that he had died, frozen to death after falling drunk in a ditch in Amarillo. She read the letter on the porch and then went around back of the little shanty she and Latrice had moved to in Chickasha and finished helping Latrice hang the laundry that was keeping a roof over their heads.

With all the lack in her life, Etta was just ripe for everything Roy had to offer her. In the manner of a starving heart, Etta had thrown herself into loving Roy Rivers, a man all bright and shining and professing to give her all she ever wanted. She had been so enamored by this knight in shining armor and the glorious prospects before her that she had rushed headlong into a most wondrous love affair, the sort written about in books, despite all of Latrice's warnings.

And warn Latrice had done. When Roy would come, tooting the horn of his sleek champagne-colored convertible, Latrice would stand and bar the front door. And when Etta, wisps of her fair brown hair flying loose in her haste, dashed out the back door and sped off in a cloud of dust with him anyway, she knew Latrice sat herself at the red

Formica kitchen table and prayed for Etta to be released from the Devil's spell.

The last thing Latrice said to her each night was, "He'll use you up and use himself up, too. Get some sense, girl."

To which Etta would reply, "I can't."

"You just don't want to."

"That, too."

Even now, remembering, she smiled and held the memory close, thinking that she had no regrets for rushing after the promises of glory. The love and high prospects at the beginning had been a very fine thing, both of them seeking the brass ring.

Only their reach had fallen far short, and everything Latrice had warned of had eventually proved out. Roy had used Etta up, and he had used himself up, too.

All these memories became windows into Etta's soul, thrown open by the shock of Roy's death. The regrets were heaviest. She did not regret marrying Roy, but she regretted not being all that he had needed her to be, regretted things left undone and unsaid.

Latrice said, "This is grief doin' its work. Let the memories come and let them go. You cannot go on until you get the grievin' out."

Etta replied, "I've wasted enough time, and I'm ready to go on right now, thank you."

She left Latrice watching television in the living room and slipped out into the twilight, onto the porch and then over to Little Gus in the corral, her body following the same pattern as her mind, trying to run when there was nowhere to run to. A person could not outrun failures and regrets.

As the fiery sun fell behind the horizon, the breeze dropped and all living things got very quiet, as if pausing in reverence. Very slowly and gently, Little Gus nosed Etta's belly, and the baby inside her suddenly kicked, as if to answer the horse's greeting. The kick was so vigorous that the horse jumped back and snorted.

Somewhat startled herself, Etta put her hand on her belly. "Oh, my gosh, Little Gus." Then she ducked beneath the fence rail and hurried to the house, running and not thinking that she possibly should not run in such a fashion. She burst through the door and hollered for Latrice.

"My land, what's happened?" Latrice said with some alarm.

"The baby . . . she really kicked hard. Oh, feel here, Latrice."

Latrice felt and said that was the baby's foot. Etta sat and stared at her belly, feeling and seeing the movements of the baby, who seemed to have suddenly decided she had not been accorded enough attention and had set out to remedy the fact. Etta got a pencil and began to list names for the baby.

"She will not be named Wysteria or Etta," she said firmly.

On the Monday following Roy's funeral, Leon Thibodeaux, the Rivers family lawyer and one of Roy's true friends, came and drove Etta into town for a meeting with Edward Boatwright, Roy's uncle and the director of the bank. He came politely to the door, with his hat in his hand.

"I'm sorry to be disturbin' you at this difficult time," he told Etta. "But there are some things we need to get straight. I'll return her safe and sound," he added to Latrice, as if he had just taken custody of Etta.

He took Etta's arm and told her to be careful while they went down the steps, watching her as if he expected her to pitch forward at any moment.

Etta had always liked Leon, but sometimes his stuffy manner could be suffocating. Leon was a very proper sort who always wore a gray suit and tie and kept his shoes highly polished. Etta's eye caught the gleam of those shoes as he slipped into the car behind the wheel, and she recalled Betsy at the funeral and thought that Leon should possibly pay more attention to wife than to his shoes.

As Leon headed his black Cadillac down the lane to the highway, he said, "You want to roll your window up, Etta? Isn't that a bit much wind on you?"

Etta shook her head. "No . . . I like the air." She had the

urge to be obstinate—she had to be widowed, had to go where she didn't want to go today; she supposed she would keep the window down if she wanted. No sooner had the thoughts come than she felt contrite. She kept the window down, though.

She and Leon exchanged small pleasantries on the drive into town—or rather Leon asked kind questions to fill the awkward time of the drive, and Etta gave him the expected answers. She could not very well tell him that she thought she had seen Roy's ghost on more than one occasion and that she might be going as crazy as her mother. Leon was not a man who would take such confidences in stride.

Leon pulled into a spot in front of the bank and hurried around to hold the door for Etta getting from the car. Then he again took her arm and escorted her throught the chrome and glass doors and across the marble floor, breezing right past Edward's secretary and through the big oak door into the banker's office, where Edward Boatwright greeted Etta in a courtly manner but without emotion. Everything about the banker spoke of discipline and restraint.

Leon placed her in a wingback chair large enough to swallow her, and from their greater height the two men proceeded to explain the extent to which Roy had left Etta totally broke. Not only had Roy left no insurance, but in the past year he had sunk the Rivers estate deep in debt. He had let the mortgage payment get six months behind, and there was nothing to be done but sell the farm or risk losing it entirely.

Edward Boatwright leaned forward and said, ''Roy and I were talkin' the day before his death, Etta. It seemed then, and it seems now, that the best course is to sell the farm. By sellin' the farm and the house, you'll come out way ahead. You'll make enough to pay off the debt and have some left to help you get on your feet again.''

''Oh,'' she said.

She kept her tightly folded hands in her lap and her back perfectly straight.

Leon propped on the corner of the desk and leaned forward on his shiny shoes. ''Etta, you will not be destitute.

You'll make enough after the debts are paid to get a nice little place and even to keep you goin' for a year or so, until the baby is a bit older. Maybe Latrice could hire out as a day maid, you know, like she used to . . ."

He continued on, and her gaze flickered to Edward, who regarded her silently. Her mind drifted, and she recalled how Roy had refused to discuss finances with her. She had her own checking account, into which he had deposited money for her to spend as she wished for herself and for running the household. On occasions when Roy had appeared in straits over money, she had attempted to be of help, but he would touch her cheek and say, "You don't need to worry your head about the Rivers estate, darlin'. I'm takin' care of it."

Feeling as helpless to change the financial situation as she had been to change her marriage, she had closed her eyes to it.

Leon had finished speaking, and both men were gazing at her, obviously awaiting a response.

"What happened to all the money?" she asked. "Roy made money. I saw him make money with wheat and oats, cattle and horses. And what about the two gas wells? Don't we get money from those wells?"

All the while Roy would tell her not to worry her head, she had been listening. She had known little of his dealings.

Edward said, "Roy sold the family mineral rights to Alice back right after the war. Alice already owned half of 'em." He paused, then added, "Roy did make money, Etta, but he spent a lot, too. And you had to know about his gamblin'."

Etta looked downward, fingering her wedding rings.

"It wasn't all that people think, Etta," Leon said earnestly. "Yes, Roy spent his money runnin' around, but he inherited a lot of debt from his daddy. For one thing, ol' Carterroy never had been able to make money or say no to anyone, most of all his wife. He let Cynthia go hog-wild on spending, let her send Roy to private college up in St. Louis where she came from, and Roy never wanted it, never was ready for it. He got into some trouble, and it cost Carterroy plenty to bail him out. After his daddy passed, Roy did no better when it came to his mama. He never would let her know how tight things were from time to time. He would send her off with Alice up to St. Louis to visit, and she'd come home with crates of stuff, and he just kept borrowin' to keep her livin' how she expected, the same as his daddy always had.''

"Cynthia's been dead for seven years. Since then he made money. What about the wheat? And there's the cattle.''

Leon opened his mouth to answer, but Edward broke in, saying, "The wheat isn't goin' to amount to much, Etta, after this drought we've had. You'd only go in deeper to get it harvested and should just graze it out. Roy never planted for wheat other than to feed the cattle, anyway, and the debt is still owed the bank for the cattle, too.''

Edward leaned forward. "Etta, selling is all that is left. I've been tryin' to get Roy to do that for two months. The bank is within its right to start foreclosure right now, but considerin' your condition and the shock that has been handed you, we are willin' to wait and work with you on this thing. As Leon pointed out, the worth of the land and house together is considerably more than the debt, so you will come out ahead.''

"I see," she said. She did see, her eyes wide open now, although she didn't quite accept.

When Etta stepped out on the street, she stopped so suddenly that Leon bumped into her. She dug into her handbag. "I need a couple of aspirins.''

"Would you like me to go down to Parker's to get you some?" Leon asked anxiously.

"No. I'm sure I have some." She began to yank things from her handbag. She pulled out a handkerchief and with it came her coin purse, which fell, opened, and sent money rolling all over the sidewalk.

"Oh!" She went immediately after the money.

"I'll get it, Etta. You don't need to be bending," Leon said.

But Etta, feeling a certain panic, kept after the coins. She couldn't afford to waste even pennies.

Going for a dime in the gutter, she suddenly found herself gazing at a snakeskin cowboy boot. She looked upward into the gray eyes of the cowboy from the blue pickup truck.

"I'll get that, ma'am," he said, stepped into the gutter and stiffly bent to get the coin. "I believe this is yours also," he said, extending several coins.

She took them. "Thank you."

For long seconds they stood there staring at each other. Etta was struck by the sunlight on the man's chestnut hair and his gray eyes, a silvery gray, bright as the coins he put into her hands shining from his very tanned face. With a suddenness she recalled his eyes from the day of the funeral. The day he had held her in his arms as she made a pure fool of herself.

"I hope you are managin' well, Missus Rivers," he said.

"Yes. I'm managing." She added hoarsely, "I thank you very much for your help the other day." It was the best she could do.

"It was my pleasure to be of assistance."

His gaze drifted past her, and then he tipped his hat and walked away down the sidewalk. Gazing after him, she noticed that he had wide strong shoulders and that he walked with a limp.

"Who was that?" Leon asked, his voice sharp.

Etta looked up to see him frowing at her. "Another man Roy owed money." Only just then did she realize she had again not gotten the man's name.

"Was he botherin' you? Anyone comes pesterin' you for Roy's debts, you tell them to come see me. I'll handle all that," Leon said firmly.

"No . . . he wasn't botherin' me." Etta felt suddenly near tears. She really didn't want to break down. She was too wrung out to break down.

Leon put the coins he'd rescued into Etta's hand. She

had not found any aspirin, and he suggested they walk down to Parker's drugstore, where they could get aspirins and have a cold drink.

Etta snapped her handbag closed with trembling fingers and shook her head. "I'd really just like to go home, Leon."

The expression on her face made Leon worry that he might have a hysterical woman on his hands. He had considerable experience in this vein, as his wife was a woman given to emotional outbursts.

People would have been shocked to know that Betsy, a plain woman who put forth a cool and collected persona, was in private moments possessed of both severe fears and severe passions.

His wife's flirtations with Roy had not been a surprise to Leon; Betsy had been in love with Roy Rivers since the two were children, and she had never stopped loving him. She had married Leon because she knew full well that she was too plain for Roy to ever look her way, at least for anything more than a dalliance. Leon had married Betsy on the rebound from a broken relationship at college. Both knew these facts going in. Betsy had been a woman who needed a man to take care of her, and Leon had been a man who needed to take care of a woman. Their arrangement had suited them both. When their union had not produced children, neither had been terribly sorry. They had the main things either needed from the other. If sometimes each was lonely, well, life was not perfect.

Some time ago, however, Leon had fallen half in love with Etta. He had never admitted this foolishness fully to himself. For one thing, Etta somewhat frightened him. There was about Etta a certain wildness that at once attracted him and put him off. He didn't often feel up to Etta.

Looking at her right this moment, as he drove her home, he experienced the rarity of feeling needed by her. It did seem that his opportunity had arrived, and that if he stepped in, perhaps something would come of it. He did not allow himself to examine exactly what he wanted to happen, but the fantasy of Etta leaning on him, in the circle of his arms, perhaps crying and trembling, and him, as the stronger, more capable man, comforting her ... kissing her ... played at the edges of his mind.

Now as he passed a cafe, he suggested hopefully, "Are you sure you wouldn't like to get a bite to eat? You really should eat, honey." He thrilled to calling her honey.

She shook her head. "I just can't eat much these days."

She put a hand on her stomach, and Leon was forced to remember that she was pregnant. He felt a little foolish for his flights of fantasy just then.

Heading out of town, he began to feel depressed that he had not done better in taking care of Etta. Here she was a widow and having to face having a baby all alone. He felt that he should have made Roy do things that would have ensured Etta's security. They had been good friends, he and Roy. But even though Leon was older, Roy had always been the one to get Leon to do things, and not vice versa.

The uncomfortable memory came to him of when he'd been eighteen and Roy just fifteen, and Roy had talked him into stealing a car from out front of the Muleshoe Bar one night. They'd just meant to joy ride and return the car, but then Leon had turned it over while going around a corner. Roy had taken the full blame, had never revealed Leon's involvement to anyone.

"Everybody expects it of me, so they won't do hardly nothin'," Roy had said that night. "I'm underage, and Dad'll get me out of it, so just let it go."

With his first year of college approaching, and knowing his own father would have skinned him alive, if not disowned him, Leon had done as Roy said. He'd never told anyone, and Roy never had told, either.

Leon had a sudden urge to tell Etta all about it. But as he was trying to get the words to his tongue, she said, "There's Obie Lee to think about. He's been here fifteen years ... since he quit playin' ball. He and Roy would fish together. He helped Roy a lot."

Leon said, "I'm sorry about Obie, Etta. But he's a capable man. You need to think about yourself and the baby.

With the sale, you'll get out from under the debts, and you'll come out with somethin'."

"Come out with somethin'? What? The farm is what I have, what gives me and Latrice a good life. It is our home. It's my baby's home."

Her tone was upset, and Leon knew dispiritedly that he had not said the right thing. He knew he'd never tell about his boyhood escapade with Roy, either, because he'd just come out looking like a coward. He knew himself to be a coward, terrified of his emotions. If he was not such a coward, he would do something about how he felt about Etta. Maybe he still would, he thought, turning into the Rivers drive. He came to a stop in front of the house, shoved the stick into park, and turned to her.

"You have no choice, Etta. The only reason the bank hasn't moved on this is that Roy's Uncle Edward is on the board. Edward's not so much charitable, but he and Alice don't want to look bad in takin' this place from the pregnant widow of their only nephew. That's all that's held them off, and frankly Edward is not gettin' a lot of help from Alice, and Alice is on the board, too." He felt stronger, giving her the warning about Alice.

"I'm sorry, Etta. Edward called me about this a month ago, wantin' me to help convince Roy to do what needed to be done. If Roy had done that, you wouldn't be in this mess right now."

"Leon, I appreciate your position, but please don't criticize Roy to me. He was my husband. I might criticize him, but I don't believe others should do so."

Hurt crossed Leon's face, and Etta regretted her sharp tone. Leon was already getting out of the car. She sat and waited for him to open her door, as she knew he preferred her to do.

"I apologize for sounding so sharp, Leon," she said, touching his arm. "God knows you've been the best friend Roy ever had—and mine, too."

Leon looked away, as if embarrassed. "Roy was a friend to me, too. More than anyone knew." His gaze returned to her. "I know Roy would want me to do the best by you that I can. That's why I'm tellin' you that sometimes you got to quit beatin' a dead horse and cut your losses. You and the baby will be better off in a house in town where you won't have to deal with all the work of this place.

"I'll take care off all the arrangements, honey. You won't have to do a thing. Don't worry about anything right now, except havin' that baby."

Leon didn't waste any time taking care of things. Only a few hours later a station wagon pulled into the lane and stopped. Seeing it, Etta walked down the lane toward the road. The station wagon had the logo for Fred Grandy Realty on the door.

She stood back and watched a man she didn't know dig a hole and bury a post upon which he hung the for-sale sign. He cast her a polite nod, got back into his station wagon, and drove away.

Etta stared at the sign and then walked back up the lane toward the house. She stopped and gazed at the house framed by the greening leaves of the tall trees. The first day she had arrived here as Roy's wife came back to her.

"Well, honey, here's where we'll hang our hats." Roy had swung her up in his arms there on the walk between the red-tipped bushes. "What do you think of it?" he had asked, his expression for that second as anxious and proud as that of a schoolboy.

"I'll live with you anywhere, Roy."

As she spoke, she had been looking at the house, though, and not at Roy, her heart already racing over the threshold to take up residence.

The memory propelled her quickly up the steps, across the porch, and in the door. She stood there a moment, looked around the entry and into the living room and up the staircase. Then she walked through into the kitchen and found Latrice on a stepstool, emptying a top cabinet of little-used glasses and jars.

"What are you doin'?" Etta asked.

"I thought I might as well start packin' away the things

we don't use much, so we're ahead of the job when it comes time for movin'."

Etta picked up two glasses and thrust them at Latrice. "Put them back. Edward said that even if the place sold, we could stay here until the baby is born. There's a lot that can happen between now and then."

Latrice frowned. "What are you thinkin' of doin'?"

"I don't know right now, but to pray, and you are the one always pointin' out the power of prayer.

"And I'll say one thing, and that is I am not a quitter. I didn't quit with Roy, and I don't see that all I've gone through ought to be for nothin' and we end up losing this house—this place that is my baby's home."

Latrice gave her one of those disapproving looks. "I don't see anything wrong with prayin' for a nice little house in town. There hasn't been anything but trouble since we came to this house, so we might be better off leavin' it behind—and there's somethin' to be said for town. Our baby could walk to school and come home for lunches. I never liked movin' out here to the country anyway. I like havin' close neighbors and sidewalks. There's a lot to be said for bein' able to get decent television reception and a grocery store a person can walk to."

Etta gazed at her. "Where are we gonna live? We live with the white, you'll be treated like a maid. We live with the colored, me and the baby will be like sore thumbs. And are you willin' to give up this kitchen? You aren't likely to find another like it, not with what we'll be able to afford."

Apparently it would be a blue moon night, because Latrice appeared not to be able to think up a reply.

Etta picked up two more glasses and handed them up, waiting stubbornly until Latrice took them and replaced them in the cabinet.

Eight

Daily the bills came, and Latrice put them before Etta, and Etta placed them, unopened, in a basket on the desk in the den, exactly as Roy had done. She did not see a reason to open the bills she could not pay.

Leon offered her money on more than one occasion, but she declined as gently as possible, mindful of his sensitivity. Leon might not consciously expect some reciprocation on her part, but such expectation would no doubt arise. Etta did not want further entanglement with Leon. As it was, he had already guaranteed her electric bill payments, adamant that she not be threatened by lack of electricity. She accepted this because her only choice would have been to be without electricity.

Etta mulled over ideas of what to do about her situation, but most of her thoughts were not really ideas at all but more like fantasies, such as the representative of *The Millionaire* showing up at her door. She kept hoping a way out of her predicament would present itself. To this end, she sat one afternoon and went through Roy's account books.

"Find any millions?" Latrice came in and asked.

Etta shook her head and closed the book. "It looks like Roy quit recording anything four months ago." She hadn't really expected to find money, but she supposed she had hoped. She supposed she was riding the wish horse.

Within the first days that the for-sale sign was up, two people inquired about the farm. The first inquiry came from a farmer, who wanted to buy part of the land only, and the second from a developer, who was building an upscale housing tract in Chickasha and was interested in building a community of country estates. Neither made a hard offer, which was just as well, because Etta wasn't interested in that happening.

The garden flourished, and Latrice pressed foods upon Etta such as mustard greens and spinach, "to build your blood," and milk from Obie's cow made into tapioca pudding, "to give you some fat for nursin' the baby."

At last Etta was able to drink coffee, as long as she laced it liberally with cream. She had, however, grown very fond of warm cola.

Each day Etta played several games of Scrabble, either with Latrice or by herself, bending the rules and using proper names, putting each on a list as a possibility for the baby. Throughout the day, Etta would speak the names aloud, "Mary Rose Rivers . . . Jolene Rivers . . . Summer Marie Rivers," repeatedly testing the sound of each and asking the opinion of the child growing inside her.

Her daughter began to move and kick with vigor that delighted and comforted Etta. The child growing inside her kept her hoping for a future. She returned to working on the nursery, which she had almost completed before Roy's death. With Latrice's instructions, she embroidered on squares to make a baby quilt and hung curtains Latrice made.

Whenever going to the nursery or the guest room upstairs, Etta continued to hurry past the door of hers and Roy's bedroom. She had not entered that room since the day of the funeral.

"You haven't seen Mr. Roy or heard him anymore, have you?" Latrice asked her.

Etta said, "No . . . but I smell his cologne, that expensive stuff he ordered from New York." She had found the actual bottle in the medicine cabinet and flushed the contents down the toilet, then had thrown the bottle away, but that had not seemed to help. Now, rubbing her shoulders, she said to Latrice. "It's like he's callin' to me to help him."

Latrice nodded. "He always called to you. Just tell him that he's dead."

"Well, I should imagine he knows he's dead."

"You haven't accepted it is all over yet, though," Latrice replied.

"All over? I don't believe our past is ever all over. It just stays around to torment us."

"Only if you allow it," Latrice said. "To let go of the past, you have to let go of anger and resentment. Time will work it out."

"Time doesn't work it out," Etta said. "It wears us out."

"That solves a lot of problems, too," was Latrice's reply.

Obie Lee worked on Etta's old Ford, which had been her car before marrying Roy. It was registered in her name alone and free of debt, so no one was going to be able to take it from her. It occurred to Etta that she might end up driving away from this house in about the same condition she had arrived, with little or nothing except poor history.

And good clothes, she reminded herself. For her entire marriage, she had been buying classic quality clothing which would see her through another decade. No matter if she lived in a shanty and drove a junker, she would be well dressed.

"This car's sixteen years old, Miz Etta, and it's been sittin' here all winter," Obie told her. "It's gonna take right much work. I may have to rebuild the whole engine. At the very least we're talkin' new fuel pump, distributor, and some wires. Likely a rebuild on the carburetor."

Etta couldn't afford any of those things. Obie said he would scrounge around and see what he could pick up from junkers.

"Thanks for tryin', Obie. We're gonna need a car."

She touched the dull fender and thought how she would

be driving her baby away from this house in this car.

"Obie, you know it looks like the farm will have to be sold."

"I know that, Miz Etta. I'm real sorry."

She peered up at him. "The land is all tied up with the mortgage at the bank, or I'd be able to just deed you your forty acres. It is yours by rights."

He removed his ball cap and wiped his sleeve over his graying hair. "I appreciate your generous sentiment, but I don't really want that land, Miz Etta. If you and Miss Latrice move off, I'd just as soon go, too. I'm not really overly fond of that cotton field." He gave a low chuckle with the last statement.

Obie's chuckles were such—dark eyes sparkled like stars—that Etta had to smile, too, although the next instant the heavy weight of dread fell back on her.

"Where will you go, Obie?"

He shrugged. "Oh, there's possibilities all over. There's a few who've wanted me to come work their farm over the years. I have considered off and on to go up to Okie City. My brother up there has a barbeque restaurant and has asked me several times to throw in with him."

After a minute he said, "You might consider movin' up to Okie City, too, Miz Etta." He looked a little hopeful.

"I don't know, Obie. I guess we could consider it. Latrice would prefer town livin'—if she could have the same modern kitchen," she said with a small grin. She looked over at Little Gus in his corral. "I'm happier here, though, where I can have my horses and things. And I think it'll be better for the baby, too."

She sighed. It seemed she was doing a lot of sighing lately, and she didn't like it.

"Have faith, Miz Etta," Obie said, his dark eyes warm. "No matter what it looks like, the Lord has it in hand."

Etta gazed for a long moment into the dark, dirty engine. "It's hard to believe that sometimes, isn't it?" She lifted her eyes to Obie. "I mean, sometimes it sure doesn't look like God has anything in hand, considerin' all the mess we get ourselves into."

Obie grinned again, sad sparks in his eyes now. "That's true." Then he paused, the carburetor piece in his greasy hand, and said, "But very often you gotta take all the wrong roads, in order to learn the right one. Our lives are school, and we have lessons to learn. Don't mean the Lord ain't right there with us, givin' a guiding hand. I've sure made my share of mistakes, but I've always thought two things: that the right place to look is at God, and you only gotta live one day at a time." He seemed suddenly embarrassed at his speech, and looked away.

Etta said, "You are right, Obie. It's just hard to remember to do sometimes." She laid a hand on his arm. "Thanks so much."

"Somethin' will turn up that will be just right for you and the baby and Miss Latrice," he said. "Right now all you gotta do is hold on and wait."

"Well, if it's right for us, then it will be right for you, too, Obie."

"Likely so," he said and turned back to the car. The hand that worked the wrench inside the greasy engine was bony and gnarled. When he shifted and stretched for better leverage he did so stiffly. He was not young.

Etta turned away and looked out across the corrals, now empty and desolate, except for Little Gus. Wishes welled up inside her. But if wishes were horses they'd all ride, and right then there was only one horse, and he was a pretty scrubby fellow who was barely green broke.

She thought of Obie's words: Look at God and take one day at a time. She supposed she wasn't in a position to do anything else.

The morning Roy's Aunt Alice showed up, she didn't bother to telephone first. She came in surprise attack was how Etta thought of it. She rang the doorbell, and back in the kitchen Latrice said, "That's Miz Alice Boatwright's ring."

"Alice's ring?" Etta was washing fresh spinach.

"It rings like her sayin', 'Get your butt in here on the double.' "

This was not a great surprise. Alice had been telephoning, and Latrice had been putting her off. It was only a matter of time before Alice reached her limit. In fact, Etta and Latrice were both surprised that Alice had been thwarted this long. Alice Boatwright wasn't one to be thwarted.

Frowning, Etta said, "Go tell her I'm on my deathbed with cholera."

Latrice raised an eyebrow. "You can either let Miz Alice come chasin' you down and catch you on the run, or you can face her and put *her* on the run."

"I don't know as God Himself can put Alice on the run," Etta muttered as she dried her hands with a towel.

She walked through to the front door, straightened her back, and gathered herself, wishing she wore something other than overalls; it was very difficult to face Alice in baggy, worn overalls.

Then she opened the door and said with all graciousness, "Why, hello, Alice, won't you come in?"

Alice was a member of the Richards family of St. Louis, as had been Roy's mother. She had married a little beneath herself when she had married Edward Boatwright, but the tradeoff had been that Edward was of the family that owned a bank and ruled a county. As Alice's branch of the Richards had come down in the past fifty years, marrying Edward was a smart thing. Rather than be a small, obscure fish in an enormous pond, Alice had succeeded in making herself an important fish in a tiny pond, and she liked it very well.

Although Latrice maintained every person had a heart, she conceded about Alice: "If there's any charity in the woman, it's well hid by power and spite."

Etta agreed, except when it came to Roy. Etta thought Alice had felt something at least close to love for Roy, even if her feelings had still carried the heavy mark of control.

The day after Etta and Roy had returned from their honeymoon, Alice had stormed over to the house and screamed at Roy, "What in the hell's the matter with you? If you wanted her, you could have just had her . . . you didn't have

to marry her, for godsakes. A man *marries* a woman like
Corinne Salyer, not some poor trash like Etta Kreger.
You're just gonna piss your life away after all, aren't you?''

Alice had not been deterred one iota by Etta's hearing
all this. When alone with family, Alice got as crude and
down and dirty as she wished.

For her part, Etta had been shocked. She had not known
that a woman of Alice's proper social standing would know
any swearwords, much less be screaming them like a crazed
shrew. Actually, Etta had not personally known any women
of Alice's social standing. But she had seen them in the
movies and had observed them entering shops on the street.
She had saved up for a month and had her hair done in a
swank salon among the ''better people,'' and they had all
appeared exactly like Margaret from *Father Knows Best*:
tranquil, genteel, and perfect ladies.

Thus Etta had been astonished and then crushed, not only
by Alice's words but by the way Alice looked at her as if
she were garbage in the street.

''Be nice to her,'' Roy told Etta later. ''She'll come
around eventually.'' Then he added how beautiful and
sweet Etta was, so Aunt Alice couldn't help but fall in love
with her as he had.

He had made Etta believe it could happen, and she had
been as nice to Alice as a person could possibly be. She
had studied books and articles on etiquette and style until
she could have been presented at a Southern League meeting. She had read *Town and Country* and the *Saturday Evening Post* from cover to cover each month and looked up
definitions and pronunciations of difficult words she came
across, all in an effort to improve so Alice would not only
like her but love her.

Her efforts had been in vain, of course. Alice did not
intend to ever accept her. Alice considered it as a mark of
her standing in society to disdain Etta. Once she had come
to accept this, Etta had ceased to be hurt or manipulated
by it.

Still, she had always done best with Alice when she had
had sufficient time to prepare to face her. Gazing at the

older woman now, Etta had the sinking feeling that she was not sufficiently prepared.

Petite and straight as a rod, Alice stepped into the foyer and eyed Etta from head to toe. "Latrice said you've been so sick as to take to your bed. It appears to me you've been farmin'."

"Are you so hard up for people to criticize, Alice, that you had to come all the way out here and start on me?" She was rather pleased with her comment, and with Alice's frown.

"I've come for my sister's things," Alice said. "When Cynthia died, poor Roy wasn't ready to let go of her things. I haven't said anything, because he's needed these pieces of his mother around him. Now, however, by rights they are mine, and I'd like to get them before they get lost from family."

"What things are you talkin' about?"

"Well, the mantel clock, for one." She strode to the mantel and gestured at the clock. "It was our mother's clock, and Cynthia said expressly right before her death that I was to have it, but Roy just couldn't part with it. And that lamp over there—it's from our family home . . . and there are several quilts that our aunt made for each of us when we were newly married."

Etta gazed at her a moment, then said, "Suppose you go around and pick out what you want."

Alice went to the door and beckoned to her maid to bring some boxes. Etta had not seen the maid, nor had she seen that the backseat of Alice's car was filled with boxes.

She felt a small flicker of alarm. She had thought she had done the right thing; she did not want Alice to go around claiming Etta had stolen what rightfully belonged to her.

Alice put the mantel clock into a box. After that she picked up not only the red glass lamp, but the small marble-topped curio table upon which the lamp had sat.

"The lamp has always sat on this table," she said.

Then she went into the den and took two prints of fox and hound hunts and then the large print of two Victorian girls from the living room wall. "I gave these to Cynthia myself," she said.

Having warmed up on those few items, Alice moved about the living room and then up the stairs to the linen closet, snatching up articles as swiftly as a challenger in one of those grocery store sweepstakes. At the linen closet, she laid claim not only to the before-mentioned quilts but to an Irish lace spread as well. "I gave this to Cynthia on her fortieth birthday," Alice said.

Etta watched with a growing amazement and dismay, realizing she had once again foolishly underestimated the woman. She watched as Alice strode into the dining room, where she retrieved the blown-glass miniature dog and horse and cat, and several vases, as well as a set of twelve crystal glasses.

But when Alice went to lay claim to the silver tea and coffee service, Etta said, "No. You can't have this."

"This set was my sister's. She bought it in St. Louis. We were there together on a trip."

"It belongs now to Roy's child, his mother's grand-child."

Alice's gaze drifted to Etta's belly. "I see. All right, but I must insist on taking the silverware. It has our family initial." She took up the polished chest of silver.

Etta reached out for the chest, too, saying, "The initial stands for Rivers. Carterroy bought this for Cynthia right after Robert's death. Roy told me so."

"Cynthia picked it out herself. I helped her," Alice said, tugging the chest from Etta.

"But you didn't buy it," Etta said, tugging it back. "And your name is not Rivers."

Alice's eyes blazed, then her mouth formed a bitter line, and Etta found herself, a woman pregnant going on seven months, in a grappling match with a petite silver-haired matron for possession of a chest of silverware.

"You little tramp," Alice said. "Roy may have married you, but you never were a Rivers."

"My child is Roy's child," Etta said.

"And are we certain of that?" Alice said.

The comment caused Etta to jerk hard on the case, using her belly as leverage. Alice held on, too, like a little bulldog. Gazing into Alice's glittering eyes, Etta realized that the fight was not really over the silverware. It was over something much larger, something she could not name but which she knew was very important.

Johnny turned his truck into the Rivers drive and slowed, looking at the real-estate sale sign. He'd heard tell how things were. The word was, though, that the bank wouldn't throw a woman and a new baby out of their home, at least not for a few months. Johnny figured he could use those few months. He felt he might be a little crazy, but there was a strong urge inside him that told him to come on to this place. The corrals were good, and there was a barn with a room. At the present, Johnny had horses, and he needed a room. He eased forward, mindful of the filly in the bed and the two horses tied to the back, and headed down the lane toward the house.

A black Cadillac sat out front, doors open, a thin young woman in a tan cloth coat sticking a box into it. Johnny tipped his hat to her and said howdy out the window, but she just sort of stared at him. He parked to the side nearer the barn and walked back to the front door. The woman in the tan coat was gone, the front door stood open. He naturally went inside. Hearing voices and noise, he walked through to the dining room, stepping carefully with his boots and spurs over the shiny flooring.

He came to a stop in the dining-room entry, right behind the woman in the tan coat, and beheld the sight of Mrs. Rivers, her and her belly in faded overalls, going round and round with a small, silver-haired woman in a skirt and sweater and pearls. Johnny recognized the elegant silver-haired woman from the funeral. The two women were having a tussle over a case.

As soon as they both saw him and the woman in the tan coat, who was shrinking backward into Johnny, they stopped, eyes wide. The silver-haired woman let go of the wooden case, which came as a surprise to Mrs. Rivers,

whose eyes sprang wider as she stumbled backward. She
lost her hold on the case, and it fell to the floor, opened,
and spewed forth shiny forks and knives and spoons like it
was upchucking, while Mrs. Rivers took hold of the buffet
to keep from falling.

Johnny didn't know what to do. He just stood there feeling awkward.

The silver-haired woman in the pearls lifted her chin.
"I'm certainly not going to fight you for any of this," she
said and stalked off past Johnny like a stiff breeze, causing
the woman in the tan coat to turn and follow as if by a tow
line.

Mrs. Rivers mumbled something like, "You could have
fooled me," and then Johnny saw her sliding from the buffet and downward to the floor. Before he could move, she'd
gone right down to her knees amid the strewn silverware.

Alarmed that she was fainting, he started toward her. At
that same moment the kitchen door swung open, and Miss
Latrice burst onto the scene.

His gaze suddenly lighting on Mrs. Rivers's belly,
Johnny stopped short, consumed by uncertainty. "Are you
all right, ma'am?"

She nodded. "Just out of breath. Anger and resentment
take a lot out of person."

Johnny didn't know what to say to that. He was relieved
to see she wasn't fainting.

Miss Latrice hardly looked at Mrs. Rivers; she knelt and
started fervently raking in the silverware, grumbling in a
low voice, "Why in the world would you let that woman
have free rein in the first place? I thought I had taught you
better sense."

"It seemed the thing to do at the time," Mrs. Rivers
said, and she was sort of chuckling, which just seemed to
make Miss Latrice look madder.

Johnny hung back. He did not know how he managed to
get into these awkward situations. It seemed every time he
deliberately set out on a course, things got all jumbled up.

Etta felt dazed. She could not look up at the cowboy.

She was too embarrassed. Did he always have to arrive when she was in a mess?

Feeling something poking her hip, she shifted and pulled two forks from beneath her and then reached for a spoon from under the buffet, handing all three to Latrice. She saw the cowboy's hands extending two spoons. She reached to take them, and because there was no way out of it, she raised her eyes.

The cowboy was gazing down at her with his silvery eyes anxious and curious.

Etta said, "I'm sorry to tell you I still don't have the money my husband owed you. I have even less now than I had the day we buried him."

He looked surprised, then said quickly, "Oh, no, ma'am. I'm not here for the money. You see, I have a little filly out in my truck." He gestured with his hat. "I need someplace to keep her, and I was hopin' we could work somethin' out."

Nine

Etta looked quickly into the man's eyes. Steely gray, strikingly bright against his rugged face. A handsome heartbreak man, she thought instantly as she averted her gaze and smoothed her overalls.

"I'm sorry, but in case you didn't notice, there is a for-sale sign in the front. There's really no way I can help you, Mr. . . ." She stopped, feeling silly about not knowing his name.

"My name's Johnny Bellah, ma'am. I guess we didn't get properly introduced the other day."

His voice was soft and deep, his face smiling, and he stuck out his hand. It was warm, moist, and rough. She was the one to pull her hand away.

He said, "I got the filly out at my truck, if you'd like to see her."

Without waiting for her to answer, he tucked his hat on his head and moved quickly across the oak flooring, his spurs jingling softly with each step, to the door that he drew open for her.

Etta hesitated and then went with him, thinking that life was just flowing on and dragging her with it.

She spared him quick glances, noting again his starched shirt stretched over broad shoulders and his lean hips. And his limp, which seemed very pronounced today.

"Got my bad knee wrenched yesterday," he explained, as if reading her mind.

Her eyes met his briefly before skittering away.

She said, "How much did you say my husband owed you, Mr. Bellah, and what for exactly?"

"Eight hundred dollars. I got the IOU right here." Stopping, he pulled his wallet from his back pocket, took out a rumpled slip of paper and handed it to her. "I sold some horses for your husband down in Fort Worth back this winter . . . but this idn't for that. This is for a poker game." His voice dropped a notch, and his eyes shifted.

"Oh."

It was Roy's handwriting all right, all his sweeping flourishes. Etta did not think she was much concerned with a poker debt.

Handing the note back to him, she looked over at his pickup parked in front of the barn. "You said you have a filly?" Shielding her eyes against the sun, she looked at his truck and saw two horses, which appeared to be tied to the back of the truck.

"Yes, ma'am." He hurried to fall in step with her again. "Little red dun, not four months old . . . and these two-year-olds, too."

"You brought them here like that?" Etta asked, finding the image of the truck trailing horses down the highway quite amazing.

"Well now, I couldn't very well put them in the back. They'd have beat this filly to death. I go slow so they can keep up."

He shoved the older horses aside and opened the tailgate. Strong, rough hands . . . shoulder muscles thick beneath his blue shirt. Etta shifted her gaze from his body.

"Easy girl," he murmured.

The filly backed up. She was so gaunt her ribs and hip-bones protruded, and her legs looked like rickety sticks. He pretty much tugged her to the ground, struggling to bear her weight with his injured knee. Etta hovered, wanting to help but not knowing how.

"They took her mama to nurse an orphaned colt," he told her, "and threw her out in the pen with the other string. She can't hold her own with them, and she would've been dead in no time. I need a place to keep her and to break these other two for a fella. Thought maybe I could use your place here, in exchange for your husband's IOU. I'll only need a month or so."

Of course he wanted to stable all three, but had mentioned only the filly at first. Etta was not at all surprised; such was the way of men like him, who were not being devious but simply assuming.

She gazed at him. He gazed at her, his luminous silvery eyes charming and expectant.

She thought she should say no, but instead she shrugged and put a hand to touch the filly's soft nose. "I guess it'd be okay. Might as well get some use out of the place while we can."

"Well now," he drawled, a warm grin sweeping his face and lighting his eyes, "I certainly appreciate this, ma'am . . . and I'll tell you what. I'll throw in breakin' that red horse for you."

Etta's head came up. She saw his eyes bright and eager and his smile as easy and sweet as slipping down a child's slide.

"Maybe," she said, then turned and walked back to the house.

Within the space of the following two days, with Etta watching from the safety of the house, Johnny Bellah not only moved his adopted filly and the two geldings he had contracted to train for Jed Stuart into the stable, but himself as well, moving his tack into the tack room and his belongings into the stablehand's room.

Early afternoon of the second day he showed up leading a string of eight horses up the tree-lined lane.

This did not come as a great surprise to Etta, as she had known a man such as Johnny Bellah would not be content with one scrubby filly and two geldings of no particular worth.

Also, at the moment he came with the herd, she was upstairs in the bedroom she had shared with Roy, sitting on the bed and crying to him things such as: "I loved you, Roy, and you broke my heart. What are we gonna do now? You left a daughter, you know. You left her penniless, damn you to hell, Roy Rivers."

She was so involved with venting her anger that she heard the horses' thudding hooves for a full minute before she responded. Finally realizing the sound was horses' hooves and not thunder, she knew instantly that Johnny Bellah was the cause. Nevertheless, she went to look out the window to make certain, and sure enough she saw him coming on the back of a big golden dun, dragging along a string behind him (only three of which were held by a rope), like a cowboy out of a picture show.

Etta ran down the stairs and out the front door, where she paused in a moment of uncertainty of her eyesight.

Johnny swept off his hat and called gaily, "Howdy, ma'am. Gorgeous afternoon, idn't it?"

Etta raced around to the side yard, completely forgetting about the child she carried and the possibility of being run down in her effort to keep the loose horses away from the yard, while Latrice, coming off the side porch, waved her apron and hollered, "Don't let them in my garden! Shoo, buggers . . . shoo!"

Grinning exuberantly, Johnny rode on by, leading the string into the big corral, turning quickly and coming out to drive the strays through the gate Etta held open. Then he jumped from the saddle, helped her shove the latch, and told her instantly how he had brought all eight head by himself thirteen miles down the county highway, with fencing and without it and with vehicles zipping past, suffering only one mishap when several horses trampled a row of rose bushes a lady had just set out at the edge of her yard.

He ended with, "This here big dun and that gray there are my own. The others I'm trainin' for Harry Flagg. I'm in the trainin' business again," his silvery eyes pleased as pleased could be.

"Mr. Bellah, you are takin' advantage of our deal. I

agreed to the filly and the two geldings—not to stablin' an entire herd.''

''Well now, I guess that's so, ma'am,'' he drawled, casting a smile calculated to be sheepish, ''but there's plenty of room . . . and the IOU is for eight hundred dollars. You got the space, and I got the talent.''

Hand on the rough fence rail, her heart pounding in a curious, frightening manner, Etta looked at the horses, at the powerful legs and noble heads, flying manes and tails, muscles moving in motion. She dared not return her eyes to the man who shifted beside her. She felt his gaze and his breath, and very nearly the cotton of his shirt and beating of his heart.

He said, ''I'll tell you what—if you'd like, I'll train that red horse for you in exchange for the extra use of your place.''

She knew in that moment that this was what he was after all along—Little Gus.

She knew, with a small heartsickness, that from his bent, once-black hat to his gleaming champion belt buckle to his spurs that never came off his boots, he was in all ways exactly like her father and every other cowboy she had ever encountered. His life and breath were horses, and he could more easily stop eating and drinking than he could stop going after them, in the same manner that Roy had gone after women and God-knew-what-all.

Turning to face him, she saw his eyes flicker downward, reach her swollen belly, and zip back upward again, his cheeks glowing slightly. He knotted his brows and waited.

''Maybe,'' she said and walked away toward the house.

At the porch she stepped up beside Latrice, paused, and looked back at the large corral, where Johnny Bellah moved among the horses and the billows of dust in the light of a western sun. It was a beautiful sight, and Etta lingered, her hand braced on the porch post, watching and not knowing why she felt compelled to do so, until she felt Latrice looking at her.

She said, ''He can be a help to Obie while he's here,'' and went inside.

*   *   *

An hour later, Johnny Bellah knocked at the kitchen door and requested Pine-Sol, in order to clean the stablehand's room in the barn, an act that immediately won Latrice's admiration, as she had never known a man to disinfect. She kept going to the screen door and looking out and tossing out comments such as, "My land, he's done thrown out that old mattress. He's hauled out the dresser and shelf and is washin' them. He's brought out the springs now and is rinsin' them . . . they'll probably rust away. Lordy, he must have had a good mama."

Latrice was in fact so captivated by Johnny Bellah's apparent bent toward cleanliness (although she would have died before admitting it) that when he returned what was left of the Pine-Sol, she invited him to supper.

"A man who works that hard at cleanin' is gonna need somethin' to stick to his ribs," she told Etta. "He loved my biscuits the other mornin' he came to breakfast."

"When did he come to breakfast?" Etta asked with some bit of shock.

"Oh, the day after the funeral, when you were sleepin' in my bed. I forgot, you missed it."

Latrice then told of the visit, and Etta absorbed the news with some wonderment. It seemed strange to think of goings-on in her own house that she was completely in the dark about.

Watching Johnny Bellah moving to and from the barn, she imagined him sitting in the kitchen, at the red Formica and chrome table, with his bright silvery eyes, eating a fluffy biscuit and drinking dark coffee with his work-worn hands, and asking to see her, while she had been sleeping in her voile nightgown just on the other side of the wall.

When he came to the door for Latrice's promised supper, he wore a fresh starched shirt, clean jeans, and polished boots and his hair was neatly combed.

As she let him inside, Etta thought she caught a whiff of an odor. Whiskey, but then she considered it could be Pine-Sol. She smoothed her worn overalls and hair, wishing she had changed and combed her hair.

Tossing off that nonsense, she straightened her back and waved him into a chair. They ate in the kitchen; Etta did not think the situation called for use of the dining room. Johnny Bellah fell into the category of a renter, a hand, not company.

Over supper, of which he ate a great quantity and with surprisingly impeccable manners, Johnny Bellah told them all about himself, with very little prodding. He had been supporting himself since arriving in the vicinity by working at the stock sale barn and for several local ranchers, and at nights he had been delivering bootleg. It concerned him some that it was illegal, but, "I don't like to judge anyone," he explained. "I like a nip myself now and then."

Studying him, Etta wondered.

"That was all just temporary anyway," he said. "I'm back to my chosen profession."

"Which is?" Etta asked.

"Horseman, ma'am," he said. He took up another soda biscuit, his fourth, and heaped jelly on it, saying, "I've cowboyed and rodeoed and done a lot of other things I'm proud of, but now I make my livin' trainin' horses. I'm a horseman."

He continued to tell them about having grown up in Fort Worth, Texas, cowboy-town-America, until the age of thirteen when his mother had died, and he lit out on his own. He had worked a number of big old ranches in Texas—the King, the Waggoner, the XIT—and other, smaller spreads all over the Texas and Oklahoma panhandles and into New Mexico.

He had been a rodeo cowboy riding a shooting star to fame and fortune as a bronc rider, bulldogger, sometimes team roper, with two bronc-riding and three all-round cowboy championships to his credit, when the army called his name and sent him to Korea. A jeep turned over on his knee in the Far East mud and knocked his rodeo star out of the sky. He was a compulsive reader of novels, liked the sound of certain words on his tongue, didn't like rising early but loved to see the dawn break over the land, favored Nocona boots, would not come in the same room with cooked cabbage, loved warm apple pie with ice cream melting on it, and Hershey bars, and red horses best of all.

All of this he told them over that one meal, which of course caused them to linger long at the table.

"You are quite a talkative man, Mr. Bellah," Etta told him, as Latrice began clearing their plates. She realized that she had not been bored listening to him, though.

"Yes, ma'am." He nodded. "I figured you ladies would want to know all about me."

Etta raised an eyebrow at that, and he added, "Since I'm usin' your facilities and eatin' at your table, you have a right to know about my caliber."

His gaze flickered to Latrice and then rested on Etta for long seconds in which Etta felt drawn to him, despite herself.

"Would you tell me about that red horse of yours, ma'am?" he said, leaning forward on folded arms.

Etta stared at him.

Then she looked at her glass of tea, fingering the moisture. "His name is Little Pegasus. He's out of a mare that Roy picked up cheap. The mare had already won a couple of races, and Roy planned to prepare her for goin' over to New Mexico."

She paused, thinking of how Roy had always had this dream of discovering a fantastic racehorse out of nowhere. She looked into Johnny Bellah's silvery eyes, and he looked back, waiting.

"When the mare got here it was discovered that she was in foal and no one knew by what stallion. It was just one of those mistakes that can happen when people aren't payin' attention. The mare died when Little Gus was born. It looked like he wouldn't make it either, but he did. He's a tough horse."

Johnny Bellah's eyes were intent upon her. "Obie tells me that you doctored him and brought him around."

"I had a lot of help," Etta said. "Obie got us a nursing mare, and Latrice helped me massage his legs, and we got him standin' every day, until he could do it on his own."

Telling of it brought it all back to her in that brief mo-

ment, the fear and the struggle, and the triumph. She realized she had smiled slightly, and Johnny Bellah smiled in
return. Etta averted her eyes and rose to get the coffee cups.

He said, ''Obie said he's been ridden once or twice.''

''Not really ridden. He was handled so much that gettin'
on him wasn't hard, but I found out I was pregnant and
had to quit on him. That was last fall. My husband got on
him a couple of times, but Gus bucked him off.''

''Well now, he doesn't look like much,'' Johnny Bellah
drawled, sitting back in his chair, ''but you never know
about some horses. Sometimes what's on the inside of a
horse can make up for a lot on the outside.''

This had always been Etta's opinion about Little Gus;
Johnny Bellah's being on the same thought wave was un-
settling.

Latrice brought their coffee and asked Johnny if he took
cream and sugar.

''Take heaps of both when I can get 'em,'' he said, his
face breaking into the sort of grin that is so pleased with
life.

That's how Johnny Bellah seemed—a man highly
pleased with life and with himself. It was an attitude that
enthralled, and irritated.

Latrice brought dishes of canned apricots with cream
from Obie Lee's cow. Johnny exclaimed over the dessert
as if he had been given a three-tier and half-dozen-egg
fudge cake.

''Uhmmm . . . you ladies have sure treated me tonight,''
he said, eyes feasting on the sweet fruit.

Then his gaze came up and met Etta's. His eyes shone,
and seemed to feast on her, too.

Etta pushed up quickly from the table. ''I don't believe
I need any dessert tonight, Latrice,'' she said and went to
the sink and began washing dishes, which earned her raised
eyebrows from Latrice.

Plunging her hands into the warm, soapy water, she told
herself that Johnny Bellah was not looking at her. He was
looking for a way to Little Gus.

She told herself not to think of his silvery eyes or the

way his dark hair curled on the back of his neck, or the foolish longings that really had nothing to do with him at all. The girl-child growing inside her, as if knowing already about a woman's foolish inclinations, began knocking inside Etta's belly, seeming to say, *Remember me.*

Despite her better intentions, as she put away the plates she sneaked looks at him, and twice she saw him looking at her. He did not hide this at all.

As he was leaving, Johnny Bellah paused at the door and said, "Ma'am, I really wouldn't mind workin' that red horse for you. I'd be interested in seeing what I could do with him. I sort of owe you."

Etta said, "I'll think about it, Mr. Bellah."

"Johnny, ma'am. Just call me Johnny." His eyes lingered on hers.

Later, upstairs in the guest-room bed, with the bedside lamp making patterns on the ceiling, Etta lay there and thought about it all: about Roy and her baby and the house, and Johnny Bellah, and the red horse, and coincidence and the hand of God. She caressed her belly through the cotton of her nightgown, feeling the fluttering of her daughter inside.

Something, some sound, made her get up and go to the window, peel back the curtain, and peer out. She saw Johnny Bellah at the corner of the barn, beneath the pole lamp. She saw him lift his head and look up at her window!

She drew quickly back, stood there, her heart pounding and the baby fluttering.

There came the sound of his truck engine starting. Peering cautiously through the curtains, she watched him drive away. She threw open the window, released the screen, and stuck her head out, watching his truck headlights to see which way he turned on the road, although that told her nothing, and she thought herself quite silly for it, too.

Closing the window, she turned, hesitated, and then walked down to the bedroom she had shared with Roy. She slowly went inside. She could see everything surprisingly well by the light of the bright moon. Roy's cologne came to her.

She sat on the edge of the bed for a long time, and Roy's cologne was there the entire time. She stroked her belly; now the child slept silently. After a while she pulled a pillow to her chest, lay over, and went to sleep.

The sound of a vehicle awakened her, and she went to the window to see headlights and knew it was Johnny Bellah returning. The hand of the bedside clock read quarter past three. The truck stopped only inches from the barn—she had thought he might hit it. Johnny Bellah got out and walked very unsteadily into the dark entry.

The sight of Johnny Bellah like that, and the horses in the moonlight, and the black hole of the barn entry struck Etta as so sad that she began to cry. She went back to the guest room, threw herself into bed, and cried until she fell asleep.

The following day, when she saw Johnny coming from the barn with a halter, Etta took up her hat and went out to watch him work with his horses. She was highly curious to decide for herself the extent of his training expertise.

Sitting on the fence rail beneath the shade of her brown Stetson, she watched and listened while Johnny gave her a running commentary on his philosophy of horse training, as if she were waiting with bated breath to hear all the magnificent things he had to say.

"No two horses are alike. They're different same as people are different. Just like teenage boys—some I grant you need a smack or two once in a while to get their attention, while most will need a bit of gentle direction, and yet still others need you to smack and then direct.

"Each horse should be treated according to his need. Now, any trainer can have a plan and go about trainin' according to that plan. What he's doin' is trainin' for himself, and if his plan works with the horse, fine, but if it doesn't, he's out of luck with that horse. Trainers like that blame the horse. What I do is study the horse and change my plan to fit him. Go *with* him—not against him."

Taking the lead rope, he strode toward the training pen without a backward glance at the brown horse, who showed signs of bolting but was forced to follow, or be dragged along. The man was clearly in control.

Although he appeared quite lackadaisical, Etta quickly formed the opinion that Johnny Bellah knew exactly what he was doing and was every inch the horse trainer he proclaimed himself to be.

While not ever looking at the horse—"To keep him guessin'," he said—he knew the animal's every movement. He shut the gate and smacked the animal's hip, hard, sending it circling the perimeter of the round pen, while he stood in the middle, smoking a cigarette and casting his pearly comments Etta's way, such as, "I call this son-of-a-buck Worthless—he's not worth breakin'." Or, "Don't look a green horse in the eye. You scare him that way." Or, "Think we'll get rain? My knee's actin' up." Despite his knee, he could run hard and threatening toward a horse.

"Domination is the key," he said. "It is the way of nature, what a horse understands. What some people don't understand, though, is that dominate means to have mastery over, to guide and influence—not beat into submission." He tapped his temple. "We got to dominate with the mind, and not the hand. If you dominate with the hand, you got to watch your back every minute. The best horse is convinced he wants to please us. That takes workin' with his mind . . . and ideally, the whole process should take months."

In a powerful motion, he grabbed the horse's lead rope and jerked the animal to him. It stood there, chest heaving, while Johnny slung the saddle pad atop it with one hand, following with the saddle in the other, saying, "But these horses here, I'll just get on and ride. The man's paid for thirty days ridin' on 'em, and he expects a three-month job done in one. So that's what I'll give."

His gray eyes flickered to Etta, down to her belly, and then as quickly away. He was decidedly uncomfortable with her pregnancy. Whenever his eyes strayed to her belly, his face would redden.

Etta, entertained quite a bit by this, kept putting her belly in his way. She took foolish pride in being able to climb easily onto the top fence rail and sit there for hours on end, and although her back would begin to ache, she would have ground her teeth to dust before allowing the ache to show.

That first day when Johnny threw himself up on top of the first horse—a barrel-chested brown, big for his age— Etta gripped the rail and held her breath, expecting to see the horse start bucking and Johnny Bellah go flying to the ground. She had watched many trainers fall to the ground in this same pen. She had once seen her own father get knocked unconscious and would never forget the horror she had felt when she had run to him, held his head, and cried, "Daddy . . . Daddy, wake up."

But the horse did not buck. He humped up, yet the next instant he was racing the circle, while Johnny leaned forward and urged him onward, faster and faster around the pen. Each time the horse slowed, Johnny snapped the end of the lead rope on the horse's hip, forcing him forward. Only when the horse looked as if he might drop did Johnny pull up.

"Whoa, boy." The horse, legs spraddled and sweat running in foamy rivulets, stood with sides heaving as Johnny slipped to the ground.

"He didn't buck," Etta said. She was at once relieved and disappointed.

"No, ma'am," he said, gasping for breath and bending to rub his knee. "I'm workin' with him, like I said. If you get a horse to runnin', they cain't buck. I'd rather run 'em any day. It's what a horse likes to do, what's his nature to do, run from the fear. Pretty soon he'll discover he doesn't have to fear me, and he'll get accustomed to me bein' there. Don't hardly ever have one buck on me when I go at it this way. I'd rather outthink 'em than try to outride 'em."

He walked the horse around, rubbing it and talking to it (Johnny Bellah talked it into submission was Etta's theory), then got on and ran it some more. The horse was tired and very grateful when Johnny finally removed the saddle and led him out of the pen.

Etta sat there watching him go at six horses in one afternoon, in a deliberate manner, sometimes standing back to study the horse, "Thinking on him," never rushing and never losing his temper, not when the horse fought him or kicked at him—or bucked with him, which one finally did and threw Johnny to the ground with a loud, sickening thud.

As Etta sat there watching with her heart pounding, not knowing whether she should go to him, he got up, dusted himself off a bit, limped over and caught the horse, swung himself up into the saddle for another go, got bucked off again, only to rise up and get back on again. Again and again, his manner neither angry nor frustrated, only intense with thought that shut out all but the conflict between himself and the horse. He became uncharacteristically silent in the process.

Etta suspected that Johnny had been waiting for a horse to challenge him like this and was in his heaven. It unnerved her to watch, however, and after a few minutes, she got down from the fence and went into the house, from where she would peek out the window every ten minutes or so. Behind her, Latrice would ask, "Is he still alive? Should I count on him for supper?"

When Johnny did come up to supper, he was limping heavily, and Etta saw the pain in his eyes. Those silvery eyes still had a glimmer of a satisfied man to them, though, and over supper he spoke of training the two horses he owned. He believed they would both be good roping horses for the rodeo.

"That big dun can stop on a dime," he said. "I'll get him in shape real quick. Guess you wouldn't mind if I use a couple of your calves, would you? I won't hurt 'em."

As he left, he again offered to train Etta's red gelding.

She said, "Maybe."

Johnny looked at her like he was about to say something more, then he closed his mouth and left to ride his two horses until full dark.

Etta watched from the fence for nearly an hour, until the air was crisp, and then she went back to the house and sat on the porch with Latrice and watched what she could from there, while the sun set and the cicadas began to chirp and the chucks-will-widow called.

When Johnny finished riding, he limped up to the porch and sat with a thud on the edge of the floor. It was too dark to see his face. Latrice brought him a cup of coffee. Etta waited for him to say something more about training Little Gus, but it was obvious he was too tired to say anything. Soon he limped away to the barn.

As Etta followed Latrice inside, she thought of Johnny in the stablehand's room, in the narrow bed.

Ten ❦

"I think I'll make a pecan pie," Latrice said. "I wonder if Johnny Bellah likes pecan pie."

"I haven't seen anything you've cooked yet that he didn't like," Etta said. "I bet you could cook up an old shoe, and he'd eat it."

She could not point her finger to the moment it had happened, but sometime in the past two weeks, Johnny had become a part of their lives.

He had fallen into taking most of his meals with them, and to bringing them his laundry. Latrice doctored his occasional wounds, and Etta took him cold drinks.

In exchange, he did things around the farm. As if by the magic of his very presence, things began to look better. Corral fences got repaired and stock tanks got cleaned. The barn seemed to sit up straighter and get more red. The water pump quit, and Johnny fixed it. A big wind blew a limb down on Latrice's clothesline, and he got it off and restrung the line. A hinge on the back screen door worked loose, and he replaced it. He helped Obie bring in the first cutting of alfalfa, and he tried to be of help in repairing Etta's old Ford. He really didn't know anything about engines, so mostly he sat in the shade with his poor leg stretched out, drinking beer, and every once in a while handing Obie a tool.

Etta pondered the entire situation. It seemed to her that one day Roy had flown away, and the next day Johnny Bellah had galloped in.

It seemed to Etta something should be made of that, and perhaps not all of it good. She was having a difficult struggle with a melancholy spirit, and nothing looked very hopeful to her.

"What you can make of it is that the man was livin' in his truck, and now he isn't," Latrice said matter-of-factly.

She glanced up from the kitchen sink, where she was washing collard greens, to see Etta standing at the screen door, looking out in a manner that had begun to concern Latrice considerably. It was only natural for a newly widowed pregnant woman to have the miserables. Latrice herself was having a struggle with the blues over the state of their future. She wanted Etta to sell the farm immediately and to move into town, although she really would miss her excellent kitchen should that happen, and there were a number of problems living in town would present.

The situation was simply too undecided for Latrice's taste. She was annoyed with herself for this sentiment. She saw that her years of easy living in the Rivers house had made her soft in her faith. Here she was putting a kitchen above everything—although God knew she was not so young any longer, and she needed a washer and dryer.

She was also put out with Etta for not being particularly bothered by the uncertainty of everything.

What Etta appeared preoccupied with was Johnny Bellah.

To Latrice's mind, Etta and Johnny Bellah were covertly studying each other in the breathless manner of a lonely man and needy woman just waiting for someone to yell, "Go!"

This was understandable. Etta was a woman long denied a lover's exclusive attention. And wild desires often plagued pregnant women, which in Latrice's opinion was why the Good Practical Lord set it down that a pregnant woman was to be married, and preferably to a man close at hand.

Now here was Etta, pregnant and alone and blue, looking time and again at a man who was looking back, and who at that particular moment, Latrice saw when she came over, was out in the sun without a shirt, handling a filly by a rope, causing his muscles to ripple and bulge.

"What's he want here?" Etta asked in a dreamy manner.

"Huh," Latrice said, "what does any man want but his food cooked and laundry done? He came along and saw an empty barn and corrals and women without a man to do for. It fit him ideally. He was drawn here without a thought, the same way a wise man is drawn to wisdom. He is in heaven." Then she pushed out the screen and yelled, "Put your shirt on!"

Johnny Bellah looked over his shoulder at her and immediately went to get his shirt off the fence post. The man had proven to have the sense to listen when she spoke.

Satisfied, Latrice went back into the kitchen. "Is the baby movin' this mornin'?" She thought it best to keep reminding Etta of the baby.

Etta smoothed her hands over her belly in a loving caress. Her face softened as it always did when she focused on the baby, her only hope.

"She's been kickin' up a storm. She growing."

Latrice eyed Etta from head to toe, judging. At seven months Etta was not terribly big. Some women were like that, and although Latrice did not say, she believed Etta would deliver early, maybe as much as three weeks.

Latrice could look at a woman and calculate her time. She had never missed by more than two days, a fact that gave her a great deal of pride. Every time she saw a pregnant woman, on the street or in a store or anywhere, she would look at her and make a mental note. Later she would try to find out when the woman delivered. She had a running tally on notebook paper stuffed in the back of her Bible.

Etta had begun to think of being pregnant as a saving grace. God couldn't totally hate her for all her foolish selfishness, since He had blessed her with this child. At times she would be seized with a great fear that she was not thankful enough, and she would pray fervently, "Thank you, God, thank you, God," in case by her unappreciation, she would lose the child.

It was hard, though, keeping this in mind. Sometimes she became overwhelmed with the state of her life—being widowed and left with the hard knot that she had failed greatly in her marriage, and that she now faced the very real possibility of losing the home she loved so much, which should be her child's home and heritage. Having never had a heritage herself, Etta really wanted one for her child.

"It is not your fault," Latrice said. "Roy Rivers ran around with women, and there wasn't nothin' you could do about it. He was addicted. And it is not your fault he ran this place in the ground in debt, either."

"I know Roy's behavior was not my fault," Etta said. "What is my fault is not giving my baby a better father."

"Well, you are probably right there. I warned you."

"Oh, please. I don't have time for that sort of thing. If you can't say something of a positive nature, please just don't say anything at all."

"You brought it up. Not I."

With a sigh, Etta went over and sat at the table where her Scrabble game remained spread out since the previous night. She began fiddling with the wooden squares of letters, trying to make a name out of an A, an E, two Ts, a B, Q, and Z. She tried the name Zetta.

"I want my daughter to have a strong name," she said. "Something strong and capable to see her through needy men that are bound to come into her life."

"You can't impart that attitude to her," Latrice said. "Just because you have been disappointed, doesn't mean your daughter might not meet with a perfectly wonderful man and be very happy. If you lead her to expect less, that is what she will find."

Latrice's critical tone annoyed Etta. She didn't think she

deserved such a tone. "You have never married," Etta said. "What does that say?"

"I'm not talkin' about me. I'm talkin' about your daughter."

"I point out that you are speaking from your own experience, which in this case is limited."

"I have a mind that is not limited by my experiences. I don't have to put my hand in the fire to know that it will burn."

Unable to immediately think of a comeback to that, Etta refused to answer further. This was her best defense against Latrice, who would argue that the sky was green once she got started.

That she could think of no retort caused Etta to feel too low to continue discussion of any kind. It seemed, she thought, to be taking all she had to simply get up each morning and keep her mind from taking off on tangents. It seemed she was expending a great deal of energy trying to control herself from all manner of foolishness which she could not exactly name.

A shadow appeared at the screen door, and Obie Lee's voice said softly, "Miz Etta . . . Miss Latrice."

"Hello, Obie." Glad for the interruption, Etta sprang up and went to the door, eagerly welcoming Obie inside.

Lately she had been having the absurd urge every time she saw Obie to put her arms around him, to hug him either because he looked so forlorn or because she needed to feel a hug, she wasn't certain which. She longed terribly to throw herself at Latrice and have Latrice cuddle her as she used to do when Etta was a child. These days, if Latrice suspected Etta might hug her, she pulled back and acted strung out about it, as if that sort of physical contact was foolish.

Etta thought she might be having a sort of craving for physical contact, as she was used to it. What had been wonderful about Roy was that he was naturally affectionate and had embraced her several times a day.

Actually Roy had been given to embracing just about anyone any chance he got. Even if that was why he was at women all the time, Etta had loved his affectionate nature. She suspected Obie was the same way and would easily return her hug, but she held control of herself, afraid she might terrify him right back out the door.

Obie carried a bulging pillowcase. "I come across some down feathers, Miss Latrice. Good clean ones—my cousin give them to me. You been sayin' you wanted a pillow for your rockin' chair, and I thought these would make up real fine."

His craggy face looked hopefully at Latrice. It was the third present he had brought her that week, the first being a whole ham and the second a basket of mushrooms he had taken an entire morning to hunt. Each time Latrice said nothing more than, "Thank you, Obie," and that's all she said now. She didn't invite him to stay for lunch, or to at least to sit down and have coffee or a cold drink.

Etta stepped in and said, "Obie, would you like an RC? We still have quite a few."

He shook his head, casting a glance at Latrice. "No, thank you just the same, Miz Etta. I promised to help my cousin with preparin' his cotton field. I'd best get over there." His lanky body seemed to fold down as he went out the door.

Etta turned on Latrice, "Why are you like this to him? He is wearin' his heart on his sleeve for you, and you are rippin' it right off. Can't you be a little nicer?"

"I'm nice," Latrice said. "I thanked him. That's enough."

Etta stared at her. "Obie's a good man and would be good to you."

In that instant she thought of Latrice going off with Obie, and her chest grew so tight she could hardly breathe.

Latrice looked at her a long moment, averted her eyes and said, "He's a good man, but he'd take too much right now. I don't need that."

Etta could practically see Latrice thinking: *And what about you? It is one thing, you and I together. It is another to bring a man into it. See what happened before?*

Etta was thinking all of that herself. She could not imagine her life without Latrice, and she was thinking: *What are we going to do? Where are we going to go?*

Latrice said, "I don't want to encourage him, when I don't know where I want it to lead. And he is a man who needs a bit of leading," she said ruefully. "Most men do, when it comes down to it." Then she added in a practical tone, "Besides, he is happy in his pursuit of me. It would be a disappointment to him if I began to give in."

"Latrice, you have wasted enough time with me," Etta said. "I don't want you to waste any more."

She knew, though, that she could not make it without Latrice.

"And who says I do it just for you, honey?"

Etta shook her head, while feeling relief near tears. She pushed aside the name Zetta, realizing it was only one letter away from her own name. That being the case, she doubted that it would be suitable as the name of a woman strong enough to handle needy men.

Johnny was nipping a bit of whiskey, when Etta came out and caught him at it. That's how he always felt—that she caught him at it—because of the way she would look at him, like she had caught him doing a disgusting deed. It seemed like every time he got ready to take a fortifying nip she appeared just to catch him.

That this time she also caught him with his pants down didn't come to him until a few seconds later, when he noticed her blushing. He was sitting on a bale of hay, with one leg out of his pants, trying to wrap his bum knee, with time out for a sip of ol' Jim Beam.

When he saw her, he slipped the bottle down beside him, but he didn't know what to do about being out of his pants. He figured it would not help to jump up and try to get his leg back in and be dancing around there in his underwear and everything jiggling.

"I'm sorry," she said, whipping her eyes straight ahead. "I came for a halter."

"No problem." He returned to wrapping the bandage

tight around his sore knee. He imagined she had seen a
man in his underwear before.

He wondered if she noticed he had rock-hard thighs.

"Maybe Latrice could help you with that. She has some
good liniments." She was looking at him again, her blue
eyes wide and round.

"It's okay. I'm used to doin' it."

She raised a doubtful eyebrow but nodded and left. He
watched her go, walking in that way she needed for balance
now, feet apart and moving from side to side in a sway that
for some strange reason always drew his eye and made him
quicken a little.

He jerked his gaze back to wrapping his knee, although
his mind remained full of the woman he could hear speaking to the gelding in the corral.

His reaction to Etta Rivers confused Johnny a great deal.
He had fallen to calling her Miz Etta, like Obie did, but in
his mind he thought of her simply as Etta. Etta with the
blue eyes. Etta with the silky hair the color of raw honey.
Etta with the righteous temper.

The clothes she wore—sometimes a flannel shirt, sometimes a blue chambray, and always the big worn overalls
and brown hat and boots—made her look like a short pudgy
man from a distance. But when you got up close enough
to see her face, all peaches and cream, and those big blue
eyes, and smelled her scent that was like Ivory soap and
sweet flowers, you could tell she was thoroughly a woman,
which was the first strong thought that always came to
Johnny, then was followed by something that went like: *By
God she's pregnant.*

Every time he looked at her, something just started
squirming inside him, so that he would have to look away.
The feelings he was having did not seem proper feelings
to have for a pregnant woman. Most especially one newly
widowed.

Johnny didn't care to look at her belly, because he kept
getting embarrassed and curious about the whole thing all
at the same time. He had flashes of imagination of what

caused her to get that way, and that unsettled him considerably.

Etta put him on edge, and he bet she knew it and enjoyed doing it, too.

Each day Etta came out and watched him while he trained. Johnny found this both flattering and disconcerting. He found himself anticipating her arrival, and worrying about her sitting up on the fence in her condition. He worried that her belly might cause her to pitch forward, or backward, or that she would go into premature labor, and he would be forced into action of a sort he might not care for. Or that in his preoccupation in worrying about her, he would make an error in judgment with one of the horses and get stomped on and thereby make a fool of himself.

Over the weeks at the Rivers farm, he learned that Etta had a fondness for coffee and warm cola, didn't read much but liked music, country and blues, that she noticed things like flowers, birds and cicadas chirping, that she liked to walk out at night—he'd watched her do this—and that she wasn't squeamish and could handle a horse.

During his sessions of working the horses, he learned a bit more about Etta's life, and he guessed that she learned a bit more about his.

"You ever been married, Johnny?" she asked him once.

"No, ma'am, never have." He added, "I've had girl-friends."

"Well, I imagine you have."

There was amusement in her voice, and he felt embarrassed for having said something silly.

He adjusted his hat and walked over to rest near her in the shade of the fence. "I guess I've just never settled down enough to get into a position of marriage. Man who rodeos and cowboys never really is set to get married. If I had the money, I didn't have the time to settle down. If I had the time, I never had the money. And I guess I just never met anyone I wanted to marry—or anyone who wanted to marry me," he added.

"How long were you and Mr. Rivers married?" he

asked, not certain that he should, but feeling it was rightly his turn.

She looked downward. "Six years."

That seemed a long time to Johnny.

"Do you have any family?" she asked. "Brothers, sisters?"

"Nope . . . none."

"I don't, either," she said, "except Latrice." She added, "And soon I'll have a daughter. Latrice says I will have a girl, and she knows these things. She has never been wrong."

Reference to her pregnancy made him uncomfortable, so he turned his attention back to the horse he was working.

Another time when he was fixing a fence, she brought him out a glass of ice tea. He saw her coming, although he pretended surprise when she got close. He was conscious of his shirt sticking to him, and of warm thoughts about her.

"Well now, I sure appreciate you bringin' this," he said, taking the glass from her and careful not to look her in the eye.

"I appreciate you fixin' the fence. You don't have to do all that you do. That wasn't part of the deal."

He looked down into her blue eyes. They gazed intensely at him, seeming to ask intimate questions he wasn't prepared to answer. He looked away across the corrals.

"Well now, you and Miss Latrice do a lot for me that wasn't in our deal, either," he answered. "And I guess I just like neatness. It seems a shame to let such a fine place run down. Not meanin' any disrespect," he added, afraid he had sounded critical of her husband.

"None taken." She sighed and looked around. "It is a shame that it got so rundown. Roy just wasn't much for keeping things fixed up. He liked them fixed up, but he wasn't handy, and the past year he had trouble affording getting it done."

She stated fact, not criticism of her husband, and Johnny appreciated this.

"Guess I'd better finish this up so I can get back to

workin' the ponies,'' he said, handing her the empty glass.

As he finished fixing the fence, he thought about why he was doing all this. He guessed he'd sort of been sucked into this place and the women's lives. They had him to their table and did his laundry, and he felt he owed them something.

They needed him, and for the first time in his life, Johnny wanted to be needed.

He thought of how he'd quit going out so much nights because he'd begun to be afraid of leaving the women here alone. They had no car, for one thing, and Obie had brought that up to Johnny, as if he should keep it in mind.

"I just cain't get Miz Etta's car goin'," he said and pointed out that an emergency could arise where Mrs. Rivers might need to get to the hospital. Miss Latrice maintained that they did not intend to use the services of any doctor or hospital, since she was a fully qualified midwife, but Obie contended that something could go wrong, and they might need a vehicle.

Since he did not have a telephone, Obie brought Miss Latrice a bugle. "You blow on this if'n you need me," he told her, "and I'll come directly."

"We had better hope the wind is favorable should I have to use this," Miss Latrice had said. She could have a pretty caustic tongue, in Johnny's opinion. Obie said he liked her sass.

Johnny thought the bugle a good idea, if Obie heard it, but there was the problem of Obie's old truck, which did not go over thirty-five on a good day. That left Johnny and his truck, and no matter how much he told himself that they were not his responsibility, he just couldn't leave the women flat.

Besides, he didn't really have anywhere he needed to go.

Finished with the fence, he began to gather up the old planks. There were several lengths of good wood, which he intended to save. As he was passing the training pen, he had an idea.

When Etta came out a few minutes later, ready to watch

him train on the horses, he was hammering in the last nail. He turned to her with a satisfied grin.

"There you are, Miss Etta. A seat ought to be more comfortable than balancin' on that fence."

He was satisfied that he had handled one big worry.

Johnny walked out to where Etta was fooling with the red gelding. She was looking his way, and she watched him come, even if she did try to pretend like she wasn't watching.

He leaned on the fence rail. This attracted the horse, who had come to learn he could get a treat of a pinch of tobacco from Johnny. Etta tugged on the lead rope to get the gelding's attention to return to her. She forced him to circle on a longe line, snapping the end of the line to get the animal to lope.

This worried Johnny. He was afraid the horse would pull her down or maybe get excited and run over her. He didn't know how to go about saying any of this, though. He didn't think Etta would accept any cautioning remarks from him.

He set about rolling a cigarette but didn't do a very good job of it, because he got so nervous and annoyed over her working with the horse that he wanted to walk off, but he couldn't go because he was afraid something might happen as soon as he turned his back.

Finally she quit with the horse and released him. He came instantly to the fence, sniffing Johnny's pocket for tobacco. Etta came more slowly.

"You ever gonna let me train this son-of-a-buck?" Johnny asked, feeding the gelding a bit of the tobacco. His gaze met Etta's, and he had to grin at the mischievous light in her blue eyes.

"Maybe," she said.

"Why?"

"What?" she said. He could tell he'd set her off balance by pushing it.

"Why won't you let me?"

She shrugged. "Why should I?"

"Because I'm a damned good trainer, and you know it,

and if you pass up my offer, you're passin' up a once-in-a-lifetime chance to make somethin' out of this cob.''

"Maybe," she said, her eyes sort of defiant.

He felt himself held by those blue eyes peering out like lights in the shade beneath her hat. Then she looked away at the horse that stood between them and stroked the animal's neck. Wisps of hair not caught by her hat brushed her soft cheeks, and Johnny stared at them, watched them flutter against her creamy skin.

Before he even knew what he was going to do, he lifted his hand and brushed the hair back. His knuckles touched its silkiness and felt the warmth of her and it went clear through him.

She jumped and looked at him, and he didn't know what to say. She stared at him, and he stared at her, and they were both thinking things they probably shouldn't have been.

Then there came a shout, drawing their attention. Latrice stood on the porch, and two men in dark suits stood beside her. Latrice hollered again; she had a carrying sort of voice and a manner that made a person pay attention.

Etta waved that she'd heard. Johnny opened the gate for her, and closed it behind her. He went about the corrals, checking the water troughs that really didn't need checking and touching the horses, while he saw Etta disappear into the house with the men in suits. He suspected at least one of them was a prospective buyer for the farm. This suspicion was confirmed when Etta and the two men came out to the barn and corrals.

Etta politely introduced the men to Johnny—a Fred Somebody, and a Somebody Fudge. Johnny wasn't particularly interested in their names, although the second one stuck, it being so unusual. Also, this Fudge fellow looked a little more like a worker; he was a bit uncomfortable in his suit, and his hands were tanned and work-hardened.

Both men were looking Johnny over good, and he imagined they were having all manner of thoughts about him being there, living in Etta's barn, which they surely could see where he was sleeping.

Mr. Fudge fellow said, "You train horses?"

Johnny thought: *No, I'm a rocket scientist vacationing here.* He said, "Yes, sir."

"I've got a few head. Might could use you." The man was really giving him a looking over.

"I'm rentin' this space from Missus Rivers for the time bein'," Johnny said, wanting to make the situation clear. "If you have space, it might be best if I come over there."

"Yes . . . well, I'll let you know. Good to meet you."

They went out and walked around the corrals and looked at the horses like they knew something, then the Fred fellow brought a pink and white Plymouth around from the front, and the three of them drove off down the pasture road to look at the land.

Watching the big car bounce off over the rutted road, Johnny felt low.

It wasn't any of his business, he told himself. Wasn't like this was his place. Maybe he had a few thoughts about it, like this would a good place to build up a good horse outfit and a rodeo stock company. He'd thought of doing that from time to time, always at some future time down the road, when he found a place that suited him to settle down.

He would be moving on from here, though, just like he always did. He'd begun to feel restless already. Damn if he knew why he'd stayed up here this long.

These thoughts propelled him to go into the barn, where he checked out his tack. He'd been using some of Roy Rivers's halters to have enough to go around, and they'd gotten all mixed in with his own. He sorted them and then admired how nice everything looked hanging on the walls. He really appreciated an organized tack room.

Etta was still off with the men in the Plymouth when Obie Lee drove up. He had a new-old carburetor that one of his nephews had come upon in a pile of junk cars along the bank of the Washita River. Obie went right to work on the car, and Johnny hung around to help, handing over tools Obie called for.

The Plymouth returned Etta to the house and then drove on away down the lane.

"That there was Fred Grandy, the real-estate man, and Walter Fudge," Obie said. "Mr. Fudge owns several farms around. His sons work 'em for him mostly, although he rents a couple. He owns the one that borders this place on the north. Only natural he'd be interested, now that this place's for sale. Heard tell the other day that Mr. Fudge is interested in this place for his youngest son."

"Well, I hope she gets a good price," Johnny offered.

"Mr. Fudge, well he's like most men, only more so— he wants somethin' for nothin'. Hand me that half-inch over there."

Obie worked clear up to sundown on Etta's Ford. Johnny hung around to help him as best he could. He liked hanging around Obie. There was something about the old man that made Johnny relaxed.

When Johnny commented on this, Obie said, "Oh, I learned to live easy a long time ago. Life, it's mostly pain. But in there is the good parts, so you better just hang on to them whenever you can."

Johnny handed Obie tools and after a while went up to the grocery store and brought back a six-pack of cold beer. Obie drank one, and Johnny drank two and started on a third.

"You need to watch that, boy," Obie said, gesturing at the beer in Johnny's hand. "That can carry you right away before you know it."

"It's floatin' me away right now," Johnny joked and went around behind the barn to pee. He wished everyone wouldn't take such an interest in how much he drank.

He watched the old man work on the engine, and he watched Etta come out on the porch and look their way, then go back inside, then come out about a half-hour later and do the same thing again.

The entire time Johnny felt an intense restlessness creeping over him.

Along about sunset, Obie got the car to start, and at the sound Etta and Miss Latrice both came out on the porch.

They were halfway across the yard when the engine died. Obie got it started again, but he couldn't keep it running.

"This carburetor is old, and likely the fuel lines are all gunked up from the car sittin' here for so long," Obie said, rubbing his head as was his habit when discouraged. "I don't mean to talk poorly, Miz Etta, but this thing's been sittin' up so long, it's 'bout froze up."

"It's okay, Obie. I appreciate you tryin'."

Johnny felt as if he should do something to help her. He had saved up a bit of money, but not enough to get her a new car. Even if she would have taken one from him. Besides, he needed that money for when he had to move on in a few weeks.

She was not his responsibility—and she'd likely make enough off the sale of this place to get her a car, if not a new one.

Latrice said, "Y'all come in for supper."

Supper was fried ham slices and cabbage, Miss Latrice obviously forgetting what Johnny had told her at the outset about hating cabbage. He smelled it the instant his foot stepped on the porch, and he almost didn't go inside, but he was at the door and thought it would be impolite to turn around and leave.

There was just something that seemed to have a hold on him and to keep him there, going in and sitting at the table and eating, all except the cabbage. At least there were Miss Latrice's biscuits. Johnny put a lot of honey on them.

The meal was what was termed subdued. Obie tried to pick things up by mentioning ideas he had yet to try on Etta's car. Latrice mentioned Walter Fudge, saying she thought he would drag his feet on making any kind of offer, in order to save two pennies if he could on buying this place.

"That's how a man like Mr. Fudge gets to be where he is," Obie said.

"Where's that?" Latrice asked. "He's got 'bout three thousand acres now, and money in two banks, and he still won't let his wife have but monthly help in the house."

Etta said next to nothing and looked so hang-dogged that

Johnny began to get annoyed with her. She wouldn't look at him at all. He wished very badly to do something for her. He felt he needed to point some things out.

"You know, all that's needed to raise some good rodeo stock is right out there. The corrals, good pasture. Could board horses, too."

He didn't know what got into him, butting into what wasn't his business. He kept his gaze on the honey he dribbled into the coffee Miss Latrice brought him.

"Mr. Roy used to board horses from time to time," Obie put in.

"That's so . . . but we can't pay the mortgage by boarding horses," Etta said, "and we sure can't start another ranching endeavor without any money."

The disparaging manner in which she spoke made Johnny shut his mouth, and he didn't linger over coffee or partake of the gingerbread Miss Latrice had made. The smell of the cabbage overpowered any aroma of gingerbread.

"I got to see the horses fed," he said.

"I'll help," Obie said, and slowly started to rise, being stiff from bending over the engine all afternoon.

"No. I can do it fine," Johnny said, sharp enough that everyone looked at him. "Thanks anyway," he added.

He set about feeding and watering the horses by the meager light of twilight and the single pole light near the barn. He tossed their grain and hay with a fervency, working quickly, eager to be done and go, and it occurred to him that he was thinking of driving over to the roadhouse.

The thing to do, he thought, was go to town and get drunk and get laid.

He had not been with a woman in months, and his sperm was getting all backed up. That was not healthy. That was why he was feeling tight and restless and irritable as hell.

The problem of leaving Miss Latrice and Etta alone niggled at him.

They had the bugle, he told himself, and knew how to make use of it should they need help. Undoubtedly Obie would stay awhile anyway. Undoubtedly nothing would happen. Etta Rivers was a woman strong enough to go climbing on fences and chasing horses, so she most probably would have no trouble popping out a baby should her time come early.

He washed in his makeshift shower—it wasn't nearly so cold these days—shaved and put on some sweet-smelling aftershave, slipped into a clean shirt that Miss Latrice had starched nicely, his best jeans, and good boots. As he went to his truck, he glanced over at the house. It was a big black hulk with yellow lights showing from the living room and Etta's bedroom upstairs. He thought he caught sight of a shadow at the window of that room.

He needed to hang it up with a woman, he thought, driving off at a good clip. That's what he needed, the same as a rooster had to crow, made by God to do so.

The roadhouse was one of the rougher places, and the women who frequented it tended to be the rough sort—the type of woman who came up to a man and asked him point-blank if he wanted a piece. This behavior unnerved Johnny considerably. He never had felt easy with lewd talk.

He drank at the bar and fell to talking with some boys he knew from the stockyard. After a while his eyes connected with a woman across the floor. She didn't look half-bad; she had golden hair. Then it seemed like he turned around, and she was right beside him. It wasn't far from there to going outside to his truck. She just seemed to lead him along.

Her name was Becky. She laughed easy and smelled like flowers. Johnny was getting good and excited and kissing her and fumbling with her bra, when the next thing he knew the door of the pickup came open. Surprised, he turned, and something smacked him upside the head. As the blackness was sucking him down, he felt someone shove him over and caught the scent of the woman.

When Johnny came to, his head felt like it held a gallon of sloshing water, and his fingers came away bloody from just over his left eye. He found his wallet lying beside him in the seat, and the glove compartment open, stuff from there thrown all over.

He'd been robbed, and he still had all his sperm blocking up inside him.

For a few minutes he just sat there. He thought of searching for a pint bottle under the seat, but he didn't feel like bending down. He thought of going into the roadhouse and finding the son-of-a-bitch who'd hit him, but he didn't see any worth in that, either. What the law said about such things was that he shouldn't have been drinking in a dry state.

At last he started the truck and slowly headed out onto the road. For a moment his head pounded so bad, he thought he might throw up, but that settled down into a severe ache.

He drove, not really knowing where he was going, just staring into the dark where his headlights faded. Then he was at Obie's driveway and turning in, coming up to the house that glowed softly. A hound as old as his master barked a warning.

Obie's silhouette appeared at the door, peering out, and Johnny felt ridiculously glad to see him.

"Good God, boy," Obie took hold of Johnny and pulled him into the house. "Come on back here to the table and let me see that."

"It ain't so bad really. Just stunned me some. And the forehead always bleeds like a stuck pig."

He followed Obie through the front room, the middle room that was obviously Obie's bedroom, and to the kitchen at the back. A radio played softly. Johnny slumped down into a chair.

Obie brought a cold cloth to press against the wound on his temple. "What happened, boy?"

"Well . . . I tried to get laid and what I got was robbed."

Obie shook his head. "How much did you lose?"

"Five dollars. That's all I keep on me when I go out to a roadhouse. If I need more, I got a pouch stashed back in the bed." He chuckled dryly. "Just about got my brains knocked in for five dollars."

Obie was shaking his head again. "Younguns ... you got to lay off that whiskey. It'll kill you. I'm tellin' you truth. I know, 'cause I been there."

"Ain't whiskey that did this. It was a woman."

Obie said, "It was whiskey that stole your senses, boy." Then he added, "Women can do that, too, I guess."

Obie made a fresh pot of coffee—the cowboy way of throwing the grounds in the water and boiling it atop his wood-burning stove—and Johnny sat there and drank it with him and talked about which team would take the World Series and the price of cattle and pickup trucks.

Johnny told about being on the rodeo circuit, and about lying in the mud with a jeep on his knee, about that being a time he knew he'd died and seen a great light and had never again feared death or God, but had not been any less sinful.

Obie told of playing baseball and how he drank and gave it up and why and how he came back here to live with his wife who six years before had died in his arms, bled to death because the only doctor had been a white one and wouldn't see to her. It seemed as if Obie was as lonely as Johnny and needed to talk.

The two of them dozed a bit in the early hours. When Johnny came fully awake, he found himself lying over on the table. The sky was growing light in the east.

He got up and went looking for Obie, who had moved to a big chair in the tiny front room. Grabbing up a small quilt tossed on the sofa, Johnny spread it over the old man. Then he went out to his truck, started it, and headed down the road to the Rivers place. A mist lingered on the ground; the silhouettes of horses moved in and out of it.

Stopping the pickup in front of the barn, Johnny sat there a moment, staring out the windshield. Then he got out and strode, limping heavily, into the barn, returning with a halter over his shoulder, saddle in one hand and the pad in the other. His head throbbed and his poor knee pained with every step. The sky grew lighter making the mist iridescent. The horses moved about with growing excitement and began to whinny.

Johnny went straight along the corrals to the one where the red gelding waited.

"It's time, buddy," he murmured.

The horse came right toward the halter, as if he, too, had been waiting and knew it was time. He trembled as the halter went on, then tried to bolt, but Johnny caught the rope and jerked hard, giving the horse his first obedience lesson. He tied the horse to the fence and saddled him up, went right about it, even when he heard the back screen door of the house squeak across the morning stillness, and Etta call out, "Johnny!"

She reached the fence as he pulled the girth strap tight. She was in a white gown and flowered silky robe, barefoot, and holding her robe closed with one hand and her belly with the other, her hair curling all down around her creamy face, and her blue eyes mad as hell.

"What do you think you're doin'?"

"I'm ridin' this son-of-a-buck."

"You have no right. He is *my* horse!"

"Yes, ma'am," Johnny said and swung himself up in the saddle, reading for the horse to go to pitching.

Etta hollered, "Johnny!" and the red gelding quivered and pranced. Johnny pulled him in a circle, and then he saw Etta flinging the gate wide. He thought for an instant that she was going to bar his way, but then the entry was clear, and he pressed the red gelding's side, sending him straight through the gate.

Johnny caught a flash of Etta's angry face and bright robe as they passed, then streaked down the alley and out into the freedom of the pasture.

They rode high and wide, Johnny ignoring his screaming knee and letting the horse have his head. Letting the horse take him back into the life he'd once had, where there never had been a horse he couldn't ride or a woman he couldn't love.

Etta scrambled up on the fence and watched him. Hair blew in her face, and she angrily pushed it back. She watched as the mist of the lower-lying pasture swallowed the red horse and the man atop him, and then out they came, brilliant in golden sunbeams breaking over the horizon.

Then she was crying so hard she could not see. Blindly, she got down from the fence and strode back to the house, burst inside, and let the screen door bang behind her.

"Johnny's taken Little Gus. I never said he could, but he's ridin' him just the same."

She went to the cabinet, got out a cup and poured it full of coffee, tossed in a heaping teaspoon of sugar, and went to sit at the table.

Latrice pulled things for breakfast from the refrigerator and spoke from its depths. "You've been holdin' that horse out like a carrot. He's gone and taken a bite."

"A carrot?" Etta did not appreciate the way Latrice seemed to be taking Johnny's side.

Latrice sent Etta a look over her shoulder. "You think that once Johnny Bellah gets his hands on Little Gus, he might discover the horse is not all he hopes it will be, or else he will satisfy all his longings, and then he will leave. You think the desire for the unknown horse is what has made him stay."

Latrice smacked the iron skillet upon the burner. Etta stared at her back, at her shoulder blades moving beneath her dark blue dress.

"You can sure make somethin' out of nothin'," she said.

Latrice cast her one of those knowing looks and then went about plopping bacon into a warming skillet.

Etta drank half the cup of coffee before it began to give her a sour stomach. She got up and went out on the porch and peered and peered, looking for Johnny and Little Gus. She saw them; they were heading back, and she waited there on the porch until they were coming through the rear pasture gate.

She went down the steps, and when she hit the yard and sharp, prickly grass, she realized for the first time that she had not put on any shoes. She ignored this and kept on walking to the edge of the yard, where she stopped and waited for Johnny to approach.

He stopped six feet away. Little Gus was breathing hard

and hung his head. Johnny was breathing hard, too. His face was pale and drawn . . . and he had an ugly wound above his eye. She gazed at it, then looked into his eyes. He regarded her uncertainly now.

"Do you intend to train him?" Etta asked.

"If you'll allow it, I will."

"It does not appear to me that I have any say in the matter."

Johnny flinched at that. "Yes, ma'am, you do," he said, and his eyes, very sad now, bored into her.

"Well . . ." Etta searched for something clever to say, but all she could think of was, "You might as well, I guess."

II

Coming Through the
Back Door

Eleven

The next day Little Gus bucked on Johnny first thing, before Johnny even got sat down in the saddle. They hadn't expected this, and Etta would have had to admit to delight that Little Gus showed his spirit, even as she held her breath, fearing Johnny was about to get his neck broken.

But Johnny found his seat and got the horse running around the training pen. He ran him there hard for five minutes and then hollered at Etta to throw open the gate. She scrambled to the ground and managed the gate, and horse and rider went shooting past her with a "Yaa!" and pounding hooves and stirring dust.

Latrice's sheets on the clothesline snapped in the breeze and spooked Little Gus, causing him to veer so fast that he appeared to have simply jumped three yards to the right, leaving Johnny rolling left but hanging on. They headed out through the open pasture gate and down the dirt track that was now used as a road. Little Gus's mane and tail flew out, and his coat gleamed in the bright sun.

Etta ran to the edge of the yard and gazed after them, going up on tiptoe and holding her hat against the wind, watching horse and rider disappear as the track dipped beyond a hill.

She stood there, waiting for their return with a type of breathless yearning.

When Johnny rode Little Gus back and stopped in front of her, he said, "This son-of-a-buck can move."

His steely eyes shone like diamonds, and his grin seemed to hang there. His pleasure was so much that Etta had to turn from it, for fear of being overcome.

She looked at Little Gus, who stood breathing hard and hanging his head. Putting her cheek against his, she hugged him and inhaled the wonderful horse scent of him. He pressed his head against her.

The following days the pattern was repeated, Little Gus pitching and Johnny running him out and down the pasture track, and each day Etta watched them go and wished to fling herself after them.

It hurt, watching Johnny ride Little Gus, *her* horse that she had saved and raised and that still belonged to her, after all, one of the few things the bank or anyone else could not lay claim to.

The "month or so" that Johnny had bargained for in exchange for Roy's IOU came and went, as did the horses he trained for Jed Stuart and Harry Flagg. Yet Johnny remained. He did not speak of leaving, and Etta would not ask him about it.

Another man brought five head of two-year-olds for breaking, and Johnny got excited about beginning with new horses, but he remained most excited about Little Gus. He said a number of times: "A few days of trainin', and that red gelding is already worth five hundred dollars, Miz Etta."

"Who would pay that?" Etta asked. It had been her experience that men tended to talk on the up side of selling a horse, but when it came to the actual selling, the price most generally was down.

"Well now, I don't know right offhand, but he's worth that."

"He's worth that to you maybe. To me, he's priceless. To anyone else, he probably isn't worth a penny."

"You could get five hundred easy, once people see him run and move."

"I thought you just said he was worth that right now."

"I think you could get that, from the right buyer, now, and I know you can get it and more once people see him move," Johnny said, getting annoyed that she was trying to confuse him. He was thoroughly puzzled as to why Etta seemed so angry at him all the time. Try as he might, he could not seem to please her.

He had the hopeful thought that perhaps if he fully explained the gelding's talents, Etta would understand, and therefore he could please her.

He said, "This son-of-a-buck can sprint right out at a run in a single stride. He can practically turn back on himself, and by golly, he could go on doin' it all day long. This horse has heart, and a horse that has that can do almost anything. You may just have a fortune on your hands here, Miz Etta."

As he spoke and watched her cool, doubtful expression, he had a sinking feeling that he was not getting anywhere.

"I have heard that song and dance before," she said, the words rolling off her tongue like beads off a table, "and what I know is that I could count on one hand the number of people who have made a fortune from a horse, and then it has been some kind of miracle. Owners of horses don't make money from horses. Trainers make money, stable owners make money, sellers make money, but it's the owners doin' all the payin'. Owners had better have a good, steady income from something besides horses, and I do not."

Johnny stared at her. Then he said, "You sure have a negative attitude," and walked off.

None of Etta's poor attitude, however, nor that of Latrice, who kept giving him the skeptical eye about like she suspected him of planning to rob the family safe, could subdue Johnny's enthusiasm for the turn toward good fortune his life appeared to have taken once again. He was riding in high cotton. The two horses he had picked up for next to nothing at the sale barn were going to get him at least eight hundred each when he got ready to sell, and he knew he had been right all along about that red gelding.

Johnny felt himself vindicated as, if not the greatest horse trainer alive, at least one of them, because he had seen the potential in the red gelding, when everyone else had missed it.

He was anxious to prove his belief in the red gelding, and when he came across the notice of a rodeo to be held at the first of the month over in Anadarko, the first one of the season thereabouts, he immediately began to train Little Gus in earnest. Their greatest potential for making money would be when the horse had not yet won a race. With his poor looks, no one would suspect Little Gus could run like he could, therefore the odds would be against him. Johnny's thoughts were to enter Little Gus in one of the rodeo races and to also get a match race.

He got carried away and showed Etta the flier announcing the rodeo. "The purse is a guaranteed one hundred and fifty dollars, plus whatever the entry fees added up to. It'll go up to three hundred easy, and Gus'll take that purse."

Etta cast him a skeptical look, and Latrice said, "You have that straight from God, do you?"

Johnny wished he'd had the sense to keep his mouth shut. Now he was going to have to defend himself, and he never liked doing that.

"It says the entry fee is twenty-five dollars." Etta was looking at the yellow flier, then raised her eyes to him. "I don't have that."

"I do. I'm willin' to pay the entry fee."

"I can't let you do that."

"Why not? I'll make it back. He'll take the purse, and bein' the dark horse, the side bets on him are gonna run five or six to one, easy. Fifty dollars will get you another three hundred in less than a minute."

"I don't have twenty-five dollars, and I sure don't have fifty, and let me just tell you that if I did, I would put it toward a car that ran, so I would have somethin' to leave here in when this place is taken from me."

Her voice started low, through gritted teeth, and she ended up very close to yelling.

After a minute of gazing into her fury, Johnny said with deliberate quietness, "Ma'am, I see your point. But I know horses—and this one is a runner." Tossing his napkin beside his plate, he got up and left the kitchen.

A second later he heard Etta at the door, yelling after him, "And what do you think everyone else is enterin' in the dang race—*walkers?*"

Johnny did not again bring up the subject of betting. Once or twice he mentioned the rodeo, in a manner of testing the waters, but Etta said nothing. She pointedly ignored him on the subject.

He wondered if she would let him take the gelding to the rodeo. He wasn't concerned with the entry fee, or betting money. He'd put up all he had. He wanted the opportunity to tell her this, but nothing about her invited him to do so.

He didn't know what he would do if she refused to allow him to take the horse to the rodeo. Likely, he thought, he would have to take the horse anyway, and the idea of doing this made him feel sick. He never set out to deliberately go against a person, and the horse was Etta's. Just up and taking the gelding was certain to border on stealing, even if he did intend to bring him back.

But Johnny knew he could not miss the chance with the horse, either. The expectation and curiosity over the animal had burrowed deep beneath his skin, taking a firm hold on him. He knew he might be getting carried away, but it was such a seductive feeling that he couldn't let it go.

He needed to prove that horse out for Etta's sake, as well as his own, he told himself. He thought it a shame that Etta had lost her faith in horses, and in horsemen. It appeared that she had little faith in men all the way around.

In mulling it all over, he began to believe that he was in a position to give the faith back to her—to show her that there were men who did know horses and could live with wagering in a knowledgeable, honorable manner, and that he was such a man.

To this end, he continued to train Little Gus and to hope that Etta would see the truth in the horse. He wanted Etta to see that he was right. He wanted to show her what he could do with the horse.

More than anything, Johnny wanted Etta to believe in him.

Johnny talking as he did about Little Gus annoyed Etta no end. It frightened her, and it disappointed her. She saw Johnny's enthusiasm for wagering as evidence of weak character.

"I don't know why you thought he had a particularly strong character," Latrice said. "He's a drifter cowboy, and you yourself has said he drinks too much."

"I don't know, either," Etta admitted. They were weeding the garden, and she jerked hard on a weed and tossed it aside. "I suppose I hoped he was stronger. He has seemed stronger at times."

After a minute, she added, "He's been a help around here. You yourself said that."

Latrice looked at her with wide eyes. "I'm not arguin' about that."

Etta plopped down in the garden row, resting her back. The baby inside her kicked and pushed up on a rib. Etta looked over to where Johnny was working his filly on a longe line. He enjoyed the filly, babied her. He said she would never be a good using horse, that she had little stamina, but he thought he might make a good rider out of her for a child. Etta had been struck by him thinking of that—a horse for a child. She had wondered what other thoughts Johnny could have that she would not expect. She suspected there was a lot she could know about Johnny, should he remain around long enough.

Etta was always wondering when she might look up and Johnny would be gone. He was, as Latrice said, a drifter cowboy, and surely before long he would drift out of their lives.

"Do you think he could be right about Little Gus?" she asked, speaking thoughts before she realized.

"Even fools make a right guess now and then," Latrice said. "It generally doesn't mean all that much. If you want to keep eatin', you had best keep weedin'."

Etta returned to pulling weeds and told herself to quit thinking crazy. She had bills stacking up and a baby on the way and a very uncertain future that could not be helped by a drifter cowboy. Lordy, had she learned nothing by being married to Roy Rivers?

Nevertheless, with caution screaming every minute in her ears, she continued to watch Johnny and Little Gus run down the pasture track. She watched Obie plow the track and rake it smooth, and Johnny mark distances of two hundred and fifty, three hundred, and four hundred yards. Johnny had Obie operate the stopwatch, and Etta would stand there beside Obie, with longing tugging at her—and worry about Little Gus putting his foot in a prairie dog hole and breaking his neck, and possibly Johnny's neck. She was still having a terrible time with hopeless thoughts.

A good deal of her watching Johnny and the horse had to do with her desire to keep connected with Little Gus. She felt it was silly, but she could not help being as jealous as a mother who'd had to give the care of her child over to a nursemaid from whom the child was learning his first steps and first words.

After Johnny would finish riding Little Gus, Etta would come forward and lead the horse away, where she lavished him with attention, washing him and grooming him, and giving him all manner of treats—of which Johnny did not approve.

She began to be very impatient for her daughter to be born so that she herself could get up on Little Gus's back and ride like the wind. Once, temptation winning out, Etta did get up on him.

She had just washed him and let him dry in the sun. Using several bales of hay as a upping-block, she slipped onto his back. Easy as could be. He was silky and relaxed. She sat there a moment, stroking his neck. Then she dared to walk him around in a circle, rocking dreamily there on his bare back, feeling the heat and power of him between her legs and the sunlight on her head and the baby fluttering inside her.

Her woman's body was a pure blessing in that moment. She stopped the horse and lifted her face to the sky, sighing.

Johnny came around the corner and came to pieces. ''What are you doin'?''

Little Gus spooked and jumped back, and Etta took hold of the lead rope and his mane to keep from falling.

Johnny grabbed Little Gus's halter. ''Whoa, boy.''

''He was whoaed until you came yellin' around the corner,'' Etta said.

''Well, it could have been somethin' other than me, and he might have knocked you right off. He's not but green broke really. Geez, Etta.''

Bent over like she was, his face was only a foot away from her own, his silvery eyes close enough to see the golden flecks there. Etta realized he had said her name without the *Miz*, as he never had before.

Then Johnny was reaching for her and pulling her from the horse's back, saying tensely, ''Are you all right?''

''Yes,'' she answered breathlessly, staring into his luminous eyes.

His grip tightened on her arms, and he gave her a small shake. ''You scared me to death, Etta.''

''I'm sorry.''

For one brief moment of insane passion, blinking against the bright hot sun and feeling his hot hands on her, she teetered on the brink of throwing herself into his arms.

Then Johnny was backing up and saying, ''I've got a stall ready for him.''

He led Little Gus away into the barn, and Etta stared after him, sudden tears blurring her eyes and frustration boiling in her chest. She had enough with which to deal, without feeling all she was feeling about this man.

That evening was the first time Little Gus had ever been closed into a stall. Johnny allowed him access to the pen outside, and Little Gus ran from the stall to the end of the pen, loudly protesting the confinement.

"He'll settle down," Johnny said.

Etta watched Little Gus repeatedly gauge the fence, thinking of jumping. From her bedroom that night, she heard him call.

Two days later, when Johnny put Little Gus into his stall, he closed the door to the outside pen, only allowing Little Gus to stick his head out the window. Little Gus protested with a vehemence.

"He'll settle down," Johnny said again.

Etta spoke with Little Gus through the stall bars. She hated to leave him. Each time she tried to walk away, he began to cry and kick the stall walls.

All through supper, they could hear Little Gus kicking rhythmically. Johnny went right on eating, as if he didn't hear a thing. Etta tried to do this. Latrice turned the radio up.

Obie arrived after the meal was over—in time for dessert, Latrice observed. "Do you know you got a horse out there kickin' his stall?" he said.

"The red gelding," Johnny said. "May I have a little more of that rhubarb pie, Miss Latrice?"

Etta watched Johnny eat and listened to the thuds of the horse's hooves against the thick stall planks. At last, without a word, she rose and went out to the barn, opened the stall door, and went inside with Little Gus. He was sweaty and wide-eyed. She put up a hand, touched his neck. He quivered but lowered his head, his muscles relaxing a fraction. "You're lonesome, aren't you," Etta crooned and rubbed his head.

Little Gus leaned into her caress. Then he sniffed her belly. The baby inside kicked, as if saying hello. Little Gus pricked his ears and blew on Etta's belly. She laughed and put her cheek against him.

"He's spoiled is what he is," Johnny said. He had come up silently.

"He hasn't been locked in a stall since he was weeks old. Why can't we at least let him into the run?"

Johnny shook his head. "He has to learn to behave, and he has to learn to be confined. When you start taking him places, he'll be confined."

Etta turned back to the horse and stroked his neck.

"Come out of there, Etta," Johnny said quietly.

His tone drew her head around. She gazed at him, puzzled by his intensity.

"You shouldn't be confined in there with him. You don't know what he might do."

"Little Gus wouldn't hurt me."

"Little Gus is a fine horse . . . but he is still a horse, and he may be gelded, but he's still male. Come out." He was opening the stall door, moving very quietly and smoothly.

Etta looked at Little Gus, who had begun to get excited by the opening door. Johnny reached in and took her arm, pulling her out. He closed the door firmly in Little Gus's face.

"The sooner he learns, the easier it will be on him," he said sharply. "You make it worse by comin' out here and coddlin' him."

"I guess I can coddle him, if I want. He's my horse."

"Yes, ma'am, he is. But I'm trainin' him. Unless you're ready for me to quit."

Etta stared at him, and he stared back. Then she pivoted and strode back to the house.

Little Gus set up a rhythmic kicking of his stall, on and on and on. Obie and Johnny drove away, and Little Gus continued to kick. Half a dozen times Etta almost went out to him, but she would recall Johnny's words, "You only make it worse." Around midnight Johnny returned, and Little Gus quit kicking. Etta breathed a sigh of relief, but within twenty minutes Little Gus began again. Etta pulled the pillow over her head and slept fitfully.

Just before dawn, Etta came awake with a suddenness. The kicking had stopped.

Both relieved and worried, Etta got out of bed and went to the window. She saw Johnny's truck and a mist wafting here and there over the ground. She listened to the silence.

What if Little Gus had hurt his leg, maybe had cast himself in the stall and couldn't move? What if he had dropped dead?

With all sorts of fears welling up inside, Etta went hurrying down the stairs, across the yard and into the barn. She stopped in the doorway, took hold of the frame. As her eyes adjusted to the dimness of first light, she stared down the alley of the barn, at the small circle of light made by a single light bulb suspended from the rafter. There was a curious object in the alley opposite Little Gus's stall. She peered at it as she went forward.

It was Johnny, she saw with amazement. He was stretched on a bed of straw covered with a blanket, propped up against the wall, with his hat over his face.

Etta stopped and looked from him to the horse, who stood quietly, dozing. She went to the stall bars and peered in at Little Gus's rear legs. One of his ankles was swollen. Otherwise, he appeared fine. A sound drew her head around. Johnny was rising.

Giving her a sheepish look, he tossed his hat aside and raked a hand through his hair. "He doesn't like to be alone," he said.

"And how is he ever goin' to learn?" Etta said, a grin tugging at he lips.

Johnny shook his head, and then he was looking at her . . . looking at her with the same fire and intensity as he had when he had pulled her from Little Gus's back. In the way that made her breath come short, made her inordinately aware that she wore nothing but her nightgown, her belly swollen out, her feet bare on the cool concrete.

"I was just checkin' to see how he was," she said, hardly even aware of her words.

"He's fine. I wouldn't let anything happen to him, Etta."

He stepped toward her. His blue shirt was wrinkled, there was a piece of straw on his shoulder, his eyes were dark and shimmering. Filled with desire.

"I know you wouldn't," she said, her voice coming hoarsely.

Johnny stopped directly in front of her. Close enough for

his scent to fill her nostrils and her to see his chest move
with his breathing.

"Well, I'd better go on back in . . . since he's okay."
Etta moved to slip past him and run for it. But then his
hand was on her arm.

She stared at his hand, rough and dark against the pale
sleeve of her cotton gown.

Then, slowly, she looked up at him.

With sweet abandonment, Etta turned into his arms and
into his warmth and into his kiss. She wrapped her arms
around his neck and welcomed his lips and his ardor, tasting him and feeling his pounding heart beat in rhythm with
her own. They kissed long and hard and demanding, and
then Johnny was looking at her, his eyes all blue silver.
She wished he would look at her forever.

The next instant, he pulled back and set her from him as
firmly as setting aside evil intentions.

A small "oh," escaped Etta. She put out a hand to steady
herself.

Johnny's face was turned from her, and she tried to think
of something to say. All she kept thinking was *Good Lord
a'mercy*.

Then she fled, not running, but walking quite quickly,
all the while listening for Johnny to call her back. But he
didn't.

Johnny stood and watched Etta disappear out the barn
door, while the warmth of her remained on his hands and
his lips and echoed in his blood. Of a sudden, he pivoted,
striding along the barn alley, unaware of where he headed,
only thinking that he had to get out of there. Things had
gotten out of hand, and he needed to throw his gear in the
truck and hit the road.

He stopped, breathed deeply, and turned to look at the
red horse in the stall. He went to the barn door and looked
at the house and thought of the women inside. The horse
. . . the women . . . It was a new experience for him. No
one had ever needed him before.

He wondered just what he should do. He felt something
was required on his part, some apology.

He knew in that instant that he could not leave Etta Rivers.

Etta went in the kitchen door, closed it and leaned against it, only just that minute realizing the kitchen light was on, and Latrice, who had been sitting at the table with her Bible open, while the radio played out *The Morning Hour of Prayer*, raised her head and stared at her.

Etta shoved from the door and went across to the back stairs and up to her room. Latrice came right behind her, saying, "You might as well tell me what has happened."

Etta shut the guest-room door against her and flung herself upon the bed and covered her cold feet and her head, while further thoughts filled her mind: *He is a wonderful kisser . . . his lips so sweet and moist . . . Did he feel my baby against him?*

Latrice knocked at the door and called to be let in.

Etta buried her face in the pillow until she could not breathe. The baby stirred within her belly. Etta thought of how she had wanted desperately to do all manner of things with Johnny Bellah. And still did. She thought of how she was pregnant, near destitution, and enamored with an itinerant cowboy.

Well, she was a *widow*. She couldn't help it that the man who had fathered her child had gone and died. She had not killed him, after all.

Latrice said through the door, "I will be waiting in the kitchen," and Etta heard her firm footsteps disappearing down the hall.

After nearly thirty minutes of considering her situation, of alternately burying her face in the pillow and dreamily caressing her belly, thinking of all of it and becoming thoroughly worn out with the thoughts, too, Etta got dressed and went downstairs to face Latrice and possibly Johnny, if he came to breakfast.

The thought of now having to face Johnny got her very nervous. She thought perhaps he would be equally nervous and not come to breakfast.

She had decided to tell Latrice that she had gone to check

on Little Gus and had been overcome by the beauty of the dawn and sadness over Roy. Her mind took instantly to this idea, and she thought she might say she was so overcome that she needed to have her breakfast alone up in her room.

When faced with Latrice's concern, however, Etta blurted out, "I kissed Johnny." She was very curious as to what Latrice's reaction would be, since she could not seem to fathom her own reaction.

Latrice said, "Out in the barn?"

Etta nodded. "It was an accident," she said quickly. "I went out to check on Little Gus—I thought he might be dead—and Johnny was there, and . . . it just happened."

Latrice frowned. "Why did you think the horse was dead?"

"I don't *know!* I just did." Etta picked up a dishtowel and ran it through her hands.

"Was it only kissin'?"

"Well, of course it was. Good grief. What do you think—in my condition?"

"No tellin'," Latrice said dryly and poured herself a second cup of coffee.

More than any silly kiss, Latrice found it disconcerting that Etta had escaped the house without Latrice knowing. Latrice had always tried to keep a good watch on what went on about her. That Etta had slipped out and about without her knowledge made her feel she had failed in her vigilance, and that they were prey to all sorts of evil that might lurk about.

She said, "You might have stepped on a snake goin' out there. We wouldn't have to think so much about snakes if we lived in town, but we do out here."

"I was not thinkin' about snakes," Etta said, a bit amazed that Latrice was.

She sat and put her head in her hands. "Oh, God, I must be crazy like Mama. Here I am kissin' a man, and my husband's grave doesn't even have grass fully grown over it, and I have his child growin' inside me."

"Your mother didn't go around kissin' men—she thought she was Carole Lombard," Latrice said. "And as

for your husband, well, he is dead. Two days or two months
or two years aren't gonna make him any more dead than
the day you buried him, so I don't think that has any bearing at all.''

Etta was gratified at Latrice's words, but her mind was
already skimming ahead, imagining having to face Johnny.
''I'm so embarrassed. I can't believe I made such a fool of
myself.''

''Oh, honey, it isn't the first time, and it won't be the
last.''

''Well, thank you for that. That is extremely helpful,''
she said sharply.

Wrapping her arms tight around herself, she went to the
window and looked over to the barn, checking for Johnny's
pickup truck, before she even realized she was doing so.
The possibility that he would leave brought a pain across
her chest, and she was further distressed to find herself
gazing out the window for him at all.

''He'll probably leave now,'' she said, deep melancholy
coming over her.

''He might.'' Latrice conceded. ''Men do tend to run off
from anything sticky. But he's hung around this long,
though, and as long as we keep feedin' him, he's likely to
stay.''

''You talk like he's a dog. I do imagine he could get fed
most anywhere. Lots of women out there are willin' to do
that, and more.''

''True, but he loves my biscuits.''

''Roy did, too. That's probably why he didn't run off
with Corinne. She doesn't look like the type who can cook
biscuits. He went over there and got what else he wanted
from her and then would come home here for your biscuits.''

Etta wondered how she would possibly face Johnny. The
way he had set her away from him played back through
her thoughts.

Then she thought of Roy.

''I was crazy for one needy man,'' she said, her voice
coming husky through her tight throat. ''I won't make that

same mistake again. I have a child to think of now.''

"Havin' a child most generally gives a woman wisdom, if they allow it,'' Latrice said. As she put the iron skillet on the burner, she added, ''Johnny Bellah isn't like Roy Rivers, though. There's more to him.''

"His boot size is larger,'' Etta conceded after a moment. She wondered if she was going to spend the rest of her life falling for the wrong men.

Latrice put her arm about Etta's shoulders, and Etta stood there, relishing the rare touch from this woman who was like a part of her. A sister and a mother and a teacher all in one.

Then, quite abruptly, Latrice broke away, saying, ''I'd better get breakfast. It will be interesting to see if that boy smells food and comes up. See what he does.''

Etta said, ''It is so gratifying that my life provides you with entertainment. God knows, I live for it.''

Twelve 🌹

Johnny telephoned, using the extension in the barn, and Latrice answered. Etta heard Latrice say, "Yes . . . Fine . . . I'll tell her," then she hung up and said directly, "That was Johnny Bellah callin' from the barn."

Etta had forgotten all about the extension in the barn; Johnny had not used it once in all these weeks.

Latrice said, "He will not be comin' up for breakfast. He also said to tell you that he had invited some men to bring their horses and have a bit of rodeo practice today. He hoped that was okay."

This annoyed Etta no end. While she had dreaded facing Johnny, deep in her heart she had looked forward to it.

She had expected something of him—an approach of some sort. She did not like that he took the easy way out by avoiding her, and she did not at all appreciate that he was right back at the horses, going on as usual, as if their kiss—quite a passionate kiss, she had thought—had been nothing at all.

Obie did not come for breakfast that morning, either, and it was a lonesome meal with just herself and Latrice. They filled the time by discussing names for the baby, but neither appeared in a truly talkative mood.

When Johnny's acquaintances started arriving, Etta was

159

highly curious. She couldn't go out with them and watch everything, of course; not only was she shy about facing Johnny, but she felt too pregnant to go out around a bunch of men.

"Pregnant or not, it's too raucous a gatherin' for a woman," Latrice said. "They wouldn't want you, either. You'd spoil their fun."

Etta went from window to window, trying to see who came and what all was going on.

Obie came. He was easy to spot as he was so tall and lean and wearing his blue cap. She recognized one of his many nephews, too, Woody, the one who rode the rodeo circuit. He was a bull rider and bulldogger. Unlike Obie, he was short and very thick in the shoulders. He went by the name of Choctaw Woody Lee. His grandmother had been Choctaw, and he avoided trouble in some rodeos by maintaining the family Indian lineage, although this could cause trouble at times, too.

She thought she recognized Jed Stuart, one of the men for whom Johnny was training horses, and she saw Walter Fudge's youngest son, Bitta. His real name was Nesbitt, but he'd acquired the name Bitta Fudge early on; Etta thought Caroline and Walter should have thought of this before they gave him the name.

Harry Flagg came, minus his old army coat now that the weather was warmer, and brought two men and five horses in his trailer. Harry always seemed to have a group with him. None of the horses he brought were ones he had taken from her.

Etta watched the men bucking out some green horses someone had brought, saw the bottle of home brew passed. Then the men moved back to the pasture track. Etta got impatient, as it was nearly impossible to see the goings-on from the kitchen or the dining room. She moved up to the east guest-room window, and Latrice joined her. They opened the window wide and removed the screen for a better view. Latrice went away and returned with Roy's binoculars, which they passed back and forth.

"They aren't much help," Etta said, waving away the binoculars impatiently.

The men ran horses up and down the pasture track. At first it appeared there were trial runs, and then Johnny ran his big golden dun against a brown horse. Etta recognized Johnny mostly by the way he sat in the saddle. He won with his golden dun. They could not see the finish line from where they were, but they could tell Johnny won by the way he came riding back, sitting high and pleased.

Handsome, Etta thought, watching him with an ache in her chest.

On the fourth or fifth run she saw Johnny riding forward on Little Gus. There was no mistaking Little Gus; even though he was a beautiful color, red as wet clay and his tail and mane soft in the breeze, he walked forward all loose and gangly. He looked decidedly awkward and small next to Woody on a stout bay.

Etta didn't realize how tense she had gotten, until the starter's flag came down, and she got carried away and yelled, "Go, Gus!"

Latrice took hold of her. "You are gonna fall out this window!"

It was most frustrating not to be able to see the finish. She strained and strained to see, until Johnny came riding back into view. He was sitting slouched.

"He lost," she said.

"Looks like it," Latrice agreed.

After a time, the men moved to the big corral, where they held runs at calf roping, and then bulldogging and indulged in a lot of laughing and horseplay. Latrice got bored and went back downstairs. Etta sat in a chair and watched the men and stared out across the land and listened to birds.

Sunset came, and the men gathered themselves, their horses and whiskey, and began to leave. Etta saw Johnny walk his grey gelding over to Harry Flagg's trailer and lead him inside.

Watching Harry's trailer rattle away, Etta wondered if Johnny would come up to the house for supper.

While she waited for him, she went downstairs and took up peeling potatoes for Latrice. She never had been very good at peeling potatoes. Latrice always complained that she took off too thick a peel, and that was the case now, as she kept looking out the window and the door, trying to see Johnny, trying to prepare herself for him, and thinking over and over of how to act completely natural, as if the kiss had never happened.

"Lord a'mercy, what is wrong with you?" Latrice jerked the knife out of Etta's hand. "Look here—you've thrown a whole potato away and saved the peeling."

Etta dried her hands and went out the screen door. She stood on the porch, gazing across to the barn lit by the golden glow of the setting sun.

Johnny appeared, coming out of the black opening. Etta's heart pattered in her chest. He saw her and stopped. Filled with yearning, she reached out and took hold of the porch post, while inside she was thinking: *Here I am . . . Will you . . . Let's . . .*

The next instant Johnny turned sharply for his pickup truck. He strode over, yanked open the door, got in and drove away.

Etta stood there, watching his truck disappear around the corner of the house, and then she listened to the sound of it until it was gone.

Obie came up for supper. He didn't bother asking if he was invited; he just came in and sat down, saying in a breezy manner, "How are you lovely ladies this evenin'?"

Latrice was a little taken aback. "You appear somewhat full of yourself, Obie Lee."

"Yes, ma'am. I'm lookin' forward to enjoyin' your meal and the company of two fine ladies. I don't think a man could ask more in this world."

Latrice raised an eyebrow at his flowery talk, but when he grinned at her, she had to grin in return. She found him quite handsome in such a rare flamboyant mood. She especially liked his even white teeth, rare for a man of his age. She had always found his teeth his redeeming grace, when he fell into acting slow and countrified.

"This is the last of our ham, so you had better take that big slice on top," she said, holding the serving platter toward him. She noted Etta's surprised glance and pointedly ignored it.

"Why, thank you, Miss Latrice. It looks invitin'."

At his eager, happy look, Latrice straightened herself up. She did not want to overly encourage him. Still, she thought, as she passed him the cornbread, she was glad he had come for supper.

Latrice, having to observe the passion vibrating between Etta and Johnny these days, had been surprised lately to find that she was lonely. There were things in her life that Etta, fifteen years younger in the bloom of youth and white as cotton, could not understand about a middle-aged Negro woman. Ironically, Roy Rivers, being nearer Latrice's age, had often been good company for her. She had known him for exactly what he was, and she believed this had given him a certain freedom to be himself around her. He used to come into the kitchen late at night, after Etta was asleep, and sit at the table with a glass of warm milk, which he got himself, and talk about jazz and blues and the dusty days. These times he would also flirt with her. Latrice had taken this for what it was: for him an unconscious, innocent act, as natural as breathing, and for her a reminder that she was indeed a woman.

Latrice did not want to let on, but Roy Rivers dying so suddenly had shaken her. She kept thinking about how she was forty-one now, and her baby Etta was having a baby of her own.

Things would change with the baby. Etta would have another person upon whom to bestow her heart. Latrice supposed that she would, too, but even as she watched Etta laugh with Obie, Latrice knew their lives were going to change in many ways she would find hard. Etta would get her own child and would finally outgrow being Latrice's child. And Etta's child would pull them all further into the white world, with school and teachers and friends. This prospect was daunting, as was their entire uncertain future.

Latrice found more and more these long days that Obie's presence had a stirring effect upon her. He had begun to show a little more determination. She wondered exactly how far he would go in pursuit of her.

"Let me get you some fresh ice tea, Obie," she said. She put her hand on his shoulder as she poured his tea, feeling the muscles hard beneath her hand.

Etta watched Latrice's unusual solicitations to Obie with some surprise, followed by a slice of self-pity that Johnny was not there with them. She definitely felt the third wheel.

"Johnny got the whole thing up this afternoon to set up the best odds on Little Gus," Obie said, grinning and plainly enjoying being the center of attention. "He wanted that horse to look good enough to run, but not so good anyone would know the little fella could really *run*. Woody was in on the whole thing, but none of those fellas would think it was like that, you know. Miss Latrice, might I have some more sugar in this tea?"

"You mean he held Little Gus back when he ran him?" Etta asked.

"Yes, ma'am." Obie nodded. "I heard Harry Flagg tell one of the boys that he thought Johnny wanted to show out that big dun. They was"—he glanced at Latrice—"*were* all tryin' to do that, put their horses either in a good light or poor light, dependin' on which way they were wantin' to go with them, sell today or get better odds later."

He chuckled and shook his head. "Those boys can sure get crazy over horses. Johnny got Harry Flagg to buy his grey for six hundred. Johnny didn't want to let him go for that, but he wanted the money. That youngest boy of Walter Fudge's—Bitta—he paid one thousand dollars for a horse from Harry Flagg. Cash money."

"Sounds like that boy has too much money," Latrice said.

"Well, Johnny seems to think that the horse was worth that. And he's thinkin' if Little Gus hit many races hereabouts, he could be worth several thousand in no time."

Etta sighed. "Obie, horsemen do one thing better than ride horses, and that's inflate prices."

"Well, I did think some of them were gettin' carried away. Seemed like the more they drank, the wilder the braggin' got about those horses. I thought maybe Johnny should wait to sell his grey, but it probably wouldn't have helped, 'cause Mr. Flagg don't drink much."

He grinned and shook his head, and then his grin faded. "Oh, Miz Etta, I almost clean forgot. I stopped up to Burgess Feed this mornin' to get that grain mixture you and Johnny been feedin' Little Gus, and Mr. Burgess wouldn't let me have it. He said he just couldn't go no more on the credit."

"Oh," Etta said, thinking of the bill that had come from Burgess Feed only two days ago. She had not opened the envelope, so she didn't know the exact amount. "Earl's been patient long enough, I guess. We'll just have to do without."

Johnny would likely be disappointed, she thought. He had put Little Gus on the grain mixture, the same thing he was feeding his own two horses, saying it would heat them up. He called it giving them "firepower." Roy used to do the same thing with certain horses he was racing or wanted to show out especially well. The proper feed gave the horse a lustrous coat and made him have extra energy. Roy called it "pizzazz."

"Well, those cattle don't need feed no more, anyway," Obie said. "I put out a little minerals, but those critters are fine since we're just grazin' out the wheat. Now, if prices weren't so far down, I'd suggest you sell 'em."

The idea of selling the cattle gave Etta a little start. "Can I sell them? I thought they belonged to the bank. I mean, I know Roy borrowed to buy them and that's still owed the bank."

"Well . . ." Obie rubbed his head. "The bank gave Mr. Roy the money to buy them cattle. The money is owed the bank, but they don't rightly own the cattle, I don't guess." He stretched his legs. "But like I said, cattle prices are bad. The other day they were down ten dollars a pound on av-

erage from the spring sell-off, which was already way
down. We didn't even much have a spring sell-off, the way
I hear it. People are holdin' out rather than take such big
losses.''

Etta rose and took her plate to the counter, her mind
revolving with the thought that she could sell the cattle.

In her mind the cattle were all bound up with the farm.
She had rather thought that when she sold the farm, everything went with it like a package, equipment and cattle,
everything. She realized she did not have an accurate picture of her position. She had not asked enough questions.

Leaving Latrice and Obie lingering over the meal, Etta
went into the den and telephoned Leon at home. She
thought of Leon with some annoyance as she dialed. Leon
should have discussed these things with her. Undoubtedly
he had not talked over any of her options because he assumed that she could not handle any of the farm business
and likely did not want to handle it.

Betsy answered and Etta heard the surprise in her voice
when Etta asked for Leon. ''Well, yes, Etta . . . just a moment, please.''

When Leon answered, he asked Etta how she was, and
she said, ''Fine. Leon, can I sell the cattle? I know I owe
the bank for them, but could I sell them if I wanted?''

''Etta, cattle prices are way down. You don't want to sell
your cattle.''

''I know I don't want to, but could I if I wanted? Could
I sell anything here I want? I mean, could I sell the tractors?''

''You want to sell the tractors?''

''I don't know, Leon. What I need to know are my options. Can I sell the cattle, if I want to? Can I sell tractors?
Can I sell part of the land?''

''You don't need to be worryin' about any of that, honey.
The bank's goin' to handle it, and Edward will see that you
get the best deals all the way around.''

''I'm sure he will, but I want to understand the situation.
What can I do?''

He sighed. ''I guess you can sell the cattle and the tractors. I didn't see anything that said the bank held the lien on them. When Roy borrowed the money, he borrowed against the farm, the house, too, which he shouldn't have done. He should have cut that out. He didn't, though, and the farm's all tied up. You can't sell the farm or parts of it without consultin' with Edward.

"But you don't want to be bothered with any of that, honey. When the farm sells, the cattle and equipment will be put up for auction. The bank can handle it, and you don't need to be concerned with it at all. I don't like to see you gettin' all wrought up about this. Who've you been talkin' to?"

"Oh, nobody, really. Obie just mentioned that it would be good if we could sell the cattle—but he told me about the prices bein' low," she added quickly, not wanting Leon to be critical of Obie.

He asked about how she was feeling, and she told him fine again and then asked about Betsy in order to deflect attention from herself. Then she was able to say a polite goodbye and hang up.

When she walked back and pushed through the kitchen door, she saw Latrice and Obie, both of them over at the sink. Obie stood behind Latrice, with his body against her, and was kissing her neck.

Etta was so stunned that she just stood there, staring.

Luckily the two did not hear her over the sound of water running in the sink. Etta backed up into the dining room and let the door close softly.

She felt so bad, so alone, that tears came to her eyes. She wondered where Johnny was and pictured him dancing with a nice, slim unpregnant woman who was not an old widow but fresh and lively. Etta felt that she had not been fresh and lively in a long time.

Obie stayed until the moon came out, sitting on the side porch with Latrice. Etta, in the kitchen, could occasionally hear the murmur of their voices through the screened door, along with the chirp of crickets. She listened to the radio the border station that played rock and roll, and made

names from the Scrabble letters, while also keeping an ear
cocked for the sound of Johnny's pickup returning.

Obie drove away, and Latrice came inside, saying, "It's
fixin' to storm."

They checked to make certain windows were closed. Afterward they sat in the kitchen, Etta at the table making
names from Scrabble letters, and Latrice in her rocker with
hand-sewing, listening to the radio, now rhythm and blues
out of Chicago.

Etta considered asking Latrice if she had changed her
mind and decided to encourage Obie after all. She decided
she didn't want to talk about it. Neither of them seemed
inclined to talk, and each fell into her own thoughtful silence, until Etta decided she was hungry for something
sweet.

"It's gettin' awfully bare in here," she said, searching
the pantry. She had developed a powerful craving for sweet
chocolate something.

The worry over buying food had been creeping up on
her. They had always bought on credit down at Overman's
Bright and White at the crossroads, but there were a couple
of those unopened Overman bills in the pile now, too,
alongside those from Burgess Feed.

She came up with rice and raisins, and Latrice volunteered to make her sweet rice, using honey from one of
Obie's nephew's hives. Just when Latrice spooned the rice
into a bowl, the storm hit, wind rattling the windows and
creaking the walls.

"We might should go down the cellar," Latrice said,
although she moved without haste to the sink and ran water
in the empty rice pan.

Etta looked out the window, heard the horses in the corral whinny, although she couldn't see them. She was glad
Little Gus was secure in the barn and out of the storm, but
she worried he might get agitated and start kicking the stall.

Neither she nor Latrice ran for the cellar, Latrice because
she did not like to go into the ground, and Etta because she
didn't care to run out into the rain to get there. She suggested the closet beneath the stairwell.

"Well, if there was a cyclone, it's already gone over," Latrice said, peering out the window. "The rain's fallin' in a steady sheet now."

"I think I'll go to the stairwell closet, just in case it comes at the back." It was all right not to be frightened of storms herself, but she had a baby to think of now.

"It won't," Latrice said, as if she knew all. Then she said, "Here comes headlights . . . guess it's Johnny." And a moment later: "Good Lord, he's gonna hit the barn— nope, he hit the light pole."

Etta rushed over beside Latrice. The night-black window reflected her own face. She flipped off the overhead light. Again peering out the window, she saw Johnny's pickup truck through the falling rain. It sat in the glow of the tall pole lamp at the corner of the barn, its front smack into the thick pole that was waving just a bit in the wind and causing the yellow light to flicker.

"Did he hit hard?"

"Not too hard."

"Maybe we should go out and check him. He might have hit his head." Etta's mind began to jump with all sorts of morbid pictures, then latch onto the worst, which was hosting another funeral.

"He's fine," Latrice said. "No doubt he was limber as a wet noodle from drink. There's no need in us gettin' soaked—and possibly struck by lightning—just to find him passed out."

"Well . . . I suppose." Etta was not eager to go outside, either.

The next instant, as she wiped fog from the window, the door of Johnny's pickup swung open, causing the light to come on inside the cab, showing Johnny with his hat on cockeyed. He slipped out of the seat, closed the door, took a lurching step, and fell facedown, splashing brown water up in a wave.

When he did not get up, Etta said, "He'll drown," and started for the door.

She was outside when Latrice caught her arm and shoved a slicker at her. Etta threw it on even as she ran off the porch and out into the rain. Behind her, above the sound of the storm, she heard Latrice call loudly for God's protection.

Johnny remained facedown in the big mud puddle, exactly like a dead body. Etta took hold of him beneath his left arm and jerked him upward, getting his face out of the water. Latrice, in Roy's old canvas duster, reached them, took hold of Johnny beneath the opposite arm. Together, struggling through the sucking mud, with the rain plastering their hair to their heads and running into their eyes, they dragged him toward the barn. Etta was amazed that he weighed so much. She had not considered Johnny an overly large man.

Just inside the barn door, Latrice let loose, and then Etta did, too, dropping Johnny on his side. For a moment both women stood gazing at each other, gasping for breath. Then Latrice knelt and put her hand on Johnny's chest. Etta leaned over her shoulder.

Latrice nodded, "He's still breathin'."

Relief washed over Etta. She stood looking down at Johnny's muddy face and chest and hearing the pounding rain and feeling somewhat dazed.

Latrice said, "We brought him this far—we might as well get him into his bed."

Each taking hold of him once again, they dragged Johnny toward his room.

"Why are we doin' this?" Etta asked, her relief giving way to annoyance. She was out of breath and miserably wet and all for a drunken man. Her slippers would be totally ruined.

"Because we are Christians," Latrice said, and not at all like she was happy about it.

Johnny gave out an, "Uhh" when they flopped him on his back on his bunk. Catching a strong whiff of whiskey, Etta had the urge to roll him off the bed and give him a good kick.

But then, after a look at his face, she insisted on wiping it off. "That mud might just cake up his nose," she said, searching around for something to use—she settled on a sock. "I sure don't want him to smother after all our efforts."

She covered him with blankets, too, while Latrice looked on and frowned.

"If he catches pneumonia, guess who'll end up nursin' him, because we are Christian women," Etta pointed out, deciding another blanket was called for.

The next morning Etta saw Johnny coming toward the house. She was at the stove, cooking the bacon. When it had begun to sizzle, she had opened the kitchen door, wondering if the aroma of cooking meat would bring Johnny, an action that made her impatient with herself.

She remained at the stove, while Latrice invited Johnny to sit at the table. With a quick glance she saw he was neatly dressed. He sat carefully, thanked Latrice for the coffee with a murmur, and drank of it deeply. When he glanced over at Etta, she turned quickly away.

Latrice took dishes out of the cabinets with a clatter and smacked them on the table, "How's your head this mornin', Mr. Bellah? You would have drowned last night out there in the mud, if we had not gone out there and dragged you into your bed."

Johnny's head jerked up and he looked from Latrice to Etta.

Then, flinching and averting his eyes, he said, "I thank you ladies. I apologize for my behavior."

"And well you should, young man," Latrice said.

Etta didn't say anything. She felt Johnny look at her, knew he wanted her to respond, but she refused.

She helped Latrice put breakfast on the table, and Johnny sat there and ate it. She imagined he was too uncertain of Latrice not to eat breakfast. He complimented them on the meal and thanked them effusively. He was desperate to please them, Etta saw. This was gratifying and strangely irritating at the same time.

His gaze met Etta's as he stood and took up his hat from the top of the refrigerator, where he had formed the habit of tossing it. His silvery eyes were very sad and uncertain, and she felt a rush of emotion. Suddenly she had the urge to gather his head down upon her breast.

Quickly she averted her gaze.

She listened to his footsteps and the screen door creak as he left. Raising her eyes, she saw him as a shadow on the other side of the screen. His footsteps scraped on the porch, and his spurs jingled and the fresh morning air puffed into the room, seeming to bring the scent of dust stirred by his footsteps.

Etta wondered if he would leave now, drive away and never return.

Listening for his truck to start, she began to shake inside. She thought fervently that she had to give up that wondering. Getting through this time was hard enough, without waiting every second for Johnny Bellah to be gone.

Later, when she was out grooming Little Gus, Johnny came up to her. "I really want to apologize for what I did last night."

Staring at her pale hand resting against Little Gus's coppery coat, Etta said, "You don't owe me an apology. It is none of my business at all what you do."

Her gaze met his then, and she saw he looked like she had slapped him.

With a nod, he turned away, all slumped down, as if she had knocked the very breath from him.

She was sorry. She wanted to reach out to him.

But she did not.

Johnny walked into the barn and over to where a pint bottle of whiskey was tucked on a wall board. He uncapped the bottle and raised it to his lips. He stopped. Then he drew back and threw the bottle with all his might against the wall, where it shattered. He stared at the stain and inhaled the sharp scent while all manner of thoughts crossed his mind, none of them hopeful.

Thirteen

Although Etta knew it was ridiculous to be annoyed with Johnny—admitted to herself that she had no right to annoyance—she remained highly annoyed. She recalled Johnny's arms around her and his lips on hers and found herself having feelings she had not known a pregnant woman could have. She blamed Johnny for stirring them, and for disappointing her.

The disappointment was so heavy in her chest that she felt she had trouble breathing. Johnny had turned from her and then shown very poor behavior in getting drunk, which was a further turning. And as always, with such men as Johnny, the horse appeared to be the most important thing to him.

After Etta's harsh words, Johnny kept to himself, until he discovered the empty grain barrel and that no more grain would be forthcoming.

"We can't have that," he said. "We've got to keep that red gelding on the rich feed."

"There is pasture now that we've had rain, and we've got alfalfa," Etta said.

Before she finished speaking, Johnny was shaking his head. "We can't stop the feed now. It'd upset his digestion and everything."

173

"Well, I'm sorry, but I just don't have any money for feed," Etta said.

Johnny went out and bought a hundred pounds of the grain mixture, the price of which had been rising daily since the dry season.

His doing that embarrassed Etta terribly. It made her feel indebted to him, and a bit more afraid of losing Little Gus. It was like she was losing Little Gus to Johnny in pieces.

She did not see any way to stop Johnny from buying the feed, though. Even if she could put her foot down, she wouldn't. Since Johnny's comment, she had begun to fear for Little Gus's digestion. Also, she didn't want to disappoint Johnny.

The morning the coffee ran out, Etta decided there was nothing else to do but see if Overman's Bright and White Grocery would continue their credit.

She dressed herself up in a skirt and blouse—in spring colors of yellow and white, her favorite of the number of maternity outfits she had splurged on during those first weeks after she had found out that she was pregnant. She put on lipstick and tied her hair back with a yellow ribbon, intending to go and be as charming and humbling as possible.

"Oh, look!" she cried and excitedly showed Latrice a five-dollar bill she found in her handbag. "It is a miracle."

Latrice said. "We'd better pray for another miracle, and that's for Mr. Arthur givin' us credit."

Etta snapped the five-dollar bill back into her handbag and thought longingly not only of coffee but of sugar and cocoa for making chocolate fudge or pudding, for which she had developed a powerful craving. She craved it so badly that she had actually prayed for some. After all, the Bible said to pray about everything.

Johnny drove them in his pickup truck. He'd been eager to do things for them in the days following his episode of poor behavior. This eagerness had had the perverse effect of causing Etta to refuse to allow him to do anything.

"I can do it," she would say tersely when he offered to

feed Little Gus, or change a light bulb, or gather onions from the garden. She didn't really intend to be so cold to him, but she could not seem to help herself. She would not have asked him to take them to the store, but on that particular morning Obie's truck broke down.

When she came out of the house all dressed up, he stared at her, and she was pleased to know he found her pretty.

"The seat's a little dusty," he said, jumping quickly to jerk open the passenger door and wipe a handkerchief over the seat.

Latrice came out, saying she was ready. "Let's hurry this up. I want to get back to see my soap this afternoon." Then she got herself up onto the middle of the truck seat.

Etta had a little trouble with the tall step. Johnny took her hand to help. She saw his face blush like it always did when he was faced with her bulging belly. He looked away quickly, slammed the door, and went around to get in behind the wheel.

They drove along the lane and turned onto the highway. Etta kept her window rolled down and her face turned toward the wind, inhaling deeply of the scents of spring full blown.

She caught a glimpse of herself in the side-view window. Her hair blew wildly around the yellow ribbon. She saw her cheeks were rosy, her eyes brilliant. She recalled how Johnny had looked at her moments before. It seemed a long time since a man had looked at her like that.

"I'm gonna get a pop," Johnny said when he pulled to a stop in front of the store.

He headed over to the dented red chest sitting at the corner of the porch, while Latrice and Etta went on through the screen door with the Orange Crush sign across the middle. Seeing the sign, Etta had a sudden craving for sweet orange anything. Orange candy covered with chocolate sounded especially good.

"You go get the coffee and cocoa," Latrice instructed, keeping her voice low and thrusting a canvas hand basket at Etta from the stack at the entry.

Etta nodded. They were acting rather like robbers, she

thought, stepping lightly and quickly to get their needs, and hoping to get out without much notice at all.

As always happened at such times, however, it appeared every woman Etta would rather not have seen had picked that particular morning to come and get groceries. She ran first into Adelaide Trueblood, the woman who owned the rose bushes Johnny's horses had trampled that day. Next she came upon Sally Mae Freeman, an old friend of Roy's mother's, and then Caroline Fudge, Walter's wife, and one of her daughters-in-law, Mary Ellen.

Etta said a polite hello to each woman and suffered their intensely curious looks. She was truly glad to see Mary Ellen; she and Mary Ellen had recognized each other as being outsiders right from the beginning. Mary Ellen was from California, and even though she had married into the Fudge family and lived for ten years one-half mile down the road from them, the Fudges would always call her the Californian.

Etta kept on moving, reminding herself of Alice as she snatched things from the shelves. When Latrice peered into Etta's basket, she raised an eyebrow.

"We might as well get as much as we can this trip," Etta said.

They set their baskets on the dark, worn counter, and Latrice took a step behind Etta, falling into playing the role of colored housekeeper in deference to white employer. Whenever they went shopping together this was the way it was played, and Etta always thought it silly and annoying. Latrice called it facing facts and getting successfully through life.

Arthur Overman greeted them in a friendly manner—he was one of those gentle giants who could not be unkind if he tried a lifetime. He gave Etta an appreciative look, and as he began to ring up their purchases, Etta thought the ribbon in her hair had likely been a good addition.

Arthur would have extended credit, Etta was certain of this. But then his wife, Noreen, who had no doubt seen them enter the store and been lurking at the edge of the back room, jumped out and put her foot down.

"I'm sorry, Etta, but we just can't carry you any longer. You'll need to pay for this today, if you please."

For a moment Etta just stared at the woman. Then she said, "I am not hard of hearing, Noreen."

That set the woman back a smidgen. "Well . . ." Speaking more moderately, Noreen shifted her stance, "We'll need payment, and we'd like some toward your account, too. It's goin' on three months past due."

Etta stared at her, and Noreen said she was certain Etta could understand their position. They were operating a business, after all. Noreen's voice was rising again; she was a shrill woman with a shrill voice, and Etta suddenly just wanted to get away from her.

"Yes, of course I understand," Etta said and brought up her handbag, digging into it. "I'll write you a check."

"I'll need cash for this bill today," Noreen said.

Etta looked up into Noreen's face. Then she slowly straightened, slipping her checkbook back into her handbag. She could not think of anything else to do but leave her cocoa and marmalade there on the counter and walk out. Get as far away as possible from the way the woman was looking at her and the humiliation squirming in her chest.

Her gaze fell on the coffee, fell to the cocoa, and she thought of the five-dollar bill in her purse.

"What's it come to?"

Etta jumped at the voice sounding from behind her left shoulder. Johnny. His eyes shone steely and bright from his tanned face.

When Noreen, her mouth looking like she'd eaten an early persimmon, just stared at him, he motioned at the groceries and asked again the total. Noreen told him, and Johnny pulled bills from his worn brown wallet with his callused hands, while Arthur hurriedly sacked the purchases. Then Johnny tipped his hat and picked up the sacks.

Poor Arthur got carried away and said, "Thank you all now, and come back."

Etta took great care not to let the screen door slam. Johnny went to the rear of the truck and lowered the sacks into the bed. Latrice got herself up in the middle, and Etta stood a moment, holding tightly to the door handle and looking back at the store.

She imagined herself getting behind the wheel of the truck and driving it right through that window.

But it was Johnny's truck, and then he was behind her, waiting to help her up in the seat. His hand was warm and gentle on her arm. Etta looked over and saw Latrice's outstretched hand. She took it and got up into the seat. Her gaze met Johnny's, and words stuck in her throat. He gave her a soft look that made her want to cry, and then he shut the door.

Latrice patted Etta's hand with her own. Etta glanced at her and then looked away.

Johnny got in behind the wheel, started the engine, and backed out. Gravel pinged as he headed onto the highway.

Etta blinked in the glare reflected from the hood of the truck. She thought of how people said money wasn't everything in life, but those that said it the loudest were those who had the most. She thought of how she had once before known life without money and was now knowing it again, and she did not like it and would not say that it added to her virtue. In fact, many people who went without money just seemed to keep getting smaller and smaller, as if all their virtue was squeezed out of them.

Her gaze dropped to the side of the road. Gravel and red dirt and green grass melding into a spinning blur. She stared at it, and the urge welled within her to open the door and throw herself out. She imagined her body hitting and being pummeled by the ground.

Startled by such a thought, she jerked her gaze upward and straight ahead and held on for dear life to the open window frame. Such thoughts were foolish in the extreme. Latrice would be highly put out. Etta throwing herself out the door of a speeding vehicle would simply make a lot more work for Latrice.

Realizing she still hung tightly to the window frame, it came to her that she had been hanging on to life ever since she was a child.

She hung on to life, she thought, but she had never fully

learned how to live it. She was still just hanging on—and usually to the wrong things.

The tense silence from the women worried Johnny. He had thought himself the hero of the day, that he at last redeemed himself, as he had been trying to do ever since he had gone crazy with drink. But Etta wasn't acting like he was a hero. She had not thanked him or given him so much as a tender look. He realized he must have stepped on her pride. He had done the wrong thing again, he thought morosely.

Feeling edgy, he said, "I think those people were right rude." He thought maybe he just had to give Etta a chance to realize his heroism.

Latrice said, "Noreen Overman was not taught manners. I knew her mother; I delivered her older sister. Her mother was stupid. She had no mealtimes but simply let the children run around the table at all hours of the day and eat off plates left there." She added, "And she went right into her neighbor's houses without knocking and was found more than once going through their things."

The picture of children running around a table, grabbing food off plates, popped into Johnny's mind. The practice seemed messy and uninviting, but he wasn't certain it was rude, at least if the children did it only in their own home.

"The Overmans have a right to want what's owed them," Etta said. "They have to pay bills, too, like everyone else."

The flat tone of her voice drew Johnny's gaze, and he saw her staring out the windshield in a manner that unnerved him further.

Latrice said, "Noreen Overman generally cannot see her own shortcomings because she is so busy pointing out those of other people. She is a jealous woman. Mr. Arthur was happy with things—with lookin' and chattin' with you. That's what the whole thing was about. Noreen didn't like Mr. Arthur lookin' at you—not today or the days before."

Etta's head swung around. "At me? Oh, Good heavens, I am goin' on eight months pregnant."

"Well, that doesn't make any difference. It was Mr. Arthur's happiness in looking, which is only natural, but Noreen can't stand for him to be happy, when she herself rarely is.''

The idea that the storekeeper had been looking at Etta perturbed Johnny, and so did the fact that neither woman had thanked him for saving the day. He thought that he had been trying and trying to please Etta, and he didn't know why he kept doing so.

In his nervousness over the situation, he broke out into whistling. He didn't even realize he was doing this until a movement caught his eye, and he glanced over to see both Latrice and Etta frowning at him. He quit whistling.

When they got back to the house, Johnny carried the sacks into the kitchen table. Miss Latrice asked for him to dig out the coffee so she could make some right away. As he did this, he saw Etta turn and go through the swinging door. He gazed after her, watching her particular soft sway.

He jerked his attention back to the bags of groceries. That he kept being drawn more and more to Etta's sway concerned him. He definitely did not need to be attracted to a pregnant woman, although in this case, he could not quite figure out why. She was not a married pregnant woman.

He got out the coffee and, after a bit of uncertainty of what was required of him, sat at the table. He thought he would have a cup of Miss Latrice's strong coffee before going out to get started working the horses.

Keeping his mood up the past days had been difficult, with Etta ignoring him and without a drop of whiskey. Johnny both wanted whiskey and didn't want it at the same time, and this confusion was wearing. He absently rubbed his knee, and his gaze kept straying to the swinging door through which Etta had disappeared. He hoped she returned and maybe sit at the table with him.

Johnny was taking his first sip of coffee when Etta reappeared through the door, awkwardly bearing a big cardboard box. He jumped up to take the box for her and set it on the table. Glancing inside, he saw things wrapped in cloths.

As Etta disappeared through the swinging door again, Latrice looked into the box. When she moved the cloths, Johnny caught a glimpse of silver, a jewelry box, piece of glass. Latrice gave out a faint "Hmmm."

At that moment, Etta returned, carrying her purse. She said, "Johnny, would you drive me up to Oklahoma City?"

The request startled him. He looked over at Miss Latrice. She quietly regarded Etta. The two women did this all the time, a silent communication that often got him all confused, because Miss Latrice would start a sentence and Etta would finish it up. This time, however, Miss Latrice didn't say a word.

"Well, sure, Miz Etta. I guess," Johnny said, becoming pleased that Etta was requesting his aid for a second time.

He got Etta and the box settled into the seat of the truck, and he was turning the key when Miss Latrice called, "Wait!" and came running out with a silver platter and a crystal serving dish. "Take these, too. This dish is true lead."

When Johnny pulled the truck out on the highway, Etta asked, "Do you know where to find a pawnshop in Oklahoma City?"

"Well now, I haven't been to Oklahoma City in a long time, but I imagine I can find one." After a minute he said, "You don't have to go all the way to Oklahoma City for a pawnshop. They have one of those in Chickasha."

He thought he should mention that, although he had sort of begun to be thoroughly pleased with the idea of driving all the way to Oklahoma City, being alone with Etta for that long and away from the farm.

"No . . . I want to go to Oklahoma City," Etta said. She didn't want to go to a nearby pawnshop and risk running into someone she knew. Her reputation was not so hot anyway; she didn't need to be seen going into a pawnshop. Besides, she felt she would do better in a bigger city.

Keeping her gaze from looking down at the side of the road (she did not want to feel again like throwing herself out of the truck) Etta looked out at the greening fields and pastures and here and there oil wells pumping beneath the bright sunshine. The sweet-smelling air blew in the window, and she began to relax.

She thought that she really liked to ride with Johnny because he did not mess around; he drove fast. Roy had always done that, too, and Etta herself loved to drive speedily. She put her hand out and felt the wind in her fingers. Johnny looked over at her, and they sort of grinned at each other.

Etta told herself to look away, yet his silvery eyes held hers and made her feel things deep inside.

Then she turned straight ahead and laid her hand on her belly, reminding herself.

They reached Oklahoma City in a little over an hour, after two stops, one for gas and another for Etta to go to the bathroom. The pawnshop that Johnny knew was in cowtown, the area surrounding the cattle market. One look at the plate glass window in which was displayed saddles and bridles and shiny belt buckles and colorful boots, and Etta knew this was not a place to sell an elegant silver service or crystal platter. She had Johnny ask several people, and they were directed to another part of town with several pawnshops and used and antique furniture stores.

"Stop here," she said, pointing at a pawnshop with a cluttered window. "This looks like a good place."

Johnny cut the wheel. "I sure wish you would give me more warnin', Miz Etta, and not just holler stop when we get right on a place."

"I didn't holler."

He looked from her to the shop, then got out and came around to help her and the box out of the truck. When she saw he was prepared to go along with her, she told him that she would rather go in alone.

At his hurt expression, Etta said, "I think being pregnant, I might do better alone."

He nodded. "Yeah, you might."

Also, Etta intended to sell her wedding rings, and she certainly couldn't do that with Johnny looking on.

He walked with her to the door, saying, "Watch the

clerk's eyes and make certain his offer matches the interest you see in his eyes."

She started inside the shop, and then a sudden uncertainty threatened to overwhelm her. She felt as if she was about to lose her grip on life. She was on the edge of turning and calling for Johnny after all, when she saw her reflection in the window glass. Looking at her swollen belly, she thought: *I have a child depending on me.*

Etta visited two pawnshops and a place that billed itself as having fine used furniture and antiques. Johnny escorted her to each one, each time waiting outside. Just knowing he was there gave her courage. She knew that if she needed to fall back on him, she could, and she followed his advice and watched the eyes of the shop proprietors. Johnny was right about that.

At the first pawnshop, she sold the ornate glass paperweight and two gold-tipped onyx fountain pens from the desk in the den, and the earrings that went with her string of pearls. (She intended to hold on to the string of pearls if possible.) When the spark in the shop owner's eyes—a woman with thick eye-liner and blue lids—was much more than the offer she made on an item, Etta declined to sell. The money the fountain pens brought astounded her. Although the shop owner was a woman and very cool acting, Etta noticed she took note of Etta's condition. She said, "Guy up and leave you, honey?"

"He died," Etta said. She saw pity flash across the woman's face, although it was quickly gone, and the woman said she was sorry, but she was after all a businesswoman.

At the second pawnshop, Etta succeeded in selling Roy's watch, the gold cuff links she had bought him on their second anniversary—getting more than she had originally paid—and her wedding rings.

"Are you sure you want to sell these?" the proprietor asked her, when she struggled to get them off her finger, which had picked that inopportune time to swell.

"Yes," she said, and handed the rings over. He peered

at them with his eyeglass, made an offer she found generous, and she accepted.

As he swept the rings from her sight, she experienced a sadness so deep as to be frightening. Watching him count out the money before her, all crisp bills, helped considerably.

When she went back outside, she waved the money at Johnny, who had been waiting right beside the door, and who gave the appearance of being a little anxious. His concern warmed her heart.

"Well now, you're doin' right well, Miss Etta," he said, giving a slow grin.

"Yes, I am," she said proudly. Some instinct caused her to take care to keep her ring hand out of plain sight.

Johnny suggested the shop of antiques and fine used furniture, pointing out the silver tea and coffee service in the window was very much like Etta's. Here she sold the silver tea service, the silver platter, and the crystal serving dish. As the man handed her a check, she mentioned that she had a number of pieces of furniture which she might be willing to sell. He passed her a card which read: Robert Lamb, Appraisals and Estate Liquidation.

Johnny worried that the check Mr. Lamb gave her might not be good and drove her directly to the bank upon which the check was drawn. The streets were busy and parking limited, forcing Johnny to let Etta out in front of the bank, while he circled the block.

Etta watched the wooden stock rails of his truck lean as he pulled out into traffic, then she looked at the building rising up into the sky and went inside. Never in her life had she seen such a bank, with ceilings rising two stories and ornate lamps and frescos and marble everywhere. She was looking so hard that she ran into a pillar.

Considering that Roy had taken her to Tulsa and Dallas and Houston, and that she had stayed in the best hotels, it seemed strange that she never once had been inside such a bank. After marrying Roy, she rarely had even gone into the bank back home. In time he had quit taking her with him to the cities, too, and her world had become the stately house and waiting for Roy to come home. She had not even realized it.

Etta counted the money the cashier gave her, then went back outside and down the wide sidewalk to where Johnny had pulled into a no-parking zone. He saw her coming, jumped out, and helped her up into the seat. When he got back inside, she looked at him for a breathless minute.

"Here's what I owe you for the groceries," she said, quite proudly bringing forth the money from her purse.

Johnny's silvery eyes went wide. He looked at the money and then at her. An angry expression crept over his face.

"I don't want your damn money."

She had never heard Johnny swear, not once, not even when he dealt with the most stubborn horse. He turned straight ahead, with his jaw hard as frozen meat.

Somewhat confused, Etta dropped her hand into her lap and stared at the money, while silence thick as heavy fog filled the truck.

"You sold your rings," he said.

Etta looked down at her hand, at the finger where she had worn her rings. There was a white place there, and the finger was thinner than the rest.

"Yes," she said, then added, "I think I got a good price."

Feelings were trying to rush in, and she pushed them out. She thought she would be crushed if she allowed them in.

"Look," Johnny said, turning to her. "You should have told me that you and Latrice needed money for groceries. I've been eatin' them for weeks now. It's only right I help pay. I could spare the money—and I wanted to do it." With each word, his voice got angrier.

She lifted her eyes to him. "Why?"

She watched his scowling face. Shifting his seat, he looked out the windshield, squinting.

"Well, you and Miss Latrice have been real generous with me," he said at last. "You let me use your barn and corrals and are feedin' me and doin' my laundry. I figure it's only right for me to chip in. I should have offered a long time ago." His eyes came around to her, and he added, "You saved my life the other night, too."

Disappointment washed over Etta. She didn't know why . . . what he said was very sincere.

She said, "I don't know if we saved your life. You probably would have rolled over or somethin' when you couldn't breathe. People do that naturally."

He shook his head, "I was drunk as a skunk and dead to the world."

"Well . . . you've done so much for us. Our deal was for you to use the barn and corrals as payment for my husband's IOU. Use of those barns for a couple of months won't add up to eight hundred dollars, not to mention you fixing the fences and everything else. I've felt that by feeding you, we come closer to coming out even."

His jaw got tight again. "Ma'am, I was raised up to look out for ladies, if I was in a position to do so. It hasn't cost me nothin' to do a little work, and I could afford to pay the dang grocery bill, so I did. It's no big deal."

He reached out and turned the key, starting the truck.

Etta said, "That's very fine, but I cannot let you pay my bills. It will make me indebted to you"—she tried to steady her lips and her voice—"and I do not intend to be relying on a man to pay my bills ever again."

With his hand on the gearshift, he gazed at her for a long moment while he seemed to be thinking very hard.

"Friends help friends," he said at last. "I figured we're friends. You saved my life, like I was a friend."

Etta nodded. "Yes . . . we're friends."

"Okay then," he said flatly. "You just keep your money and go on feedin' me for a few more weeks. I guess we can call it even after that."

He shifted into gear and pulled out into the street.

Etta gazed at Johnny's strong tanned hands on the steering wheel, and then her gaze dropped to the money she still held in her hand. She had been gripping it so hard that her palm had grown moist.

If Johnny insisted on being foolish, there was nothing she could do about it—she couldn't very well dash him in the head and stuff the money into his pocket. And she could use it, she thought, as she opened her handbag, slipped the bills deep inside, and closed it with a snap.

Her gaze lit on the pale skin of her finger where the rings used to be. She saw herself and Roy in the small office at the courthouse that had smelled like oiled wood, and the judge who'd kept blowing his nose in a handkerchief, and how when Roy had put the wedding ring on her finger she had known a terribly frightening feeling, like knowing she was about to get hit by a car but that she could not do anything about it because she was already in the middle of the road. There was no going back, only going forward and hoping for the best.

That's exactly how things were now, she thought.

Lifting her gaze from her empty finger and empty memories, she looked out the window at the city buildings and lots reflecting brightly in the sunlight and the people walking along, each with his or her own troubles and pain that could not be seen from the outside, each going onward.

On the outskirts of the city, Etta spied the familiar sign with the flying red horse. "Would you pull into that station? I need to use the restroom."

Johnny turned into the gas station, saying, "Geez, Etta, you can sure startle me with those requests to turn. Would you start givin' me a little warnin?"

"I'm sorry, but I just now saw it."

He had called her Etta again.

She slipped from the truck before Johnny could come around and open the door for her, and hurried away to the ladies' room. When she came out, she found Johnny sitting at one of the picnic tables at the edge of the parking lot. He had them each a hot dog and drink—an Orange Crush for her, root beer for himself.

"Oh, gosh, we never did have lunch, did we? Thank you—I'm starving!"

Johnny looked highly pleased.

She adored hot dogs with only mustard, and when she

remarked on this, he said, "I remembered once that you said that."

He had remembered that.

She gazed at him. It was nice to sit in the shade beneath the minuscule awning above the picnic table, nice to feel the cooling breeze and look across into Johnny's bright silvery eyes.

As she bit into the warm hot dog, it struck her that no matter the blows one took, life—appetites and distractions and annoyances—went on. There was a certain comfort in this.

Stretching out beyond a barbed wire fence was a pasture in which several horses grazed. Gazing at the sight, Etta asked, "How many acres do you suppose I'd need just to operate a stable? Maybe raise and train good riding horses?"

She was a little shy about bringing up the subject, since she had initially thwarted the idea when Johnny had suggested it.

He didn't seem bothered. "Depends," he drawled. "If you kept grazing pasture, you'd save some money. If you weren't using your grazing pasture, you could always rent it out. I'd say you could manage easily with twenty acres, but you'd probably want forty, so you could keep that alfalfa field."

"I'd need enough property for people to ride on, if I rented boarding space."

"That'd be nice, but what would bring renters is an arena for training."

"I don't think I'll make enough money to go sinkin' it into building an arena."

"Well, not at first, but later," Johnny said, warming to the subject.

He then went on describing the various setups of stock ranches he had seen and worked for, in the manner as only Johnny could, talking endlessly yet interestingly. Etta listened and ate her hot dog and watched Johnny's eyes and voice grow intense with his subject. He had a way of really drawing out his words when he got intense; she liked to listen to his tone.

She ended up eating two hot dogs. She might have had another Orange Crush, but she didn't want to keep having to stop to go to the bathroom. The public restrooms between Oklahoma City and Chickasha were not of the quality she preferred.

"How 'bout a Fudgesicle?" Johnny asked with a tempting grin.

"Well . . . okay," Etta said, grinning shyly at the quantity of food she seemed to be able to consume these days.

Together they went into the small store. While Johnny paid, Etta stepped back outside. Inside the store smelled heavily of tobacco and pickle vinegar, making her feel a little sick.

As she stood beneath the portico and unwrapped her Fudgesicle, an old, battered Dodge pickup pulled up to the gas pumps. The man and woman in the cab looked used and worn out. The woman stared out the windshield, looking neither right nor left. She didn't even blink when the man got out of the truck and slammed the door. She looked like one of those living dead in the horror shows, Etta thought.

Etta caught a whiff of the man, about a week's worth of sweat, as he passed her going into the store. The woman continued to stare out the windshield. She gave no sign of hearing the children fighting in the back of the truck.

The woman so disturbed Etta that she started to move away. Then her gaze connected with a girl in the back of the truck. About seven, stringy hair not combed in a month of Sundays, snotty nose and dirt-streaked face and shirt torn at the shoulder. A child neglected and forgotten. She stood holding on to the side of the bed and stared at Etta with big eyes, while two younger boys wrestled behind her.

For an instant Etta was a child again. She recalled riding in the back of her father's pickup, how hot the steel got in the summer, how the wind batted her ears until she couldn't see, and the dust choked her throat. She would cry, but her father and mother never paid any attention.

She blinked and saw the little girl again.

Slowly Etta extended her Fudgesicle. The child gave the frozen chocolate a startled look. Her eyes, hazel, darted back at Etta, and Etta smiled. Just as the little girl reached out her grubby hand to take the Fudgesicle, Johnny came out the door. Clutching the treat, the little girl looked at him.

Etta turned and walked quickly away. Johnny followed.

"That mother doesn't care for those children," Etta said. She was shaking. "She never once looked back at them," Etta said. "Why does God allow things like that?" She peered up at Johnny and then looked over at the children. The three were now solemnly sharing Etta's Fudgesicle.

"There's a lot of mysteries in this world, and that's one of 'em, I guess," Johnny said. He didn't quite know what was required of him. The sight of the poor couple and the children had definitely unsettled Etta.

The old pickup pulled away, and the little girl waved. Etta waved back. Then she looked up at Johnny. "I was like that little girl, but I had Latrice. I wonder if that child has anyone."

"Well, she has your Fudgsicle," Johnny said and was relieved when she smiled.

He held the remaining half of his melting chocolate ice toward her. "I'll share mine with you, Miz Etta."

Her grinned widened, and then her eyes sparkled. Leaning forward, she licked the frozen chocolate. Then he watched her suck it into her mouth and slowly release it, her blue eyes sparkling up at him the entire time. Keeping his eyes on hers, he took his turn at sucking on the frozen chocolate, and gave Etta another lick. He watched her tongue move on the sweet ice, then watched it move over her lips.

Feeling things he didn't think he needed to be feeling, he tossed the now empty Fudgesicle stick away. "Guess I'd better get you home, or Miss Latrice will come after me."

He rested his hand on her back as they walked to his truck. She seemed to like his nearness. He put her in the truck from the driver's side, and she didn't scoot over to the passenger side, but sat next to him.

"Johnny," she said, after he got in beside her. She looked at him with a shy expression. "Thanks for all you did for me today . . . for drivin' me up here and waitin' for me. It helped to know you were just outside those shops, waitin' if I needed you." Her cheeks got very red.

He wanted to kiss her.

"It was no trouble . . . glad to do it," he said and started the truck to give him something to do, while inside he was jumping around, excited to have finally pleased her.

Once out on the road, he slipped his arm behind her on the seat. Then he slipped it onto her shoulder. She glanced at him and looked a little hesitant, but she didn't move away.

The next thing he knew she was drooping against him. She had fallen asleep.

When Etta awoke, she found she was lying against Johnny's shoulder. The scent of him, of warm male and starched cotton, was all around her.

Coming fully to herself, she jerked up straight, smoothing her hair and clothes. "I hope I didn't bother you."

"Nah. I didn't have to shift."

Etta's gaze fell to his shoulder, and she wished she could put her head back there . . . and rest there for days and days. Jerking her eyes away, she looked out the window, watched the farmhouses and little roadside stores flash past.

When she saw the curve of the cemetery arch approaching, she said, "Oh, could you turn in here?" and pointed.

Johnny cast her a surprised look, braked, and turned quickly with a squeal of the tires.

As they drove beneath the white stone archway and the cemetery was spread out before them, Etta suddenly wished she hadn't asked him to stop. Her spirit did not feel up to looking at Roy's grave. But Johnny had gone to the trouble of making the turn, and she couldn't tell him to just drive out again.

The grave site looked so different without the canvas

awning and stacks of flowers. Etta felt a little guilty for not coming earlier and putting fresh flowers on the grave. Then she noticed that there was a small bouquet. Corinne, no doubt.

She sat there, gazing at the grave from the truck. She might not have gotten out, but Johnny came around and opened the door for her, took her arm to help her to the ground.

"Are you all right?" he asked, his eyes anxious. She nodded. "I'll just be a few minutes." She pressed a hand on his forearm, feeling the strength and warmth of him.

Slowly she walked across the deep green grass; it had still been brown when they had buried Roy. Bermuda sod had been carefully placed over his grave, and it was taking hold, as if sealing Roy there with his family. She gazed at the little bouquet of wilted daisies and reached down to toss them aside. She stopped and drew back. Throwing them aside seemed disrespectful and callous.

Kneeling, she put her hand to the ground, trying to feel something . . . wanting so much to feel something warm, not the cold of guilt and resentment.

She gazed at his headstone, for long minutes at the words: Roy J. Rivers, Beloved Son, Beloved Husband. Pain came across her heart. She squeezed her eyes closed, and when she opened them her gaze fell upon the headstone several yards away. "And forgive us our debts, as we forgive our debtors."

The line was part of the Lord's Prayer, which was carved in entirety upon the headstone for one Orton Wood. His family must have had money.

Etta looked again at the words, and then scanned the headstones surrounding her, some large, some small. Many names, people who had once lived and loved the best they knew how.

A warmth swept her, seeming for an instant to fill her heart. It quickly passed, but Etta knew she had felt it. Then quite suddenly the baby inside her kicked. Etta put a hand on her round belly. The baby kicked more.

"Thank you, Roy. You really tried to give me a child
. . . and honey, you did."

Seeing Etta remain crouched for a number of minutes,
Johnny got worried and started up the hill toward her.
When he reached her, she looked up at him, and he saw
tears in her eyes.

"I guess I got stuck," she said, extending her hand.
"Can you help me up?"

"Sure." He took her hand. When she was on her feet,
he kept hold of her, as she seemed a little wobbly.

He saw she was crying and pretending not to, and he
became nervous. He hoped she didn't start crying really
hard. She was a lot more pregnant than she had been the
last time she had cried in his truck, and anything could
happen.

Casting a glance at Roy Rivers's headstone, Johnny
thought with irritation that he did not appreciate the man
interjecting his dead self into their day.

He kept hold of Etta's arm as they walked back to the
truck, and he helped her up into the seat. "You sure you're
okay?"

She smiled at him. "I'm sure."

Feeling relieved, he hurried around, started the truck, and
pressed the accelerator, sending the truck flying down the
highway, hoping to get Etta home as soon as possible. He
was afraid any moment she would turn and work herself
into a state.

After several minutes, however, she blew her nose and
sighed calmly. "Roy and I had two really good years before
it all fell apart. And you know, I tried real hard and Roy
tried real hard, too."

She seemed to be speaking to the world at large, but
Johnny felt it was up to him to answer. "I know that you
must be disappointed about things," he said, "but you
know, just because somethin' doesn't quite turn out the way
you expect, doesn't make it not worth the attempt."

She looked at him for a long minute. "That's so true.
And thank you for sayin' it."

The way she spoke and looked at him made Johnny feel ten feet tall.

"I guess, even when it may not seem like it, we are all doin' the best we can," she said. "And I wouldn't wish I hadn't married Roy, because then I'm wishin' away the good right along with the bad."

He didn't quite follow exactly what she said, but he glanced over to see Etta's blue eyes gazing at him, clear and strong. As if she was seeing him, and not thinking of Roy Rivers at all.

"How about some music?" he said, reaching over and turning the knob.

On passing Overman's Bright and White Grocery Store, Etta had Johnny stop. She made the request when they were still a fourth of a mile away, so as to give him plenty of warning.

"I'll only be a minute," she said.

She went into the store and paid Noreen Overman the entire overdue account, all the while having the satisfaction that she behaved with more grace than Noreen would ever know in a lifetime. When she came out, Johnny stood holding the truck door open for her. He gave her a little grin, and she grinned in return. Then they headed home, Elvis singing out from the radio and the sun casting long shadows.

Johnny pulled the truck around at the back door and shut off the engine. Etta glanced at him and then looked out the windshield at the horses in the corrals. She heard Little Gus whinny from the barn. Johnny got out, and she watched him through the dusty glass. She recalled how he had kissed her that morning, a thought that had played at the edges of her mind all day.

Their gazes met when he reached her door. He opened it and helped her to the ground.

Etta dropped her gaze to his blue shirt, having the strange urge to put her hand there, on the starched cotton just above his heart.

"Are you comin' in for supper? Latrice will want to

know—if she hasn't already started somethin'."

"I guess the hot dog is about gone," he said, with a bit of a grin. "Maybe I could force down a biscuit or two and a glass of ice tea. I'll see to feeding the stock first, then I'll be up."

She watched him walk away, limping slightly. An emotion that she couldn't name but which made her feel weak and warm washed over her.

Pivoting quickly, she strode into the house. She straightaway placed the money on the table in front of Latrice, who was snapping green beans. Latrice dried her hands and began to count it.

"I stopped and paid the Overmans."

Latrice's eyebrows rose. "You might should have postponed that. We're gonna need the cash."

"I know . . . but I couldn't. We'll just have to go on trusting to be provided for." Etta lifted the hair from the back of her damp neck. "I'm gonna go wash up. I'll be back down to help with supper. Johnny said he'd come, too. He's feedin' the horses first."

Her hand on the swinging door, she stopped, looked around. Then she rushed over to Latrice and hugged her. "I love you, Latrice. I'm so glad I've always had you."

Latrice jumped and stared at her. "Well, I'm grateful to be here," Latrice said, looking a little confounded.

Etta went on through the swinging door. Passing through the living room, she paused to touch the stained glass lamp with the cat-statue base that sat on the the table with the telephone. She had seen a similarly ugly lamp at the fine used furniture shop. Opening her purse, she brought out the card the man there had given her. Thoughtfully she slipped the card beneath the edge of the telephone and then proceeded on upstairs.

In the bathroom she stripped off her clothes, took a sponge bath, and got into her robe. She considered what to put on to go downstairs. She thought she would wear the blue dress. Johnny seemed to like blue.

Passing hers and Roy's bedroom, she stopped. The door was ajar. She pushed it open and looked inside. Golden beams from the setting sun slanted through one window and made a pattern on the flowered wallpaper. Faintly, Roy's scent came to her.

She walked over to the bed and ran her hand along one of the dark, smoothly turned posts. She wondered how much money she could get in selling it.

She had bought the bed on a trip to Dallas, during the first weeks of their marriage. She had seen it on a shopping expedition and had returned to the hotel all excited and wanting Roy to see it—wanting his approval, his interest at the very least, but he had only kissed her and said, "You buy anything you like, honey. I don't need to see it."

Sitting on the edge of the bed, she grew very still. The child inside her fluttered, and she caressed her belly.

"Roy . . . I sold a bunch of your things, and your family's things today. You surely don't need them, and I need the money. I have to try to save this place for me and the baby and Latrice."

It came to her that if anyone could appreciate her financial position, Roy certainly would. He had willingly given her all he could while he was alive; she didn't think his being dead would change his sentiment.

"I did pretty good," she told him. "You know your gold cuff links—the ones I gave you on our second anniversary? I got ten dollars more than I paid for them."

After a moment, she added, "I hope your mother isn't too upset that I sold the silver tea set. I did not sell her clock. Alice took it."

For another few minutes she sat there. Then, hardly realizing, she lay over on the pillow, closed her eyes, and slipped off into a deep sleep in which she dreamed vibrant dreams all night long, awakening only when Latrice came and nudged her.

"Wake up. Are you all right?"

Etta opened her eyes to see Latrice's face very close. "Yes . . . of course." She was having some confusion with where she was and why Latrice would ask her such a strange question.

"Are you ready to take up residence in this room

again?'' Latrice asked as she began to raise windows.

"No," Etta said, throwing back the cotton spread with which Latrice had covered her in the night. "I'm gonna see if we can sell this bedroom set. Roy told me in a dream to ask two thousand dollars for it."

Fourteen

Etta telephoned Robert Lamb, the estate appraiser and auctioneer, who had given her his card. A slight man who wore a black bow tie, he arrived just after noon in a van with a burly driver, saying he came prepared to buy. He had also come with cash, which so favorably impressed Latrice that she served him coffee and pound cake on the good china.

"What would you think this china is worth?" she asked him.

Going through the house with Mr. Lamb, Etta managed to get past an attack of uncertainty and began to bargain over pieces with a fervor. Latrice followed, pointing out any items or particulars she felt went overlooked.

Mr. Lamb bought on the spot the stained glass lamp with the cat-statue base. He called it Art Deco and said it dated from the twenties and was still in demand in the right circles. He also bought the cherrywood Texas settee from the entry hall, the cane-bottom chair from the upstairs hall (which he estimated was a hundred years old), the marble-topped dresser from the small dressing room off the bathroom, and the set of ruby glasses he spied atop the china cabinet.

Etta showed him the silverware service she had fought

over with Alice, and he would have bought it, but Etta
decided she was not ready to sell.

After some deliberation, Etta settled upon consigning for
auction her bedroom set, which Mr. Lamb agreed not to
sell for less than two thousand dollars. He expressed interest in purchasing the dining set in the future.

When Johnny came around, curious as to what a van was
doing at the front door, Etta told him excitedly, "I'm making more money."

He grinned at her and said, "Well now," and then
pitched right in to help the burly driver load furniture.

"That Mr. Lamb's a pretty puny-lookin' fella," Johnny
said in a whisper to Etta. "You wouldn't want him to have
a heart attack before he pays you."

Etta also thought Mr. Lamb looked puny, but then she
worried about Johnny's leg. This caused her to hover as all
three men worked to move the furniture. Thankfully, when
it was time to load the heavy pieces of the bedroom set,
Obie and his nephew Woody showed up to help.

Watching her bedroom set be carried from the room,
piece by piece, as she had imagined the day of Roy's funeral, she felt strange. She felt she should cry, felt she was
crying inside, yet she felt oddly excited—as if embarking
on a trip around the world.

Then into all this came Fred Grandy's pink and white
Plymouth, speeding up the gravel drive. The real estate broker had brought Leon and Walter Fudge. The three men
got out of the car, and Leon came forward across the yard
speckled by sunlight.

"What's goin' on here, Etta?" He surveyed the sight
with knotted brows as he came up the porch steps.

Etta explained that she was selling some of her things,
and Leon's frown deepened. Then Johnny came backing
across the porch with his end of the big headboard.

"I'd appreciate your movin' out of the way," Johnny
said in a rather forceful manner.

"Who is that?" Leon asked with some annoyance, gesturing at Johnny with his hat as he followed Etta out into

the yard. "Isn't that the guy you met that day on the street?"

"Yes. That's Johnny Bellah. He trains horses here." She looked questioningly from one man to the other.

Leon cleared his throat and said with a nod, "Walter here has made an offer on the farm, Etta."

"Are you still wantin' the whole thing, Walter?" Etta asked. "I am certainly ready to sell, but I've decided I want to keep the house and the half-section that stretches down to include Obie Lee's cottage and fields. Any or all of the rest, I'll sell to you."

She sounded more abrupt than she had intended, but she was a little unprepared and distracted.

The men looked surprised, and Leon said, "What are you talkin' about, Etta?" He flipped back his coat and propped a hand on his thin belt.

"Well," she pushed stray hair out of her eyes and felt the need to take something of a stance, "I've decided to try to keep the house and a half-section of land. I was going to call you later today to talk about this. I rather got distracted when Mr. Lamb came down. How much do you think you want to offer for the land, Walter?"

Etta felt she was on something of a roll now with bargaining and was disappointed when Walter pulled at his ear and declined to make a concrete offer.

"I'll have to think it over now," he drawled. "I was really wantin' the house and barn up here for my boy. If I can't get it, I might have to go buy a farm I've found over to Ninnekah."

"I guess you'll be the one to decide that," Etta told him bluntly, annoyed by the way he spoke.

Walter looked about like a rooster who'd had a pan of water tossed on him. As he got into Fred Grandy's car, Fred followed after him, apologizing profusely for the turn of events.

Leon said to Etta, "I don't know what Edward is goin' to say about this. Sale of the land only is not goin' to repay the entire mortgage. It's just not."

"I know that. But it will pay the biggest part of the

mortgage, and then I can pay the rest little by little. Besides, if I can sell the land in smaller chunks, I'll get more money from it. Isn't that true?''

He frowned. "It can be true, and it might not be. Etta, the mortgage is past due. The bank isn't goin' to wait years while you pay five dollars here and five there.'' He looked anxiously at the van. "Do you know the worth of some of those pieces you're sellin', Etta? Do you even know what you're doin'?'' His neck and face were turning really red.

Etta swallowed. "Maybe I'm not certain about what I'm doin', Leon, but I do know that I am doin' something now, rather than just waitin' to lose everything that means anythin' to me.''

"You weren't gonna lose the farm, Etta. You were sellin' it.''

"It amounts to the same thing. I don't want to sell it. This is my home. I want to stay here.''

Leon gave a disparaging shake of his head. "Edward's gone to Chicago for the rest of the week. We'll discuss this with him when he comes back. Maybe . . .'' He shook his head. "Etta, you think about this," he said, pointing his hat at her for emphasis.

Then he slipped into the car, and the three men drove away. Etta gazed at the dust billowing up behind the winged rear fenders of the departing Plymouth and wrapped her arms around herself and held tight.

Then Latrice was hurrying across the yard and saying that Mr. Lamb wanted to buy the wool rug from in front of the fireplace. "I've already sold it to him," she said in the next breath.

When everyone was gone, Etta went upstairs and looked into her and Roy's bedroom. Latrice was folding Roy's clothes they had hastily emptied from the chiffarobe and dresser drawers and putting them into cardboard boxes; Obie was going to take them to distribute among his brothers and nephews. Etta's things were tossed into laundry baskets.

"I want Obie to take the oak valet, too," Etta said and slid it out into the hallway.

Then she began going through the final odds and ends of Roy's personal belongings. She ended up dumping everything, even the lemon drop candies, into a cigar box. All the while they worked, it seemed the scent of Roy grew fainter and fainter, until Etta could hardly smell it when she took the cigar box down to the guest room and placed it, along with the photograph of herself and Roy, into the back of her lingerie drawer.

She returned and stood in the empty room, looking around. She spied a worn path on the carpet in front of the windows and realized it had been done by her pacing during Roy's absences.

Latrice came through the door and looked around. "It'll sure get easier to clean around here, this keeps up." She raised an eyebrow. "You gonna move the guest-room stuff down here now?"

"No," Etta said. "I kind of like the guest room now. I like the morning sun. Let's move the nursery over here. It's a big room . . . plenty of play space."

As she spoke, Etta threw up the windows, letting in fresh spring air. After that she began to remove the draperies, which were not at all suitable for a nursery.

Latrice made her quit stretching upward. "You are gonna misshape that baby girl's head stretchin' like that."

The next afternoon, Johnny drove off and returned within an hour, followed by a hand driving Harry Flagg's two-ton truck.

Johnny said, "I told Harry that you had some first-cuttin' alfalfa left, and he said he'd take it all, providin' you want to sell, Miz Etta."

He raised an eyebrow, and she asked, "How much are we gettin' for it?"

The men loaded the hay from the barn, and Harry Flagg's hand paid Etta in cash. The money joined the wad stuffed into an empty five-pound Folgers can in the chest freezer. Latrice decided they did not need the freezer and tried to sell it to her cousin Freddy, but she asked as much as a new one in the store, and Freddy would not pay it.

That evening at suppertime Obie showed up with one of his many brothers, who said he was interested in purchasing the old Allis-Chalmers tractor.

Obie said, ''I figure we can get by with just the Massey, seein' as how all we're doin' is cuttin' and balin' these days . . . and if you sell off most the land, we sure won't need two tractors.''

More money went into the Folgers can. Etta counted it and then counted it again. The entire time she ate supper and carried on conversation with Latrice, Johnny, and Obie, she thought about the money and the upcoming rodeo race.

She told herself not to even think of it, but she still did.

After she had finished helping Latrice with the dishes, Etta slipped outside to find Johnny. He was over at Little Gus's pen, and the instant she laid eyes on his back, she felt shy. It was not an easy thing to swallow one's words. She wanted to please him but was embarrassed to have him know this. She felt excitement about the possibility of Gus racing at the rodeo, but she was embarrassed to have him know this, too.

The silvery moonlight lit on Johnny's hat and fell down over his shoulders and poured over Little Gus, too. Since Little Gus had finally exhibited a bit of patience within the stall, Johnny would allow him the run of the pen until late at night. Johnny was giving him a pinch of tobacco. Little Gus saw her and pricked his ears, causing Johnny to turn and look at her. She went toward him slowly, out of the glow of the pole light and into the softness of moonlight.

She said, ''It's a nice night, isn't it?''

Johnny nodded and agreed. Little Gus poked his nose at her, and she stroked his forehead. He lowered his head and blew on her belly, as if exchanging breaths with the little girl inside. Etta put her nose against Little Gus and inhaled the familiar musky horse scent of him.

When Johnny, uncharacteristically, said nothing more, Etta asked, ''Do you still plan to race him over at the rodeo tomorrow?'' She kept her gaze on the horse, stroking him.

"I'd like to." Johnny looked down at her. "Are you goin' to let me?"

She grinned at him. "Do I have a choice?"

"Well now," he said, "I wouldn't feel right about takin' him, if you were against it. He is your horse."

"But you would take him," she said.

He raised an eyebrow and stared at her, and she didn't think he was thinking only about horses and rodeos. He said in a slow drawl, "Are we goin' to have to find out . . . or are you gonna let me take him?"

"I'd like to take him," she said. She watched Johnny's strong, callused hands reach out to reach out to pat Little Gus's forehead. She wished he would touch her.

"Okay. I've lined up Woody Lee to ride him—he'll do better than I can with my poor knee."

"I have the entry money," she said, making certain he understood she was paying her own way. "And I plan on going along. I'd like to see him race."

"Well now, that's fine, Miz Etta," he said, and his eyes rested on her thoughtfully. Then he added, "I figure we'll run him at least twice. I've already set up a match race for him before the rodeo, with a horse of Bitta Fudge's."

"You made an awful lot of plans with my horse," Etta said.

"Directing a horse is a trainer's job," he replied. Then he surprised Etta by saying, "I think I'll turn in. Good night, Miz Etta." He gave her a tip of his hat and walked away.

Etta was thoroughly annoyed. She had somewhat expected him to kiss her. To at least exhibit a possibility in that direction. She almost called after him in the darkness to take him to account for it. Closing her mouth tight, she walked back to the house.

Johnny dropped himself down on his bunk, tossed his hat aside, and raked his hands through his hair. He felt all tight. He ached, and he rubbed his knee absently, but it wasn't his knee he needed to rub, so much as his groin.

He was wrought up about how he felt about Etta and

about the prospects ahead of him, racing the red gelding
and having himself proved out as a man who knew what
he was talking about. After a minute he stretched out, took
up the detective novel he had begun, and tried to read. But
his mind kept wandering. He finally got up and went to the
barn door and smoked a cigarette. He never would let himself smoke inside the barn.

As he stood there, he looked at his truck and considered
driving down to the roadhouse and getting a few drinks to
relax him. Maybe a woman, too, although after what had
happened to him the last time, he was hesitant in this direction. He considered the few drinks, imagined them, even
tasted them, but he didn't move, except to throw the butt
of his cigarette in the dirt and step on it.

It was a heavy thing he had taken on, he realized—Etta
had put her trust in him, and he sure didn't want to disappoint her.

Thinking about her trust suddenly made him very worried. What if Little Gus did not win?

The possibility jumped out at him as unexpectedly as a
spook from a closet. Amazingly, he had not heretofore considered that the horse could lose. Where before he'd imagined over and over the red gelding gleaming brightly across
the finish line, was certain of it, he now saw with stark
clarity the horse losing and all the consequences this would
bring.

If Little Gus lost, Johnny would not only disappoint Etta
in his abilities, but he would lose her money, too. This
possibility grew in his mind by leaps and bounds. He realized that he had put himself into a position of responsibility such as he never had in his life. Etta was not believing
in the horse; she was believing in *Johnny's opinion* of the
horse.

He had managed to get himself in a good predicament
again, he thought morosely and looked toward his truck,
stepping out toward it, although he did not move, except
in his mind, which pictured him behind the wheel and driving away to get just one beer. He felt it cold in his hand
and sharp on his tongue and landing warm in his belly.

But he knew it wouldn't be just one beer, once he started. He'd end up being a disappointment to Etta even before they got to horse racing.

Turning, he went into the deep dark of the barn, pulled on the light, went into Little Gus's stall, and closed the horse in from outside. The horse pricked his ears and sniffed Johnny's shirt for tobacco.

"You are gonna win at least one of those races tomorrow," he whispered, scratching the horse's forehead. "I know you can do that."

Then, speaking even lower, his voice barely a whisper, he added, "You and me, we're gonna be her heroes, boy,"

Returning to his bunk, once more taking up the paperback, he glanced out the small window that faced the house. He saw the lights in the kitchen and imagined Etta and Latrice there in the warm glow, radio playing, Etta at the table and Latrice in her rocker. Imagined the delicious scent of Latrice's biscuits and the heady scent of Etta's skin. Imagined their feminine laughter. Imagined himself looking through the door, then going in and sitting there among them, and their welcoming, Latrice handing him a cup of coffee, and Etta . . . Etta touching his cheek, then bending to kiss his lips, seductively, her silky hair falling over his face . . .

He suddenly saw her belly and realized that his fantasy had neglected to recall Etta was pregnant. He backed up and thought of how she would look and be, not pregnant. He let himself see how he would be with her then.

"How much are you gonna bet on the horse?" Latrice asked. She sat in a kitchen chair, and Etta sat on a pillow on the floor below her. Latrice was rolling Etta's hair in cotton strips. "Hold still," she added when Etta went to look up at her.

"I haven't made up my mind to bet," Etta said. "I think maybe I should stick to just entering the race. Twenty-five dollars will be enough to lose, if Little Gus doesn't win. I don't need to gamble. That way is just foolish."

"What do you think payin' an entry fee is, if it isn't gamblin'?" Latrice asked.

"It isn't the same thing," Etta maintained. "When a person pays an entry fee, he is buyin' time to put his horse on the track. I get to race Little Gus for that entry fee, and if he wins, I'll get the purse. It's an honorable exchange."

Latrice gave a grunt. "It is gamblin', and if you're goin' to gamble, you might as well make it worthwhile and go for as much as you can get." She jerked tight the last cotton strip and rose.

"Puttin' up an entry fee is not the same thing as wagerin' all around. When I put up an entry fee, I'm buyin'. When I just bet, I'm just betting."

Etta got herself to her feet and gathered the brush and comb and remaining rag rollers. She wished her hair was not in these silly rags, because it was difficult to hold what was amounting to an argument with Latrice with her hair looking like that of a sock doll.

"I am not talkin' of gamblin' every penny, but a couple hundred out of that Folgers can won't keep a roof over our head, so you might as well give it a try on the horse. We have more furniture we can always sell."

"How many times do you think Roy probably said the same sort of thing?"

"I don't think Roy Rivers ever sold his furniture or much of anything else. He simply owed people," Latrice muttered, wiping the table with a cup towel. Then, hand to her hip, "I have never seen the sin that has been attributed to gamblin'. Gamblin' itself is not the sin—people gamble that they are goin' to live a few more days everytime they buy green bananas. The sin is in the extreme. Moderation is the key to life, and Roy Rivers was an immoderate man. He kept dropping the key."

"Moderation is what I intend to keep," Etta said. She paused and looked at Latrice. "I wish you would change your mind and come with us tomorrow."

Latrice shook her head. "I'm not goin' to go. I have no desire. A rodeo is no place for a middle-aged colored woman."

"Oh, Latrice," Etta said, "over at Anadarko there'll be lots of different people—whites and Indians and Mexicans and Negroes, and all ages, babies on up to grandmothers. You know that. You've been over there when Daddy was rodeoin'."

"I was a young woman then and mostly I went because you were too small to be goin' on your own. I never liked any of it, except the flirtin' with young bucks. I don't flirt any longer, so why should I waste my time?" Then she added, "You know what my mother used to call rodeos? The endeavors of idiots. I agree. I think I'll have a holiday while you and Johnny are gone tomorrow."

Etta regarded her. "A holiday with Obie?" she asked, raising an eyebrow.

"Perhaps," Latrice said, turning to wipe the sink.

"Just what is goin' on with you and Obie?" Etta asked.

Latrice looked over her shoulder. "You are pryin'."

Etta got rather piqued at that. She put her hand on her hip and opened her mouth, but feeling her rag curls bob she felt a little silly, so she toned herself down. Still she said, "I don't think it can be called prying between two people as close as we are. I just want to know if you have decided to encourage Obie."

"Obie Lee has never needed any encouraging. If you are asking have I decided to enjoy him, the answer is yes. I have—and to what extent is yet to be decided, but is definitely my business."

"Well, I'm glad for you," Etta said. She made herself say it. She was glad for Latrice, but a little disconcerted as well. It was difficult to fathom, Latrice having a boyfriend. Perhaps a lover. And it made Etta feel very sad and envious.

For some reason, she felt called upon to go across and kiss Latrice's cheek before she took herself off to bed, where she lay gazing up at the dark ceiling for quite a while before she could fall asleep. During this mulling time she considered Latrice's opinion about betting and thought she found merit in the idea.

If she could not have Johnny Bellah, she might as well

bet. She needed to break out somewhere. It would be good for her spirit.

Latrice made her nightly inspection of the kitchen, putting everything exactly as she liked it. Etta generally dried and put away the dishes, but Latrice checked behind her, making certain the glasses were set just so.

When she was certain Etta would not be back downstairs, Latrice went to her own room, bent down, and removed a small section of baseboard, drawing out a bulging stocking. From it she pulled out a tiny black book, flipped to the last entry, stared at it, debating. Then she dug into the stocking, extracted a roll of bills, pulled off two hundred dollars in twenties, replaced the black book into the stocking and the stocking into its hidey-hole. She folded the money, went out the back door, and hurried across the yard lit by bright moonlight, to the barn and Johnny Bellah's room.

Low yellow light spilled from his doorway. He reclined in his bed, reading a paperback novel with a trashy cover by the light of the rusted metal desk lamp. He was surprised to see her, of course. For an instant he just stared at her with his mouth slightly open. Then, as she came into the room, he scrambled himself up and buttoned his shirt.

"I have some money," she said. "I want you to bet on that horse tomorrow." If he could be more surprised, he was.

"Me to bet?" he repeated.

"That's what I said. What do you think the odds will be?"

He swallowed. "Well, I don't know. Four or five to one maybe, depends."

Latrice decided she was not likely to get exactly the information she wished, so she said, "I have two hundred dollars here. Do not tell Etta about this. It is not lying to simply not mention it. It is my own money."

He stared at the roll of money she extended toward him. "Yes, ma'am."

"You bet it all on the match race, and then two hundred of what you win there on the rodeo race." When he didn't take it, she poked it at him, and he at last got his hand moving to take it.

"I can't guarantee the horse will win that match race," he said.

She shook her head, chuckling. "I didn't think you could. That's why it is considered riskin' money."

She turned and left him, went back to the house and to bed, sleeping soundly, as she always did when she followed her inner direction. She thought perhaps she would write a book on following the Inner Guide. Maybe that's what she should do with the second half of her life.

The afternoon was cloudless and bright, the sun warm and the wind yet cool with spring, perfect in the way days in Oklahoma could be. The sort of day on which it seemed to Etta only good things could happen. She tried to convince herself of this, to look for signs that things would go as she wished.

Etta dressed in a blue skirt and maternity blouse, and tied her curls back with the yellow ribbon. At a last check in the mirror, she decided to add tiny dangling earrings, turquoise disks that brought out her eyes. To help shade herself from the bright sun, she took along a wide-brimmed straw hat.

When she stepped out on the porch and Johnny looked at her, she could tell he liked what he saw. He was up in the back of the truck with Little Gus, whistling, and he let out a low wolf whistle on sight of her, then ducked his head and fiddled with securing his saddle on the top rail.

Johnny had decided to leave his golden dun behind, and Little Gus was nervous about being alone. He moved, and his hooves made a sharp staccato on the wood floor of the truck bed, startling him and making him dance and make more noise. Johnny put a hand on him and spoke soothingly.

Latrice brought a large picnic basket, and Obie put that into the middle of the seat, then he helped Etta into the truck.

"Thank you, Obie."

He grinned at her as he firmly shut the door. "Good luck to you, Miz Etta."

Etta thought his words and smile amounted to a blessing.

Johnny came around and got behind the wheel. "All ready?"

She nodded, and Johnny started the truck away, slowly, glancing in his rearview mirror and listening for Little Gus, making certain he got his footing in the moving vehicle.

Etta turned to wave out the window at Latrice and Obie standing side by side on the porch. Obie's hand was around Latrice's shoulder. The sight of them like that struck her. Obie grinned and waved in return, but Latrice just stood there looking at her, like she always did. "I'll call you!" Etta yelled.

Then they were going down the drive and up onto the highway. Etta glanced over at Johnny. He laid his hat on top of the picnic basket and let the wind blow his hair.

A sense of relief swept Etta. She hadn't known until that minute that she'd been worried about a number of things. That the truck might pick that morning to break down, or that it would rain, or that Johnny would be suffering a hangover, or maybe not show up that day at all. She saw his eyes were clear, and he smelled of aftershave and sunshine, not whiskey.

Gazing out the windshield, squinting in the brightness, Etta didn't know why the day and racing Little Gus was all that important. She could win money, yes, maybe as much as a thousand dollars—Johnny was speculating that morning about the odds and what could be won, and no doubt inflating everything, Etta thought but did not say, not wanting to damper him.

Just then her eyes met his. His were so bright and warm upon her that she had to turn away or risk throwing her arms around him. She had the curious thought that she had just started her first day around the world, and it seemed as if she had started it riding the red winged horse.

"If wishes were horses"—she heard her mother's voice, saw her sweet, sad face—"we'd all ride."

Fifteen

The rodeo grounds weren't much more than a wooden grandstand and some fencing rising up out of the flat bottomland at the edge of town. Even though it was hours before the performance, people were already coming on a bright Sunday afternoon, to visit friends and to be daring in showing off skills and horses, or to watch others be daring in showing off their skills and horses.

Trucks and cars pulled into the surrounding area, bouncing over the grass, parking in a more or less orderly fashion, with men directing participants one way and attendees another. Horses were brought in the beds of pickup trucks, in trailers of wood or steel, and quite a number were ridden to the rodeo. Etta and Johnny passed three groups of riders along the highway.

Johnny, keeping a sharp eye, drove through the clumps of vehicles, trailers, people, and horses to the far side of the arena and grandstands, where he drew to a stop, saying, "This looks like it's gonna be the place." At her puzzled expression, he gestured and added, "Those cars and trucks make up the outer line of the racetrack there."

Looking out the dusty windshield, Etta saw the dirt track made in the flat ground and the vehicles parked in a line at the edge. It looked rather like a string of trucks and cars in a parade.

It was what was known as a bush track. There were hundreds of them throughout the rural areas, had been since there were horses and men on the land. As a child, Etta had often tagged after her father to such races at rodeos, and on a number of occasions, she and Roy had attended racing of this sort, although Roy preferred the stock shows and sales held in big cities, or going back East to the sophisticated, fancy tracks.

Etta had been to those tracks, too, and bush tracks held little resemblance to them. All it took to have a bush track was enough flat land on which to plow a track. There were no rails, no starting gates, no official time clocks. It was wild and woolly, without benefit of colors and professional jockeys. Most riders rode their own horses, and the horses were more often everyday working horses, used during the week to work cattle and brought for a day of fun and frolic, raced in Western saddles or no saddles at all.

Johnny's door creaked open, drawing Etta's head swinging around to see him, hat in hand, alighting from the truck. Etta peered through the rear window, seeing Johnny go directly to the rear to unload Little Gus.

She sat back in the seat, stared a moment out the dusty, glaring windshield, waited for Johnny to remember her. He didn't.

She opened her door and slipped to the ground. Standing beside the pickup bed with a hand resting on her belly, she watched Johnny tie Little Gus to one of the stock pen rails and looked around at the commotion. Little Gus was not used to all the activity, and he pranced on his short lead, wild-eyed, snorting and whinnying.

Johnny said, "I'm goin' to go get Little Gus entered in the rodeo race and see if Bitta Fudge's here yet. You might should just stay here in the truck, keep out of the sun, and watch Gus."

"Okay," Etta said.

He walked off toward the arena. Etta watched him go,

then looked at Little Gus, who was prancing and tugging on his lead.

"He'll be back," she said, reaching upward to stroke the horse's neck. She tried to soothe him with her touch and voice, but he began pawing impatiently, and after coming close to getting her foot stepped on, she left him to his temper fit and got back into the seat of the pickup.

Sitting with her legs out the open door, she surveyed the activity around her. She saw a man leading a sleek, hot-blooded grey, no doubt of racing stock. Among these horses would be an occasional mount that had racing potential and whose owner wanted to try on the bush tracks, before sending it on to bigger tracks in New Mexico, or even perhaps back in Kentucky. The horses didn't need to go on to bigger tracks to make a nice sum of money and fame, though. While the sophisticated amenities and rules might be somewhat missing, the racing at a bush track was every bit as exciting as a big fancy one—more at times, when things got crazy. And anything from five dollars to several thousand on a single bet could change hands.

Over at the arena pens, men were unloading cattle, and riders were entering the arena to exercise their horses. Several young men practiced roping a saw horse. Nearby two men with weather-toughened faces, wearing Stetsons with the brims curled up so high on each side they were more or less useless, leaned on a pickup, talking and having beers, and next to them two women, in summer blouses, sexy, slim-fitting slacks, and little flat shoes, chatted. Noticing their short hair, Etta touched her own, which curled to her shoulders. She had been considering cutting it off to be more stylish.

A family of Indians rode past, one after another, father, mother, three children, grandfather, each with long braided hair, each on a fine pinto pony, riding straight-backed, looking neither right or left, exactly as if coming right out of an old museum photograph.

Etta stared, not realizing that she was doing so until the old, weathered man winked at her and grinned. She grinned

in return, and then he turned his head once more stoically
straight ahead.

The sky stretched like a clear blue ocean. The sun beat
down through the windshield, and the breeze died, causing
sweat to trickle between Etta's breasts. People passing nodded politely, saying, "Howdy," when they came within
range. She recognized a few faces, but could not put names
to them. After fifteen minutes, Little Gus quieted, although
his ears remained pricked and his eyes wide.

Etta dug in the picnic basket and brought out a mason
jar of cool tea, sat there drinking it and searching for sight
of Johnny. Ten minutes more, and she got out of the truck
and went to look for the restrooms. She kept an eye out for
Johnny but did not see him.

Johnny was at the truck when she returned. "Are you
okay?"

"Yes."

He often asked if she was okay these days. She wasn't
certain what he meant by it. She was annoyed with him for
leaving her so long, which didn't mean perfectly okay, but
she did not elaborate.

He was already going on to his intentions, anyway.
Looking off and pointing, he said, "I'm gonna move the
truck up a bit—there to the middle of the line. You'll have
a pretty good view of the track. These unofficial match
races have to run on this outer side, 'cause of the riders
practicin' in the arena. When Little Gus runs the rodeo race,
though, he'll run right in front of the grandstand. He's up
against three others in that race so far, but I imagine more
will be comin'."

Etta got herself up into the truck seat, and Johnny moved
the truck up where he wanted it, trailing Little Gus behind.
Then he got out, threw the pad atop Little Gus with one
hand and his saddle over that with his other, all in a smooth
movement. It was a Western saddle, but lighter made, a
saddle Johnny kept for racing.

Etta watched through the rear window, deciding that she
didn't need to get out of the seat again.

Trailing Little Gus by the reins, Johnny came over to her

open door and told Etta that he needed to exercise Little
Gus and get the lay of the land, so to speak. Then he swung
up into the saddle and rode off.

Etta, again sitting with her legs out the open door of the
truck, watched Johnny join some other men on horseback
beside Harry Flagg's big two-ton truck. The distance was
too great to clearly recognize the men. A couple of women
rode up to them. Etta craned her neck to see. She judged
the women to be barrel racers by the way they were
dressed. They wore pale cowboy hats and pale blouses; one
had a flourish of flowers on her blouse. After several
minutes the group rode beyond the parking area, out of
sight.

Etta sighed and eased her back. Her gaze rested on a
brown horse tied to the back of a nearby truck. He looked
back at her and blinked contendly.

Some activity began on the track, drawing her attention.
She watched men measuring, and a Popin' John came chugging up with a small disk and began to work the ground,
extending the track at the curve to give a longer straightaway. The heat gathering in the cab made Etta sleepy. She
laid her head over on the seat back and dozed, waking with
a start when a shrill cheer went up.

Lord a'mercy! She'd fallen clean asleep and missed a
race.

Standing on the running board, holding the door frame,
she tried to see which horses had been racing. It would be
just her luck if she had missed Little Gus.

No—with relief she saw it had been a brown and a bay
that had raced. The rider on the bay looked vaguely familiar, but this might have been because he wore jeans and
shirt and hat just like every other man within sight.

Glancing around for sight of Johnny, Etta saw more vehicles and people had come. Two women walked past in
slim-fitting riding pants and boots and spurs, pale blouses
and Stetsons. They cast her curious glances and whispered
something to each other.

Etta sat back down in the seat.

She caught a glimpse of the women between vehicles,

saw how the sun seemed to shine on them and make them glow. Digging a lipstick from her handbag, she wrenched the rearview mirror around and colored her lips. Another look in the mirror, and she turned it away, threw her lipstick in the picnic basket, and sat back with a disgusted sigh. The baby inside her kicked. Then it seemed to wiggle round and round. Etta pulled the expensive blue linen blouse tight over her belly and watched the movement.

Tiring of this, she sighed deeply. The musky smell of sun-warmed dust closed around her. When she'd been standing on the running board, she'd caught a sweet cooling breeze, but she couldn't go standing on the running board for any length of time, as her back began to ache. She looked back at the brown horse tied to the next truck, who was dozing with one foot cocked, quite satisfied with himself and his life.

Squinting in the bright light, she searched for Johnny. Activity down at the start of the track drew her attention. Not Johnny, but two riders positioning their horses, both paints, side by side at the starting line of the track.

One of the riders was an Indian, had braids whipping around when he turned his head and a tall feather in his dark hat. The other looked like a young boy; his dark, battered hat was so big it came halfway down his head, as if it stopped only by his nose.

Suddenly the horses sprang forward. Etta rose up on the running board for a better view. People were yelling, the horses were pounding over the ground, the riders bending low over their necks. The Indian won all the way. Turning his horse, he stood in the stirrups and gave a whoop. Several men held money high, and he rode by, snatching it out of their fists. The boy who lost rode off, no one watching him, Etta guessed, but her.

She sat back down and gazed out the dusty windshield. The baby inside her stretched, putting a foot painfully into her rib.

As far as Etta was concerned, the day was not turning out to be the highlight she had anticipated. She was not

certain exactly what she had anticipated, but she had imagined more of Johnny in her day.

Johnny sat atop Little Gus beside Harry Flagg's two-ton
truck. Harry's truck had become the gathering place for
brisk bet placing. At the moment, Harry stood behind the
flatbed, counting out money and paying off to outstretched
hands. "Here you are, Miss Annabelle, you were right
about that paint—those were wings shaped on his butt,"
he said, handing bills to a rather plain woman in a shirtwaist
dress.

Up on the flatbed, Harry's serious-faced thirteen-year-old
daughter sat furiously recording figures on a Big Chief tab-
let; Harry said of her, "She's gonna be my accountant
someday," while three of Harry's younger children ran all
over the truck like wild things. Johnny had heard Harry
Flagg had ten children.

Wiping his face with a handkerchief, Harry lowered himself to sit on the truck bumper. One of the wild children
came and threw his arms around his neck, but Harry didn't
pay any attention. A plump girl came running. "Daddy,
Mama wants ten dollars." Harry produced several bills and
told the child, "No more," exactly as Johnny had already
seen him do twice before.

The young Indian who'd earlier won a match race on his
paint pranced his horse around, seeking a challenger. He
rode over to Johnny and Little Gus. "You want to give me
a try?"

Johnny shook his head. "I'm waitin' for Bitta Fudge."

Everyone had been laughing about that, which was fine
with Johnny. The more people laughed, the higher the odds.

"Well, race me instead. You might stand a chance, since
my horse has worn down some," the young man said, his
eyes dancing.

Johnny acknowledged this as true, then added, "I'd say
your horse is better than Fudge's, so I'd better save mine."
The boy gave a shake of his head and went off to find
someone who'd race him.

"You think Bitta Fudge done decided not to bother?"

asked one of the men propped against the rear tire of Flagg's truck.

"Maybe he doesn't see the challenge," another ol' boy put in, chuckling and casting a disparaging eye at Little Gus and Johnny.

Johnny had grown a little worried that Bitta Fudge had decided not to come, or that something had prevented him coming. Either circumstance would mean Johnny would not get to race Little Gus against the horse he had specifically chosen, thereby lessening his chances of proving himself to Etta. The possibility of this happening caused Johnny's hopes to dip low, but he tried to hold on to them. He could not afford to be down if he was going to race Little Gus at all. He had to keep his energy flowing.

At that particular worrisome moment, someone called out, "Here comes Bitta Fudge."

Johnny looked over and saw the tall, thin man riding forward on the sleek blue roan he'd purchased from Harry Flagg. Mostly thoroughbred, the horse was quite a looker; it had won one out of the two races it had run, and expectation ran high for a great future.

To Johnny's eye, the roan was one of those horses who was a lot more looks than substance. The roan's legs were finely drawn, and it was light in the buttocks, and in clocking it running, Johnny saw the horse ran fast between two and three hundred feet, then petered out—which was exactly why he had chosen this horse for Little Gus's first race. Little Gus was quick on the first stride, but his strength lay not as much in his speed but in his ability to go a distance and keep on going as hard as any horse Johnny had ever been privileged to ride.

"How-do, Johnny," Bitta Fudge said. He was a friendly sort, if a little flashy. That was his weakness—flashy man liked a flashy horse. Today he wore a dark blue shirt with stars embroidered above the curved slit pockets, about like Roy Rogers would wear.

"Howdy, Bitta." Johnny smiled; it was hard not to smile when he said the name.

All around them people were looking from the sleek roan

to the squatty red gelding and shaking their heads.

Fudge said, "You can't really want to race me on that horse, John." He looked at Little Gus intently, as if seeking the trick of the thing. Fudge wasn't stupid.

"Call me crazy," Johnny said. "And I ain't racin' you—Woody Lee's gonna ride him for me. I got a bum leg, you know."

Woody was over shooting the breeze at the pens with some bull riders. Johnny lifted a hand and gave a shout, which was passed along to get Woody's attention. Woody started forward at a trot, the fringe of his chaps fluttering. Johnny had begun to wonder if Woody slept in his chaps, as he'd never seen the boy without them.

"I don't think another rider is gonna make any difference, seein' as how that scrub only has about half the legs mine has," Fudge said. "What did you come up with to bet?"

Johnny grinned and got out of the saddle. "Well now, I got six hundred dollars here, Bitta. Harry, what'd you say on the odds?"

Harry rubbed his chin. "I'm gonna call it four to one . . . the roan the favorite of course," he added, as if he needed to be exact.

Johnny looked back at Fudge. "You heard the man. I'll go with that."

"You're crazy, John."

"Maybe." Johnny shrugged, then peered up at the man. "And if you think that, I guess you don't mind coverin' my money."

Fudge looked a little edgy at the taunt, but he didn't take it. "I know my horse's gonna win . . . anyone with any eyes knows it."

"Then you'd get an easy six hundred dollars, wouldn't ya?" Johnny shook the money in the air. "I got six hundred dollars here, bettin' at four to one and cash only. Any takers?" He handed the money over to Harry Flagg.

Bitta Fudge jumped in and produced enough to take two hundred and fifty of the bet. As Johnny handed Woody the reins, he heard behind him other men stepping forward, saying things like: "I'll take fifty of that crazy boy's money," and "That ol' boy must have gotten his head kicked, here's a hundred says so."

Woody winked a velvet eye, and Johnny clapped him on the back, then gave him a boost up into the saddle. While he adjusted the stirrups up three notches for Woody's shorter legs, Johnny cast a glance at Bitta Fudge. Fudge, a man caught between what his eye told him and what his intelligence whispered, was looking at him intently.

Johnny patted Gus's chest and told Woody to ride like hell. Woody headed Little Gus away at a trot toward the starting line, his tail high and flicking. "I've bet on your red cob, sonny," an old man with no teeth told Johnny.

At that particular minute, as if she'd called him, Etta popped into his mind. Good golly, he'd all but forgotten about her!

He peered over at his truck, but was unable to see Etta. He looked at Little Gus, still heading for the lap and tap starting line, then started off at a jog for his truck, casting glances down the track to see Woody, who was positioning Little Gus at the start.

"Etta!" Johnny reached the truck and looked in the open door.

She was sitting there, eating a ham sandwich. She looked at him, startled.

"Little Gus is about to race," he told her. It seemed strange that she hadn't been watching.

"Oh!" She threw aside the sandwich and shifted her legs out the door.

Johnny put out a hand to help her, and then he was tugging her along down the line of cars, to the finish of the track, while he strained to see the start. Doby Brown stood with the red flag, made from an old shop towel, held out for a full minute, and then it flashed downward, and the horses sprinted forward, tossing spirals of dust with their hooves.

From so far down the track, Johnny could not tell which horse took the lead. He could only hope Little Gus made his usual running start on one stride. He knew it would take the roan two, possibly three.

He and Etta reached the finish line, and he looked down the track at the horses and riders coming on like bandits running from the law.

Woody was low over Little Gus, his body compact, like a walnut growth attached there. Bitta Fudge's hat flashed bright in the sun, and one of his arms was flailing wildly. Up and down the track people were screaming and yelling.

Johnny's heart seemed to pound in rhythm to the horses' hooves. He saw the horses' legs a blur of motion, while he remembered how he had bet the entire six hundred dollars, and if Little Gus did not win, the money would be gone, and Johnny himself would look ridiculous, something he had not allowed himself to think of, but wished now he had considered.

Etta was suddenly gripping his arm, pressing her body against him. Then he saw Little Gus was ahead, by God, and pulling farther in front of the roan, coming on hellbent to win, and Johnny himself was yelling and urging the horse onward with every cell in his body.

When Little Gus crossed the finish line, Johnny jumped clear in the air. The next instant he realized he'd sent Etta stumbling backward. He grabbed her just in time to keep her from falling to the ground. She stared at him.

"He won, Etta."

She didn't seem to quite understand what had happened. In fact, her expression, sort of in shock, unnerved him.

"He won," she repeated in a breathless manner, her gaze shifting beyond him to Little Gus, whom Woody was riding in circles, bringing the gelding back down. "Oh, my . . . he won!" she said in a most peculiar and laughable way.

"Yes, ma'am, he most certainly did," Johnny said, and then he swept her to him and swung her around right up off the ground.

"Johnny . . . oh . . . I think I'm gonna faint."

He quick got her over to sit on the bumper of a Buick and put her head down, while people crowded around to congratulate them. His elation was overwhelmed by his concern for Etta, and he worried that he never should have brought her, never should have brought the horse. He might end up being responsible for something dire happening to Etta and the baby, and he cursed his propensity for getting into predicaments.

At last, however, Etta raised her head and said, "I guess I should have bet, like Latrice wanted me to."

Laughing, Johnny got thoroughly carried away, grabbed her cheeks and kissed her. Immediately embarrassed by what he'd done, there in front of everyone, he was relieved that Woody Lee appeared with Little Gus, so the attention turned to the horse.

"Can you believe it?" Etta said to Latrice several times on the public telephone. She gazed out the glass of the booth, squinting in the bright sunlight, her eyes watering and a great lump in her throat.

Latrice said, "Well, you're tellin' me. Don't you know?"

"I keep askin' myself," she replied. "Maybe I'm dreamin' all this."

She told Latrice everything she could think of as fast as possible, until her change ran out, and the operator cut them off. The line went dead right in the middle of Latrice telling Etta that she should bet all she could on the next race.

Etta thought it was a good time for the conversation to be cut off. She was somewhat amazed at Latrice's predilection for wagering now that she was being given the chance. This was an entirely new side to Latrice, who had always been so very conservative. Although when Etta thought of it, Latrice had always been a big one for playing the Bright and White bingo game on the radio. When they had lived in town, Latrice and several of her neighbors would bet on the game.

Etta hung up the phone, stood holding on to it a moment, until a young man came running up wanting to use it.

Heading back to the truck, she ducked into the restroom on the way, then walked behind the grandstand, where children played, boys pretending to be cowboys and girls making hopscotch squares in the dusty ground. One woman rocked a baby in a stroller while talking with several other women, and one of them was pregnant, too, making Etta feel a little less odd. A line formed at the concession stand; a voice blared from the loudspeaker, testing. Two cowgirls sat atop their horses, talking and laughing with a number of fellows around them.

When she reached the truck Johnny was wiping Little Gus with a wet rag and whistling happily. Seeing him, a sharp emotion, something like a mixture of extreme happiness and extreme fear, swept her. She was so very happy he had come into her life, and she wondered how she would do without him, when it came time for him to go to wherever he would go.

He straightened and leaned against Little Gus. "Well now, Miz Etta, what do you think of your horse?" He was plainly cocky.

Etta knew what he wanted, and she gave it to him, saying, "I think he has a great trainer."

"And I was right all along," Johnny prompted her.

She laughed. "And you were right all along."

She and Johnny gazed at each other, and the air seemed to grow very warm. She saw him gear up to say something, but at that moment Bitta Fudge came sauntering up.

Bitta slipped off his hat and gestured at Little Gus, saying, "That ugly son-of-a-buck sure shut our mouths, Etta. Congratulations."

She said thank you, but she did take exception to him calling Little Gus ugly.

Bitta said to Johnny, "Man, you think you might train a horse or two for me?"

"We can talk about it, I guess," Johnny told him, managing to look both proud and humble.

And next Harry Flagg came over to say he wanted to stable four horses at Etta's barn, so that Johnny could break them.

"I don't know how long Johnny's gonna be stayin' at my place," Etta said. She looked squarely at Johnny. "Are you goin' to stay long enough to break Harry's horses, Johnny?''

He looked at her and blinked, then said, ''I imagine I will. Harry, you bring those horses on over.'' He gazed at Etta as he spoke.

''I'll pay your goin' fee, of course, Etta,'' Harry said, ''and I'll spread the word that you're boardin' now, if you think you'll have room.''

''I'll have room for a few more,'' Etta said, her gaze still on Johnny.

''Looks like you're in the stable business,'' Johnny said, when Harry walked away.

''Yes . . . I guess I am.''

They looked long at each other, their eyes asking questions and seeking answers, while their tongues tried to form them.

Etta turned toward the truck cab, saying, ''Would you like a ham sandwich?''

Johnny said he would and quickly volunteered to go get her an Orange Crush at the concession stand. ''We should celebrate.''

Etta thought he might kiss her when he left, but he just grinned and sauntered away. She watched him go.

When he returned, he had a woman walking beside him—a very pretty woman, with blond hair curling out from beneath her buff-colored hat, wearing a white Western shirt and turquoise pants and custom-made boots with roses embroidered on them.

Her name was Sissy Post, and she was a barrel racer, Johnny said, making the introductions. And she wanted to buy Little Gus for a thousand dollars.

Etta stared at her, then looked at Johnny standing there with a bottle of Orange Crush in each hand and gazing expectantly at her.

Etta said to Sissy Post, ''I don't believe we're wantin' to sell.''

''Well, I could go to fifteen hundred,'' the woman said, just like that, almost without a blink of the eye. Then she added, ''Cash money.''

Etta thought that maybe if she just stood there staring at Sissy Post, the woman might keep on going upward with her offer. Then she gathered her senses and said, "I appreciate your offer, Miss Post, but Little Gus is not for sale. I just couldn't sell him."

The woman frowned and then shrugged. "Well, I'll be around, if you change your mind." She turned smartly and walked away.

Etta looked at Johnny. He grinned. "Don't you sell this bugger for anything less than five thousand . . . and if you wait, chances are you can get eight, maybe ten."

Etta did not care for Johnny talking about selling Little Gus. Then she wondered. Would she have sold Little Gus, if she'd been offered five thousand? Would she sell him for ten? It was a good thing no one was likely to offer ten thousand, because she'd have to make a decision then.

The sun had just set and the pole lights come on when Johnny took Etta to the grandstands to watch the rodeo race. He took her hand, cautioning, "Watch your step."

The seats were crowded, but they found a place not too high up yet high enough to see well, and with some shorter people in front, so Etta would have no trouble seeing above their heads. An older man in overalls and battered straw hat took a look at Etta, saw she was pregnant, and moved over to give her plenty of room.

When Johnny said he was going down to Harry Flagg's truck, Etta knew it was to place a bet.

"Johnny, would you place one for me, too?"

His eyes went wide, and she ignored him. She thought if she said something, she would just be opening the way for him to make an I-told-you-so comment. She gave him two hundred dollars that she had brought with her, just in case, then changed her mind, and took one hundred back. Then, as he rose to go, she called to him and reduced her bet by fifty, saying, "He's won one race today."

"What's that have to do with it?" Johnny asked.

"It's not likely he can win two."

"Thinking that way, we shouldn't enter him."

"Oh, no," Etta said quickly, "we have to enter him."
She tried to act like she thought Little Gus had a chance in
the rodeo race, but she found it very hard to believe that,
having won one race, he could win a second. Wasn't that
too much to ask of God and the Universe?

Johnny shook his head as he went away. Etta followed
his progress for a moment, until her attention was drawn
away by two children riding their horses in a circle outside
the cattle pen. More people came and squeezed into the
row in front of her, and Etta had to look around a tall,
skinny man.

The wind had picked up, and goosebumps rose on her
arms. Etta put on her sweater, which she had been using
as a cushion on the wooden board seat. The hope that Little
Gus would win the race slipped across her thoughts. Johnny
would be over the moon if Little Gus won. Roy had won
two horse races in one day once, although not with the
same horse. She did imagine that a single horse had been
known to win two races. Gosh, Johnny had told them stories of horses that had won races all day long, to hear him
tell it anyway. She did think he exaggerated; he was a
horseman.

She thought that she was in a very strange place, sitting
in a crowded grandstand, a baby kicking up a storm inside
her, while she thought about a horse and a man, one who
was not her husband.

Two races had been run and a third was about to start,
when Johnny returned. "He's up against eight horses," he
told her. "I bet at five to one odds."

Etta thought of her fifty dollars. Maybe she should have
bet more. She didn't want to lose more, though, which was
why she didn't bet. It was just too nerve-wracking.

"Little Gus has stamina," Johnny said, easing down on
the seat, relaxing his bad leg. "That's his edge, and this
race is gonna go four hundred forty yards. That's why I
entered him in it."

The old man in the overalls sitting next to Johnny picked
up on that comment and struck up a conversation with
Johnny, and in the process learned Etta's name. "I knew

your husband, Roy. He owed me for a ton of alfalfa,'' he said flatly.

Etta told him to see Leon Thibodeaux about it. She thought this sort of thing might continue to happen for the rest of her life.

For his race, Little Gus was lined up second from the inside. Etta was about to ask Johnny who decided the positions, when the horses were off and running. She watched them all, then kept her eye on Little Gus. Four horses went out in front of him. She thought maybe he would catch up, but told herself it would be all right if he did not. She struggled to keep calm.

Then there he was, catching up, and then he was catching up to the lead horse ridden by a man in a blue plaid shirt and not wearing a hat. Woody's big brown hat and the other man's head were side by side, and then Woody was ahead, Little Gus just flying.

What Etta had thought too much to ask had happened.

She looked at Johnny. His eyes were soft with wonder and emotion. And she knew in that moment that the entire thing was for Johnny. That he had needed Little Gus to win, and that for some reason the day would always be there to bind them together, no matter where each of them went.

"He won, Etta," Johnny said, a grin blooming on his face. "By damn he did it, just like I said he could."

Then he took her face between his rough hands and kissed her in a way that a woman treasures until her dying day.

Sixteen 🌹

Johnny brought the winning check and the cash from her bet to Etta at the truck. She took the money, then watched Johnny fold his own winnings and tuck them into his boot. He obviously had made quite a bit, which meant he had bet quite a bit.

"It's a good thing Little Gus won," she said, "or you would be broke."

But Johnny shook his head. "No, ma'am. I always save some back." He cast her a crooked grin. "I know when to bet, and when not to."

His cockiness both perturbed and charmed her, although she didn't think she should let on how much he charmed her.

Etta put her money deep into the bottom of her purse, closed it securely, and tucked it way behind the seat. For an instant she thought of Roy and more clearly understood his weakness for gambling. Self-control was perhaps the biggest problem for a human being, and everyone had weaknesses in this area. Poor Roy had been overcome with it in all areas, and it had broken him, she thought.

Johnny touched her elbow. "Etta?"

His voice seemed to demand she return to him. She looked into his eyes and was so very glad he was there.

229

"Would you like to watch the rodeo from the truck?" he asked. "The view won't be as good, but the seat will be more comfortable. And you know, now that your horse is gettin' to be worth a lot, we might not should leave him alone." He smiled with that.

Johnny was able to position the truck nearer the arena, although their view was obstructed by the railings and occasionally by men and children climbing on the railings. They watched the bronc riding, the bulldogging, in which Woody competed and took first place, and the barrel racing. Sissy Post ran the barrels on a stocky bay and came in second place with a time of twenty-two seconds, which Johnny said was not bad and might have won at some rodeos.

Etta had seen barrel racing a number of times before. After the first run, she got out and climbed up on the fence for a better view, while Johnny hovered behind, as if ready to catch her.

She got very excited when the barrel racer came charging into the arena and rounding the barrels. Her heart beat wildly, and she cried with others, urging the horse and rider on. At one point during a rider's go, however, Etta got so excited that she lost her hold on the fence and toppled backward, right into Johnny's arms.

Breathless and shaking, she hung on to Johnny, pressing against his strong chest.

He looked down at her and said in a husky voice, "I think we need to get you sittin' back in the truck."

He carried her back to the truck and sat her in the seat.

Etta, whose thoughts had been absorbed with barrel racing, found herself a little dazed. She watched Johnny walk around the front of the truck and then slip in beside her. She looked down at her belly. How she thought and felt did not seem to match her pregnant state. She felt suddenly frustrated and tired and told Johnny that she was ready to go home.

"Okay," he said, clearly puzzled at her sudden change in attitude. "I guess if we go now, we'll miss all the traffic anyway."

As they were leaving the rodeo grounds, Sissy Post rode her bay mare up beside Etta's open window and said, "I'll give you two thousand dollars for that gelding."

When Etta declined, as politely as possible, the other woman rode away mad, evidenced by the way she jerked on her poor mare's mouth and spurred. Etta was glad she had not sold Little Gus to a woman with a temper, even as the thought of two thousand dollars echoed in her mind. Thinking of the money in her purse and Sissy Post's offers for Little Gus, Etta pondered the fact that things were looking up.

"We're gonna have to start keepin' an eye on this son-of-a-buck now, Miz Etta," Johnny said. "He's gettin' valuable enough to steal. It was simpler when everyone thought him a cob."

He pulled onto the highway and headed in the direction of home. Etta rolled up her window. Johnny turned on the radio, and country music came softly: Kitty Wells singing "Making Believe."

With the sultry song filling her ears, Etta looked at the blackness beyond the truck, then looked over at Johnny. Her gaze moved over his profile and lingered on his lips. She thought of how he had kissed her. She gazed at him and was swept with the pure passion that comes when a person is exhausted and can no longer keep a firm hold on common sense.

Taking a deep breath, she moved the picnic basket to the far passenger side and scooted herself across next to Johnny. She might have thought about what he might think, but she was too tired and knew only what she wanted to do.

He glanced at her, his eyebrows rising, then returned his gaze to the road. She waited, gazing at him, at his eyes that stared intently out the windshield. Slowly but deliberately, he put his arm along the back of the seat, brought it down to her shoulders, and drew her against him. She relaxed with a sigh onto his shoulder and let her heart start beating again. Her hand rested on his leg, the denim stiff and warm beneath it, while she looked at the silvery glow of the dashboard and how it reflected on Johnny's legs. She thought, with the emotion filling her chest and slipping warmly through her limbs so that she felt fairly weak, that maybe she should tell him she didn't expect anything, that this was no promise and didn't require any, that she simply had not been able to resist tender emotions and needs at this moment.

Then all thought went flying as his hand came to her neck, and his thumb moved on her skin in little, tingling circles. With a silent intake of breath, Etta lifted her head and buried her face in his neck, pressing her lips ever so gently against his skin, tasting the wonderful saltiness, and rubbing her nose there, smelling the delicious warm maleness of him, in this almost innocent way pulling him into her.

She felt a tremor shake him. He kissed her forehead and rubbed his cheek against her hair. She closed her eyes and let herself drift on the sweet sensations like drifting on a cloud in the summer. Like riding that red flying horse up into the sunlit sky.

Thus swept away, Etta was only vaguely aware of Johnny taking the route that went through Chickasha. Then the truck began slowing and doing a peculair chugging. Pulling herself out of her very pleasant lethargic doze, Etta saw they were turning into a gas station. Apparently unwilling to disturb her, Johnny had been letting the truck slow without shifting. She straightened, and he quickly shifted the stick and rolled the truck to a stop in front of the gas pump.

She raked her hands through her hair, while Johnny told the attendant to fill it up. With a bit of a grin at Etta, he said, "I guess I can afford to go around with a full tank now, thanks to your horse."

His gaze lingered on hers and then moved all over her face, while a smoky expression slipped into his eyes, before he jerked them away and leaned out the window to tell the attendant to check the oil.

Now it was little awkward, neither of them able to look at the other, while their bodies seemed to radiate desire for touch. Etta felt this, felt her body leaning toward Johnny, as she looked through the back window at Little Gus. She was fairly certain Johnny felt it, too. It did not seem that she could feel something so strongly, and Johnny *not* feel it.

The next instant Johnny said, "He's settled down now that's he's tired," and as he spoke, he reached for Etta's hand, entwined his fingers through hers.

"Yes," Etta agreed, gazing down at their hands.

Just then a car came speeding into the gas station, braking with a squeal of tires on the opposite side of the gas pumps. Etta and Johnny both looked that way. A black car, Etta saw, a Buick convertible, with white seats, and two women in the front. The car looked familiar.

Recognition came over Etta like a cold splash of water. She instantly sat back against the seat, jerking her hand from Johnny's and barely even realizing, wanting to hide, even casting her eyes about, as if looking for a place of shelter.

Corinne Salyer. Etta had seen Corinne drive that car on numerous occasions. Fleetingly she thought she might duck down in the seat, if Corinne got out. Then it came to her that Corinne would not expect to see Etta in this unfamiliar truck, was not likely to pay the truck any attention at all. And what further drew Etta out was hearing sharply spoken words.

Peering cautiously at the car, she saw Corinne was behind the wheel and her mother, Amy Salyer, sat on the passenger side. They appeared to be arguing.

Her eyes glued to the car, Etta turned down the radio. Johnny cast her a puzzled look. He started to speak, and she waved him quiet.

The women's angry voices came in snatches: "That's not true, Mama." "You and your father . . . humiliate . . . married . . ." "Rest . . . Oh, good Lord . . ."

The next second Amy Salyer turned, and her door flew open. "You don't know any of it, what I have to put up with your father flyin' around with that piece of trash . . . and then you . . . You both hate me." Then a woman's legs swung out, feet in dainty black open-toed shoes. Head bent, with a rose-colored pillbox hat over silvery hair. "I've tried with you, and your father, but you two never have appreciated any of it!"

"Mother, get back in the car." Corrine's voice was commanding.

Then Amy Salyer got back in the car, more or less collapsing on the seat, crying.

The attendant came to get his money, cast a frown at the convertible, and said, "I see all kinds of stuff in this job."

Johnny pocketed his change and gave Etta a curious look.

She said, "That's her—the woman Roy died with. The young one with the brown hair. That's her mother with her, the woman who was gettin' out."

He turned his head to the car, then swung his gaze back to Etta. She sat back in the seat and looked straight ahead and fought a ridiculous surge of shame. The harsh voices, murmuring now, continued from the Buick.

After several seconds, Johnny started the engine, but no sooner was he pulling away from the pumps than the convertible started forward, too. Johnny had to brake to keep from hitting it. The convertible lunged ahead and squealed tires as it pulled onto the street, Corinne's dark curls flying all over her head. Etta wondered how Amy Salyer managed to keep her hat on.

"Well," Johnny offered, "she isn't much of a driver."

"She no doubt has other talents," Etta said, feeling great sadness.

Then she took hold of herself. She was not going to let the appearance of Corinne spoil a very special evening, she thought. And since she wasn't moving away, likely she would see Corinne from time to time in the future—a thought that made her sick to her stomach—and she might as well get used to it.

Johnny put his arm up on the back of the seat, as if in invitation, and Etta returned to the hollow of his shoulder and tried to return to the sensual lethargy she had been experiencing, where there existed only herself and Johnny.

It helped that he slipped his hand down her arm.

Etta kept peeking through her lids, seeing the trunk of the Buick and the two women's heads ahead of them, as if to torment. At last, at the edge of town, the convertible pulled rapidly ahead and was swallowed up in the darkness. Etta breathed a deep, lovely sigh and enjoyed feeling the warmth of Johnny against her side and the sensation of his rough hand on her arm.

Timidly, hesitantly, she brought her hand to his stomach, a very flat, hard stomach, and encircled him with her arm and thought of how it would feel if he were naked. Tormenting herself now, she thought.

Some ten minutes later, Johnny braked. Etta opened her eyes. There was the convertible again, ahead, its rear shining brightly in the truck's headlights. It veered sharply left, over the line, then came back. Johnny said something under his breath, quickly removed his arm, and downshifted.

"Good heavens . . . what is she doin'?" Etta said.

"Looks like they're havin' a fight."

More exactly, Amy Salyer was attacking Corinne, beating her with her patent leather purse that caught the gleam of Johnny's headlights every time she raised it. Corinne put up a defending hand, and the Buick went all over the road, and it all kept unfolding like a moving picture rolling ahead of them. Amy Salyer lunged at Corinne, flailing at her head and arms, and Etta heard a scream. The Buick went off the road, came back on, then went off and, rather gently, it drove down the embankment, its headlights flitting like a moth on the siderails of a bridge, brush, and trees, just before it seemed to drop headfirst off the earth.

As Johnny pulled off the road and came to a stop, Etta breathlessly leaned forward and peered out the windshield at the red taillights of the Buick poking the air. *OhmyGod . . . oh, my, God*, Etta thought.

Johnny eased the pickup forward over the clumpy grass. Etta looked behind to check Little Gus, who was thumping around in an effort to remain standing.

Johnny's headlights hit the convertible. The car had not gone into the creek, but had been stopped by a tree, which seemed to have smacked the convertible right between the eyes.

"Stay here," Johnny said, as he got out of the truck.

She came right after him, folding her arms around herself, peering into the shadowy light. Closer, and she heard the hiss of steam coming from the Buick.

The driver door swung open, and Corinne got out. Her dark hair shone silvery in the dim light of the truck headlights. She wore a dark, tight skirt and reached out to the car for support. Her face came up, white and ghostly, eyes like a frightened deer.

"Ma'am, are you all right?" Johnny said, his voice slicing into the night.

Etta stopped where she was, unwilling for Corinne to see her.

"I . . . my mother . . ." Grasping the car, Corinne hurried around the rear of it, calling, "Mama? Mama . . ."

Johnny went forward to help get Amy Salyer out of the car. Etta, with her arms still wrapped around herself, hung back. As Corinne and Johnny brought Amy Salyer across the sloped grass, she stepped backward. She had the urge to move into the darkness, but reached the truck and held her ground behind the opened door, watching the three people come forward. Apparently the elder Salyer woman was not seriously injured, as she tried to hit both Johnny and Corinne with her purse and screamed at them that she was not going to any hospital.

"I'd be best dead," she yelled.

Then Corinne looked up and saw Etta standing within the open passenger door of the truck. She said, "Oh, my God."

Etta said, "Not exactly."

Another moment of staring, and then Etta moved quickly out of the way for Johnny to bring Amy Salyer, who had slumped against him, around to the seat.

Corinne came behind, her head down. Etta stared at her, then she pulled herself together and wet a gingham napkin to put on Amy Salyer's head. Mrs. Salyer did not have a wound, but Etta could think of nothing else of a soothing nature to do. The elder Salyer's previous frenzy appeared to be fading. She had turned limp as a dishrag, although she kept on talking, murmuring now, something about needing pills.

"Does your mother have medicine?" Etta asked Corinne, feeling worried about an imminent heart attack or stroke. "She's asking for her pills."

Corinne tiredly shook her head, pushed her hair from her face. "That's her problem. She's taken too many of her little pills."

Etta noticed Corinne's smeared red lipstick. Apparently the woman had a propensity for it.

Corinne's eyes lit on Etta's, and she said flatly, "My mother has . . . episodes. She's windin' down now. A little late, but better than never."

The two of them gazed at each other, and Etta, looking into the other woman's eyes, felt a knowledge fall on her which explained everything between her and Roy and this woman and herself. It was not something she could put into words, and not something she appreciated in that moment, either.

Overwhelmed, she averted her eyes, poured cool water into an enamel cup, and extended it to Corinne. "Why don't you sit on the running board," she said. There seemed nothing else to do but accept the dark situation handed to them by the busybody forces that brought such things about.

Corinne sank down, very elegantly even there on the dirty running board. Etta saw Corinne's hands around the enamel cup were white and tender, and shaking. Looking at them she thought: *the hands that pleasured my own husband.* She glanced at her own hands, darker, capable, with blunt nails.

Between sips, Corinne felt it necessary to tell them that she had been taking her mother to her aunt's in Wichita Falls, for a rest. Her mother had been suffering increasing episodes of depression and hysteria, which sometimes led to her overdosing on her medication and becoming quite erratic. "Aunt Joan is the only one who can seem to handle her and get her back on track," she said.

In between these enlightenments, which Etta felt she could have lived without, Amy Salyer kept up her muttering. With all of it, Etta experienced flashbacks to her own childhood and had to attempt to regulate her breathing and act totally rational, as Johnny was looking at her, and Corinne seemed to be looking at her, too.

No other car came. There was nothing to do but drive the two women back to the gas station at the very least, as Corinne also vetoed the hospital, and this produced quite a discussion. Amy Salyer had begun to cry, and Corinne was not inclined to ride squished in the cab of the pickup truck with her mother.

"We simply can't all go the distance in that tiny space, and with that horse looking on from behind," Corinne said, giving a wave of her hand. "Mother and I will wait here, if you will kindly send help."

Johnny rubbed the back of his neck and whispered, "That old lady might kill her."

Etta, gazing at the two and finding them pitiful, wondered if they would kill each other. "I think I'd better wait here, and you can take them to Chickasha. Maybe you could just drop them at that all-night gas station."

"No," Johnny said tersely. "I'm not leavin' you here."

Ten minutes and a lot of wrangling later, Johnny found himself behind the wheel, wondering exactly how he had gotten there, heading in the opposite direction of home, with Etta squeezed against him, the dark-headed woman on the far side, and her slight, silver-haired mother sitting slumped on her lap. The older woman had passed out and snored gently the entire trip back to the big house in Chickasha where Johnny had driven Etta on that first day, and Johnny wondered bleakly how he managed to get into these sorts of situations.

Seventeen

"We got to get up and get dressed," Latrice said to Obie. "Those two are goin' to be here soon."

She slipped out of bed and put on her robe before turning on the lamp. There was enough light for Obie to catch a glimpse of her body; in the low light she knew she looked very good, and she thought this was enough for him. When she switched on the lamp, she looked down and saw him grinning at her.

"Get up . . . get yourself dressed," she said, trying for sternness but feeling a weakness inside from the way he looked at her.

Obie grabbed her arm, but she shook him off and slipped into the bathroom to dress, tossing over her shoulder, "I want you dressed when I come out."

A moment later, his voice came through the bathroom door. "You gonna marry me, Miss Latrice?"

She didn't answer. She buttoned her dress and gazed at her reflection in the mirror. Quickly and adeptly, she pinned her hair in place. She looked again at her reflection and saw evidence on her face of passion. She didn't think either Etta or Johnny would notice, however, taken up with themselves as they were.

She was annoyed with herself; she had been rash in let-

ting passion so carry her away. The Bible teachings were
not high concepts—they were good sense, and she was
stepping over the line into foolishness that would cause all
sorts of unwelcome complications.

Straightening herself, she jerked open the bathroom door.
Obie was now sitting on the bed, his shirt on but not buttoned, putting on his socks. His fumbling got on her nerves.

"Will you hurry up. Johnny and Etta are liable to come
any minute."

Obie looked surprised at her tone. Then he seemed to
make an effort to comply. Latrice didn't know what irritated her more—his lingering, or his trying to comply when
she fussed at him. She left him and went into the kitchen
to put on a pot of coffee. She thought the coffee would
make everything seem natural. She was so nervous, though,
that she kept dropping things.

At last Obie came out of the bedroom. He was still tucking in his shirt. She looked at him, then finished making
the coffee. He came up behind her, stood very close so that
she could not move. He just stood there, quiet yet unre-
lenting, and of a sudden Latrice felt herself melting.

His arms came around her, and he pulled her back
against him. His body was rock hard. He put his lips next
to her ear and whispered, "How was it?"

Latrice sucked in a breath. "It was fine."

"Fine?"

"It was . . . unexpected," she said finally, and both of
them laughed.

"So . . ." he asked her. "Are you gonna marry me?"

She turned, and he stepped back, giving her room, his
eyes intent upon her.

"I've gone my life without marryin'," she said. "I don't
see that we can right things by making another terrible mistake." She paused, then added, "You can keep comin'
around if you want."

The disappointment that crossed his features made her
feel bad, but she remained firm. He put his hands on her
shoulders and bent to look her straight in the eyes. "At my
age, I know a man can't get everythin' in this world. But

I also know that ain't no reason to give up."

Latrice shook her head and shoved at him, beating at him with her hands because she was so touched and felt she might give in. "Go on. Get out of here before they show up. I don't like everyone knowin' my business."

She shooed him out the door, stood on the porch, and watched his taillights disappear down the dirt road to his cottage. She thought of his cottage. It was poor, the kitchen one from about a hundred years ago. She did not think she wanted to marry him and go to that. And likely if she married him, he would change into a man who thought he could tell her what to do.

Yet, now that he was gone she felt a distinct loneliness and absurd longing for him to return and sit with her and talk with her. Maybe what she liked best was that he listened to her talk.

Then she recalled what she had shared with him in her feather bed. Obie had in fact greatly amazed her with his capabilities.

She saw headlights flicker up on the highway, and a moment later she heard a vehicle pulling into the drive. She ducked back into the house to look around and make certain there was no telltale evidence left about.

When Johnny pulled the truck into the yard at the back door, Etta was again leaning against his shoulder, feigning sleep and wishing she could stay there forever resting in his musky male warmth, trying to stretch the seconds of bliss in which reality had no place.

Johnny stopped the truck and sat there with the engine running, his foot keeping the clutch pressed in for long seconds, until he simply let up and the truck gave a lurch and died. Etta remained against his shoulder. His hand stroked her neck, and his thumb began the delicious circles.

At last, stirred into reaction, Etta raised her head and looked at him. The dashlight shone silvery on his features, dark and rugged, before he quite suddenly brought his lips down onto hers. They pressed fiercely, his tongue forced entry, and desire came charging up Etta's chest. Tears of yearning for something she knew she could not have sprang into her eyes. She grasped him and he grasped her, all heavy breathing and urgent kissing and pounding desire.

The next instant, Johnny went still as stone. Her belly was pressed against him, she realized, and the baby inside kicking. Etta took in a deep breath, watched Johnny pull back and look down at her pregnant belly. Slowly she, too, looked downward.

For a long minute they sat thus, both gazing at the mound, while Elvis sang softly from the radio.

Then Johnny very hesitantly put his hand on Etta's belly. Placing her own hand over his, she guided him to the spot where the baby poked her foot. The foot drew back and kicked, and Johnny jumped, and Etta had to grab his hand to keep him from pulling away.

Another kick and Johnny whispered with awe, "She's strong."

His eyes, filled with a mixture of sadness and wonder, came up to hers. She was a little surprised by his wonder. Surely he had been around many a pregnant horse.

And then again they were both gazing down at Etta's belly, which sat there between them, an elemental barrier.

Johnny said, "We'd better go in before Miss Latrice comes out."

Etta watched him slip from the truck and come around the hood. She felt tears choking her throat and held them back with all her might.

He did not enter the kitchen but stood in the door and bade both Etta and Latrice good night. Etta watched through the screen, as he got back into his truck. Then she closed the door and turned to Latrice, who waved her to sit and brought forth a steaming cup of cola.

"Okay. Tell me all about it," Latrice said.

Etta attempted to give a synopsis of the happenings of the day and evening, although it ended up being a very brief synopsis as she was tired and in such a fog of emotion that she really did not want to reveal to Latrice. Her feelings about Johnny were her own, dear and confusing, and there existed the enormous possibility of being misunderstood about all of it.

About the incident with Corinne and her mother, Etta concluded, "I know now that Roy was drawn to her for the same reasons that he was drawn to me. Whatever we are, we are each the product of crazy mothers. She is worse off than me, though," she said. "She can't manage to keep her lipstick from smearing all over her face."

Etta went up to bed, complacent in the way exhaustion brings, and wanting only to hang on to the vibrant tender feelings regarding Johnny. She fell into her feelings like she fell into her feather pillow, completely and gratefully, letting them surround her, comfort her, and choke her all up at the same time.

Latrice was sitting in her rocker and listening to the radio and musing over life in general, when Johnny came to give her the winnings from her bets. She saw his face peering cautiously in the window before he opened the door.

"You are not a very adept Peeping Tom," she told him.

He still had not learned to recognize her sarcasm and quickly defended himself. "I wasn't tryin' to peep, no ma'am. I thought I should check to make sure Etta was gone, before I gave you your money. I thought you wanted it that way."

She eased him with a gesture, and he handed a wad of money to her. It was warm, obviously from his body heat. Pointing at it, he said, "I could have gotten down to Mexico and had a pretty good time on that."

She shook her head. "You wouldn't. You might take a horse or a woman, but you wouldn't take money."

He gave a sad little smile, as if he was sorry she didn't think him capable of stealing her money.

She said, "I will make fried ham and apples for breakfast . . . and biscuits, of course," offering it as her thanks for him betting her money.

"I'll be here," he said, looking pleased.

He opened the door and was through it and pulling it closed behind him, when Latrice stepped forward, caught open the door, and told him, "You won't have to wait

much longer for her. From what I observed of her a bit
ago, she will likely have the baby tomorrow evening.''

His eyebrows jumped, and he reddened as his eyes
avoided hers.

''She'll be nearly three weeks early, but the barometer
is goin' to drop tomorrow, so that baby will come on. You
had better decide where you're sittin' in this thing, hadn't
you?''

She saw clearly that he didn't know what to say, and she
expected nothing from him in any case. She told him good
night and shut the door.

She thought that her talent for discombobulating people
was grand, and that perhaps she should feel a little ashamed
at such pride. In her own defense, she believed that if the
Lord wanted her to behave better, He would have changed
her.

Counting her money, Latrice returned it to her hideaway
with satisfaction. She could have paid at Overman's grocery, but that had been handled for her, so she continued
to save for dire circumstances that could come about in the
future. Oh, yes, things were tight, but not dire yet. This was
a hedge against starvation, and if they were fortunate for
that threat to never come about, then it would send Etta's
daughter to college and perhaps provide for Latrice and Etta
in their old ages.

She had recently been reading the newspaper and teach-
ing herself about the stock market. There was an electronics
company in Texas that looked to be a secure investment—
when she could get enough saved. Electronics was coming
on like gangbusters these days.

The following morning, as she brought his coffee to the
porch, Latrice told Obie that Etta was likely to have the
baby that evening and asked him to stand ready. She didn't
know exactly ready for what (and she had never asked anyone's help in delivering a baby), but feeling the need for
explanation, said she might need him to calm Johnny.

When Walter Fudge called a little later, at only quarter
past eight, which revealed his lack of manners, requesting

to speak to Etta, Latrice told him Etta could not be disturbed. "Miz Rivers is on the brink of delivery and needs to rest. You'll have to wait, like everyone else."

She told this to Leon Thibodeaux and then Corinne Salyer, when each of them telephoned, too, later in the morning. Leon Thibodeaux was so stunned that he stumbled over his words, then managed to get straight and say he'd come to the hospital right away. Latrice screamed into the receiver for him to stop, afraid he would hang up and run out like a mad man in a useless trip and perhaps kill himself in a wreck.

"She's not deliverin' *yet,* " Latrice said, going on to explain that she expected the event to take place that evening. "And you might as well not go to the hospital, because she'll be here, in my bed."

Mr. Thibodeaux was not happy about that, and Latrice had to wear herself out reassuring him. She gave him enough references that he would keep himself busy all day calling around. She promised to notify him when the event took place. And she wondered at his wife's crying her heart out at Mr. Roy's funeral and now Mr. Thibodeaux showing such a personal interest in Etta.

When Miss Corinne Salyer phoned, she was insistent. "I really need to speak to her," she said, urgency and hysteria vibrating in her voice and annoying Latrice, who was not nearly as soft-hearted and forgiving as Etta.

"Write her a letter," she said, and hung up.

After that she took the phone off the hook. The dang thing had not rung so much in a month of Sundays.

During all these calls, Etta slept away, until almost eleven o'clock, when she finally appeared in the kitchen, still in her gown, looking like someone dazed. "Were you goin' to let me sleep the day away?" she said, a little crossly.

"I figured you needed sleep after being up half the night."

Latrice made no mention to Etta of the ordeal she would face in a few hours. She thought that if she told Etta, the knowledge might interfere with nature. She said calmly,

"Here . . . drink this warm Co-Cola, while I make you some spoonbread."

"I want some eggs," Etta said, as if she had just thought of them, "and can you fry these leftover biscuits?" She took one, nibbling.

Latrice made Etta all she wished—she had not changed her opinion that the event would take place that night, so there was as yet no danger in Etta's overeating. While she cooked, she watched Etta go to the screen door and look out at Johnny, who was in the corral with a horse. He had his shirt off, Latrice saw, and his tanned skin glistened with sweat in the sun. She mused that Etta's body was stirring harder than ever at that moment, filling and budding in readiness for delivery . . . and things would be no less stirring after the delivery of the baby, with breasts making milk and womb drawing tight.

She was shaking her head with it all, when Etta asked what was the matter.

"The weather's gonna change . . . rain tonight," Latrice said.

If she had had any doubt in her prediction that Etta would go into labor that evening, (and she didn't have much, but she always allowed for changes in fate) they faded as the day wore on, and she watched Etta set into washing things: showering and washing her hair, and then bedsheets, and the pillowcase of laundry that Johnny brought to the door.

Johnny did not come in with his laundry. He seemed vaguely afraid of what Latrice had told him was going to happen. Or perhaps vaguely afraid of his own feelings. If he was going to leave, Latrice thought, it would be now.

Etta complained that her back ached, but she continued around the house, as if she could not be still and could not settle her mind on any one thing. She started outside once to see the red gelding, but then she stopped at the door and simply gazed out for long minutes at the horse, rubbing her hands over her upper arms. Then she said she needed to count the money and get it to the bank, yet she never did get the money but went off to dust the baby's room. She returned with the telephone book, looking up the bank's telephone number.

"I want to get an appointment with Edward. I'll do better to talk to him myself, instead of leaving it to Leon. Leon has his own opinions and forgets mine."

Then she set the telephone number aside and started re-folding diapers, changing their shape slightly, while at the same time fooling with the Scrabble game letters to make girl names.

"Everyone will tell her about Corinne," she said out of the blue, raising dark eyes. "What will we tell her?"

"The truth," Latrice said. "These things happen . . . and it has nothing to do with her."

Etta frowned and rubbed her hands in a circle over her belly, appearing deep in thought. The next minute she went to the pantry in search of a snack.

The afternoon stretched long and humid, with clouds blooming in the sky and growing ever darker and thicker. Latrice prayed that fierce storms would pass over and dump further north, on Tulsa perhaps. She did not look forward to having Etta give birth beneath the stairway, or worse, down in the cellar.

She decided instantly that was how Obie could help, and she slipped out to request he clean the cellar, just in case, while she made soup and cornbread, which would digest easily for Etta, for supper. Pitching in to help, Johnny came and requested the Pine-Sol, for cleaning the cellar.

"Anything yet?" he asked in a low voice, casting an anxious glance at the kitchen, while he remained safely outside the door.

Latrice shook her head, and to forestall him asking the same thing in another hour, she said, "About midnight tonight." Since Johnny appeared hesitant about coming into the house, she added, "Are you comin' in to supper tonight, or do you wish to eat it on the porch?"

He looked puzzled. "I'll come for supper," he said.

Latrice had not truly known the hour, but as if she had set an appointment, Etta's water broke at five minutes before midnight, just when the wind rose and the sky rumbled. She came down the stairs and into the kitchen with her eyes wide, already going into her first hard contraction. Latrice had everything in readiness, her bed with the rubber sheet over the feather mattress, towels and baby blankets neatly folded, medical kit open nearby.

"You're gonna do just fine, honey," Latrice said, taking hold of Etta around the shoulders. For the first time in her life, Latrice herself felt the pain, too, as if it were her own.

Etta said, "Damn," and gritted her teeth, then relaxed and breathed deeply.

Latrice made her walk around the kitchen for ten minutes, while she observed the contractions and the sky, trying to decide whether it would be the bed or beneath the stairs or the cellar. The storm appeared to be blowing by, so Latrice helped Etta into the bed.

Etta, finishing a hard contraction, said breathlessly, "Go call Johnny."

Etta labored a bare two hours to bring forth her baby. She did not particularly find it hard going until the last twenty minutes, when a number of ripe moans escaped. Latrice told her that it might be better to let out her pain in a few good whoops, as Indians used to do to build courage when they attacked.

"I don't want Johnny to hear . . . he's out there isn't he?" Etta said breathlessly and sucked the sweat from her upper lip. Her body was soaked with it.

"Yes, honey . . . I told you he's been out there the entire time. He's 'bout to wear out the floor."

"Well, I hope he isn't drinkin'," Etta said, and then was taken up into a great wave of pain that seemed to have no relation to her at all.

Latrice went to commanding her to breathe and to push. She came and took Etta by the shoulders and helped her into almost sitting position, and then the baby was coming, slipping right out of Etta and into the world, ready or not.

Etta lay back, dizzy, trying to find the breath to ask if the baby was okay . . . please, God, let her be okay . . . then being rewarded by a lusty cry, and causing Etta to cry, too, and to thank God.

. Moments later, Latrice placed a wriggling, warm, slippery being on Etta's chest. The soft lamplight encompassed them, and it seemed that Etta's mother was there, and Roy, too, and all the seasons and feelings of her entire life, as Latrice leaned close and held the baby in place on Etta's body with her dark hand on the baby's pale skin, while she murmured a blessing upon the precious new soul.

"Her name is Latrice Katherine Rivers," Etta said, the name coming in a commanding rush into her mind and out her lips.

Latrice stared at her. "We'll get confused. We'll have to call her Kate," she said, turning quickly away.

Out in the kitchen, Johnny was standing, staring at the door. He had gotten to his feet at the sound of the baby's cry. Now there was only silence. He looked questioningly at Obie.

"We appear to have a baby born," Obie said with a wide grin. He snatched off his blue ball cap and slapped it against his thigh. "Hot dog! A new baby round this place."

"But why isn't it cryin'?" The silence worried Johnny. He thought the baby should be crying.

"There's some that cry, and some that shut up," Obie said. "The ones that shut up are preferable."

Johnny was a little comforted, yet he still worried. He'd been waiting two hours, since Latrice had telephoned him in the barn. The telephone ringing like that had jangled his nerves in the first place, and he'd come running over, only to sit in the kitchen since, drinking Obie's coffee, which was not at all the quality of Latrice's, and occasionally pacing. He really wanted a nip of whiskey, but not only did he not have any since he had broken that one bottle, he didn't dare get any, because he did not want to suffer a weak spell and get drunk and disappoint Etta at this most particular time. He tried to play cards with Obie, but mostly he walked a bit and then stepped to the door and smoked.

Obie said that two hours wasn't much to wait at all. He had been present at the birth of ten of his nephews; he had waited once with one of his brothers for two days for the birth of a nephew. This report contrasted highly to Johnny's experience, which was only with mares, who most generally gave birth within thirty minutes. If a mare's labor went on much longer than that, more than likely either the mare or the foal, or both, died.

Just then the telephone on the wall rang, causing Johnny to about jump out of his boots. He and Obie gazed at it, dumbfounded. It had been off the hook when Johnny had come into the kitchen, and sometime during his pacing he had replaced the receiver.

It rang again before Johnny reached it and said hello in an angry manner—the telephone ringing and disturbing them at that crucial time annoyed him considerably.

"Who's this?" a vaguely familiar voice demanded.

"Well, who in the hell is this?"

"Leon Thibodeaux," the man said with some righteousness. "I want to speak to Etta, please."

"It's two o'clock in the mornin'," Johnny pointed out.

"I can tell time," the man said, then spat out a bunch of questions all strung together: "How's Etta? Has she had the baby? I want to speak with her. Put Latrice on the phone."

Johnny almost told Thibodeaux to make up his mind, then said simply that Etta had just given birth and therefore was unavailable, and that Latrice was with Etta. "I'll tell them you called," he said and hung up.

"That Thibodeaux fella," he told Obie, and thought to take the receiver off the hook in case the fool or someone else tried to disturb them again.

It was another fifteen minutes before the door of Miss Latrice's bedroom creaked open, and Miss Latrice stood there, disheveled and sweaty but smiling—at least what passed for smiling for her. She motioned, saying, "You may come and meet Miss Kate."

Johnny could not move. Obie smacked him on the back, saying, "Well, boy, we got us a girl," and gave him a shove forward.

Etta was sitting up against puffy pillows in the soft glow

of two lamps. Johnny stopped just inside the room, gazing at her and at the small bundle she held in her arms. He thought suddenly that he should have washed his hands and combed his hair . . . and possibly put on a suit and tie, and bowed down, too.

Etta smiled at him. "Come see her . . ."

Johnny went to the side of the bed and looked. Overcome by the sight of Etta so beautiful holding the tiny baby, he went down on his good knee, peering closer at the tiny creature in her arms. Such a tiny, wrinkled thing, with the reddest face, like a turnip plucked out of the red mud, although he didn't think he was supposed to say anything like that.

"She's sure pretty," he said.

Then Obie was leaning over Johnny's shoulder and poking a finger at the baby and murmuring to her. Latrice sat on the opposite side of the bed and told them they didn't have to whisper.

Looking around at all of them, Johnny felt oddly like crying. He would have gotten up and left, but Obie was blocking his exit, so he made himself go on acting natural. He had to blink really hard a couple of times.

At daybreak Johnny was sitting on the porch steps with a cup of coffee, admiring the day and thinking wonderingly of the new baby, when Leon Thibodeaux came driving up, all the way to the back door in his big car, where he got out and slammed shut the car door.

"I've been tryin' to call," Thibodeaux said. He shoved his coat back and put a hand on his belt.

"Took the phone off the hook," Johnny said. "We didn't need disturbin'."

Thibodeaux glared at him and then stalked across the porch and opened the kitchen door, going on inside without knocking. Johnny, following, told him that Etta was asleep.

To Johnny's satisfaction, Latrice wouldn't disturb Etta for Thibodeaux, either, but she brought the baby out for him to see. Since the baby had been born, Latrice had appeared strangely pliable and agreeable, even speaking in a softer voice. She didn't let Thibodeaux hold the baby, though, much to Johnny's satisfaction.

Johnny said, "She's a tiny thing, only weighs about six pounds," letting Thibodeaux know that he had held her.

Thibodaux gave him an eye then told Latrice he would take a cup of coffee, if she was so inclined. He tossed himself down in a chair before she even answered, as if she were expected to wait on him.

Johnny said, "I'll get it, Latrice."

She went back into the bedroom, and Johnny strode to the percolator on the counter, poured a cup of coffee and set it in front of Thibodeaux, who eyed him.

"Nice to have seen you," Johnny said and left to go feed the horses.

When Latrice came out of the bedroom, Mr. Leon was sitting at the kitchen table. She had been so preoccupied with the baby that she had sort of forgotten about the man and had to bring herself around.

"How is she?" Mr. Leon asked quickly, half-rising from his chair so that his tie swung lose. "Did she get along okay?"

"As fine as any I've ever attended," Latrice said.

She felt a sudden tenderness for him, recalling that his wife had lost a child, and the two of them never did have another.

"She's sleeping," she said, "and she needs to do that. I'm in a position to see she gets the best care, so I'm not lettin' anyone disturb her. She's had a lot on her recently, and she needs peace."

He nodded, accepting. "Well, that's good. It's good she has you to help her, Latrice."

Latrice was pleased that he noted that fact. He seemed a right pitiful man who was having some inner emotional struggles, which caused him to keep bouncing his leg and stare broodingly into his coffee. Wanting to nurse him in some way, too, Latrice offered him breakfast.

He at first declined her offer, saying he didn't really have time, but then, catching sight of her pan of biscuits, he changed his mind. As she prepared his plate, he asked, "Who is that cowboy?"

Latrice glanced at him, then focused on bringing his plate. "Well, that's Johnny Bellah."

"That's what everyone keeps sayin', but who *is* he? What's he doin' around here?" he asked in an aggravated tone of voice.

"Well . . . he's livin' here. Out in the barn," she added firmly, not wanting him to get indecent ideas. "He came around lookin' for Mr. Roy, as Mr. Roy owed him some money, and then he and Miss Etta worked out that he could use the corrals for training and stay in the room in the barn. He's been awfully handy around here, too," she told him with a certain deliberateness.

"I just bet he has," Mr. Leon said.

Latrice began cleaning the dishes, waiting for Mr. Leon's next words, for she felt certain he had more to say.

"Latrice, it is foolish of Etta to try to hold on to this place. You need to speak to her about this. She can sell this place and end up with a good profit and get her a place in town. It'd be a lot more convenient and comfortable for her."

Not looking at him, Latrice said, "She has what she wants here. This is a very comfortable house," she added.

"The house is grand," he allowed, "but this kind of life . . ." He shook his head. "She'll have to work hard, and she's likely to wear herself out and lose the place anyway, and then what's she gonna have? She's gonna end up back in one of those shacks like y'all came from."

Latrice found the man a definite pessimist. She said, "Etta has a mind of her own, and she knows what she wants."

She decided she wasn't going to try to explain any of it to the man. He had his mind set, as Etta had observed the previous day. He wanted Etta in a certain place for his own reasons that even he did not recognize nor understand. Latrice could speculate as to those reasons, but she didn't think any of it mattered. People went through these spells. Hopefully Mr. Leon would get over his.

He ate the rest of his meal in silence, then wiped his mouth and tossed his napkin on his plate, saying, "I sure thank you, Latrice. This was the best breakfast I've had in six months."

"You're welcome," Latrice said. She saw him to the door and returned to clean the table. That he had thrown a cloth napkin onto a dirty plate irritated the daylights out of her. She hated napkins thrown on a plate.

When Leon Thibodeaux came out of the house, Johnny was at the large corral, filling the stock tank with water from a hose. Looking but taking care to not appear to be looking, Johnny saw Thibodeaux pause at the edge of the porch and hitch up his trousers. Then he saw him coming across the yard, walking purposefully yet mindful of his shiny shoes with each step, a manner which put Johnny in mind of a tom turkey.

"I guess it's you who has encouraged Etta in this dang fool notion of keepin' this place and runnin' some sort of horse farm," Thibodeaux said without preliminaries.

Johnny looked up from the water rushing out of the hose. "I haven't discouraged her. But Etta has a mind of her own choosin'."

"What is it you want here, buddy? You want this place?"

Johnny said, "I rent this space from Miz Etta, and I train her horse. Critter won two races on Sunday over to Anadarko. She got offered two thousand dollars for him." He took great pride in the telling, and in Thibodeaux's raised eyebrow and startled glance over at Little Gus, who was grazing and looking as scrubby as ever.

Frowning, Thibodeaux looked again at Johnny. With a disparaging shake of his head, he pointed his hat at Johnny and said, "Look—Roy tried this horse farm business, and he ran this place in the ground. This was a fine place, and he just wrung it dry . . . and Etta, too."

That sat there between them, and Johnny let it lay. He certainly couldn't dispute the facts.

"Etta doesn't need to be doin' this," Thibodeaux continued. "She can get some security from this place, if she'll just sell it."

"Well now," Johnny said, focusing Thibodeaux with a firm look, "far as I could tell Roy Rivers didn't operate this farm, and he didn't do much more than play at horses." He paused, then added, "And Etta idn't her husband by a long shot. She has some sense."

"That may be," Thibodeaux allowed, "but this isn't any life for a woman. Etta does not need to be throwin' herself into a life of hard work and heartache all over again with another no-account man who can't grow up. At least Roy could give her this place. Just what's some hard-luck ol' boy like you gonna give her?"

That question and the intent look on the man's face went clean through Johnny. He stared at Thibodeaux and Thibodeaux stared back. Then Johnny brought the hose up out of the stock tank and sprayed straight down at Thibodeaux's shiny shoes.

Thibodeaux cursed and hopped backward.

"Man with such shoes shouldn't be comin' out around corrals," Johnny said.

Thibodeaux stalked back to his car and drove away fast enough to be out of sight before the dust settled, while his voice lingered in Johnny's mind like the smell of burnt cabbage in the air.

Johnny checked the level in the stock tank, then stopped, gazing at the face reflected there in the murky water and thinking: *Man like me . . . what can I give Etta?*

Eighteen 🌹

Etta fell immediately into calling her daughter Lattie Kate. She liked the feel and sound of it rolling off her tongue.

Latrice did not. She said, "Do not saddle that child with such a arty name. No tellin' what it will lead to: runnin' around without shoes and no bra and draped in perfume and feathers. Kate is a good, honorable name of a woman who can handle life, and a man, too."

Etta believed what Latrice said was true, and she tried calling her daughter simply Kate, and she tried Katherine, but Lattie Kate just seemed to keep coming out. She could not help smiling as she held her baby girl close and waltzed gently around, singing softly, "Lattie Kate, lovely Lattie Kate," in a melody to fit her tiny, exquisitely beautiful daughter, who at the instant of her birth became Etta's moon and stars.

The first days following Lattie Kate's birth, Etta kept thinking profoundly: *I have become a mother.* Of course she had known she was to be a mother, but she truly hadn't *known*. Certain things took on new importance far and above piddly things like bills or mortgages or racing horses. Now all Etta could think about was nursing correctly and learning lullabies and keeping her hands washed, and making certain anyone who wanted to hold Lattie Kate had their hands washed. She felt such a strange combination of wonder and reverence and duty about the whole thing that she worried that she might be going a little loony like her mother.

Latrice said, "You are fine. You are healthy and had an easy time and aren't so worn out that you can't think of how you have been blessed with this angel," she said, taking Lattie Kate (whom she insisted was just Kate) and hugging her and smiling one of those rare beautiful smiles that she could when extremely happy.

Etta thought that perhaps Lattie Kate's arrival had caused everyone to go a little loony. Latrice smiled a number of times a day, and cooed and spoke in a childish voice to Lattie Kate. Obie did likewise, although this did not seem strange for him—with all his nephews, he was the most adept with Lattie Kate.

Several times a day Johnny came up to the house to see the baby. He would sort of wander in and would gaze at Lattie Kate for long minutes, with an expression somewhere between puzzlement and awe. When Lattie Kate let out any kind of a wail, he seemed to jump clean out of his skin and would say, "What's wrong? Do you think her diaper pin is stickin' her?"

Etta had gotten along so well during her delivery that after a few good hours of sleep, she was on her feet, and that very first afternoon of Lattie Kate's life, Etta took her daughter outside to see the sun and the sky and Little Gus. She wanted to introduce her child to all the world, to share the things she herself loved and hoped her daughter would love, too.

"Oh, look, darlin', it's a bright world and the sky is blue as blue can be . . . this is a blade of grass, and this is a tree . . . well, you'll feel it when you're older. And here is a horse . . . this is Little Pegasus."

Etta held Lattie Kate up for Little Gus to sniff; he blew on her face, and Lattie Kate did not flinch but looked up at the horse with eyes that seemed to see.

"Look," Etta said to Johnny who'd come up beside them at the fence, alerting him to her daughter's certain magic with the horse. "Oh, look . . . how gentle he is to her."

"She's already a charmer," Johnny said. He leaned close to Lattie Kate, grinning at her and calling her a beautiful doll, his rugged features all soft and gooey. "Can I?" he asked with a suddenness, indicating that he wanted to hold the baby up to the horse, too.

Etta hesitated slightly, worried about Johnny's dirty hands, but his face was so concentrated on Lattie Kate that she could not disappoint him. She slipped the bundled baby carefully into his arms. "Hold her head . . . there you are . . . oh, darlin', look at who's holdin' you."

His hands dark and rough against the soft, fine baby blanket, Johnny held the baby up to Little Gus, and Little Gus blew and sniffed on her in an unusually quiet manner, as if he was very aware of the preciousness of the child. Etta leaned close to Johnny, hovering, sharing the moment.

Then Latrice was hollering from the porch: "Bring my baby back in this house. It's too bright for her eyes out there."

Although Etta did not want to let Lattie Kate out of her sight, she made herself be generous and let Latrice hold and rock Lattie Kate, while Etta napped for long hours. She would wake up, and Latrice would bring Lattie Kate for nursing, and then take the baby afterward, getting the burps out of her. Etta would drift into sleep again, listening to Latrice sing a lullabye and thinking that the child belonged to Latrice, too.

Leon Thibodeaux returned that first evening to see Etta and Lattie Kate. He came alone, as he said Betsy had a cold and didn't feel she should be around a baby. He brought a little stuffed lamb that played "Mary Had a Little Lamb." Etta was glad to see him and so very excited to show him Lattie Kate, although she worried when he held her. Leon had a habit of bouncing his knee in a nervous tic, which jarred Lattie Kate just a little too much in Etta's opinion. She quickly retrieved her daughter from him.

When Leon was leaving, he said, "We'll need to discuss

the mortgage, Etta. Edward is back from Chicago and ready to settle this."

Etta looked at him for a moment, then down at Lattie Kate. "Oh, I'm sure we will, Leon," she said and kissed her baby, whispering, "Mama loves you so much." She let Latrice see Leon out the door.

Later in the nursery, Etta changed Lattie Kate's clothes, then turned out the overhead light, leaving on the dim clown lamp. Humming, she scooped Lattie Kate up into her arms and swayed her around. The next instant, she found herself looking into the shadowed recesses of the room that had belonged to her and Roy together. She saw nothing. His scent was gone, too. The only thing she smelled was baby lotion.

"Here's your daughter, Roy," Etta said, just in case. "You made a beautiful baby. I'm so sorry you aren't here with her. I'll take very good care of her."

Etta kissed Lattie Kate's sweet-smelling head and, humming, she danced her across the room and out the door and down the hall to the guest room that had become Etta's own now. She placed her gently into the bassinet sitting on its stand beside the bed. Lattie Kate, her eyes squeezed closed, made a funny face. Etta slipped into bed and lay there for fifteen minutes, before bringing Lattie Kate into bed and holding her close.

Sometime in the night she opened her eyes to see Roy standing beside the bed, looking down and smiling sadly. "She's beautiful," he said, and Etta said, "Oh, yes."

Then he was gone, and Etta came fully awake to find herself staring at nothing but the window curtain, which stirred softly in the night breeze. She felt, however, that Roy truly had been there, but that now, with Lattie Kate's birth, he was gone, never to return. She hoped wherever he was, someone was looking out for him. Some strong angel could no doubt do better than she, a mere mortal.

*   *   *

Latrice considered the first days as those of Kate's newborn life and Etta's newborn motherhood. They were needed days of discovery and adjustment, and Latrice was intent on providing her charges with peace in which to discover and adjust as required. She screened telephone calls, and she herself went for the mail and set it aside on the desk in the den, not even looked at.

It was not hard to screen the calls, as Etta had no desire to answer. She had no eyes for anything or anyone beyond her little daughter. Latrice would see Etta holding her baby and gazing lovingly at her, and Johnny Bellah sitting there lovingly gazing at Etta.

Leon Thibodeaux came the second day, too, which caused Latrice to wonder about him, and caused Johnny Bellah to come inside and sit right there with them in the living room, in his dusty clothes and spurs, too, until Mr. Leon left. Mr. Leon and Johnny Bellah looked at each other as if they were squaring off, but Etta never really saw them, as she was so thoroughly focusing on her baby and her motherhood.

Heloise Gardner, Roy's cousin, came bringing a big box—a new dress for Etta and a fancy one for the baby, too, who Heloise laughingly said would be a future Style Shop customer. Latrice's cousin Freddy, the cab driver, surprised them by bringing by a Raggedy Ann doll for "the new little girl God sent Latrice."

The third day Harry Flagg came driving in with a bunch of his horses, and Etta took Kate outside to Harry to show her off. Latrice had thought herself immune to life's surprises, but she was a little amazed when the big man came, hitching up his sagging britches, and sat for an hour on the porch, giving forth the entire time on his vast knowledge of children at every age.

Etta sat there with little Kate and sopped up his words, most of which seemed sound to Latrice, except the one about putting a clove of garlic beneath the baby's pillow as a cure for a cold.

Mr. Harry was still sitting there when Johnny Bellah, sweating from the work of putting Mr. Harry's horses in the barn, came up and joined them, gazing at Etta and the baby, while she listened with rapt attention to Mr. Harry. Every once in a while, she would look at Johnny and smile, showing that she had not completely forgotten him, and he would sort of glow.

Latrice watched this and wondered at what was being built in these days that Etta discovered another facet of herself and the life stretching ahead of her. If Johnny Bellah did not get tired of waiting this out and take his leave, undoubtedly things were going to get wild and crazy around there.

On the fourth morning of Kate's life and Etta's motherhood, Miz Alice Boatwright made her appearance. When Latrice opened the door to the ringing doorbell, she almost shut it again. She and Miz Alice stared at each other, Miz Alice saying with her eyes: *You'd best not shut this door.*

Then Latrice saw the woman carried a very pretty pink package.

"I want to see my nephew's daughter," Miz Alice said and stepped forward, and there was nothing to do but step out of her way or be run down by her tiny ass.

Watching the woman breeze on past into the living room, Latrice mused that for some peculiar reason she always found herself admiring Miz Alice's gumption. She closed the front door and went upstairs to where Etta was dozing with Kate.

"Miz Alice has come to call," she said.

Etta surprised her by jumping right up and putting on the new dress Heloise had brought—the only one Etta could now fit into (Heloise was a very smart woman)— while Latrice put darling Kate into her best gown and booties. The three of them went downstairs, where Alice Boatwright waited regally in the tall, wingback chair.

Etta stopped in the living room archway, gazing with sudden apprehension at the woman. She had not thought of anything but showing off her little princess; she had forgotten exactly who Alice was. Now their previous encounter came full-blown into her mind, bringing swiftly the anger and the shame.

Then came a surge of confidence, however, with the thought: *I am a mother now*, sending Etta stepping out and crossing the room to show Alice the perfect treasure Etta herself had produced.

"May I hold her?" Alice asked, her pale eyes looking upward with combined eagerness and anxiousness.

Carefully, magnanimously, Etta relinquished her daughter into the older woman's arms. She saw Alice's hands with sudden clarity; they were finely drawn, veined by the years, and—most surprisingly—shaking. The lonely hands of a woman who had never held her own child.

Etta backed up to sit on the sofa, on the edge. Beside her, Latrice propped herself on the arm, keeping one foot on the floor as if to be ready for any contingency.

Etta watched a slow, gentle smile soften Alice's pinched face as she gazed at Lattie Kate. She gazed at her for long minutes, rocking her back and forth, beginning to murmur baby things and actually seeming a little foolish, so that Etta and Latrice glanced wonderingly at each other.

Alice finally said quite clearly, "She looks like my sister," and looked at Etta. "What have you named her?"

Etta told her, "Latrice Katherine . . . we call her Lattie Kate." Latrice did not contradict.

Alice tightened her lips, obviously disapproving. Looking again at the baby, she said, "Well, you will bear up underneath that, won't you, Katherine Rivers?" She smiled. "Katherine was my mother's name," she added with some triumph.

She seemed lost again for long minutes of rapture with the baby, then she said to Etta, "Won't you please open the gift I brought her?"

"Oh, yes . . ." Etta took the pink box. She opened it, peeled back tissue paper, and beheld a silver cup and spoon and rattle, all bearing the letter R.

"You know you should have called me," Alice said, her voice both wounded and accusing. "It was despicable to hear about the birth of Roy's daughter by way of Leon Thibodeaux."

Etta gazed at her, thinking and swallowing each comment that came to mind, intent on keeping peace if at all possible.

Latrice said, "Miz Alice, would you like some cake and coffee?"

Alice's eyes jumped. Then she said, "Yes, thank you," and again looked down at the baby and swayed her back and forth. "You look like your daddy, too, sweetness . . . beautiful like he was when he was born. All of our family, the Richardses of St. Louis are a handsome people."

Observing her appreciation of Lattie Kate, Etta felt her heart grow more tender toward Alice. There were so many sides to people—a revelation that made her think of Roy and smile inwardly. She supposed she could learn to get along with Alice. She knew in that moment a sense of power over the woman. It came, she thought, from a fresh, and surprising, recognition of her own strength.

Latrice brought coffee and chocolate cake she had just made, and Alice stayed an hour in which she alternately cooed at Lattie Kate and commented on what she had heard (apparently by way of Leon) about Etta selling the furniture and deciding to keep the house.

"You have Katherine to think of now," Alice said. "You really have to consider practicalities. Leon seems assured that you could get a nice profit from this place. And you can't keep all this up by yourself, a woman alone. Besides, it would be better for Katherine in town."

She continued on about the better schools and the hospital being in town, and how her sister had never been happy this far from town, and that she herself believed her sister would have lived longer, if she had been closer to a hospital.

"I think Lattie Kate will do well here," Etta said.

Alice's eyes rested on her. "We own several nice rent houses in town. There's one I think would be right for you—and Latrice, too, of course. I'm certain we can work out an arrangement where you can afford it."

Etta, somewhat stunned, said, "Thank you for the offer, Alice, but this is our home."

"You won't need to worry about runnin' into Corinne Salyer. I had a talk with her and made her realize that it would be best for her and everyone if she moved away. Her mother agreed, and persuaded Corinne to go down to Wichita Falls to live for a while with Amy's sister, I believe."

"I'm sorry you did that," Etta said tightly. Her spine had gone suddenly rigid, her lungs compressed. "It was none of your business. Corinne had every right to remain where she was."

"Her rights weren't at question. The best thing was. She would never really find happiness because people would always talk, at least for a number of years."

With great surprise, Etta saw Alice's lips quiver. Then she breathed deeply. "I really was tryin' to help. People talk for a long time about such juicy gossip, but without her around, it will all be forgotten. She'll have a new start, and you will, too. Without Corinne there, you and Katherine and Latrice can move into town, and Edward and I would be able to help you when you need it."

Etta said, "I appreciate what you tried to do in my behalf, Alice. But this is our home and where we wish to live."

Alice simply blinked and said, "Yes . . . well, I imagine you'll want to think it over," and then returned her attention to cooing at the baby.

When Lattie Kate began to fuss to be nursed, Alice finally took her leave. On her way out, she stopped and said to Etta, "Thank you for letting me see her." Her eyes were blank as a blackboard, but there was something in her voice that touched Etta.

"You can come out and see her anytime you like," Etta said.

Etta and Latrice, holding Lattie Kate, stood in the doorway and watched Alice's Cadillac drive away—and Alice even waved out the window.

Latrice shook her head. "Looks like Kate has turned that

woman to butter . . . well, strong sour cream anyway.''

Etta chuckled and waltzed Lattie Kate across the entry and through the house, singing, ''Lattie Kate, sweet Lattie Kate, you melt hearts wherever you go.''

III

Love Rides a Dark Horse

Nineteen

Saturday came, and Johnny took Little Gus to a bush track he had heard of over in Caddo County. It was nothing more than a track scratched into a flat piece of ground owned by a farmer who also raised horses, where riders and owners gathered to race and bet and have a good time now and then. Obie went with him, and Woody met them there.

Etta remained at home. She could not leave Lattie Kate for an entire afternoon, nor did she believe Lattie Kate, at only a week old, should yet be taken out and exposed to the sun and wind. Etta missed going terribly, though, and the instant she heard Johnny's pickup coming up the drive, she raced out onto the porch.

Johnny came tooting his horn, and Obie waved his blue ball cap out the window, instantly setting Etta's heart thumping. Johnny stopped the truck, leaned his head out the window and smiled at Etta.

"We won another, Miz Etta," he said, his eyes twinkling like bright stars.

This was good news. It appeared the most natural thing, too, as if the horse had been predestined for this winning, and Johnny awfully smart for seeing it.

After putting Little Gus away in his corral, Johnny came into the kitchen for supper and waved bills at all of them, licked his fingers and counted out Etta's share with exaggeration. She had given him twenty dollars to bet, should it turn out he could get a promising race for Little Gus. He put sixty dollars in her hand, so very proudly.

"The boy's in tall cotton," was Obie's expression. Etta just had to grin at him. She took his hat and put a cold drink in his hand and set a plate of pork chops in front of him. She didn't know what she enjoyed most—that Little Gus had proved out again, or that Johnny was so happy about it.

Obie was already telling tales of the afternoon, and Johnny jumped in with further elaborations as to how after Little Gus had won his race, a number of men had wanted to match their horses against him, but Johnny would not.

"The less we race him, the more unknown he is, and I think we'll do better to keep him that way. I want to save his best for some real races with good-sized purses."

With the added work of Harry Flagg's four horses being stabled in the barn, Etta arranged for Obie's youngest nephew, who was actually named Nathan Lee Lee, to come clean stalls and help out after school each day. Johnny gave him free riding lessons, and Etta paid him a small salary, which she had to increase when Jed Stuart brought two three-year-old geldings to stable.

Jed was the first man of the area who had given Johnny horses to break; after hearing of Johnny's success with Little Gus, he wanted Johnny to train two of his geldings, who were bred of quarterhorse racing stock.

"Jed told me to name a price, and I did—and he paid it," Johnny said with such a sense of wonder that Etta had to laugh.

"Of course he did. He knows enough to know that if he wants the best he has to pay for it," she told him.

He blushed bright red and looked down at the leather he was braiding.

It was evening, the sun just setting and the warm breeze easing down. They were sitting on the porch, their feet on the top step. Etta had come out to join Johnny, leaving Obie and Latrice in the kitchen. While Obie held Lattie Kate,

Latrice taught him words from the newspaper crossword puzzle. Latrice had embarked on a new project to improve Obie's vocabulary, and Obie was set to please her.

Etta had looked out and seen Johnny on the porch and known he was waiting for her, in the way women knew these sorts of things. As she sat down beside him and arranged the skirt of her summer dress (one Latrice had let out in the waist and tried to let out in the bosom) over her bent knees, she mused about how a woman simply knew some things and how just that day she had seemed to look up from Lattie Kate and see Johnny looking at her. She had looked right into his silvery eyes, and in that instant she had felt much more a woman than a mother.

This had been disturbing, but not unpleasantly so. It was as if it had only just then occurred to her that she was both a mother and a woman.

Watching Johnny's strong, rough fingers work the leather, Etta said, "You know, I really need to start payin' you for trainin' Little Gus. Our deal was for you to break him. You've more than done that."

His eyes came up, and he gazed at her intently. "You start that, and I'll have to start rentin' corrals and stalls, and payin' for my room and board, and then we'll have to figure my hourly wage for doin' occasional repairs, and it'll just get all confusin'. I'd just as soon call it even, if you will."

Of course she was relieved to hear this, as she had no idea how she would pay him, but she had thought she should offer. Then she was gazing into his eyes so deep and silver, and they seemed to be saying a lot more than about the horse.

She looked quickly away, out at the corrals.

"Why is it so hard for you to let me do things for you?" he asked, his voice sharp and bringing her eyes around to him.

"Because it's frightenin' to me," she said at last while she smoothed her skirt tightly over her knees. Searching for the correct words, she glanced at him and saw his puzzled frown and his eyes so silvery.

"I feel like I owe you so much," she said. She gestured at the corrals and Little Gus with the golden sunlight shining on him. "I never would have him like he is, if you hadn't come that day, and I'd likely be banned from Overman's Grocery, and I wouldn't have have gone up to Oklahoma City to the pawnshops, and I sure wouldn't have anything like it is around here—rentin' stalls and makin' a little money from Little Gus . . . none of it without your help. I owe you, and I'll never be able to repay you," she said, at last bringing her gaze back to meet his.

He nodded, a softness coming over his face. "Well now, you've done a lot for me, too," he said, thoughtfully running his gaze over to the door, up at the porch ceiling, out at the corrals. "You've given me a place. You and Latrice . . . well, I guess this is as close to a home as I've ever known. So you don't need to let your pride get all bent. It's even, like I said."

His gaze moved over her, lingering on her breasts, before returning to her eyes. Etta felt the strong urge to lean over, put her hand on his cheek, and kiss him fiercely.

She looked away, resisting all that swelled and churned inside her. Emotions that could not be trusted—she had learned that well enough. She wanted to tell him how glad she was that he was here, and that she needed him, but that same need scared her socks off, and she wasn't ready to trust him with her fear. She kept thinking that she would say these things, and away he'd go, or maybe come and go, or maybe stay and end up being not at all the man she had thought.

It seemed that her newfound self-confidence was not quite so sturdy as she had believed, and this brought a gloom over her.

She said, "I might not be able to hold on to this place, you know. Edward might force me to sell. He's stretched the bank's patience as it is. And likely he'll say that I'm a woman and can't be doin' any of this." The gloom deepened. If she could not hold this place, she and Latrice would be gone, and so would Obie and Johnny and his training.

"There's always another place to go to somewhere," Johnny said after a long minute.

She shook her head. "I don't want to do that. And I wouldn't ever get enough money to go elsewhere and get a barn like this and the corrals, and the pasture and alfalfa field." She gazed at it all. "No, this is it."

"I think you might could," Johnny said, "if we threw in together to do it."

Etta looked at him, startled. He kept his gaze on the leather he braided.

"Together?" she said breathlessly, her eyes searching his tanned cheek.

"It's somethin' to think about." His voice was even and low.

"It is?"

He raised his head, looked at her, his silvery eyes sharp. "Well, we seem to want the same things—a house and barn and corrals, a place to raise and train horses. I've thought about that sometimes, but I just never had a reason to go to all the trouble, I guess. It's not so important to a man alone."

"No, I imagine not," Etta said, staring into his eyes. Her thoughts skipped around. *She needed a man to help her . . . and she would lie naked with him in bed . . . He would continue to train Little Gus . . . He would make love to her . . . likely he would make decisions . . . She would have him to make repairs . . . She would have him . . .*

Johnny said, "I think we could make a go of it, both of us . . . and Latrice and Obie, too."

"And Lattie Kate," Etta said.

"That goes without sayin'."

Etta looked away at the corrals that were no color now as the evening got darker and cooler. Johnny returned to braiding, and Etta sat very still, feeling Johnny's heat beside her. The scent of him, all male and musky, came strongly to her.

After a long silence, she said, "I have this place, and this is where I want to stay. I think we might do just as well together here."

She listened intently and found it a little annoying that he did not answer right away. Then, to her suprise, he pushed to his feet. He looked down at her, and his face was shadowed with the twilight.

He said, flat and hard, "This place is yours. I don't know about fittin' here." Then he shook his head. "And I guess I haven't never stayed in one place, anyway, Miz Etta, and likely you couldn't count on me to. I guess it is sort of pie-in-the-sky talkin', idn't it?"

And with that he walked away.

Etta jumped to her feet and yelled after him, "Well, you seem to have been fittin' here pretty good so far—you even said that!" and her tone was as flat and hard as his had been.

When he didn't stop, she went into the house, letting the screen door slam. Obie and Latrice looked at her in surprise.

Pretending not to notice, she went to the refrigerator and pulled out an cold Orange Crush. As she opened it, she heard Johnny's truck start. She went quickly to the door and watched his truck drive away. Turning, she saw Latrice eyeing her.

"That was Johnny drivin' off," Etta said.

"Well, I didn't think it was one of the horses," Latrice said.

Obie looked edgy, as if feeling he must leave in the midst of whatever crisis had suddenly fallen, but casting regretful glances at Latrice. Etta did not think that she needed to spoil their time and told them both she was going to take a bath.

"Would you please watch Lattie Kate while I go get a bath?" she asked Obie.

"Well, of course, Miz Etta. I don't want to give up this jewel until I have to." Then he added, having become bold with Latrice's recent attention, "I'm not as stupid as Johnny and runnin' off from beautiful women."

He sought her smile, and Etta gave him one, touching his shoulder gently as she passed. When she got in the dining room, she found she was close to tears. She thought that was foolish. Tears were not going to solve any of her problems, and she really didn't have energy for them, either.

The entire time Etta bathed, she thought of Johnny and their conversation, which she began to wonder if perhaps she had misinterpreted. She had thought he had been asking her to marry him and move away. On further consideration, she became totally uncertain.

He had not actually mentioned the word *marriage*—although she could not imagine what else he could have been saying. Two together, he had said, and he had not seemed to be speaking of a platonic partnership. He had not looked at her in a platonic fashion.

One thing she was certain about was that Johnny had been uncertain.

Etta did not appreciate this. She was uncertain enough, without Johnny adding to it. She supposed it was old-fashioned thinking, and maybe a little irrational, but she believed women were naturally uncertain. Uncertainty was a product of their changing emotions, and also a woman's open-mindedness. She expected men, however, to be certain. Especially if they were going to start bringing up marriage.

It was all a terrible muddle, and the thoughts went round and round in her head as she washed her hair and brushed it shining and sprayed on perfume. She tried to put on a summery dress, but it would not fit over her motherly breasts or thicker waist. At last, promising herself a shopping trip for new clothes, she settled for a cotton gown and her silk robe and a blue ribbon to hold her hair.

For the next hours, she kept looking out the window for Johnny's return. She hoped he would return sober because she did not think she could handle him drinking. Every bit of hope she was having about them might just be killed outright, should he come in drinking.

It occurred to her that he might not return at all.

Johnny returned at quarter past ten. Etta had just sat down in the rocker in the kitchen and was putting Lattie Kate to her breast. She heard Johnny's truck pull in, imagined it over by the barn. Listened to the engine shut off, closed her eyes, and sighed. *He had come back.*

Then she immediately wondered if he had returned drunk or sober. She thought to look but kept herself in the chair, rocking harder.

The next instant, when she heard his boots on the porch, she turned her head and saw his shadowy form at the screen door. He rapped lightly, and she said, "Come in," and quickly threw a diaper over her shoulder, covering her breast and Lattie Kate's head.

"Oh, I'm sorry," he said, backing out the door when he saw what she was doing. "I didn't mean to interrupt."

"It's all right . . . come on in. Latrice's takin' a hot bath, but she made coffee about an hour ago, if you want some." She spoke quickly, trying to cover any nervousness, while her heart beat rapidly with the thought: *Don't go!*

If he left, she would just have to chase him down. She had things to say. She intended to get some things clear.

His eyes, shadowed by his hat, met hers, then skittered away. Lifting his hat, he tossed it atop the refrigerator, then sauntered over to the counter. He walked straight, although there was the scent of the roadhouse about him, cigarettes and whiskey and a hint of pool playing.

Lattie Kate began to fuss because Etta's tension had allowed only a trickle of milk to flow.

Johnny, pouring a cup of coffee, asked if Etta wanted any, and she said no. "It's not so good for Lattie Kate."

He leaned against the counter and sipped his coffee, gazing down at the floor, as if he dared not look at her. Etta was noticing the way his jeans stretched over his thighs, when her milk suddenly let down. She felt the languid heat flush her body, Lattie Kate's tugging on her breast, and the tugging deep in her womb. And she felt Johnny's gaze.

She lifted her head to look at him.

He looked at her for a long minute, then he moved to sit at the table and began to tell her about racetracks he'd heard of in the northwest part of the state.

"They got racin' every weekend at some of those places," he said, "and they get pretty good money goin' once in a while. Some of those ol' boys bring their horses to try out before goin' on over to New Mexico and Arkansas. We might could take the son-of-a-buck up there and make us a bit of money and run his worth up. Wouldn't take but a time or two. Woody couldn't go up there, though, so we'll need to find someone to ride for us.''

There, surrounded by the glow of the warm kitchen light, Etta listened to him tell her all about it and rocked softly and felt her daughter tugging on her breast and stirrings deep inside, and thought how she was no longer pregnant and Johnny had asked her to marry him. Again and again, she felt and saw Johnny's gaze upon her, and again and again, she looked at him, at his dark hair shining in the kitchen light and his sweat-dampened shirt over his thick shoulders and his rough, thick fingers holding his coffee cup.

Latrice came out of the bathroom, looked into the kitchen and said hello to Johnny, met Etta's gaze, and then closed her bedroom door, leaving them alone again. The refrigerator made a noise, and Lattie Kate sighed a snuffly sigh as she slipped into sleep.

Etta said, ''Let me put Lattie Kate in her bassinet, and we can step out on the porch.''

''Okay,'' Johnny said, somewhat startled. His gaze hit on her breast, and he caught a glimpse of creamy flesh as she took the baby from her breast.

He rose as she did, and he watched her lay the baby into the basket that sat on the table, watched the opening of her robe hang, revealing the white skin of her neck and swell of the tops of her breasts. Etta straightened and tightened her robe, and Johnny leaned over to gaze at the baby.

He always found himself drawn to doing this. He was nervous about touching the baby, but he was drawn like a magnet to look at her. She looked then as she always did, like an angel sleeping.

Then Etta was at the screen door and looking back at him in an expectant manner.

He followed her out, feeling nervous about the situation.

Feeling much as a schoolboy being brought to account for his foolishness.

Johnny had spoken rashly a little earlier, which now meant some serious talking, of a sort he did not feel at all comfortable with, but which he felt he'd come to have because he just could not stay away from Etta—or from looking at her hips. He really should stop that, he thought, as he pulled the kitchen door closed behind him.

Etta stopped at the edge of the porch and tucked a strand of her hair behind her ear. The glow through the door window and from a nearly full moon lit all around them. The flowers in Etta's robe appeared purple, her face and hair somewhere between bronze and gold.

She looked at him, and he looked back.

He was not about to begin when he wasn't certain where this was headed. Letting her lead seemed the wisest choice. It had been Johnny's experience that women liked to lead.

She said, "This evenin', earlier, when you said we could build together—were you askin' me to marry you?"

One of the things Johnny liked about Etta was that she could, when she wanted, get to the heart of a matter, although at this moment, he didn't care for the way she pinned him down.

He nodded. "I guess it's a pretty wild idea," he admitted, feeling foolish.

He shifted his stance and propped against the porch post. He did not think she would appreciate the entire truth, which was that his recent successes with the gelding and Etta's eyes looking at him like they had that evening, when she sat beside him on the porch, had caused him to get carried away with something he wasn't at all certain could, or even should, happen. Sometimes a man could think crazy thoughts, but usually, if he kept them to himself, they were harmless.

She stood there now, with an expression that demanded more of an explanation.

"It seemed sort of practical. There is something between us," he said, firmly, because he knew this was truth.

"Yes, there is."

Her voice was husky and breathless and her eyes were on him, and it all made his palms sweat. She looked away, folded her arms and rubbed her elbows, causing her breasts to push out full.

She said, "You didn't seem all that certain."

Johnny shifted his stance. "Maybe I wasn't. I guess I was wonderin' what you might think of the idea. Let's just drop it, okay?"

"You were the one who brought it up," she said.

He sensed he'd insulted her, and he was getting aggravated with her and himself. He stood there trying to get past his fears to find the words to set things straight.

Then she said, "I don't think it's a wild idea. I think it's quite practical, too." Her eyes searched him. "I . . . would you still want to marry me, if we stayed here?" Her voice was earnest, her eyes wide.

"I think I'd need a place we can build together," Johnny said after a second. "Here, I think I'd always be lookin' around and knowin' I came and took somethin' you already had."

"But you wouldn't be. I wouldn't even have this today, not like it is, without you."

He shook his head. "I just don't think we can make it like this. I'll always be lookin' over my shoulder at the shadow of Roy Rivers."

"Only in your mind," she said, her voice a little sharper than he thought necessary.

"Maybe that's so, but I guess that doesn't change how I feel. This is your place, and it always will be. When I get ready to settle down, I want a place I can call my own, and not something I married to get."

Etta fixed him with an annoyed eye. "If I left here, I'd be goin' to your place. It'd be a place I got by way of you. Now, tell me why it should be different for me and not for you?"

The only answer Johnny had for that was that he was a man. Since he was fairly certain an answer of this sort would not do, he kept silent. He didn't see any need in continuing what was turning into an argument.

"Johnny . . . this place is here, and it's a really good place. A house and a barn and corrals . . . twenty acres of alfalfa already planted and growin'. Obie's cottage down there across the creek. It's here and all we'd have to do is work it, build it up. You could do that and make it your own, the same as any other place."

She fell silent, her eyes on him.

"What you say is true," he said, "but this was still Roy Rivers's place. It will always be the Rivers farm, Etta."

"It is mine, too. I think it is more mine because I have stood by it." She paused, then added quietly, "I can't just up and leave this place and run off with you. I just can't."

She half-turned from him. He thought to reach out for her, felt he wanted to do something to draw her to him, yet he couldn't seem to move.

Then she rounded on him, saying, "But what I can say is that I don't want you to leave, Johnny. I really don't. And I guess maybe you didn't really mean to ask me to marry you or want to hear all that, but that's how I feel."

He heard tears in her voice as she offered him all she could. What she said made him feel foolish and angry and desperate all at the same time.

"Damn, Etta . . . you ask a lot from a man."

Then he stepped over, slipped his hand to the back of her neck, hauled her against him, and kissed her, hard and thorough. Kissed her until she was weak against him and moaning softly and pressing her lips and pelvis hungrily against his. When he couldn't breathe, he came up for air and buried his face in her hair, then went back greedily for more at her lips. Finally, out of breath and almost out of his mind, he lifted his head and saw triumphantly that her eyes were glazed.

He said with a ragged, angry voice, "I'll tell you the truth, you are the first woman who has ever made me think of settlin' down, and I'm not certain I can even do it for you. I guess we're just gonna have to let this dark horse run, and see how it goes."

Then, quickly shoving her from him because he could part no other way, he walked down the steps and away across the yard as fast as his bad knee would allow, quite fully satisfied that he had left her wanting more.

When he got to the barn, he realized he'd left himself wanting more in a way that he himself could not satisfy. He ended up going out back of the barn, stripping naked in the moonlight and spraying himself with cold water from the hose, dancing around from the shock of it, all the while telling himself that Etta was a woman who had recently given birth and didn't need to be messing with a man anyway.

Etta stood in her bedroom looking out the window. She saw Johnny's pickup drive off. He didn't head for the highway, though, but turned down the track to Obie's cottage. She breathed a little easier, seeing that.

She went to the bassinet and checked Lattie Kate, tucked the cotton blanket that didn't need tucking, stood gazing down at her tiny jewel of a daughter.

Was it all for Lattie Kate? she thought. Is that why she would not leave?

She brought her hand up, making a fist and pressing it at her midriff, thinking without words that there was so much more to why she clung to this place. It had to do with what she had given up to be here, with all that she had lost and with all she was finding again.

She had given up a lot for Roy Rivers. She had given up herself, and she could not allow herself to get that lost in a man ever again.

Twenty

The following day, Johnny came to breakfast, tagging in behind Obie Lee. The two were discussing the condition of the water pump, and Johnny barely paused when Etta put a stack of pancakes in front of him.

His eyes met hers, and then he was reaching for the syrup and going on talking, changing the subject to the various rodeos and races to be held during the coming Fourth of July holiday, about the good chances of Harry Flagg's horses and the poor ones of Jed Stuart's. He certainly gave no sign of the intimate conversation he had held with her the previous evening.

Etta had come to the conclusion sometime in the hours since that Johnny had made a rash proposal when he had proposed marriage, and that he regretted it. He obviously wanted to back up and go on as if he had never spoken. The idea depressed Etta, and she did little more than push the food around on her plate.

Since she was already depressed, after breakfast Etta decided to tackle the mail that had stacked up during the days since Lattie Kate's birth. Bills mostly, although there were a few nice cards of congratulations on Lattie Kate's birth from people Etta saw on rare occasions. She read them with small slices of wonder and joy.

There were many more people who wished her well than she had imagined—there were congratulations cards on Lattie Kate's birth from Caroline Fudge and Mary Ellen, and Noreen Overman. Betsy Thibodeaux sent a lovely card and a clipping from the headlines the day of Lattie Kate's birth, and Maveen, Latrice's cousin, sent Lattie Kate's horoscope.

Then Etta came across a letter from Corinne Salyer. There was no return address, but the handwriting was that of a woman, and Etta opened it, looked at the signature at the bottom of the page, and saw Corinne's name. She jumped up and hurried to the kitchen, where Latrice was mixing headache powders.

"Did you know I had a letter from Corinne? When did it come?"

"Last week, I believe, 'long with the rest."

"You should have given it to me," Etta said, now scanning the letter.

"You were busy learnin' to be a mother last week. What does it say?"

"Well . . . she says she's leavin' town, like Alice told us. She's gonna stay with her mother for a while in Wichita Falls and then maybe go to Dallas." Etta read aloud: "I hope it will be better for both of us if I go. And here's a parting gift—I heard the other day that you have cattle you can't sell without a loss. You should see Bill Flowers. Back last winter, he contracted to buy cattle from Roy." She signed her name with a flourish.

Etta cast Latrice a puzzled look. "Contracted to buy cattle from Roy? What does that mean?"

Latrice frowned. "I think that means this Flowers person was supposed to buy the cattle at a set price. But I really don't know."

"I'd better ask Johnny," Etta said and went flying out the door, looking for Johnny or Obie, certain either could tell her.

Both men were out behind the barn, where Obie was preparing the old tractor to cut the alfalfa, and Johnny was standing nearby holding tools in the same inept manner he would have held surgical instruments.

Etta showed Johnny the letter and hovered at his elbow, watching his face as he read it.

"Well, now . . ." His eyes came up to hers, and a small smile spread over his face. "You may have just made a bit of money, Miz Etta."

"How . . . what does it mean?"

Passing the letter to Obie, he carefully explained to her, "Bill Flowers is a broker, buys and sells cattle hereabouts. He likely contracted with your husband to buy the cattle at a set price on a set day. And likely he hasn't stepped forward, 'cause he stands to lose a bit of money, prices bein' what they are."

"He ain't stepped forward 'cause he's a crooked son-of-a-gun," Obie said. "Miz Etta, you might best go see if you can find a copy of that contract in Mr. Roy's papers."

She looked from Obie to Johnny, then whipped around and went flying back to the house, through the kitchen, and on to the den, with Latrice coming in her wake. Immediately, tossing things topsy-turvy, they searched the single file and desk drawers.

"There's a lot here to be thrown away," Latrice said, coming upon receipts dating from ten years before.

"I found it!" Etta exclaimed, actually before she was totally certain it was the contract she was looking for. She checked the date and saw the name of Bill Flowers. She waved the paper at Latrice and ran to holler out the back door at Johnny, who was just then coming across the yard. "I found it! Let's go."

Twenty minutes later she was getting into Johnny's truck, with Latrice saying, "You have about two hours, and you'd better get back here to this baby."

"Take care of my angel," Etta said, blowing a kiss to the baby. She smoothed her dress—the one Heloise had given her, and she really was going to have to get another one—and waved at Latrice and Obie standing side by side on the porch.

Her gaze lingered there with them and her baby in Latrice's arms, experiencing a surge of hope in her life. Then she faced forward, clutching the contract in her hands. *I can do this*, she thought. Then: *And Johnny is here to help me*.

The last thought seemed foolish, contradictory to what she felt she needed to be learning to do, but she did not feel up to figuring it all out. She gazed ahead with nervous anticipation.

Johnny knew who Bill Flowers was and that he had an office at the local stockyards. Other than that, he held no personal knowledge of the man, although from this situation he had formed the loose opinion that the man appeared less than forthcoming and was taking advantage of a widow.

During the drive Etta made comments, such as, "It won't pay the mortgage, but at least it will clear the debt for the cattle. Maybe it's a mistake, though. Maybe he and Roy canceled the contract. I shouldn't count on it until we see. Do you think he'll give me a check straightaway?"

Johnny made appropriate answers, but he could tell Etta was so excited and nervous that she didn't half-hear him. She kept chewing on her bottom lip and looking at the contract and skipping all over with her comments from the cattle to the weather to needing to get back to Lattie Kate within two hours to nurse her.

Johnny would just as soon she not mention nursing because that made him feel very awkward.

As it was, he could not seem to keep from noticing things about her, like her larger breasts and curvy hips. He wished his imagination was not so keen. It seemed like he had to struggle so hard not to think certain thoughts that sweat popped out on his forehead.

When he pulled to a stop, Johnny cut the engine, glanced at the clapboard building that housed the sale barn offices and then at Etta, who was looking apprehensively at the building.

"Would you like me to go in and take care of it?" he asked.

The sale barn was pretty much a male domain. There

were a couple of women secretaries, and on occasion a woman might come to do business, but generally she would be a woman who had done so all her life. He was quite certain Etta had never set foot in a stockyard sale barn.

But she shook her head. "No," and opened the door.

Johnny hurried around to help her out of the cab. She shook wrinkles out of the skirt of her flowered dress, and looked again at the white clapboard building.

She said, "I guess I would appreciate if you went with me, though."

Her wanting him made him feel good. He nodded, falling in step beside her, leaning ahead to open the door and putting a hand to her back as they went down the hallway.

"Let's take a look at the prices," he said and led her over to the board and pointed to the price they were looking for. Etta peered at it, looked down and checked the amount on the contract, then looked at him with wide eyes.

Tickled almost to laughing, Johnny said, "You're gonna make a profit, Miz Etta," then put a hand to her back and directed her toward Bill Flowers's office. It only just then occurred to him that the man might not be in, a concern he decided not to mention.

Bill Flowers was there, jawing and laughing with some fellows. Etta might not have known who he was, but by his expression Johnny could tell Flowers sure enough recognized her; as Johnny made the introductions, the man stared at Etta about like he'd seen a ghost. The two men with him nodded politely and made quick goodbyes.

Johnny looked at Flowers and took it upon himself to say, "I believe you owe Missus Rivers for cattle you had contracted to buy about six weeks ago."

Etta stepped forward and handed Flowers the contract. "I found this in Roy's papers."

Bill Flowers cleared his throat and looked curious as he took the contract. "Well, what have you got here?"

He appeared not to understand as he read. Then he started rubbing the back of his neck, as if thinking very hard of how to get out of this hole because paying for the cattle was going to cost him terribly.

"I forgot all about this . . . I sure did, and I'm sorry, Miz Rivers. My secretary quit on me 'bout then, and everythin's been in a mess."

"I'd like a check," Etta said very simply and making Johnny have to choke back a laugh. "And you can come get the cattle anytime you want. There's two new ones, too," she added.

The man started to hem and haw about prices, trying his best to come up with a way out of it, but then his gaze met Johnny's. With a resigned sigh, he sat down and opened his big checkbook. "You're gettin' a good profit. I guess Roy knew what he was doin' after all," he said as he handed Etta the check, acting as if he wanted to jerk it back.

"Yes," Etta said. "Sometimes Roy knew exactly what he was doing, and no one expected it. Thank you."

She turned for the door, and Bill Flowers called after her that he'd send a couple of trucks for the cattle.

Walking so swiftly that Johnny had to hurry to catch up to her, she burst out of the office doors.

Whirling around to face him, she cried, "Oh, Johnny!" in a way that made his heart fly up. The next instant she was hugging him, and he felt her warm feminine body beneath his hands, smelled her fragrant hair, for an instant before she was racing away to his truck.

"We have to go to the bank right now," she cried. "I have only a little over an hour before I have to get back to feed Lattie Kate."

Etta was kept a good many minutes waiting to see Edward Boatwright. This gave her more time to compose exactly what she wished to say to him, but it was also time that her breasts kept filling with milk, and she began to get very nervous. When at last she was shown into his office, she sat on the edge of the chair, gazing at Edward, who looked back at her and not at all inviting.

"Leon tells me you don't want to sell the house, Etta. He said you have decided to keep it and a section of land, but what he didn't say was how you plan to pay the bank."

Etta passed him the check she'd received from Bill Flowers, and then everything she'd planned to say came rushing out like a river, how she hoped to sell the land to pay off the biggest part of the mortgage, and then how she planned to raise horses—not fancy stock like Roy had done, but solid ranch and rodeo stock, and to operate the place as a stable and sell hay. She did not plan to be rich, but to live simply and quietly and provide for Lattie Kate.

"I can go back to waitressing, too, and if you'll let me make small payments, I know I can repay the loan."

When she was finished, she realized how tense she had become and made herself sit straight but relaxed. She thought she ought to have learned something from Roy about maintaining composure while going after what she wanted.

Edward stared at her for a long moment, probably the longest he had ever looked at her. There was actually no expression on his face. She had the disconcerting thought that his expression might be the same if he were dead. Yet she felt suddenly his power, and she forced herself to look him straight in the eye. She was not helped at that particular moment by the realization that her breasts had begun to ache.

He leaned forward, folding his hands together on top of the desk. "I have no problem with you sellin' off the land in parcels. Likely you will get more for it that way than if it is auctioned as a whole. But the mortgage is overdue now, and I really don't foresee that it is in your interest to be payin' on the mortgage for the rest of your life, which could happen with the interest accruing like it is. The debt is gettin' larger with every day. Do you understand this, Etta?"

She nodded. She did understand, although she hadn't really thought of it. "When I sell all the land and pay that on the loan, can we then refigure for the house? And if anything happens to me, it would be the same—the bank could take the house."

Edward gazed at her again. "How much time do you want?"

"Oh." She swallowed, thinking, "Six months . . . six months to get on my feet."

"To get on your feet." He smiled wryly, "No wonder you married Roy. You believe in miracles."

She did not care for his sarcasm, but she didn't think she was in a position to make a lot of it. "No," she said. "I'm just not one for givin' up."

Again his cool blue eyes rested thoughtfully on her, and she figured he was going to say that there was no way. She was already so far behind; it was not likely she could ever catch up.

"The only smart thing Roy ever did was marry you," he said, to Etta's great amazement. "You're right about not givin' up—you showed that when you stayed with him. And that's what makes me inclined to go with you now." He nodded. "Okay. Let's see how much land you can sell in three months. That's the best I can do."

Stunned, she gazed at him, thinking she may have misunderstood him. And she had questions.

But Edward said brusquely, "Go on and get busy. You got land to sell and money to raise, and three months go fast," and turned his attention to folders in front of him, pushing the buzzer for his secretary, as if he was ready to forget all about Etta.

She turned and hurried out, halfway expecting him to call her back even as she softly shut the door. She walked through the lobby and out the door, stood blinking in the bright light, peering down the sidewalk in search of Johnny. She saw him waiting, leaning against his truck parked at the curb. She walked toward him, and he opened the truck door for her. She started to get inside, then paused and looked over the top of the door at him.

"Edward's given me three months more to sell land and catch up some of the mortgage," she said.

"Well, that's what you were wantin'."

"I asked for six," she told him absently as she slipped into the truck seat.

Johnny shut the door, came around and started them for home. Etta decided that she didn't want to pick up the conversation again because what was on her mind was to ask if he was going to stay and help her. Her pride held her quiet on that score.

But she was so wound up over her meeting with Edward that she ended up telling Johnny about it, in short sentences which made what had transpired sound all choppy. At last she fell silent and looked away out the window, watching the passing scenery and wondering about her mood, which had begun declining.

Only a few minutes ago, she had been so excited. Now, thinking of it, she began to feel overwhelmed. What had she done? If she could not pay back the bank, they could take the farm from her. She'd have nothing then. She and Lattie Kate and Latrice would be destitute and all alone.

She suddenly felt so sad and tired, and what was more, her breasts had grown very hard and painful. She sat as still as possible, hoping to prevent them from leaking all over her dress front and embarrassing her to pieces—and Johnny, too.

The very next morning Fred Grandy called to say that Walter Fudge had made an offer on the section of land to the east that bordered his own property. The price he offered to pay was a hundred dollars an acre less than what the land was worth. Etta decided to discuss the matter with Johnny before she answered.

"It's your place, Miz Etta. You have to decide."

"I know that," she said, annoyed at his reticence.

She followed after him as he strode down the barn alleyway to a stall. "I'm askin' your opinion."

He reached to open the top of the stall door, stopped, turned, and looked at her. "You can sell now, and have the money hard and fast, or you can wait the man out. Do you think he wants it more than you want to sell it?"

"Well, he wants it—he's wanted it for years. But he doesn't need it as badly as I need to sell it."

"Probably nobody is gonna need or want it that bad," Johnny said dryly, going on into the stall and putting the halter on one of Harry Flagg's horses.

Etta knew that was so. "He's the only one who's been interested, too," she said, hardly aware of speaking out loud.

Johnny went on with his attention on the horse, haltering him and stroking his neck. Experiencing a sinking feeling, Etta turned and walked away down the barn aisle.

Then Johnny's voice came after her. "You know . . . if Fudge has wanted that land for years, he's likely to still want it a couple of months from now."

Etta paused, looked back at him, and then headed on to the house, her stride getting faster and firmer as she went. Immediately she telephoned Fred Grandy and told him to tell Walter that she could not take his offer, that he would have to come up to a fair price. She added, "Fred, if you can't find a buyer for my land in the next two months, I'm goin' to go with a different realtor."

Fred said something about an agreement with Leon, and Etta told him righteously that he would have to see Leon about any agreement, but that she expected results.

After she hung up, she sat there once more feeling herself sink into a blue mood. Her tone of voice had been rude to Fred.

It was, she thought, the effect of desperation over money so overcoming her that her virtue was leaking out and turning her into a rude individual. Money troubles could make one go clean out of one's mind. This low and disturbing thought mushroomed in her imaginaion, until she saw a picture of herself like her mother, spending afternoons in a ratty dress at the movie theater, eating popcorn and growing fat, and then going out and wrecking a car and killing herself, leaving Lattie Kate motherless.

Jumping to her feet, she went to ask Latrice if she would go shopping in town with her and help with Lattie Kate, who Etta would rather take along. For some reason, the image of herself in a ratty dress had lodged in her mind. If she could correct nothing else, she was determined to be dressed nicely.

Latrice was so taken with the idea of shopping that she

telephoned her cousin Freddy right away to come as soon
as possible in his taxi.

That evening, when Etta came down to help with supper,
she found Latrice wearing a new blue dress. "You weren't
the only one shoppin'," Latrice said.

Etta had known Latrice had been shopping, too, but she
had not seen Latrice buy the dress, nor had she ever seen
Latrice wear one so pale blue. She even had black onyx
earrings dangling from her ears.

Etta herself was wearing a new dress and had her hair
curled and upswept. She was very curious to see Johnny's
expression when he saw her, but when he came up, he held
out a bouquet of yellow wildflowers, and her eyes so focused on them that she forgot to see his reaction at seeing
her.

"They're a little wilted," he said, as indeed they were
drooping sadly.

"Wildflowers do that—they'll be fine when I get them
in water."

She took them so quickly that she practically dragged
him into the house on the wake of the fast-moving air.

She put the vase of flowers on the table, where her eyes
had to slide by them every time she looked at him.

Obie also came bearing a gift—banty hens and a chicken
coop for them, too, which he brought in the back of his old
truck. Latrice was thrilled, although she would not let herself act like it.

"I'm not messin' around chickens and an old coop in
my new dress, Obie Lee."

He responded with something that Etta could not hear,
but she saw Latrice blush, something she had rarely in her
lifetime seen. It was truly an eventful evening, Etta thought,
moved almost to tears.

After the meal, Johnny asked Etta if she would like to
drive into town for some ice cream. She nursed Lattie Kate
and left her with Latrice and Obie, again working with
words from the newspaper crossword puzzle, then drove
off with Johnny into town to a drive-in ice cream shop. She

had a hot fudge sundae, and he had a banana split. They shared, each feeding the other spoonfuls, while talking about horses and books and music and all manner of things that were of no importance but gave them something to say while they each tried to read the other's true thoughts.

They also took every opportunity to touch. Etta wiped a napkin where she missed Johnny's mouth with the spoonful of fudge, and he dabbed one where he dropped cherry sauce on her dress. Once he brought his hand up and brushed the back of his knuckles on her ear.

A minute after that she said, "I think we need to get back. Lattie Kate may be cryin' for me."

"Okay." He started the truck and headed it out on the highway.

The summer night air blew in, and she shivered. He put his hand up around her shoulders and drew her close, into his heat and his scent.

When he turned into the drive, Johnny came to a stop before passing beneath the darkness of the trees. He turned off the engine and the lights, saying, "The stars are really bright."

They looked up through the windshield at the stars, marveling at them. Etta was seeing the stars but having a hard time paying attention, and she did not think Johnny was thinking about stars, either. A sudden shyness overcame her, and she couldn't look at him, until he sat back, and she felt his eyes on her.

Then they were gazing at each other. She waited, and Johnny put a hand on her cheek and kissed her. She thought she might split right in two from the sweet desire that welled up from her belly and went out her lips. She was filled with his scent all summery and male, and she could not seem to move her hands. It was as if she had gone suddenly paralyzed, except for her mouth and between her legs, which seemed to give little jumps.

Johnny took a breath and kissed her again, deeply, causing a flame to burst in her belly and lick up her ribs. She strained toward him, wishing to press the length of him, while he just kept kissing her and kissing her and taking her breath and her senses.

He lifted his head, and they were both gasping, and Etta was trembling so hard she could not control it.

She couldn't look at him, and then she found herself staring at his crotch, which so unnerved her that she closed her eyes tight. The next instant Johnny's hand was stroking downward, along the skin of her neck and further, to brush her breast and then to hold it, and Lord a'mercy, she felt it tingle, just like the milk was letting down!

She got very still, and he did, too, as if he sensed she was about to go to pieces. Or maybe he was, too. She looked at him, and found him gazing at her with eyes so hungry she could not bear it. In that moment she would have spread her legs and taken him then and there.

He swallowed and said, "I'd better get you home."

Etta realized she had gone a little crazy. She nodded and tried to deal with the desire roaring inside her. It was a stunning thing to realize she could feel so strong a desire. She could not recall ever feeling this before in her entire life, and all he'd touched were her lips and her cheek and the side of her breast, both of which were beginning to feel damp.

Latrice had forgotten to turn on the porch light, and Johnny was glad. He felt the need to stay in shadow.

He walked Etta up to the door, and he just had to kiss her again, but he touched her only with his lips. As she went inside, he thought that it should help that she wanted him, too, but it just made it all worse.

He had not intended what had happened this night. He had considered kissing her and told himself that would be unwise, and the next thing he had been kissing her. It was unnerving to have gotten so carried away. It made him think he was capable of something like killing a person and not even knowing it.

The following day, when he and Obie went to sit in the shade after helping with the final load of Etta's cattle into one of the two-ton trucks Bill Flowers had sent for them,

Johnny asked the older man how long a woman had to wait after she had a baby. The most he knew about this were crude remarks he'd heard but had never taken as actual fact, and that a mare would be brought to a stud one week after giving birth to a foal in order to breed again.

"Wait for what?" Obie asked, mopping his forehead with a handkerchief. He asked the question to tease; he knew exactly what Johnny was talking about and was experiencing both amusement and anger.

"You know . . . a man."

Johnny thought Obie was teasing, but he figured he had better be specific, if he wanted a correct answer. Even so, he was embarrassed by his lack of knowledge, and also by revealing himself so much. Now Obie would know he was both uninformed and hot for Etta. He ducked his head and focused on getting a drink of water out of the hose.

Obie waited for him to finish and look up. "That's Miz Etta you're talkin' about," the older man stated.

Johnny didn't say anything.

Obie said, "Well, the doctor's general word is six weeks, but I knows a lot of folks don't wait so long.

"My second oldest brother got impatient before three weeks, and I'm here to tell you he got his wife pregnant again, purely disprovin' that old wives' tale 'bout a baby at the breast keepin' one out of the womb. So, boy, you'd best be rememberin' that, too, and make damn sure you do somethin' about it. Miz Etta done had enough trouble without you makin' more. I'll go further and tell you, you get that gal knocked up and I'll kick your ass from here to the river, and don't think I can't do it."

Johnny believed Obie could whip his ass, and he found a tale about a nursing woman not being able to get pregnant awfully farfetched, considering mares. It hurt that Obie could think so poorly of him, too, after all this time.

He said, "Obie, I've asked Etta to marry me."

Obie's eyebrows went up, then his eyes narrowed. "Did you need to know how long to wait to get married?"

Johnny shook his head. "She didn't say yes. It's all pretty complicated."

"I sort of imagined that, I guess," Obie said wryly. "Miz Etta'd have a hard time lookin' trustfully on another man, after Mr. Roy."

"I suppose that's it, but mostly it's that she doesn't want to leave this place, and I want us to move and build a place together."

Obie gazed at him thoughtfully. "Well, son, gettin' Miz Etta to move from here might be a pretty good job. You'd probably do better to just settle down and, well, concentrate on just what you were concentratin' on before. You'll get that afore you get her to move off from here."

Johnny thought Obie could be right. He figured Etta cared a lot more about this place than she did him. Thinking drearily of it, he picked a blade of grass and began to strip it.

He wanted his own place, and at the same time he didn't want to leave here. But the thought of marrying Etta and sticking here sort of chilled him to the bone.

Johnny figured he was in big confusion about the entire thing.

"Would you come with me, Obie? If I can find a place, will you come partner in buildin' it?"

He thought if he could at least get Obie to come, Etta would think of following. And he just couldn't do it alone, in any case. If he left here alone, he'd just be drifting again.

"Ah, John . . ." Obie shook his head. "I'm gettin' old for that kind of physical work. And 'sides, I ain't got much of any money to contribute."

"You got yourself. I'll need help, and I'll tell you, Etta sure isn't gonna come without you and Latrice."

Obie looked at him a long minute. "I'll think about it. And I appreciate the offer," he added, his dark eyes glowing softly.

He looked at the house. "But I have to tell you, Etta and Latrice stay here, I'll stay here. Otherwise, I might get myself on up to Okie City. I've been thinkin' on that. I've got a brother up there runs a good barbeque joint, and he's been askin' me to come help expand it. I can cook barbeque." He added ruefully, "That's my own damn recipe for that barbeque that my brother's been usin' for five years now, and he's makin' a pile from it.''

Johnny found the thought of them all going their separate ways depressing. It seemed to him that these people had become his family. He swiftly got so depressed over it that he almost could not move. He wished very much for a bottle of whiskey and thought that when he could find the strength to stand up, he would go and get one.

Then Obie took a foot and prodded him. ''Get up, boy, and go bounce your balls around on one of those horses you're supposed to be teachin' some good sense. Bounce around on them enough today, and you won't be worryin' so much about what you and Miz Etta can be doin' tonight.''

Not wanting Obie to realize the low state of his mood, Johnny shot him a grin and got to his feet. He spent the rest of the afternoon riding hard and fast, thinking there was merit in what Obie had said and hoping to be so tired and battered come nightfall that he wouldn't be able to think about either whiskey or what he wanted to do with Etta.

Also it was truth that a horse could generally take his mind off anything else in this world. He was a horseman.

Twenty-one

At Overman's Grocery and the feed store and in the newspaper, Etta posted notices of boarding services and the availability of a horse trainer. She calculated the alfalfa already baled, figured what the entire season would bring, and judged how much she could safely sell. A lot of this seemed pure conjecture on her part and quite risky business. Obie told her that was the nature of farming.

"When it comes to growin' things, Miz Etta, a lot of it is just trustin' it will work out. It's just that way."

It occurred to Etta that a lot of life was lived the same way, so she might as well get used to it.

Harry Flagg bought all the alfalfa she would sell him, and then he sent around a man who rented a section of land from her to run his cattle on. Fred Grandy brought a prospective buyer around, but the man did not make an offer, and Walter Fudge held his peace.

Obie, with Nathan Lee's help—Nathan Lee was something of an artist—built and painted a very classy sign with the silhouette of a horse in the middle, the words Rivers Stables arched at the top, and Horses Boarded and Trained below the silhouette. Below that Etta had Obie paint Johnny's name as trainer, and they saved this as a surprise on the day they erected the sign up near the road.

Johnny didn't react as Etta had wished, though. She stood there with Lattie Kate on her shoulder, watching his face in anticipation. But he didn't say a word and acted as if he hadn't even seen. She kept waiting for him to see, but he just finished tamping the dirt in around each post, then gathered the shovels and unused bag of concrete and threw it all into the back of Obie's battered truck, where it fell with loud clattering and thudding.

It was hot, Etta thought, and he'd had to dig one of the posts and was now pouring with sweat. She wondered if perhaps he hadn't seen his name, had simply stared without seeing, like a person could do when they were very hot.

"Did you read the sign, Johnny?" she asked.

He looked at her then. "I saw it." He glanced at little Nathan Lee, who was staring at him. "It's a real nice sign, too." Then to Obie, "You ready? I need to get back for Miz English's lesson."

Obie looked at Etta.

"Y'all go on," she said. "I want to get the mail. I'll walk up."

The black truck chugged away up the drive, and little spirals of dust rose behind the back tires.

Etta took her eyes from the dust spirals and looked again at the sign. Obie had done four layers of enamel white, and it shone in the sun. The deep blue, not black, lettering came from stencils to get just the right shape. Etta's eyes lingered on Johnny's name.

He had not seemed to be in a good humor lately, she thought. She supposed she hadn't either. She wanted what she wanted, and he wanted what he wanted, and there was only one thing they each wanted together, and this one thing had all kinds of problems attached to it.

Lattie Kate squirmed and emitted an impatient cry. Etta shifted her from one shoulder to another, thinking that it was nearing time for her precious angel to eat. Etta at times felt like an overworked cow, although Lattie Kate had extended her time between nursing to almost three and a half hours. At five weeks of age she was growing quite fat.

Etta turned to walk toward the mailbox, but upon seeing

the white Buick approaching along the highway, she stopped and waited. She was fifty feet from the driveway, but she did not trust the woman behind the wheel of the Buick—it was the Miz English Johnny had referred to, who was really named Mrs. Winslow, and her daughter Amy, come for their riding lessons. Mrs. Winslow, a very prosperous woman, drove as if she owned not only the road but the universe. Etta was certain she could, and possibly had, mowed people down and never even known it.

The white Buick turned into the drive, one rear wheel narrowly missing the ditch, and sped toward the house, while hands came out the windows and waved. Etta waved back, but the car was already halfway up the drive by then.

In the two weeks since posting her notices, she had rented boarding space to Mrs. Winslow/English, the wife of an oil geologist from Pennsylvania, and Mr. Hornbuckle, a retired farmer.

Mrs. Winslow/English had ridden as a girl and wanted to introduce her daughter to the sport—English riding, to Johnny's annoyance, and the reason he called her Miz English. To Johnny's further annoyance, her horses were thoroughbreds, but he sought to accommodate her, as she was not only renting stalls and buying feed from Etta but willing to pay Johnny for lessons.

Etta felt a little sorry for the daughter, who was overwhelmed by her forceful mother and also quite afraid of horses. Etta would walk out and watch through the training pen fence, and in her new capacity as a mother, she would give the girl encouraging smiles whenever possible. Johnny was very good with the child, and within her first week of riding, he'd had her gaining confidence. By her third lesson she was experimenting with letting go the front of the saddle and had taken to grabbing the horse's mane instead.

Johnny went around asking people what they knew about English riding, and each night he sat at the kitchen table, poring over books about it and discussing his findings with Etta, who was not a lot of help, for she knew nothing about English riding. She read with him, however, and sought to boost him as much as possible.

Etta glanced at the mail she pulled from the box. Right on top was an envelope from Mr. Hornbuckle. His first payment for boarding his old mare, Etta thought appreciatively.

Mr. Hornbuckle was an elderly man who'd brought his beloved gray mare to Etta's stable when he recently sold his country home and moved into town. So far he came every couple of days to visit the mare but had ridden her only once out in the pasture.

They still had two stalls in the barn Etta would like to fill, and just that day a man had telephoned from up in Canadian County, asking to speak to Johnny about taking on a racehorse he had that had been crazed by a barn fire. It appeared that Johnny's name as a trainer was spreading.

Etta was excited and pleased for Johnny, but she was rather unsettled for herself. It appeared that their relationship was in great question, neither of them certain of what move to make.

Twice more Johnny had brought her wildflowers, and she had baked his favorite peanut butter cookies. They had gone on short dates, into town to get ice cream or cold drinks, a drive to a ranch to see prospective colts for sale.

On occasion they would touch. His hand might brush hers as she handed him a glass of ice tea, or she would lay her hand on his shoulder when passing behind him at the table, or his shoulder would press hers when he came up beside her at the corral fence.

Once he had kissed her there at the fence. They had been standing and talking about purchasing breeding stock. Their eyes met, and Johnny leaned down and kissed her, swiftly and touching her only with his lips. Another time she had gotten carried away when they were alone in the kitchen, and she had leaned over his shoulder, looking at something in one of his books, and the next thing she had been kissing him.

They had not, however, spoken another word about getting married or what was going on between them.

Time and time again she would find him looking at her with his steely gray eyes. He seemed to be waiting for her.

She knew he wanted her. She wondered if he still wanted to marry her. Was he waiting for her to say she would go with him? She wouldn't, and this made her very sad.

That Johnny would leave had become one of Etta's big fears. She had seen him scanning the real-estate section of the classified ads. One morning he had brought the paper to breakfast, and she'd seen an ad circled when he'd left the paper by his plate. It was for a small farm down in Cotton County, house and hay barn on a half-section of land. He had wanted her to see the ad, of course, and she had carefully pretended not to see it.

She realized, though, that if he did leave, she would be heartbroken.

Having her heart so thoroughly broken by Roy made her terrified; she thought she might die if she got her heart broken again. This fear had opposing effects on her, causing her at times to reject all her feelings for Johnny, and at other times causing her to want to throw herself at him, do anything to make him stay.

Then she would get hold of herself and realize she was reacting to the situation in a manner similar to the way she had with Roy. She knew that way she would lose herself. Much larger than the fear of Johnny leaving and causing her to have a broken heart was the fear of losing the self she was at last finding.

She walked up the tree-shaded driveway and let herself in the front door. It was cool in the living room, with windows providing a pleasant cross-breeze. She sat on the sofa to feed Lattie Kate and look through the mail. The bills were fewer these days. People were smiling at her now when she came into their stores, asking her how she and Lattie Kate and Latrice were getting along.

They were getting by, just barely, but they were not paying off the mortgage. Etta tried not to worry over it, most especially when she nursed Lattie Kate.

She came to a long white envelope—from Robert Lamb, the estate liquidator. She tore it open, and a check fell out onto Lattie Kate's belly. The next instant the breeze lifted the check and seemed to wave it in the air in front of her face, before depositing it on the couch beside her. Etta smacked it with her hand, then lifted it and looked at it, then at the note accompanying it.

Clutching Lattie Kate to her breast, Etta jumped up and ran to the kitchen.

"The bedroom set sold," she told Latrice, who was altering an old dress of Etta's. "It sold for three thousand dollars!" She tossed the check down in front of Latrice.

"Well, that Robert Lamb is a sweet-talkin' man." Latrice gave the check a highly approving look.

"Are you gonna put all the money on the mortgage?" Latrice asked, after Etta had dragged over the rocker to finish nursing Lattie Kate, who had properly thrown a hissy fit about her meal being interrupted.

"No." Etta shook her head thoughtfully. "If I'm gonna start raisin' rodeo stock, I've got to buy some."

Latrice looked at her. "You take some of this and you save it in the bank for an emergency."

"What do you think we're livin', if it's not an emergency?"

"You put some aside, for the rest of your life, so that you don't ever get stuck again," Latrice said. "So that you can feel a slice of freedom."

Looking at her, Etta said, "You're right. I'll put some of it aside . . . but I've got to buy some breeding stock."

For an instant her thoughts flashed back to the day she had been told Roy had died. It seemed so long ago, much more than months she could count on her hand. She saw herself, how frightened she had been, cowering in her bed and fearful that her entire world was crumbling around her, which it was. It had crumbled and it remained that way.

Her position was not greatly changed. She was still trying to hold on to her place and provide a home for herself and her child and Latrice. What had changed was herself.

Latrice spoke of putting money away for a bit of security, but Etta thought the only true security a person had was in her ability to cope. One could not prevent sadness or tragedy from coming into one's life, and one could not help but make mistakes, too, which seemed a quite frustrating fact of existence. One could, however, develop the ability to cope with it all.

Etta felt she was at last getting ahead in learning to cope.

She rocked Lattie Kate at her breast, and Latrice finished her sewing and took up the Sunday paper, which she had not gotten to read on Sunday, and read aloud items of interest, which she and Etta discussed in soft voices, laughing now and again.

That night at supper Johnny spoke of their choices of Fourth of July rodeos that would have racing opportunities. He'd also learned of some good breeding stock that Etta needed to look at. He had found all this out at the feed store that morning. Whenever Johnny went to the feed store, he always had a lot to talk about. Everything from the price of grain to the sale of stock to who was sick, who was in debt or jail or having an affair.

"People just tell me things," he said with some perplexity. "Today all I did was say a polite hello to Gabe Pickett, and the next thing I knew he was tellin' me how his father has been pesterin' women at the rest home, so they had to tie him down. Now, I really don't want to be privy to stuff like that, but people just tell me, like I want to know."

Etta thought that Johnny did like knowing. He liked to be able to tell the story later, and usually they all wanted to listen.

"What about the Fourth?" she prodded him, anxious to get back to the subject of racing Little Gus. Johnny tended to get off on tangents.

"I'd like to take him up to Woodward, but that's a long drive," he said, frowning. "Anadarko's closer, and there'll be good racin' there—more than before. But we're gonna have to find someone to ride for us. I found out this mornin' that Woody's gone down to Bonham and he's goin' on to Fort Worth and maybe Waco after that. He won't be back for at least a month. I've been askin' around, and I've gotten the names of a few fellas who might could ride for us."

He and Obie started discussing these few fellows, and

Etta looked from one man to the other, listening.

"I can ride Little Gus now," she said.

Both men's eyes swung to her, Obie's coffee-dark and Johnny's shimmering silver. Etta gazed at Johnny, and he gazed back with a somewhat stunned expression.

"I haven't raced," she said, "but I used to gallop some of the horses Roy and I were getting ready for sale. I can ride pretty well. And I want to learn to barrel race, anyway."

She watched Johnny's gaze flicker down her body and then quickly back up, splotches blooming on his cheeks and making Etta feel self-conscious. His steely gray eyes held hers, and she knew he was thinking about more than riding, just as she was.

Then slowly Johnny nodded. "You just got to get him to run, and he's willin' to do that." He raised an eyebrow. "You know it can get a little dangerous? Gus is a pretty steady son-of-a-buck, but some horses you might race with can be crazy."

"I know," Etta said with a nod, "but it's been my hope all along to ride him. And I do seem to be the most logical choice."

Johnny, sighing and laying his napkin on the table, said, "Well, if you're gonna ride this weekend, we need to get you some practice. You ready to start tonight?"

He didn't wait for an answer but was already rising and reaching for his hat. Etta jumped up, saying that she would be only a few minutes, and then she hurried upstairs to change clothes, only to be confronted with the fact that she still could not button any of her riding pants.

Throwing the last pair on the floor, she was about to despair when her gaze lit on the laundry on the line in the backyard—Johnny's three pairs of jeans blowing stiffly in the breeze. She called down the back stairs to Latrice to please get them.

The first pair she tried fit fine, a little loose but a belt solved that problem, and his inseam was the same as her own. Quite satisfied, Etta nursed Lattie Kate, then handed her to Latrice, grabbed up her old brown hat, and raced out the door to Johnny and Little Gus waiting in the training pen.

Johnny didn't appear to look at her, so she could not tell if he noticed that it was his pants she was wearing.

"I think we should start in the pen and see how it goes," he told her, as if to forestall any protest on her part.

She said, "Fine," and took Little Gus by the reins.

She caressed his neck, anticipation rising in her chest. The time had come at last, and she hadn't even realized it until there at the supper table.

Automatically she checked the tightness of the girth strap before swinging up into the saddle. Little Gus stood there, and she felt his tenseness as he awaited instruction. The late sun hit her, and the breeze tugged at her hat. She shifted her buttocks and legs, getting the memory of her seat, and the horse pranced. Having been conditioned to run, he anticipated the command. Easily he walked, and then he trotted, and then Etta kicked his side, sending him loping around the pen. His trot was hard and bouncing, but his lope was as if he changed into a winged creature. He seemed to float above the ground, and there atop him, Etta's spirit began to fly, up and up and up.

"He's beautiful," she called to Johnny.

The next instant Johnny threw open the gate, and Etta and Little Gus shot out, across the yard and straight for the open pasture track, never slowing.

It had been so long since she had enjoyed this pleasure, and she reveled in it. Reveled in the power and beauty of the horse beneath her and the wind on her face, the turquoise sky stretching above and the golden glow of the evening sun on the trees and hills.

She thought she could gallop forever, but eventually she and Little Gus came to a sharp turn in the road at the fence line, and she brought him down because she was a little afraid of the turn. She had always been afraid of turns when galloping. She would have to get over that, but she didn't think she needed to do so immediately.

For that moment, she would enjoy the sheer bliss of the time, the place, and the movement. It seemed like she had not ridden in years, instead of months. Well, it had been nearly a year. A really trying year, she thought, except for Lattie Kate. And Johnny.

Thinking of Johnny made her turn Gus for the house.

Johnny was slouched atop the corral railing, when she rode across the yard. The final rays of the sun hit his hat and face and shoulders. She stopped in front of him.

"He's wonderful. You have done so well with him," she said, the words coming in a rush.

He didn't smile, and he didn't praise her riding, but something in the way he regarded her made her instantly aware of being a woman. She tightened her legs enough that Little Gus thought they were to run again, and she had to hold him back.

Johnny said, "Well, Miz Etta, I guess you can ride. Now you have to learn how to run him."

Stiffly he climbed down from the fence and started in with directions about how it would be against other horses and how sometimes she would need to hold Little Gus back and know when to let him go. He walked beside her and Little Gus to the pasture road and sent them galloping up and down it for half an hour, until it was getting too dark to see, and Etta told him she had to get back to Lattie Kate.

She got stiffly out of the saddle, her legs hurting and buttocks bruised, although she immediately tried to cover the fact. She was also a little annoyed at Johnny's attitude, which was cold and authoritative. Etta never had responded well to an authoritative attitude.

"You'll need to ride every day," he said to her. "You have to learn to push him hard and get him right up into the bit. He likes to run, but sometimes he needs remindin'."

"I'll ride," she said, handing him the reins and turning toward the house.

He caught her wrist and jerked her around, pulled her against him and kissed her fiercely.

In an instant, her annoyance melted away. She wrapped her arms around his neck, crying out from inside, kissing him for all she was worth. When he lifted his head, he would have pulled away, but she would not let him go. She threw herself against him, whispering his name.

"Johnny."

He held her tightly for a moment in which she felt him quivering. Or else it was her own trembling. Then he set her from him.

"You'd better go in to Lattie Kate," he said.

Somewhat stunned, she stepped out toward the house.

Johnny called after her, "You can keep the pants!" and there was amusement in his voice.

"I think I will," Etta returned. "They fit just fine."

Twenty-two 🌹

That night when Etta showered, she found a raw blister on her buttocks. Before riding the next day, she put a bandage over it.

By the third day of running Little Gus up and down the pasture track, she had another blister, but her muscles were stronger and she fit once more into at least one pair of her jeans. For practice, though, she continued to wear Johnny's pants.

Johnny would sit on his golden dun beneath the hackberry tree and watch. He would sit slouched, with his good leg hooked over the horn, peering out from beneath the brim of his hat and calling out directions.

"Learn to feel him. Learn to tell how your weight affects him. Keep right in the middle of his back and out of his way. Get the feel of how tight to hold the reins."

Etta began to believe she would never please him. "Would you just leave me alone? I can't ride with you yelling all that at me!"

She pressed her right leg into Little Gus, and he pivoted, and they ran off down the track, flying over the ground. When Etta returned with Little Gus, she found Johnny sitting there on his horse, waiting.

"You need to figure out when to tap him to push him

up into the bit,'' Johnny said, as if he'd never been interrupted. ''You need to let him build steam, and know when to release him.''

Etta set her jaw and returned to practicing.

On the fourth afternoon, Johnny had Etta riding bareback. He said he thought this would help her get the feel of Little Gus. ''And you might want to race bareback sometimes,'' he added. ''Sometimes you can give the horse an edge without the weight of the saddle.''

Etta was nervous to ride like this, and her nervousness did not help Little Gus. On the second run, she fell off. Little Gus felt her tilting and slowed, so at least she did not go off at a full run. She simply slipped off his side like a rag, while Little Gus circled and looked at her from several feet away, hanging his head, as if he might be in trouble.

Johnny came racing over and jumped down beside her. ''Are you okay?''

''I don't think it is as easy as it used to be, but I'm okay.''

She found it gratifying that he hovered, clearly somewhat undone. She walked over and got Little Gus by the reins. ''Will you give me a boost up?'' she asked, squinting at Johnny, who stood there, looking uncertain. She liked that he worried about her, but she didn't want him to think her incapable.

He came forward and formed his hands into a prop for her foot. She got back on the horse and kept at it because she loved the riding, and because she didn't want Johnny to be disappointed in her. Also, she wanted to win races all over the place.

While Etta practiced, she and Johnny shared the endeavor. He the teacher, she the student, and both reaching for the same end, and both occupied with a goal outside their relationship.

As soon as Etta quit riding for the day, however, it seemed that they would look at each other and be struck shy.

It was be getting more and more tense between them.

Etta would be all hot and her clothes stuck to her, and she would feel Johnny's eyes on her, but when she looked at him, he would avoid meeting her gaze, and she would suddenly find herself uncertain of what to say to him.

She would say normal things like: "I'll wash down Little Gus," or "Will you empty grain sacks into the bin?" while her thoughts revolved around how she would like to touch him and tell him her heart.

She imagined saying, "I think you are a superb horse trainer and a wonderful man, Johnny." And she would imagine him smiling and saying to her, "I've reconsidered, Etta. I think your idea of me staying here and marrying you is a fine idea. Let's just sit on the porch and plan our future together. It is going to be perfect and we will live happily ever after."

What he actually said to her was, "I'd better get started on Harry's horse," and he would take himself off to get up one of the horses. Later in the afternoon, he would drive away on some sort of errand, having his suppers in town and returning late into the night.

Etta wondered where he ate, what he did. She wondered if he was meeting a woman and would imagine him walking down the sidewalk beside a pert woman in heels and red and white dress with a swirling skirt, both of them entering a darkly lit bar and sitting with their hands all over each other.

Having wonderings like this made her get so angry that she ended up slamming cabinet doors.

The morning of the rodeo they were all up before the sun and doing the chores before leaving for the Fourth of July festivities. In addition to the rodeo, there would be a parade and a carnival, a chili cook-off, Indian dancing, and all manner of goings-on. People would come from miles around and stay with relatives or camp on the grounds. The rodeo was to be so big there would be cutting competition and trick riding acts, too.

The plan was to go over in the morning, return home that night, get up again Sunday morning and do it all again, for two full days of holiday. It was all very exciting, and Etta rushed around, trying not to forget anything that would be needed for their comfort. She did not trust Latrice's memory, because Latrice had only reluctantly agreed to go.

"I am a town girl," Latrice said. "Just because I've lived out here for six years does not mean I like the country or rough things like rodeos and smelly animals that go with it."

Still, she went because she was needed to take care of Lattie Kate when Etta rode Little Gus or otherwise got pre-occupied with the rodeo doings. Obie went because Latrice did, and to drive her over he had completely cleaned his old pickup truck and had tuned it up so that it could get up to fifty miles an hour.

"You'd better put these porch chairs in the back of Obie's truck," Etta told Johnny, when they began loading up for the trip. "Latrice will have a fit if we don't have a chair for her."

She went inside and returned with two quilts and Lattie Kate's baby carriage. Johnny grinned at her and said she might as well bring the sofa, too.

"Don't forget to get the new umbrella," Etta told him. "I put it in the shed."

He went off, shaking his head, and Etta turned back to the kitchen. When she looked through the screen door, she paused.

There at the table, loading into the picnic basket the fried chicken and potato salad Latrice had been up since dawn cooking, stood Latrice and Obie side by side. Latrice looked up at Obie, who had come dressed in a starched white shirt and creased khaki trousers, and who had ex-changed his ball cap for a new straw hat for the occasion. Obie bent his head slowly and kissed Latrice.

Etta saw to her astonishment a man and woman kissing with great passion. Quickly she stepped back and waited, her heart pounding in her chest with embarrassment and anxiety as thoughts raced across her mind of what might happen to her life should Latrice finally give in to Obie's love.

When she heard the water running in the sink, she went inside. She couldn't look at Latrice, which didn't matter, because Latrice ordered her to take one of the picnic baskets out to the pickup truck. Obie was leaning on the kitchen counter, charming Latrice with a smile whenever she happened to look his way.

"Help Etta carry out those baskets," Latrice ordered him, and he readily complied, casting a wink at Etta to show he was not bothered by Latrice's brusque manner.

Etta looked at his hands as he lowered the two picnic baskets into the back of his truck. Then she found herself looking at Johnny's hands as he closed the rear of his truck. She wondered what his hands would feel like on her skin.

At the last minute, Etta ran back inside and upstairs to comb her hair and put on lipstick, before coming back down, jumping into the cab beside Johnny and taking Lattie Kate into her arms for the drive. Johnny's hands shifting gears caught her eye, and then she looked upward, meeting his eyes that grinned at her.

Facing forward and holding Lattie Kate firmly, Etta thought excitedly about the day ahead, about getting away from the everyday and enjoying everything with Johnny. And she found herself repeatedly looking at Johnny's hands.

The rodeo grounds, indeed the entire town of Anadarko, swarmed with people and vehicles and horses.

"It's a wonder people aren't being run down or trampled all over the place," Latrice said. "I imagine we'll see plenty of that before it's all over."

She had brought her medical kit in case of emergency, and she voiced what amounted to anticipation that she might be called upon to attend someone. This seemed to mollify her annoyance at having to come. Once she was ensconced in one of the chairs beneath the big umbrella, she was satisfied and indeed interested to watch the sights, which she now expected to be interesting.

"This many people and animals, we're bound to see some good foolishness," she said.

Etta, having grown so excited that she was afraid she

might be one of those acting foolish, contained herself and
even managed to act a little nonchalant as she tagged after
Johnny to get the lay of everything. She saw Sissy Post,
the barrel racer whom she'd met at the previous rodeo and
who had wanted to buy Little Gus. This day the woman
was riding a different horse, a very flashy roan. Sissy, flam-
boyantly dressed in white shirt with fringe from the yoke
front and back, and white pants, gave her a nod, but she
was not an overly friendly person.

For Etta's first race, Johnny entered her in one of a
shorter length, which filled rapidly to thirteen entries. Two
of those were young women, one a girl of no more than
fifteen.

It seemed to Etta that one minute she was sitting there
on top Little Gus and watching a race, and the next she
was lining up to be in one. All the horses and commotion
had Little Gus prancing. It was the first time Etta had been
atop him when he was agitated, and she was agitated, too.
Little Gus and the bay next to him got into it, the bay trying
to kick Little Gus. Etta began to understand a bit of
Johnny's concern about the whole thing. Riding hell-bent
alone on the pasture track was a whole lot different than
on a track alongside other agitated horses and riders of all
types.

They all struggled to get their horses lined up for the lap
and tap start. Etta tried to hold Little Gus steady while she
listened and watched for the signal. She made the mistake
of blinking, and the next instant Little Gus was bounding
forward with all the other horses. It seemed to Etta that he
took off on the fly.

Down the track, people yelling on either side and from
the grandstands, all a roar of sound and color, Etta passing
a rider and riders passing her, and then she panicked to see
many horses' tails in front of her.

Everything went so fast that Etta didn't have time to
think of deliberately pushing Little Gus up into the bit or
to even be afraid of possibly being shoved out of the saddle.
It was over in a matter of seconds, and she'd come in fifth.

Etta was stunned to realize she had lost. Little Gus had

won all the previous races, and in her mind he was going to win forevermore. She vaguely recalled the possibility of him losing crossing her mind, and Johnny mentioning it, but still she had not considered it seriously, so fixed into her consciousness was the image of Little Gus like the red winged horse and herself winning races all over the place.

Now she had lost the race, her entry fee, and the twenty dollars she'd had Johnny wager for her. He'd had a good laugh at her twenty, too, thinking it of scant worth.

The thought of losing that money made her sick. And remembering how happy Johnny had been at Little Gus's previous times of winning, she had trouble going back and facing him. She felt she had let him down.

Johnny said, "It was your first time out—and you didn't come in last. You did okay." Etta could tell by his attitude that he was not surprised at all.

"If you had expected me to lose, you should have warned me and saved me my wager," she said sharply.

She had been angry at herself, and now she was annoyed with Johnny. She was hot and dusty and ready to go home, where she would not further exhibit her foolish tendencies.

"You can't be runnin' home," Johnny said with a shocked expression. "We got Latrice over here, and she isn't gonna take kindly to be jerked away."

This was true. Latrice was now happily chatting with an old friend she had not seen since schooldays, while Obie sat quietly beside her, content to listen to tales about the life of his love when she was young. Etta's news of having lost the race was greeted with the barest of comments, before the three returned to their conversation.

And Etta really didn't want to go home. She was irritated that Johnny wouldn't see this, irritated that he looked so worried.

"I didn't mean it," she said. "I was just lettin' off steam."

"Oh." He looked vastly relieved. And as if to escape something he didn't understand, he eagerly took the opportunity to walk Little Gus and cool him off.

Etta sat in the truck, taking comfort in holding and nursing Lattie Kate. That she knew herself to be a good mother helped her to accept her imperfect riding abilities and foolishness at betting.

When Lattie Kate tired of smiling and sucking and finally fell asleep, Etta laid her in the seat, looked in the mirror and refreshed her lipstick, then slouched on the seat back, thinking that Johnny really should not have let her bet, if he had expected her to lose.

Having risen before five, Etta was dozing when Johnny returned.

"Etta," he said, bringing her up quickly. "Are you ready to ride again? I got you a match race."

He took hold of her hand and told her to come on, although she still hadn't answered him. She was coming fully awake, realizing she must have been dozing for quite some time.

He called for Obie to watch Lattie Kate, whom Johnny himself gathered from the seat. Etta hovered, as she was never certain about Johnny's expertise with the baby; he always seemed a little uncertain when handling Lattie Kate. At this moment, however, in a motion much like handing off a football, he quite capably handed the baby to Obie. Etta put her foot in the stirrup and flung herself atop Little Gus. They started away, Johnny leading the horse, but Etta made him stop and return for her hat. The sun was so bright she could barely open her eyes.

"Who am I racin'?" she asked.

"Sissy Post, that barrel racer."

Etta experienced a slice of alarm followed by increasing curiosity. She wondered if she could beat the woman in a race. She really wanted to beat her. She would be awfully embarrassed if she lost.

A race was about to get under way on the track, and people were calling odds and bets to each other. Little Gus, having had the edge run off him, was no longer agitated and stood calmly, although his ears twitched with interest in the goings-on around him.

Sissy Post rode up, making her horse prance by tapping

it with her spurs, causing it, and herself, to appear quite flashy. "You ready?" she asked.

Etta nodded. She thought that she could be equally as cool and crisp as the other woman.

Johnny sent a message to the announcer's box with word of their match race, and they had to await their turn, as this sort of thing was being done again and again, races being vigorously drawn up between competitors. Harry Flagg and his daughter were holding furious bets again over at his flatbed truck.

It suddenly occurred to Etta to wonder about the wager Johnny had made with Sissy. She had neglected to ask him, and she could not now, as he was talking with several men.

She had been remiss in allowing herself to be dragged along almost like an observer, she thought, and felt a little sick with the memory of the disappointment she had suffered at losing the earlier race. It was not a feeling she wanted to repeat, most especially with this flamboyant, confident woman.

Yet Etta also found a spirit of competition rising in her. This was a revelation, as she had never before felt such a sense of rivalry. Usually she was trying too hard to be refined to pay attention to competitive feelings.

At this moment, the sense of competition caused her heart to beat faster and anticipation to rise at an equal rate to apprehension. She gave up a little prayer for God to understand that she didn't mean to be petty, but she really would like to win. She studied Sissy Post's roan and thought that it seemed a little narrow in the chest.

Then Johnny was leading Little Gus to the track and helping to line him up beside Sissy Post on her roan.

Resting a warm hand on Etta's knee, Johnny beckoned with his callused finger. She leaned toward him. His eyes were bright and shining.

"Little Gus can take that roan," he said. "It's fast, but it'll give out at three hundred feet, and you're gonna go four. Let Little Gus jump out like he does, then hold him while the roan wears himself out getting a length ahead. Then just lean forward and go."

Looking into his eyes, Etta believed every word he said, as if it had all already happened.

The next instant he put his hand to the back of her head, pulled her down and kissed her hard and fast right there in view of everyone.

She straightened, blinking and seeking to calm herself. She realized then that she could feel Little Gus tensing beneath her, could feel him draw back into his hips and gather his energy in a way he did not do when practicing on the pasture track.

At the instant the flag went down, Little Gus sprang forward as if shot out of a cannon. He was instantly in front, but the roan gained. Etta, although frantic, held Little Gus, while the roan and Sissy Post's fluttering fringed shirt went past. She counted seconds in her head and then let Little Gus go, leaned forward, thinking: *Go . . . Go . . . Go!*

Little Gus came up on the roan and went past him so quickly that Etta had the urge to wave goodbye. Seconds later Little Gus flew over the finish line, way ahead of the roan, just as Johnny had said he would do.

Etta leaned down and hugged Little Gus's neck, then she looked around for Johnny and rode eagerly toward him, as he smiled his I-knew-and-ain't-life-grand smile.

"We won," she said.

"Yep," he said, his eyes bright and grin wide.

Sissy Post came over at a run, then pulled her horse up quick, sawing on his mouth. Her face was red. She dug into her pocket and handed Etta a couple of folded bills. "Congratulations." She turned the roan and spurred him and was off.

Etta slipped to the ground and unfolded the money Sissy had given her. It was two hundred-dollar bills.

"What if I had lost?" she said, frowning.

Johnny grinned. "Then we would have had to pay up. But we didn't lose. And seein' as how we're sort of partners, are you gonna split that with me?"

He stood very close, was gazing down at her with his eyes warm and bright and making her think of all manner of things that had nothing to do with money. She folded one of the bills and gingerly tucked it into the pocket of his starched shirt. Her fingers felt his chest muscle jump at her touch.

"Is that what we are—partners?" she asked.

He shifted, looked off over her head for several seconds and then back into her eyes. "I guess that's what we are for now."

There was a sort of sad questioning in his voice and in his eyes, and she thought he seemed as wanting and confused as she felt.

She saw, too, what he left unsaid, which was that he was making no promises for anything except that day.

She touched his arm, her hand coming up as if of its own accord to lie lightly on his forearm and to feel the strength and heat of him. A crooked grin came on his lips, and he pressed his rough, scratchy palm to her cheek for the space of seconds.

Then, with a hard sigh, he took the reins from her, saying, "Well now, I guess I'd better cool this son-of-a-buck down."

He did not ask her to walk with him. She watched him lead Little Gus away toward a more deserted area along a creek bed with tall trees. Then she looked down at the bill she still held in her hand.

Turning and tucking the money into her pocket, she went back to Latrice and Obie, who were unpacking the picnic basket and preparing to enjoy the feast Latrice had prepared. Etta sat on a blanket in the shade of Latrice's big umbrella, with Lattie Kate cooing beside her, and told about winning the match race and how Sissy Post had been mad enough to pull her hair out. This was the part that most interested Latrice.

That afternoon, before the nightly rodeo events got under way, they all toured the carnival. Etta pushed Lattie Kate in her carriage, with Johnny walking alongside. Ahead of them Latrice, wearing a wide-brimmed straw hat Etta had bought her, walked with her hand in the crook of Obie's

arm. At the pitching booth Obie threw balls and won Latrice an entire set of red glass plates. Johnny stopped at the
shooting booth and won a stuffed panda for Lattie Kate.
When Obie and Latrice decided to play bingo, where they
could sit for a while, Etta and Johnny left Lattie Kate with
them and strolled on. Johnny took her hand, as if they were
on a date.

"I saw Latrice and Obie kissing this mornin'," Etta told
Johnny. She did not know why she picked that moment to
say this. She had been dying to discuss it with him, to see
his reaction. She wondered if he had known about it all
along, but when surprise crossed his face, she knew he
hadn't. She was glad of this.

"Kissin'? Really?" he said.

Etta nodded. "Obie has been in love with Latrice for
years."

Johnny averted his eyes. "I know."

"I guess he finally wore her down."

"He has seemed pretty happy recently," Johnny said.

"He has, hasn't he?" Etta wondered how far this thing
had gone. It was a little disconcerting, thinking of Latrice
and Obie having sex. Surely it had not gone that far. Latrice
was a very proper woman.

Johnny stopped walking. "You want some cotton
candy?" He gestured at the booth where there was a machine making pink cotton candy.

Etta said she did, and he bought a big stick of cotton
candy to share. They each peeled off small pieces and ate
them. Then Etta tore off a piece and put it up to Johnny's
mouth. He smiled and took it, his lips touching her fingertips. Then he fed her a piece. He looked at her in that quiet
way that seemed to say: *Well now.*

She thought to say, *Where are we goin'? Are we headin'
in the same direction as Latrice and Obie?* But she decided
not to complicate the day.

They continued to stroll, took a ride on the small carousel
and rode the Ferris wheel, where Johnny put his arm around
her shoulder. Laying her head back on his arm, she let

herself feel the heat of him and the sweet stirrings his nearness wrought inside her.

Later Latrice and Obie kept Lattie Kate with them at the truck, and Etta and Johnny went to watch the rodeo from the stands. During the bronc riding, Johnny left her and went down to the chutes, speaking to men he knew. Etta watched him there climbing up the rails and helping this one and that one position himself. It came to her that this had been his world, something he had loved to do and had excelled at, and had been forced to give up when he'd had his knee permanently damaged.

He was back at her side for the barrel racing, which she watched with avid fascination, plying Johnny with questions as to each rider's technique and the horse's ability. When the rider would round the third barrel and head for home, Etta would get so excited that she would jump up and down, while shaking Johnny's arm.

"I can see that you are enthused, Miss Etta," he said, laughing at her.

"I think I can do that," she told him. "I really think I can."

"I have no doubt," he told her.

Etta was pleased at the confident light she saw in his eyes.

After the rodeo they returned to Johnny's truck. Things looked different in the pitch dark and with occasional headlights shining in their eyes as vehicles left the grounds.

When Etta and Johnny did reach his truck, they found Latrice over at a nearby car, tending a man who'd had his foot run over by his wife as she was backing up, trying to get their car out of a tight parking spot. The woman had so panicked that she had almost fainted and been of no help to the husband. In the low glow of the car interior light, Latrice got the man's boot off and studied the foot, finding it swelling quite rapidly. Latrice instructed the woman, who seemed recovered enough to follow instructions, to take the man directly to the emergency room to have the foot checked for broken bones. Luckily the man was not in a great deal of pain, as he was drunk.

Obie reported that this was the second accident Latrice had attended during the time the rodeo was going on. She had also helped a man whose horse had gotten spooked by a car, thrown him, and then stepped on him. She had been certain the man's collarbone had been broken, so she'd tied his arm up and sent him on his way to the hospital, too.

"I think I should stay on duty for accidents for a while longer," Latrice told them, when she returned to Johnny's truck and sat down in one of the porch chairs. "At least until everyone who's leavin' tonight gets gone and things settle down."

Johnny said to Etta, "In that case, would you like to go over and have a couple of dances?"

Etta, quite excited by the prospect, looked over at where the lights were strung and the band already beginning to play. She nodded. "Yes . . . that'd be very nice." She sounded so formal, so silly really, when inside she was already dancing.

Johnny's hand closed around hers, and he held on to her all the way there. Etta felt her breath coming very shallowly, which seemed absurd, but she couldn't help it. She wanted to fling herself at Johnny and have him hold her tight.

When they reached the dance, the band happened to be playing a slow tune. Johnny pulled her into his arms and waltzed her around, with amazing smoothness, considering his bum knee. The next tune was a little faster, but they could still dance in each other's arms.

He gazed down at her, and she gazed up at him, or she laid her head on his shoulder, and he rested his cheek against her hair. His shoulder was strong beneath her hand. Their thighs brushed.

Then the band played a swinging tune, and they stood on the sidelines, watching couples square dance. Etta clapped in rhythm as everyone else did, while she wished very hard that the band would get back to a slow tune. When it did, she turned to Johnny and rushed into his arms, causing him to give her that easy grin. For a long minute after the band finished playing, while everyone melted off the dance floor, the two of them stood there gazing intimately at each other.

At last Johnny said, "Well now . . . if we're gonna do this all over again tomorrow, we'd better get home."

He slid his arm around her and led her back across the fairly empty grounds beneath the starry sky to where Obie and Latrice sat beside the truck. Latrice, still keeping a lookout for an injury that might require her attention, reluctantly agreed that it was time to leave.

They drove home through the summer night, Etta holding Lattie Kate in her arms and leaning into the curve of Johnny's shoulder.

The next day, just after noon when church let out, they returned to the rodeo grounds. This time Latrice was eager to go, as she was certain there would be further accidents to which she could attend.

"And I rather enjoy Obie's company," she said privately to Etta. "He dresses up very fine, doesn't he?"

Etta agreed, but held her tongue against asking if Latrice was going to marry Obie. She did not want to face it, and she did not want to get into a deep discussion when she was in fact focusing a great deal on her own affairs—and the particular affair that was not happening with Johnny.

Somewhat to Etta's surprise, Latrice asked how things were progressing between Etta and Johnny. Etta was struck by the word *progressing*.

"We're partners," she replied, then took Lattie Kate up and went out to the truck, where Johnny was already waiting.

Twice that afternoon, Etta again raced Little Gus, both times in races with a purse, which she preferred.

The first race was three hundred and fifty feet against a field of eight other horses, six of those seasoned ones. "Just lean forward and ride like hell," Johnny told her and smacked Little Gus on the rump as she rode over to the starting line.

She had barely gotten Little Gus straight at the line before the flag went down and they were off. Little Gus sprang forward, and Etta crouched on top of him, letting him have his rein and thinking with all her will, *Run, Gus, run,* while she held on tight and the wind beat in her face.

The race was so quick that she held her breath the length of it and gave out a cry when they went across the line. She thought they had won, but there was some discussion, as a black horse had been very close. But then Little Gus was declared winner of the race and the purse of a hundred dollars. On hearing this news, Etta slid off Little Gus and threw herself into Johnny's arms, almost unbalancing him.

They had not planned to race Little Gus again, but then they got drawn into a sort of match race with two other riders. It began with a young man, who was very Indian and of the wild-living sort that Roy had been. From listening to the young man pester Johnny about racing, Etta got the idea that he had wanted before to race Little Gus with his paint horse. This paint horse looked awfully fast to Etta, and the young man a very good rider.

"I'll bet you a hundred and fifty dollars that my pony can take yours," he said.

"There's no need to bet," Etta injected into the men's conversation. "I imagine he can."

This made all those around her chuckle, and Etta assumed they were all used to flimflamming each other and did not take to the truth stated.

Johnny rubbed the side of his nose and whispered, "Let me handle it."

She whispered back, "Maybe a hundred and fifty dollars is not a fortune, but I don't care to flush it down the toilet. I think we ought to save his strength for races with purses."

He gave her that "Well now" grin, and said, "I'll get you a purse, Miz Etta."

Etta raised an eyebrow at that. One thing she knew, and that was Johnny Bellah could talk the stars from the sky.

As it turned out Johnny worked it around so that Jed Stuart and the owner of the Western Auto store each put up added money to see a race between Little Gus, the young Indian's paint horse, and Bitta Fudge's horse, a deep brown gelding. Etta heard someone say the gelding had won a hard race up at Woodward the day before. Each rider put in fifty dollars, and with the added money the purse to the winner would be three hundred dollars.

Etta thought fifty dollars a lot to risk, but Johnny reminded her they were partners, so her share would be twenty-five.

"Have I steered you wrong before?" he asked.

Etta brought up the first race she had lost, and he told her he had known she would lose that, just like he knew she'd win this.

"I know horses," he said, and then added, "It's women that puzzle me."

And again he was right. Little Gus ran the four hundred and forty feet like he could run forever, leaving Bitta Fudge's pretty brown gelding dropping back at three hundred and fifty, and the paint horse losing enough ground at four hundred that Little Gus was able to pull ahead and win by a neck.

The young man softly rode his paint pony up to Etta and Johnny. With a wry grin, he swept off his hat to Etta. Then he told Johnny that he'd like another match sometime at a length of three hundred and fifty feet. Johnny laughed and said he was smarter than that.

"I'd like to come by, talk to you sometime," the young man said, his black eyes intense.

"Come on," Johnny told him. "I'm over at the Rivers Stables for now. I'd be pleased to talk with you."

Etta heard Johnny's words, *for now.* She looked at him and wondered and thought of how she wanted to say, *Marry me and stay.* And likely, if he said he would marry her at all, he would say, *Marry me and go with me,* and there they would be, each asking of the other what the other was unwilling to give.

The four of them ate their picnic meal on the blanket beneath the big umbrella, which today was trying to blow away, and then strolled the carnival, where Obie pitched and won Latrice a set of red glass goblets to go with her red plates, and Johnny shot targets and won a teddy bear for Etta. Again while Latrice and Obie played bingo and minded Lattie Kate, Etta and Johnny rode the carousel and the Ferris wheel and ate cotton candy. Again that night Etta watched the rodeo from the stands, while Johnny sat beside her, giving her a sort of running commentary of each contestant's effort in each event.

There was no dance that night. The booths closed at the carnival and the grounds quickly emptied. Everyone packing up, loading horses, and moving on.

When Etta and Johnny returned to the truck beneath the stars, they found Latrice a little disappointed, as she had only been called upon to assist in a very minor emergency of a man walking past with a bloody nose. She showed the man how to press a penny on his gum beneath his upper lip and stop the flow. That had happened early in the evening and nothing had happened since. "I might as well go home," she said.

Johnny helped Etta, with Lattie Kate, up into the truck seat. Etta nursed Lattie Kate, who fell asleep, and then Johnny reached for her, and she scooted over beside him and into the curve of his arm. On the way home they talked about this horse and that, funny things that had happened or been said. Etta told Johnny again that she wanted to learn to barrel race.

"Will you help me?" she asked.

He nodded. "Yeah," he said.

And then he rested his hand on her shoulder, and her skin grew moist with the weight, while his thumb drew tingling circles on her neck.

Twenty-three

That first week after the Fourth of July rodeo, Johnny set up barrels in the big corral, and Etta began to learn the art of racing Little Gus around them.

They went at this early in the morning, before the heat of the day, oftentimes before the sun became more than a rosy glow in the east and while cool still radiated from the dusty ground.

Johnny sat on the fence and gave direction. "Don't lean into the hole," he would say, or, "Push him around with your leg—you're forgettin' to use your leg."

"Why don't you yell at the horse once in a while," Etta said to him in a snippy tone.

"Because he's not the one havin' the trouble," Johnny answered patiently.

That Johnny remained so even-tempered aggravated Etta. He sat there, and his eyes would follow her in a lazy, seductive way, yet he did not exhibit impatience or nervousness. His being right about the horse did not improve her temper, either.

Little Gus took instantly to running at top speed around the barrels, while Etta had trouble riding atop him running around them. The horse exhibited the wonderful ability to turn sharply, and Etta had to fight her fear of these racy turns. She had not known before that her fear of such turns amounted to stark terror. Little Gus felt her fear. It slowed him down and often confused him, too, as he kept watching for a possible threat from somewhere.

Again and again, Etta forced herself to face the fear, knowing that only by gaining confidence could she communicate that to the horse, and thereby win money at racing barrels.

Money was one of Etta's major concerns. The days and weeks were adding up to months, and she still had not sold any land. She struggled to pay the everyday debts and had nothing left to put toward the mortgage debt. For every dollar she spent, she worried of a way to earn another. She managed to rent two corrals to people who needed a place to keep old horses they didn't want to send to the slaughterhouse, and she went through the attic and the house again, hauling out anything that she could part with and that could possibly be of value. She had the good fortune to come upon an entire set of china packed away in the attic and an old rocking-reclining chair, both of which Robert Lamb readily bought from her.

"This is good," Latrice said. "We're gettin' less to pack everyday, should we end up havin' to move."

"We're not goin' to move," Etta said vehemently. She was often vehement these days. "I'm tellin' you we have put our hand to the plow and are not lookin' back," she added, purposely using analogy Latrice herself might have employed.

"You have put your hand there," Latrice said. "Don't include me."

"I have always included you," Etta told her. "For twenty-six years I have included you in my life, so I do not think I should change now, unless you yourself decide otherwise."

She looked pointedly at Latrice, who said with vehemence of her own, "I guess I've put my hand to the plow, too. It's a different plow, but it seems to be hooked to the same horse."

Etta stubbornly clung to her intention to stay right where

she was, with the belief that she could will everything to turn out. She made herself believe that she was going to ride her wishes just like she was riding Little Gus. She was riding with fear, but she was riding.

She was, however, far less believing about Johnny.

Etta's feelings for Johnny appeared to be in a constant pivotal state. Although she realized that she depended on him every day, she could not decide whether she should allow herself to do this, whether she wanted to continue doing this. She knew she loved him, but she could not decide if she was going to allow herself to love, or if she was going to firmly reject it.

She was certain of one thing. She wanted Johnny.

Without the enforced discipline of her pregnant state, Etta began to be overcome with this wanting. She wanted him to kiss her, to touch her, to make love to her until she was sweaty and breathless and could not move. Recalling his kisses, this wanting increased daily, until she had intervals of thinking that she might go crazy with it.

It would sometimes come as a surprise to her to find herself going about the normal activities of helping with laundry or setting Johnny's plate in front of him and asking him if he wanted coffee and then discussing the front page of the newspaper with Latrice, while in the back of her mind teemed steamy desires. She and Johnny had ceased to touch each other, fearing it, Etta supposed, as one would red-hot flames. She would catch him looking at her, though, with hungry eyes. And she occasionally slipped up and let him catch her looking at him in the same way.

As a remedy for the condition, a control over it, Etta tried to wear herself out by taking care of Lattie Kate and thinking up ways to earn a dollar, or by tending horses and learning to race barrels, until she had to drag herself up to the house and was too physically sore to anticipate a man's touch.

Once Latrice said, "You two are exhausting my patience. I wished you'd both get it over with."

At first stunned, Etta then came back with, "Yes, I

should fling myself at a man just so you can have your patience soothed.''

She left the room because she wanted to prevent getting into a good argument. Of late she and Latrice had been picking and sniping at each other, and Etta had discovered her best defense was to leave while she was ahead. She also knew this was a way of winning, as it drove Latrice crazy. Now she went into the den and took up the bills that needed to be paid.

Latrice came after her, entering the office with a burst of frustration. ''What I am sayin' to you is that you are gettin' nowhere in this state. You two need to get it settled between you before you both burn right up.''

Etta looked at her. ''I apologize for my distracted and somewhat ill humor; however, I am now forced, since you are pursuin' the subject, to bring up that you yourself could settle a few things with Obie. He moons after you, and you have left him hangin' for reasons of your own. Suppose we agree that I have to work my own problems out, and you do the same.''

Seeing what she interpreted as a confused, sad expression on Latrice's face, Etta felt badly and softened her tone.

''I know that you have held yourself contained out of your responsibility toward me. I urge you to do exactly as you wish with Obie and know that I'm agreeable. You should know by now that I want nothing more in the world than for you to be happy. You have given up so much for me, but I'm grown now, and you don't need to do that. And should you marry Obie, we'll always remain close.''

To this Latrice said, ''Huh. I'll have you know that I am doin' exactly as I please with Obie. I always have.'' Then she pulled the leaving-the-room ploy.

Etta sat there, staring after her, with lips trembling and tears threatening.

The memories flashed across her mind. Memories of childhood, pulling at Latrice's skirts, and being in Latrice's comforting arms. Memories of the many nights when she had left Obie and Latrice working over the newspaper crossword puzzle when she went to bed. And many morn-

ings that she came down and found Obie sitting at the
kitchen table with coffee, mooning over Latrice while she
awaited her breakfast.

She had assumed that Obie had left and returned early,
but thinking of it now, she realized he might not have left.
That he might have been staying the night was a startling
idea. An image flashed across her mind, and she swept it
right along.

Latrice generally did exactly what she wished at any
given time, Etta thought. This should be a good example
to her to follow her own mind. Although, with a sinking
feeling, she knew that choices were sometimes very difficult indeed. She did not want to be tied up in the angst of
an affair, but neither did she want to be celibate.

Neither choice was appealing, she thought, getting up
and switching on the fan sitting on one of the bookcases.
She unbuttoned the top buttons of her blouse and leaned
over to cool herself.

That night she was awake and in front of her opened
bedroom window when Johnny came home from wherever
he had been. She imagined lipstick on his cheek as she
watched him walk beneath the pole lamp and enter the
darker barn.

Watching the light come on in his room, she gathered
up all she had not to run down there and throw herself on
him. Even while she clung to her determination, she
thought that it was foolish to remain this wound up and not
do anything about it. Why did she not doing anything about
it?

Fear of appearing foolish, she thought, going to her bed
and slumping upon it and crying into her pillow.

The next morning, clearing the breakfast table after
Johnny had left, Etta dropped a plate and cracked it. She
broke out in immediate, hard sobs.

"Good Lord a'mercy," Latrice said. "It was only one
of those Duz plates."

"He doesn't care," Etta said through her sobs. "He
doesn't want me like I want him." She had a headache and
was feeling very weak, and her hunger for Johnny had so

consumed her that the words simply poured out on their own.

"I think you are wrong there," Latrice said, handing her a dishcloth to dry her tears. "He can't keep his eyes off of you."

"Well, he hasn't made any move toward me. He doesn't even look at me these days."

"Exactly. He is containing himself, as a gentleman should do. If you want something differently, you'll have to go to him."

"Oh, Latrice, I don't want to end up like Corinne!" Etta said and broke out in fresh sobs.

"Why should you end up like Corinne? Roy's dead, and your mother's dead."

"I'm afraid that if I make love with Johnny, I'll never be able to let him go. I'll end up losing my body and my soul." With her mind filling with morose pictures of herself as a lost woman, Etta sat staring at the linoleum.

Latrice said, "I do see your point, however, you could just as well sleep with him and find relief, and find, too, that your mind made it out to be much more than it is. Making love with a man is a wondrous thing . . . but it can also be a little disappointing."

"You seem to have more knowledge about this area than I ever knew," Etta observed dryly. She was perturbed that Latrice had not said something more soothing.

"I have a lot of experience in things that you never knew about."

Then Etta dared, "So what about Obie? Is it all you imagined?"

Latrice gave her a look. "It is more, although my ima-ginings had never been much," Latrice said and pushed her hip against the screen door, opening it to carry a pan full of grain out to the chickens Obie had given her and leaving Etta puzzling about her answer.

Etta decided she did not like speaking about intimate things with Latrice. It was just too embarrassing and cer-tainly no help.

She went to the door and saw Johnny riding one of the

horses around in the big corral, chasing around several other horses, playing as he sometimes did. She sighed, thinking that she had a very good imagination.

Johnny helped load the two horses he had trained for Jed Stuart up into Stuart's truck, then slammed the tailgate closed. He gave Jed an overview of what he thought the prospects were for each horse, and Jed paid him.

"Can you take two more horses?" Jed asked him. "I picked up two fillies the other day. All I want right now is for you to break 'em."

"Give me a couple of weeks. I'll let you know," Johnny said. He felt restless, the thought of committing himself to the responsibility of training more horses at that minute seemed beyond him. He still had Harry Flagg's four and the lessons he had going, and he felt trapped by all of it.

As Jed drove away, Johnny saw Etta come out on the back porch. She was carrying a basket of laundry for the line. She paused at the top step and looked his way. It was like heat came out of her eyes and fell all over him.

Etta had been looking at him a lot lately, as if she was just waiting for him to say the word and she would jump naked into his arms.

Johnny wanted to say the word, but caution kept his lips shut. This was not all good sense and valor on his part. For one thing, there was the problem of where they could do it. His single bunk in the barn did not add up to the romantic imaginings in his mind, and he couldn't see strolling past Latrice and up to Etta's bedroom. The thought of Latrice looking at him tended to cast cold water on his desire.

Johnny kept wondering where having sex would get them both. He felt fairly certain that Etta would take this as a commitment on his part. He himself felt it would be commitment, and he felt trapped enough, without digging in deeper.

She went to the clothesline, and he turned and rounded the barn, sauntering over to where Obie was working on Etta's car. She'd finally managed to get enough money to buy the needed parts. It looked like Obie had most of the motor spread out around him, while he bent all the way underneath the hood. Johnny took off his hat and wiped his forehead with his shirt sleeve.

"Whew, it's hot."

"It generally gets that way 'bout now in Oklahoma," Obie drawled. "Hand me that half-inch over there."

"Why is it that the particular tool you need is always just out of reach?" Johnny asked, handing over the tool.

"One of them Murphy laws, I reckon."

Johnny stood in the shade of the barn and watched Obie for some minutes. He asked if Obie thought he might get the car going sometime soon, and Obie said he thought he'd have it by the following afternoon. Johnny had heard the car start once, but it wouldn't keep running, so Obie had to tear it all down again. Something about clogged fuel lines and a messed-up carburetor.

Johnny said, "Well now, seein' as how it's so hot, why don't you take a break for a couple or three hours? I'd like you to drive with me and see somethin'."

Obie glanced over at him. Johnny tried to look casual, but he figured Obie picked up a sense of his intensity, because Obie set down the socket wrench and said, "Okay. You can buy me a beer on the way."

After a stop for cold beers, Johnny drove south along the highway for nearly an hour, the windows down and the wind buffeting their ears, with country music blasting over this. Every once in a while Obie would say, "I hope what you have to show me is worth the distance."

What Johnny had to show him was a small farm of a hundred and sixty acres, plantings of alfalfa and cotton, fields that usually grew winter oats and maize, and a small orchard of apples and peaches. It had a house, a tin barn that had two rough stalls and room for two more, a second tin hay barn of a large size, a number of falling-down sheds that needed to be torn down, and two fenced corrals. The house was of fieldstone, solid, with two bedrooms and a small extra room made of the closed-in porch. It had a fireplace in the living room, too. There were forsythia bushes in the frontyard and half an apple tree in the backyard; a large limb had split out of it in a wind, and it lay dead on the ground.

Johnny showed Obie how he could fix the barn with four stalls and a tack room and how he wanted to build new corrals and a training pen. He showed him how the house had a small room upstairs and about all it really needed was painting.

"It's all fine," Obie said. "Mighty fine. You must have searched for this one, boy."

Johnny nodded. He had searched, and this was as close as he could come to the best that he could afford. "The man who owns this is willin' to rent it to me, and if I decide to buy, he'll take part of my rent as payment for the pur- chase price," Johnny said.

Obie propped his foot up on the dead limb that was still connected to the apple tree. "Is this what you want for yourself . . . or for Miz Etta?" he asked, fixing Johnny with a hard eye.

Johnny sighed heavily. "Both, I guess. I've thought for a long time about settlin' down and starting a stock-raisin' business. I'd like to . . . well, the long and short of it is that if I want Etta to go with me, I got to have her a place to go to. I don't have a lot of money, Obie, but I thought this place was pretty nice."

"It is very nice. The house is real nice, but"—Obie pulled at his ear—"I'm not sure Miz Etta would leave her place if you bought her a mansion."

Johnny looked over across the grass growing tall and waving in the wind.

"It doesn't have to do with you, John," Obie said. "It has to do with where Miz Etta feels secure. She has scrapped hard for that place. Ever since Mr. Roy brought her there, she has had to try to survive. And once you scrap for a place, it becomes part of you."

After a moment, when Johnny stared at the ground, Obie asked, "What's wrong with stayin' up there with her any- way? She's got a good start there." He pointed a bony finger at Johnny. "*You* have a good start there. Why you want to leave that, boy?"

Johnny shook his head. He had trouble finding an explanation for something he didn't quite understand. "Because it's hers. If I marry her there, I'm just comin' in to what she already has—just fallin' into it is how everyone'll see it. Like I married her for all that. Maybe this place isn't so much as what she's got, but it would be somethin' I could give her." Saying it out like that, he felt foolish. He couldn't give her nearly as much as she already had, so he didn't know why he was even trying.

Obie said, "Now, John, don't discount yourself, boy, when it comes to givin' to Miz Etta. You have a lot to offer her just in yourself."

Johnny shook his head sadly. "You know what I am, Obie? I'm a man who never got past the eighth grade, and I only got that far because I skipped a grade. I'm a man who hasn't lived in any one place since I was thirteen years old. I can't hardly imagine doin' so. It makes me a little sick to even think of it. The truth is that I dream of marryin' Etta like a man dreams about Marilyn Monroe. But when it comes to the actual fact of marriage, I don't know if I could stick it out day after day. I guess that's some of why I want to start my own place, scrap for it like you said, and you got roots to hold you there. But even if I do that, I may not be able to stick it out. Etta knows this, too."

Obie looked like he felt sorry, and this was embarrassing, so Johnny quickly said they needed to get on back.

"I got Miz English comin' for a lesson this afternoon." He started for his truck, turning his eyes and mind away from the small rock house.

"That woman's comin' around for a bit more than ridin' lessons," Obie observed as he bent himself into Johnny's truck. He thought a bit of teasing might cheer the younger man. And he also thought Johnny could use a bit of warning about a ripe middle-aged woman who wasn't getting what she needed at home.

He said, "You know that Miz Winslow is a woman who is bored at home and lookin' around. Woman like that can be dangerous. You might better watch out."

Johnny glanced at him as he headed the truck down the

country lane. "All women are dangerous," he said in a dispirited tone. "They really get a man tied up."

"Well, I can't argue with you there," Obie said, thinking of Latrice.

Obie felt profound gladness for having at last obtained Latrice's favor, however, such favor appeared so often in jeopardy that he felt constantly walking against the wind.

"You and Latrice are gettin' along pretty good, aren't you?" Johnny asked, drawing him from his thoughts.

Obie sort of smiled. "Yeah. 'Course Miss Latrice is not one to let a man get too very certain. She gives, and then she takes back about twice."

"Are you gonna marry her?" Johnny asked.

Obie shrugged. "Miss Latrice is not one who favors marriage a whole lot. Don't get me wrong . . . she's strong about propriety. It's just that she has her ways and she is not a woman given a lot to changin' them. She don't look kindly on my kitchen, either," he admitted a little sheepishly, "which I can't say as I blame her, bein' as she's been enjoyin' that fancy one up there at the Rivers place for quite some time now."

He gazed out the window and recalled lying in Latrice's featherbed. "There's a lot to be said for small favors, John." Then he pulled at his ear. "Truth to tell, I kinda like my space, and Miss Latrice does, too. I've lived a goodly time by myself, and I might not accommodate myself so well at this late stage, if Miss Latrice came in my place and went to fixin' everything up. She feels about the same, so it's workin' for us."

"What if they up and move?"

"Well, I guess I'll just have to go along. We'd work it out, I guess," he said. "You just got to live one day at a time, John. All of them together are too much."

Obie reflected that there were many things the years took from a man but they also gave. He was older than Johnny and had learned the difference between true pride and ego pride. He supposed he had faced the fears inside himself long ago and had gotten past them in the manner of a man who trusts himself and his God.

"You know," Johnny said, breaking the thoughtful silence. "Long as I have my hands, I don't need a woman for anything."

Obie laughed long and hard at that, then he observed, "Hands can do a lot, boy, but they can't kiss. And yours can't make coffee as good as Latrice's by a long shot."

Twenty-four

Harry Flagg tried to talk Johnny into taking his horses over to New Mexico to race them, but Johnny told him no. He finished getting the horse that had gone through the barn fire back into some semblance of normal and sent it back to the owner, and every once in a while a guy or gal would come out and bring a horse for a day or two for Johnny to evaluate and tune, but this was the most he would allow. He steadily refused to take on the responsibility of any new horses.

Etta rented two of the now-empty stalls to a couple of barrel racers, so Johnny found himself being drawn more into that sport. Etta began riding at play-days and pasture rodeos around the area. Johnny was proud of Little Gus's abilities, born a lot from Johnny's own training, and he was proud of Etta and the gumption she displayed. She continued to be frightened about racing around turns, but she didn't let that stop her.

Each Saturday and Sunday, Johnny would load Little Gus and drive past the back door of the house for Etta to race out and hop in the truck, saying, "Let's go!" and they'd be off for five or six hours. Johnny more or less went along for the ride—a driver and helper with the horse and admirer of Etta.

She'd race Little Gus around the barrels a time or two, and on occasion, when she was in high spirits from winning the jackpot, she would consent to a match race on a straight track. More often that not, she won then, too. Almost always she made money enough to cover their expenses of entering and had some to bring home, too.

A couple of people wanted to buy Little Gus. Once Etta came to Johnny and said, "I just got an offer to buy Little Gus for three thousand dollars."

"Well now," Johnny said, with a smile. He thought what she told him was a pretty good thing, but Etta was not looking at him like it was.

"Do you think I should do it?"

Johnny had come to understand that Etta had moments when she truly wanted him to tell her what to do, yet if he did, she'd always back away from whatever he told her.

He said, "What do you want to do?" He was thinking that she did not want to sell the horse, that she would never want to sell the horse, so why didn't she just accept it? Of course, he knew it was not wise to say this. Words of this sort tended to bring out her fire.

"What I want to do and what I should do might be two different things," she said, giving a little impatient jerk of her body that was becoming a lot harder and firmer from all her riding.

Averting his eyes from her body, he grinned sadly. "It's that way a lot, idn't it?"

She looked at him a long minute, before going off, presumably to say no to the buyer, as she came back with Little Gus in tow, and happily, too. Johnny was happy that she didn't sell the red gelding, too, so much so that it startled him.

"We need to get home," she said.

After her barrel racing rides, she was always anxious to return home to Lattie Kate. Johnny didn't know how much of this was due to mother-worries and how much was due to her still nursing. He didn't see a need to probe into such an intimate detail.

A thousand times during these weeks, Johnny thought of

ranchers he had worked for in Texas and New Mexico and how they would be happy to have him come work for them now. He also considered going on down and renting the farm with the rock house and beginning his own place.

Yet he stayed at the Rivers farm, keeping himself steady by thinking each evening that maybe he would leave the next day, or the day after that.

He came in the barn and found Etta sitting on the stacked hay. "You got a letter," she said.

She wore a sleeveless dress, one she often wore while working around the house. It was of some thin, flower-sprigged fabric that flowed over her body, showing all the curves. Her hair was pulled up off her neck. The strands that escaped in an unruly manner at her temples and nape were damp with sweat, as was the skin beneath her blue eyes. She looked tired, as if she'd just had to sit down.

Johnny, feeling the humming he always felt in her presence, tossed aside the halter he carried and took the envelope from her. He didn't often get mail and was curious.

"I think it's from Harry Flagg," Etta said. She remained sitting there.

There was no return address, but Johnny, too, recognized Harry's scrawl. "Yeah, looks like it."

Removing his hat, he tossed it on the hay and wiped a sleeve over his forehead. He opened the envelope. It was a little hard to read, feeling Etta's eyes on him. The letter was from Harry, who began with, "Hello, you son-of-a-buck," and Johnny thought fondly of the big man's voice.

Johnny read it, then said, "Harry wants to know if we can take on another six head for him. If we can, he wants me to come out to Sayre and get them next week and bring them back and get them ready for fall racing. He says he has a good barrel racing prospect for you."

He looked at her. Her blue eyes were studying him.

"What do you think? Want to take them on?"

She blinked and looked down at her bare leg that she stretched languidly. He looked at her leg, too, at the skin so pale and sleek, and his eye traveled up to where the dress collapsed between her thighs.

"We have the room now," she said, "but do you want to take on trainin' them?"

Johnny's gaze returned to hers. He had difficulty thinking much about horses in that instant. He felt his heartbeat in his groin.

"I don't know. It'd take a couple of months, but it'd mean boardin' money for you, and Harry is reliable to pay."

He noticed the hollow of her neck shone with perspiration. With heat.

"What does he say about the barrel horse?" she asked.

"Oh . . . just that he has one he thinks you'll want to look at."

She sighed a sort of dispirited sigh, put her hands on her thighs in an unconscious gesture and moved the fabric of her dress. "It's too hot to be thinkin' about horses right now," she said.

Her dispiritedness pricked at him. "Yeah," he said absently, folding Harry's letter and stuffed it back in the envelope.

For an instant he had felt anticipation at taking on new horses for Harry, but now he didn't think he wanted to do it. But he recognized that he could just be in a low moment and the next moment he might pick up and change his mind. He wished he would get himself straightened out.

He was brought up short by Etta getting to her feet. She seemed about to say something, but then she was just looking at him. Her eyes pinned him, and he felt like a buck caught in headlights.

The next instant she was coming to him with parted lips, and he was taking her into his arms. He saw her lids slowly shut over her blue eyes, as she wrapped her hands behind his neck and brought his head down to her.

Supreme relief was the first emotion that flashed through him. At last he had her against him.

She was hot and damp, smelled of sweat and sunshine and Ivory soap. Her lips were sweet as honey, seductive, and trembling. Her entire body started trembling against him, and Johnny felt as if he were dropping down into her. He tried to resist, tried breaking away, but smoky desire closed around him.

He kissed her lips and then down her neck to the silky swell of her breasts at the neckline of her dress. He savored the smoothness of her skin and the salty taste of her. He opened his eyes and looked at her skin, saw the delicate fabric of the dress against it and the way the dress was pushed out by her breasts, which were heaving up and down. Her breath was hot in his ear, calling his name over and over in a breathless whisper that about drove him senseless.

"Johnny . . . oh, Johnny . . . please . . ."

He thought of the prickly bales of hay only a foot away, of his hard, narrow bunk covered in a worn flannel blanket, of Etta's bed that he had seen only in his imagination but pictured with soft white sheets and plump feather pillows against which to lay her down and kiss her until she cried and took him into her.

Then Latrice entered his thoughts, and Obie's caution about getting Etta pregnant came to haunt him. It was as if the cooling breeze of hard sanity swept over his back.

He placed his hands on either side of Etta's flushed cheeks and pulled her from him.

"Etta . . ." He saw tears squeezed from her closed eyelids. "Etta, is this what you want?"

Her eyes flew open. They looked confused, glazed and shimmering with heat.

"Etta, all I got is a bunk in there, and this isn't the way I want it to be. Where will we go from here? Sneakin' around?"

Thinking that she would do this made him angry, and he gave her head a little shake. "Do you want to marry me?"

"Yes," she said breathlessly, desperately. "I'll marry you, if you'll stay here."

He noticed she said, "I will," not "I want to." He thought of it and felt the sense of being closed in a box.

With a shake of his head, he dropped his hands and

turned from her. He heard her say something, but couldn't quite make it out over the anger and confusion roaring in his head.

Then he heard her walking away out of the barn.

Drawing back, he struck out at a bale of hay, which sent pain reverberating up his arm. He welcomed the pain. It was better than the ache inside him. He looked around for something else to hit, but there just didn't seem to be anything.

With heavy footsteps, Johnny went into his room and sat on his bunk, raking his hands over and over through his hair, calling himself all kinds of a fool for not accepting what Etta had offered him.

Disappointment sliced through him. She wanted him, and maybe she even loved him, but she would not give up this hunk of land and house for him.

The way Johnny looked at it, he wanted no part of being second fiddle to a piece of land and collection of buildings.

Feeling in something of a wild and distracted state, Johnny washed his hands and face, put back on his dusty, sweat-stained hat, got into his truck and drove over to Beetle's roadhouse, where he proceeded to toss back drinks in the refreshing coolness of air-conditioning, and to convince himself that he did not need to get married.

Just when he was about to get drunk, he looked up and saw an old man drunk at the bar.

After a minute of gazing at the miserable sight, Johnny put down his drink, took up his hat, and left.

He drove over to Obie's cottage. Obie was picking tomatoes. Johnny helped himself to making them each cold glasses of tea from Obie's refrigerator, took them out and sat with Obie beneath a big hackberry tree. It was a lot cooler there than in the house.

"I'm thinkin' I need to head on down the road," he said to Obie.

"And what are you runnin' from, son?"

Johnny shook his head at that and shrugged. "You know, I've never in my life really had to make a decision more weighty than whether to have a hamburger or steak for.

supper or stay in my truck or a rented room. My mother dyin' started me off on the rodeo circuit, and Uncle Sam chose me for the army and sent me to have my knee ripped apart.''

"You can't decide whether or not to marry Miz Etta?"

Johnny waved a fly from his glass, drank the remainder of the tea and threw the ice into the grass. "I gotta take a lot I may not be able to live up to, if I marry her.''

"Well, most anybody does that when they join up with another person," Obie said wryly. "I had to take on my wife's mother, and that wasn't easy, I'll tell you."

Johnny chuckled.

"What about Little Gus?" Obie asked, his voice growing serious again. "What will Miz Etta do about him if you leave?"

"I've pretty well finished all I can do with Gus," Johnny answered. "Etta's fully capable of doin' anything she wants with him now.''

"You do know, John, if you leave, you're likely to cause Miz Etta to lose a lot of boarders. And there's other things. She's come to rely on you, boy." Obie's attitude was definitely critical.

"I know that, Obie." All of it was a weighty burden, something he did not take lightly, and it hurt that the older man would think he did.

Then Obie nodded in a sympathetic way and said, "Life's a puzzle, son. It's meant to be a challenge, not a burden, but I guess sometimes the two come so close together it's hard to tell the difference.''

After a long minute of silence, Obie said, "What you need, son, is to go fishin'.''

"I don't like fishin'," Johnny said.

Still, he went along with Obie because it was something he could see to do, and afterward he went back and fed the horses in the same manner of doing something because it was there to do.

The next morning Etta did not come out to ride Little Gus as she had been doing. Uncertain of what to expect, yet pushed by a certain perversity to see Etta, and a craving for Latrice's coffee and biscuits, Johnny joined Obie in going up to the house for breakfast. He sat down at the table with the three people he had been having meals with for months and spoke of the weather and baseball and that Nathan Lee was riding good enough for his father to buy him his own horse.

Etta did not say anything directly to him, and he didn't say anything directly to her. He watched her cross the room and bring back the coffee pot and refill his cup. He felt her eyes on him. He looked at her, then quickly away, saying, "Thank you."

He drank his coffee and watched Etta bring Lattie Kate into the room and sit with her at the table. He noticed Etta's skin, although darker, was as smooth as the baby's. Then he left to begin his day that stretched before him with dust and heat and vague inward questions he didn't understand and couldn't answer in any case.

Friday afternoon, Johnny was mending a fence when Leon Thibodeaux drove up. He came to the back door these days. Johnny watched him go inside, and fifteen minutes later, he came out with Etta, and the two drove off together.

Curious and trying not to be, Johnny went up to the house to ask for a glass of tea and to find out exactly why Etta was going off with Thibodeaux. He didn't have to ask.

Latrice handed him the cold glass of tea and told him as fast as she could talk, "Mr. Leon took her over to Fred Grandy's office to meet with a man from Oklahoma City. Some big-shot builder. It's the same man who inquired about some land back right when the place first went on the market. He wants twenty acres up by the highway. He's gonna chop it up and build houses on two-acre sections. I tell you, if he buys that land, Walter Fudge is gonna come runnin' and pay whatever Etta wants him to."

Johnny agreed with Latrice on this. "How much is this builder goin' to pay for the land?" he asked.

"Maybe twice the goin' rate per acre, since he just wants a chunk. Mr. Leon said the man was not set on exactly how many acres he wanted. Maybe twenty acres, but maybe more like forty.''

A couple of hours later, Johnny was out back of the barn, trimming hooves, when Etta came looking for him. She stepped out of the barn, and he saw by the excitement on her face that she had sold land and sold at a good price.

For several seconds she just looked at him, as if so happy she couldn't bring all her words out.

Then she said, "Oh, Johnny, I sold forty acres. Forty acres for as much as sixty, and right while we were signing the papers a man called about the east section, and he wants to buy it. Can you imagine? He called while I was right there signin' papers to sell the forty acres.''

"I guess you got an angel workin' for you," Johnny said, giving her the smile required. "I'm real happy for you.''

She gazed at him and bit her bottom lip. He thought for an instant that she might be going to press him to stay and say that she wanted to marry him. He had a little panic, hoping for this and afraid of it, too.

She said, "Should we count on you for supper?''

"No," he said with a shake of his head as he gathered his farrier tools. "Not tonight. I gotta run over to town and see a fella.''

"You just go on, Johnny.''

Startled, he looked up to see her eyes shooting fire.

"Don't let us keep you here. We'll be fine, so you don't need to put yourself out by stayin' around at all.''

She whirled and walked off through the barn, and Johnny stood there, watching her silhouette.

Twenty-five 🌹

Within days Etta sold forty acres to the builder from Oklahoma City as well as a half section to a farmer to the east. When word of this reached Walter Fudge, he got into a panic and bought all the rest of the land that Etta intended to sell, paying the going rate per acre with no quibbling.

Edward's final solution to the remaining amount owed on the mortgage was to pay the bank himself, drawing up a personal loan that Etta would repay at a low monthly rate for the next twenty years.

"I don't want to have to deal with this any longer," Edward told her. "The way you go at things, we would likely be tied up for a decade tryin' to get you off that place."

"I'll pay you, Edward. I promise I will."

"I know you will," he said quietly. Then he gave one of his cool grins. "It's a very good deal for me, you know."

Several days later, Etta was quite thrilled to drive herself into town for signing of the official paperwork for the sale of the land and closure of the mortgage. Obie had at last gotten her car going.

It had been over six months since she had been behind the wheel of a vehicle, and she headed away down the drive with fits and starts, with Obie and Latrice watching wide-eyed, and Johnny limping alongside, calling to her through the window instructions about the use of the clutch. Johnny was something of a fanatic about the proper use of a clutch.

By the time she returned from the.meeting at the bank, she sped smoothly up the drive and came to a quick stop in front of the house.

"Latrice! Latrice, it's ours!" she called as she raced up the steps and through the house.

Latrice was in the kitchen starting supper. Etta could smell the aroma of meat and onions—the roast Latrice was cooking in celebration of their good fortune. Bursting through the swinging door, she saw Obie sitting at the table, holding Lattie Kate, and Latrice, in her lovely blue dress, standing beside him.

Etta thrust the papers at Latrice, took Lattie Kate from Obie and danced her around, singing, "Lattie Kate, sweet Lattie Kate, Mama's gonna love you twice your weight."

She coaxed a smile from Lattie Kate, and then she said to Latrice and Obie, who now held the papers Latrice had passed to him, "Isn't it wonderful, Obie? We can all stay right here. We can raise Lattie Kate right here where she belongs. Where's Johnny? I want to tell him. He has all the time in the world to take on new horses now."

She handed Lattie Kate down to Obie again, intending to go and find Johnny outside. All the way home she had thought that maybe now she and Johnny could settle things between them. She didn't feel so frightened anymore. She felt things were falling into place and surely they would with Johnny, too.

"Johnny Bellah's gone, honey," Latrice said.

Etta, already halfway across the room, stopped and slowly turned. "He's gone? Where'd he go?"

Her gaze moved rapidly from Latrice to Obie. Seeing their drawn expressions, she tensed with dread.

Latrice took a deep breath. "That I don't know. He just came up here earlier this afternoon and said he was leavin'. He had his truck packed, and that golden horse of his in the back."

"You mean he's gone for good?" Etta again looked from Latrice to Obie, who averted his eyes.

Latrice's expression was filled with pity. "That's what it seems, honey."

"Do you know where he went, Obie?" Etta asked quickly.

Obie shook his head. "He told me goodbye, but that's all."

Latrice held out an envelope. "He left you a note."

Etta slowly took the envelope, saying faintly, "It looks like one from my stationery."

"It is, honey. He asked to borrow paper and an envelope," Latrice said. She had not called Etta *honey* so many times in a row since the morning they'd been told Roy had died.

Etta read her name written upon the envelope in a careful hand. She raised her eyes to Latrice. "He couldn't wait to speak to me?"

"I guess he thought it was better like this."

Holding the envelope tightly, Etta left the room, walked through to the stairway, where she sat without thinking three steps from the bottom. Slowly she opened the envelope and took out her own watermarked stationary. She noticed a thumbprint smudge on the fine ivory linen.

It was the first time she could recall seeing Johnny's handwriting. Before she took in what he said, she noticed how perfect his hand was, and that his wording was much more proper on paper than when he spoke. Still, she clearly heard his voice.

Dear Etta,

It is time for me to go along down the road. I have stayed longer than I had intended. You are doing fine with Little Gus now, and I am confident that you can do anything you should take a mind to do with him. You might want to remember to use your legs more. I have arranged for Bennie Nightingale to come take over my training and lessons. Bennie is that young

*man with the pinto that you raced. He is of fine cal-
iber and a good horseman. It is likely he will bring
you more business, too. I greatly appreciate my time
spent at your farm and thank you and Miss Latrice
for your hospitality.*

With warm regards always, Johnny

A tear fell from Etta's cheek and blotted the Y of
Johnny's name.

Through blurred vision, she read the note over twice,
thinking she must have missed something. He had hardly
said anything at all. He hadn't said he loved her, that he
was sorry to leave her, that it killed him to leave her, but
that he just had to go because it was hard on both of them.
How could he not say any of that?

Dropping her head upon her knees, she cried profusely.

Latrice, who had slipped through the swinging door,
heard Etta's sobs. She went back into the kitchen and demanded of Obie, "Are you sure that boy didn't tell you
where he was goin'?"

"He just told me that he was goin' along. And besides,
if he had told me, I wouldn't be able to tell you, if he didn't
want me to."

Latrice didn't know what to think. She did not know if
she should be glad that Johnny Bellah had gone on, or if
she should be disappointed. With a single whack, she put
a butcher knife through a turnip.

"I suppose it's for the best," she said bitterly, "if this
is the type of man he was goin' to turn out to be, it is better
to happen now rather than later."

"Now, Miss Latrice, Johnny is a fine man. He and Miz
Etta just didn't see things quite eye to eye."

"He apparently is not strong enough for her," Latrice
said. "It takes a strong man to stick with a woman moody
and stubborn as Etta." Glancing over, she saw Obie casting
her a speculative grin.

"It takes a strong man to keep up with Latrice Wilson,

too, and I'm up to the job,'' he said, coming to put an arm around her.

"Not tonight," she said firmly. "Get any thoughts of my bed tonight out of your mind. Dealin' with Etta will wear me out."

She felt badly at the disappointed look that came over Obie's face, but not badly enough to change her mind. She was put out with men in general at that minute. She knew it was not fair, but she blamed Obie in part for not stopping Johnny Bellah from going. She also thought that he did not need to get too complacent about her affections.

The next instant Obie, holding Lattie Kate, creamy white against his dark arm, put his free arm around Latrice from behind and pulled her against him. He bent low to her ear and said, "I'm strong enough for whatever you throw at me, Miss Latrice. I ain't the one who left, and I'm never gonna stop comin' in that door."

Latrice pressed her head back against his rock-solid chest.

Then she told him to sit down and mind the baby before he dropped her and broke her neck.

That very evening, just at the time Etta and Obie were preparing to feed the horses and the light was golden over all the corrals, Bennie Nightingale pulled up in a red truck, bringing two beautiful paint horses. He jumped out with the ease of a very young man and ran to take the wheelbarrow of hay out of Etta's hands.

"I'll get it, Missus Rivers. Johnny told me feeding time was 'bout now, and I'll see to it. It'll give me a good chance to see what stock you got here."

Etta stood there a minute, and then she followed after him to tell him a little about each horse and each horse's owner. Bennie listened and eagerly threw in comments crafted to show that he knew horses. He was very proud Johnny had asked him to come take over.

"They don't come better horsemen than Johnny Bellah," he said fervently. "I'm like Johnny. I've been with horses all my life, and my father before me, too."

Etta tried to act pleased that he was there; she didn't want to dampen his enthusiasm. But she had to drag herself around. Johnny's abandonment had caused her to lose all interest in her horse operation. She felt as if she had little interest in breathing, and this so scared her that after showing Bennie Nightingale around, she rushed in and held Lattie Kate the rest of the evening. She held her most of the next couple of days, too, so much that Latrice fussed at her: "You are goin' to make that baby sore."

It seemed strange that Etta's life could be so changed and yet everything could continue along not only as normal but progressing. Bennie Nightingale proved out a charmer, as most horsemen were, and all Etta's boarders stayed. At the end of the second week after Bennie had taken over, Mrs. Winslow caught Etta at the barn and told Etta how pleased she was with him.

"Bennie has gotten my Amy interested in ridin' again," she said in her very cultured Virginia accent. "He is so encouragin', where Johnny had become a little discouragin'. Bennie really knows how to sweet-talk a woman," she added with a womanly smile.

Etta had indeed noticed how animated Mrs. Winslow had become around Bennie. The woman had taken to putting her hair in a ponytail, the same style as her daughter wore.

"Yes, and Bennie's equally good with horses," she replied dryly.

As Johnny had believed, Bennie did bring in a couple more customers he had already been working with. Very shortly, all the stalls in the barn were occupied, and several more of the small corrals employed.

Bennie mentioned that more corrals would need to be built. He could not be expected to build them, however, or make any repairs. He drove over each morning from where he lived with his parents and returned there each evening, and in between he ate and breathed horses, with no eye for anything else. Obie's private opinion was that Bennie did not know the name of any tool that was not connected with dealing with a horse.

Nathan Lee, Obie's nephew, could help with feeding horses and some less-strenuous chores, but he was too young to be expected to sling hay bales. He could manage to drive the tractor and pull the trailer, while Obie and Etta loaded the bales from the field, something Johnny had helped do during the previous two cuttings.

Leon came out one afternoon while Etta was doing this. He drove his Cadillac across the clipped alfalfa.

"Good God, Etta," he said immediately, "you don't need to be out in the field like this." His eyes fell on her bare arms sticking out from her sleeveless shirt. Etta followed his gaze and saw how tanned, sinewy, and hard her arms were.

"That's what I tell her," Obie put in. "But she don't listen to me, either."

"Where's that Bellah fella?" Leon asked.

"He's moved on," Etta answered. She was rather pleased with the way Leon seemed appalled at her arms. She had to deal with a perverse streak these days. Latrice kept telling her she had a poor attitude.

"Can't you hire someone?" Leon asked.

"Hirin' someone costs money, and it isn't always easy to get good help, either. What do you need, Leon? I presume you didn't come out here to stare at my arms."

Leon blinked and reddened. Shoving back his coat, he said, "You know that ten acres you have left between here and Obie's cottage—it borders the highway?"

"Yes?"

"Well, I think we have a buyer for two of those acres if you're not too stubborn to sell. A fella wants to build a house, and he's payin' cash."

In two days, Etta had sold the acreage. She took the money and bought the barrel racing prospect Harry Flagg had written Johnny about.

"She's beautiful," Etta said, when Harry himself delivered the mare.

"I told Johnny she'd be for you."

Etta stroked the mare's neck. "Have you seen Johnny, Harry?" She stared at the horse as she spoke, then looked over her shoulder at the big man.

He shook his head and looked regretful. "No, Etta. I haven't. I'm sorry."

Bennie took her and Little Gus to a couple of rodeos where she raced barrels, but she did not succeed in drumming up any real interest in the competition. Little Gus felt her low spirits and did not perform well. He lost the first competition and won the next only because all the other horses and riders were so poor.

Etta's true reason for attending the rodeos was her hope of running into Johnny. She asked Bennie and several others if they had seen him, but no one had.

She supposed he had returned to Texas, and she would imagine him out on the plain, chasing horses around a training pen made of rough cedar posts.

Sometimes she imagined his blue truck speeding up the drive, and Johnny jumping out and running to her and saying, "I made a mistake, and I've come back, and I want to love you for the rest of my life."

In these fantasies she would either reply, "Oh, my darling," and throw herself into his arms, or "You idiot," and slap his face, depending on her mood at the moment.

"You haven't heard from Johnny, have you, Obie?" she asked impulsively one evening, while they paused in feeding the horses. "I . . . I was just wonderin', you know. Hopin' he's okay."

Obie averted his eyes, looking uncomfortable and sad. "No, ma'am, I haven't heard. I imagine he's okay, though."

"I guess you couldn't tell me, if he told you not to." She thought that she was being a little irrational.

Obie shook his head. "I don't know about that . . . but I haven't heard from him."

There was a heaviness in his voice, as if he were as disappointed as she. She gave in to the urge and hugged him, and he awkwardly patted her back.

Feeling foolish, nevertheless Etta continued to hope each day when she checked the mail, thinking that perhaps Johnny would write. Just some little note, to say he was doing okay, and that he missed her. Something maybe to say what he had not said in his parting letter and now needed to say.

She would hurry to the mailbox, and then, when no letter came from him, trudge back up the lane, her heart dragging around until she could boost it up again.

At night she would look down from her bedroom window at the empty place where Johnny's pickup truck usually sat, or she would gaze up the lane, looking for headlights.

All of this was most wearing on her nerves, and Latrice's constant observation was not a help in the matter.

"I wish you would not watch me as if you are certain I am about to either expire or turn into a raving madwoman," Etta told her impatiently.

"I wish that Johnny Bellah had never showed up," Latrice said. "You need to just forget him."

"I imagine I should forget him . . . and I imagine I will in time," Etta said. "But I'm not sorry he came here. I wouldn't throw away all he brought us."

She pushed through the screen door and went out on the porch, looked out over the dusty corrals, where Johnny should have been.

Latrice came behind and put a tentative hand on her shoulder. "I only want you to be happy," she said. "That's all I've ever wanted."

Etta laid her paler, rougher hand over Latrice's. "I know that. I've always known that, and I count on it." They shared a grin.

"I don't know how to pray," Etta said then in a hoarse voice. "It doesn't seem right to pray for Johnny to come back. It seems like that's tryin' to order his life. But sometimes I can't help but say that."

"It's okay to tell God how you feel, honey," Latrice said. "That's what prayin's all about. I pray that boy gets the whippin' he deserves, but God knows what I mean is please take it all and make what's best for us. God knows the heart, honey."

Etta noticed Latrice's abundant use of *honey* again and was comforted.

Twenty-six 🌹

One afternoon when Etta and Bennie returned from a rodeo in Lindsey, Obie and Latrice were waiting for her on the porch. Lattie Kate had at last accepted a bottle, so Etta had been gone since early morning.

"We won," Etta told them happily.

That day she had felt more like her old self than she had in weeks. It had shown in her riding, and Little Gus had beat all other riders' time by a full two seconds. She and Bennie had discussed taking Little Gus to a big fall rodeo in Oklahoma City the next weekend.

After she put Little Gus up and waved goodbye to Bennie, Etta walked over to the porch and took Lattie Kate into her arms. She noticed then that Obie and Latrice seemed to be glaring at each other.

"What's wrong? You two look like you might be ready to shoot?"

Latrice kept her jaw clamped and looked straight ahead.

Obie rubbed his hair and said, "Miz Etta, Johnny come by this afternoon."

Etta felt as if she'd been hit in the stomach. "He did?"

"Yes, ma'am. He and I went out and had lunch and had us a real nice visit."

Latrice was still staring straight ahead and rocking heartily.

"Well, I'm glad you had a nice visit, Obie." Etta's heart was clogging her throat. "I'm sorry I missed him."

To that, Latrice said, "Huh!"

"Miz Etta, I thought you might like to know he came by and that he has a place down in Cotton County, south of Lawton. He's started a horse operation there."

"He has?"

"Yes, ma'am."

Latrice sprang out of her chair. "I'll throw the leftovers from the noon meal on the table. If you're hungry, come on, if you're comin'."

No more was said about Johnny. Indeed, the meal was very subdued. Etta gave an account of her and Little Gus's performance, and that was short in the telling, as her mind kept drifting to Johnny and the possibility before her. She did not ask anything further about him, however. She didn't see any need in getting Latrice worked up any more than she was.

Just after lunch the following morning, Etta rose from the table and asked Latrice to please watch Lattie Kate for the afternoon.

"You're goin' to go see Johnny Bellah, aren't you?" Latrice said.

"Yes."

Latrice, obviously bursting with opinion, but trying to restrain herself, said, "Are you sure? You might should pray over this some more."

"I have prayed," Etta said, as she left the room and went to shower and change into her prettiest dress.

Several times as she was getting ready, Latrice popped in to offer further cautions. "You should wait for him to come here. He came once, likely he'll come again. You're rushin' headlong."

The cautions did not deter Etta; she had made up her mind to go to him.

But seeing Latrice getting quite wrought up, Etta said,

"I am not going to abandon my home and take off with him. I am simply going to go see him."

Latrice said shortly, "I guess I might as well save my breath. I have never deterred you when it came to a man."

"No, you haven't," Etta said.

Her car sped swiftly along the blacktopped highway. The sun was bright, and even wearing sunglasses she squinted slightly. She had the vents open and the windows down slightly for the breeze. She did not want to arrive with her dress unattractively plastered to her body. Obie had given her careful directions, and she did not have any trouble finding the dirt road turnoff. From there it was a dusty mile east, another half mile south, and then she saw the rock house off to the south. She turned down the rutted drive and drove slowly until she reached the house.

She sat there a moment, her hands dropped between her spraddled legs.

The yard needed mowing, except right near the front door. She rolled down the window and smelled the scent of apples. She thought maybe Johnny would come out.

He didn't.

Likely he was out back. The thought that he might not be at home caused her already tense spirit to droop.

Getting out, she shook her dress from her sweaty legs, went up and tried the door. It opened. She stepped into an empty living room. It was immediately cooler, the windows closed and shades drawn against the sun on this side of the house. The walls needed painting, but the rock fireplace was really striking.

Curious, she went on through the house, peering into the rooms. She stopped at the door of the bedroom Johnny was obviously using. The windows were wide, letting in fresh air. The walls were newly painted, as was the iron bed. There was only the bed and a dresser in the room. Boots and two stacks of books on the floor. A cotton spread, tan, with stripes of blue and green, covered the bed.

Etta went over and sat on it, put her hand out to smooth over the spread. Then she got up and proceeded on through

the kitchen, half newly painted and with a green Formica
table and chairs, to the back door.

Through the window in the door, she saw Johnny's truck
and then Johnny out back in a corral. No shirt, his tanned
skin glistening beneath the sun, his face shielded by a wide-
brimmed hat.

She looked at him for several minutes before she opened
the door and stood there.

Johnny saw the horse he was attempting to capture prick
his ears and turn to look at the house. Johnny followed the
horse's gaze and saw a woman in the back door of his
house.

Etta.

Her hair blew around her head.

Surprised, he blinked and peered harder. Then slowly he
took his shirt off the fence post (recalling Latrice yelling
at him for the shirtless infraction) and slipped into it as he
walked toward the house.

Several feet from the back step, he stopped and looked
up at her. He had to smile. "Hello."

"Hello," she said, giving only a small smile. "I missed
you yesterday when you came by."

He wasn't certain what to say. He turned his head and
looked away in the distance, before he looked back at her.
"I'm glad you came down," he said.

Then he started up the stoop into the house, and she
backed up to allow him entrance. He tossed aside his dusty
hat and went to the sink, turned on the water and began to
wash. Etta sat at the table.

"It's very nice, this place," she said. "The house can
be lovely."

"I need more barn space, more corrals first," he said.

She didn't reply. He finished washing and turned to face
her while he dried off. Her body was more compact than
when he had last seen her, but her eyes were as blue and
beautiful as ever. He thought of kissing her, but all he could
do was stare at her while wanting grew inside him.

Then she was standing and coming toward him with a
deliberate light in her eye. "Oh, Johnny," she said just

before she wrapped her arms around his neck and brought her lips to his.

Johnny knew there was no stopping this time.

He kissed her and kissed her, moved his lips across to her ear and down her throat. She pulled away and took his hand, and he followed her into his bedroom. Jerking her into his arms, he leaned her backward and kissed her some more and ran his hands up and down her back and once over her breasts, enjoying the jump of desire into her eyes. He captured her mouth again and unbuttoned her dress at the same time, while her hands were shoving his shirt from his shoulders.

Their breaths came hot and fast. Johnny pushed her dress off her shoulders but could get it no further. She stepped away and began to remove it herself, and he hurriedly went to work stripping out of his own clothes, all the while watching as her dress fell to the floor, followed by all the rest.

The breath went out of him when he saw her naked body, and all of him that was male stood at attention.

She lay on the bed and lifted her arms to him. He went down on her feeling as if he was dying and going to heaven and singing hosannahs.

They breathed each other's names and kissed and touched and grasped. Johnny felt himself drowning in her scent and warmth and passion. She opened herself completely for him, responding to his every touch with a fire that startled him. He thought he wanted to go slower, but quickly she was whimpering and pleading and pulling at him, and he was covering her with his body.

When he slid into her, Etta lost all cohesive thought. She knew only that she had to have him, had to have all of him. She met him urgently, knowing nothing but the shimmering rise of glorious passion, and reaching the peak, she teetered there in a shaft of pure, bright beauty. Johnny buried his face in her hair and moaned deeply and quivered, and she held him, feeling him flow into her, feeling his body throb and all her heartache fade away.

*   *   *

"Oh, I'm sorry," Etta said, embarrassed to notice her breasts were leaking milk.

Johnny, his face flushed, wiped the dribble away with his finger. "I guess you're needin' to get back to Lattie Kate."

"Yes."

Etta raised up to sit on the side of the bed. Johnny came up behind her, lifted her hair and kissed her neck. A lump came in her throat.

Johnny slipped off the bed. She looked at his hard thighs, and the scar on his bad knee. "Here's your dress," he said, handing it to her.

"Thank you."

Etta hugged him after she had gotten dressed, words clogging up inside her. She kept thinking he would speak first, but he picked today to be reticent.

Johnny walked her out to her car. The sun was far to the west, and she would get home just at dark. Her breasts had begun to hurt, and no doubt Lattie Kate would be crying for her.

They stopped at the car door. Johnny bent his head and kissed her softly, dragging his lips away.

She gazed into his silvery eyes, wondering if she should tell him that she loved him. She didn't want him to feel trapped. She was frightened to bare herself.

"I love you," she said, quivering and watching his eyes.

"I love you, too."

The rush of warm light in his eyes made Etta want to cry.

"I want to marry you, Etta. I want you to be my wife."

"I want to be your wife, Johnny."

He smiled a crooked smile. "We got that to agree on then, don't we?"

She nodded, both smiling and tearing up.

He shifted and looked over her head into the distance. She looked up the dirt road.

"I got a good place here, Etta," he said. She raised her eyes to see him still gazing off into the distance. "I've never had anything of my own like this."

Then he looked down at her. She smiled softly and laid a hand on his chest.

"I understand. That's how it is for me, too."

Her gaze fell heavily to his shirt. She felt as if her life were draining away.

Johnny took hold of her cheeks, raised her face and kissed her hard and demanding. He pressed her back against the car door, kissing her again and again, as if to take her very soul.

She began to cry.

He pulled away.

"It's my home," she said, gazing at him through tears. "My husband died this year, and I've had a baby, and I've fallen in love . . . and now you want me to up and leave my home. I love you, but I can't . . . oh God . . . I . . ."

She pressed against the car to keep from throwing herself onto the ground.

Johnny gathered her into his arms. "Shush . . . it's okay. We don't have to do anything right now. It's okay. Oh, don't cry."

He held her so tightly against his own quivering body that she could hardly breathe. And then she felt her breasts tingle urgently.

"I have to go," she said, feeling herself getting panicky. She got behind the wheel, and Johnny closed the door after her.

"You okay?" he asked through the open window.

His silvery eyes were very dark and concerned. She smiled at him and nodded. It was on the tip of her tongue to ask him if he would come to see her, but she didn't want him to feel trapped.

He leaned through the window and kissed her softly, then straightened and stepped backward. He didn't ask her to return.

Etta cast him another look, and then she started the car and drove away down the rutted lane. She looked once in the rearview mirror to see him standing there gazing after her.

Thirty minutes after she had returned home, while she

sat rocking Lattie Kate, Johnny telephoned. Etta heard Latrice answer, and instantly she knew it was Johnny.

"I'll put her on," Latrice said, then listened again, said,
"Okay," and hung up.

"He just wanted to make certain you got home safe, but
he didn't want to talk. Costs a lot, you know," she said,
as if hoping to make Etta feel better.

"I know," Etta said.

Gazing down at her peaceful, and now full, sleeping
daughter, Etta remembered being in Johnny's arms and
gave thanks. She didn't want to be ungrateful for all she
had.

Etta hoped Johnny would come to her. She would have had
to admit she hoped he would chuck his ranch and come to
her. It struck her that this was a wild hope, and an equally
selfish one. She prayed for God to forgive her, and then
she prayed that Johnny would come.

She kept remembering his touch and how it had been
between them, and marveling. She would smile to herself.
In fact, she continued to have these episodes of smiling to
herself for several days.

"I'm supposin' you found it to be all you had anticipated," Latrice said dryly.

"Yes," Etta said in a dreamy fashion.

She began again going out on the porch and looking
toward the highway with yearning. *Oh God, make him
come.* She knew He understood.

"Why don't you just go in there and write him a letter?"
Latrice said. "Ask him to come. I imagine if you ask him,
he will."

Etta shook her head. "No, I can't do that. I went to him,
and now it's his turn. Besides, he loves his place, like I do
here. It wouldn't be right to ask him to give it up."

"From what you and Obie tell me, this place is a lot
better than his. It would be the practical thing to settle
here."

"How good it is has nothing to do with it," Etta said.
"Now leave it alone, please."

Once she overheard Latrice berating Obie, "Look at her. She's moonin' after him again. This would not have happened if you hadn't told her where he was. She's likely to lose her mind if he doesn't come."

Etta slumped back against the wall with the thought that Johnny might not come.

She forced herself to go out and ride Little Gus and talk to people and make plans to take Little Gus to the rodeo in Oklahoma City. She would not let herself sink as she had done before. She could not afford to do that.

She cried into her pillow, and held Lattie Kate to her breast and gazed into her daughter's face, and thought that a man did not matter. She told herself to be grateful for the one time with Johnny. She was not sorry about making love with him, and even though her love for him hurt, she did not regret it, either.

It was late at night and moths beat against the screen door. Latrice brought paper and pen to the table. She put on reading glasses she had recently bought; she hated having to wear them, which made her doubly annoyed with Johnny Bellah, since she was having to wear them to write to him.

Dear Johnny,

There is more than one way to skin a cat. If you will come up here and marry Etta, it is likely that she will in time become so attached to you that she will go with you anywhere.

I realize this is a gamble for you, but the odds are in your favor. She loves you. Should she never be willing to leave this place, you have not lost much, except a little pride. That seems a small price to pay for love and my biscuits.

She deliberated a moment as to just how to sign it, and ended with: *Yours truly, Latrice.*

The next day, she took the envelope to the mailbox at

the time the mailman came by and placed it directly into his hand.

Johnny had been checking his mailbox each day. This day as he opened it, he cautioned himself not to be disappointed in not finding a letter from Etta. He had not written her, either. He had wanted to write her, but he'd been too confused, and starting up correspondence seemed like it would make everything worse.

Yet he went to his mailbox each day with a small hope in his chest, and this day he was surprised to see the familiar envelope. He drew it out and saw the unfamiliar handwriting. Then he opened it and read Latrice's words.

Throwing back his head, he laughed.

Starting for his house, he then began to run eagerly. Halfway there, he had to stop, as his knee was giving out.

Etta was in the barn helping Nathan Lee clean stalls, and was sweaty and dirty when Johnny came.

She heard a vehicle and recognized it instantly as Johnny's truck. She set aside her pitchfork and hurried to the barn entrance, her heart beating wildly. *Of course it isn't him,* she told herself, *do not get overwrought.*

Then she saw his blue truck coming slowly. She saw he had his golden dun in the back and another horse tied to the rear. He came to a stop in his usual place in front of the barn. She gazed at him through the dirty windshield. He got out slowly, and came around the front of the truck. He was limping badly.

Noticing her see his limp, he said, "I got kicked good yesterday."

He stopped and looked at her, giving her a lopsided, hesitant grin.

Etta told herself not to jump to conclusions. She went forward slowly, stopping several feet in front of him. "Hi," she said shyly.

He opened his arms, and she went into them and thought she would just go to pieces.

He said, "I've come to stay, if you'll have me, Etta."

Letting out a sob, she threw her arms around his neck.

Johnny, feeling like he'd done a very good thing, whispered, "You ask a hell of a lot from a man . . . but I'm up to it."

"Oh, Johnny, I love you."

"I love you, too, darlin'," he said through his choked throat.

He turned her toward the house and walked with her in the curve of his arm. Just as he entered, he experienced an instant of uncertainty. Etta, ahead of him, was saying how Lattie Kate had grown. Latrice was looking expectantly at him.

He saw the chair at the table where he had normally sat the past months, and although Obie was not there, he knew the older man would come later, and that they would all sit around the table. They would talk of Lattie Kate growing, and of the weather, and of the worth of a horse and the price of alfalfa.

He looked again at Etta, who smiled at him a smile that said she was thinking of his touch, and he thought of holding her in his arms in the night. Taking a breath, he stepped inside the house, and he knew with that act he made it his home.

Epilogue

"Lattie Kate, come out from under that porch," Etta said, feeling something of a panic. There could be snakes under the porch.

"I had to get Thomas," her daughter said, coming forth with a smudged face and a big yellow tomcat. "We can't leave Thomas behind."

"Of course we won't leave Thomas, honey. Obie has a cage for him." She wiped the dirt from her daughter's chubby cheeks and picked a dead leaf from her flaxen hair.

They got the cat into a cage in the back of Obie's old black pickup truck, right alongside crates of chickens and a slatted box with a blue tick hound.

Etta helped Latrice carry out the last boxes from the kitchen. Obie took up Lattie Kate, who wanted to ride with him in the old truck.

"I'm ridin' where I can spread out some," Latrice said and got into the passenger seat of Etta's new Impala. Etta called it the car that Little Gus bought, as she had purchased it largely from his barrel racing winnings.

"You forgot to shut the door," Latrice told Etta.

Etta hurried back to the house and across the porch.

When she took hold of the knob on the kitchen door, she paused and gazed into the now empty room.

Her heart seemed to pause, and she heard echoes of voices. Latrice's voice singing hymns along with the radio, Roy hollering out that he was home, Obie asking after Latrice, Johnny asking for Pine-Sol that first day he moved here, and Lattie Kate crying to be fed.

She blinked, and the kitchen was empty again. Etta shut the door firmly.

"We're off," she said, plopping herself into the seat behind the wheel. "Anything that's forgotten, the new owners can have."

Shifting into gear, she headed away down the drive, passing beneath the tall elms for the last time. Obie followed behind. When she turned onto the highway, Etta gave the land and house a wave out the window, then pressed the gas pedal and never looked in the rearview mirror. She was already eagerly thinking of Johnny waiting for them.

Etta spied him as soon as she pulled beneath the sign: Bellah Quarter Horses. He came down the steps of the front porch of the frame house he had bought years before.

Now the house was bigger, boasting not only the front porch, but a side one as well, and two more bedrooms. Johnny was planning ahead, hoping for a new baby. On the other side of the orchard was a small cottage; this was for Latrice and Obie, their own place at last, without a kitchen, because Latrice said the one at the main house was enough for her. She did not care to have to clean two kitchens.

Before Etta got out of the car, Lattie Kate was running toward Johnny with her arms outstretched. "Daddy . . . Daddy, we're here!" Etta watched him pick her up and hug her tight.

"Well, here we are at a new home," Latrice said.

Etta looked over at her. "Yes, here we are."

They grinned knowingly at each other.

Then Etta got out of the car and walked to meet Johnny. "I was gettin' a little worried," he said.

"A lot more last-minute things than we'd thought," Etta

said, and he looked around to check out the backseat of the Impala.

"We didn't forget Thomas or Blue," Lattie Kate told him. She had her arms tight around his neck. "They're part of the family, too."

"Yes, they are, darlin'."

Latrice right away put together a meal, and they all sat around the table to eat and talk about the day and ones to come. Afterward, Obie Lee read Lattie Kate a story, and Etta and Latrice cleaned the kitchen, arguing over where to put things, while Johnny checked on the stock. Then Latrice and Obie went to their cottage, Lattie Kate slept instantly in her new room, and Etta waited for Johnny in their bedroom. She had bought a new gown for the occasion.

"We have to move the bed over to there," Etta told him, when he came.

"You move that bed anywhere you want," Johnny said.

Then he came over, drew her up to him, and kissed her thoroughly, until she could hardly stand. She wrapped her arms around him, and pressed her cheek into his shoulder.

"You aren't sorry for movin' down here . . . leavin' the other place?" Johnny said, and she felt him tense.

Drawing back, she looked into his eyes. "I have all I want right here. I know exactly the horse I'm ridin', and it's a sure winner.

"I love you, Johnny Bellah, with all my heart." Then she kissed him.

Author's Note

While I am the one putting forth the endless hours in the chair, I could not get any book written alone. My everlasting gratitude goes to the following people who generously gave me their time, their knowledge, and their encouragement:

Carrie Feron, my editor, who provides valuable guidance and suggestions, and continued faith in my work.

Gordy Whitman, horseman and storyteller, who has fascinated me with tales of horses and Western life for as long as I have known him; and to Rick Ketcherside, for his experiences with horses and bush tracks in Oklahoma, as well as for always lending a neighborly helping hand.

Melva and John Gorham, for their recollections of life in Grady and Caddo counties; and Machelle Courtney, who shares with me her women's perspective of farming, and who manages to urge me out of the house for horseback riding when I most need it. Champion barrel racer Carol Goosetree was kind in relating much about the sport of barrel racing and her love of horses.

I am indebted to Christina Owen of the Anadarko Library for the information about the rodeo grounds, and to the Oklahoma Historical Society, a truly magical place where I lost myself in perusing back copies of newspapers of towns throughout the state. From the National Cowgirl Hall of Fame I received much inspiration for this book and others to follow.

My appreciation to the people at Computer Plus, who are very patient when I telephone, wailing that I have once more confused my machine.

I am grateful to my mother, who reminds me of Southern traditions too precious to let pass—such as the term Co-Cola. And to my dear friends who boost me when I get tired and discouraged that my talent is not all I wish—Dixie Browning, Karen Coughlan, Mary Doyle.

My husband's contribution was to drive me all over the dusty backroads, to be at my side when I accosted strangers, very often men who uneasily suspected me of being some sort of investigator for the racing commission, with questions. My son helped by making me laugh at the right times, and by checking the oil in my truck.

I am grateful to God for putting me down in Oklahoma, a truly grand place with very special people. And thank God I'm a country girl.

Cogar, Oklahoma

Dear Reader,

If you haven't yet become a fan of the incomparable
Loretta Chase, then April's THE LAST HELLION will
introduce you to one of the brightest stars in historical
romance. And for those of you who already love Loretta, I
know this is the story you've all been waiting for. There's
all the witty banter and sizzling sensuality you've come to
expect from Loretta, and in THE LAST HELLION there's
also an unforgettable hero — Regency rake Vere Mallory —
who meets his match in the impertinent Lydia Grenville.
Don't miss this wonderful Avon Romantic Treasure!

Also Coming in April from Avon Romance, THE PIRATE
LORD by Sabrina Jeffries — a deliciously fun romp about a
group of pirates who decide to give up their lawless ways,
settle down and get married! So they kidnap a shipload of
women, who aren't about to give in easily. This is romantic
fantasy at its very best.

And don't miss Linda Needham's latest HER SECRET
GUARDIAN. Linda, author of EVER HIS BRIDE, has
penned a romance brimming with passion. To honor a
deathbed request a young woman agrees to marry against
her will, little knowing she has just consented to wed her
secret guardian.

April's contemporary romance, IF I CAN'T HAVE YOU,
is the latest sparkling love story from Patti Berg. Patti's
funny, sexy stories have a touch of magic and characters
who are utterly irresistible. Here, a seductive hunk of the
silver screen is transported through time to the 1990s,
where he encounters a very attractive, very adoring fan!
Can their love withstand the test of time?

Don't miss any of these sensuous, scintillating love stories
from Avon Books!

Lucia Macro

Lucia Macro
Senior Editor

AEL 0398

Avon Romances—
the best in exceptional authors and unforgettable novels!

SCARLET LADY   **by Marlene Suson**
78912-4/ $5.99 US/ $7.99 Can

TOUGH TALK AND   **by Deborah Camp**
TENDER KISSES
78250-2/ $5.99 US/ $7.99 Can

WILD IRISH SKIES   **by Nancy Richards-Akers**
78948-5/ $5.99 US/ $7.99 Can

THE MACKENZIES: CLEVE **by Ana Leigh**
78099-2/ $5.99 US/ $7.99 Can

EVER HIS BRIDE   **by Linda Needham**
78756-0/ $5.99 US/ $7.99 Can

DESTINY'S WARRIOR   **by Kit Dee**
79205-2/ $5.99 US/ $7.99 Can

GRAY HAWK'S LADY   **by Karen Kay**
78997-3/ $5.99 US/ $7.99 Can

DECEIVE ME NOT   **by Eve Byron**
79310-5/ $5.99 US/ $7.99 Can

TOPAZ   **by Beverly Jenkins**
78660-5/ $5.99 US/ $7.99 Can

STOLEN KISSES   **by Suzanne Enoch**
78813-6/ $5.99 US/ $7.99 Can

Avon Romantic Treasures

Unforgettable, enthralling love stories,
sparkling with passion and adventure
from Romance's bestselling authors

EVERYTHING AND THE MOON *by Julia Quinn*
78933-7/$5.99 US/$7.99 Can

BEAST *by Judith Ivory*
78644-3/$5.99 US/$7.99 Can

HIS FORBIDDEN TOUCH *by Shelley Thacker*
78120-4/$5.99 US/$7.99 Can

LYON'S GIFT *by Tanya Anne Crosby*
78571-4/$5.99 US/$7.99 Can

FLY WITH THE EAGLE *by Kathleen Harrington*
77836-X/$5.99 US/$7.99 Can

FALLING IN LOVE AGAIN *by Cathy Maxwell*
78718-0/$5.99 US/$7.99 Can

THE COURTSHIP OF
CADE KOLBY *by Lori Copeland*
79156-0/$5.99 US/$7.99 Can

TO LOVE A STRANGER *by Connie Mason*
79340-7/$5.99 US/$7.99 Can

Discover Contemporary Romances
at Their Sizzling Hot Best
from Avon Books

TILL THE END OF TIME *by Patti Berg*
78339-8/$5.99 US/$7.99 Can

FLY WITH THE EAGLE *by Kathleen Harrington*
77836-X/$5.99 US/$7.99 Can

WHEN NICK RETURNS *by Dee Holmes*
79161-7/$5.99 US/$7.99 Can

HEAVEN LOVES A HERO *by Nikki Holiday*
78798-9/$5.99 US/$7.99 Can

ANNIE'S HERO *by Maggie Shayne*
78747-4/$5.99 US/$7.99 Can

TWICE UPON A TIME *by Emilie Richards*
78364-9/$5.99 US/$7.99 Can

**WHEN LIGHTNING
STRIKES TWICE** *by Barbara Boswell*
72744-7/$5.99 US/$7.99 Can

America Loves Lindsey!

The Timeless Romances of #1 Bestselling Author

KEEPER OF THE HEART	77493-3/$6.99 US/$8.99 Can
THE MAGIC OF YOU	75629-3/$6.99 US/$8.99 Can
ANGEL	75628-5/$6.99 US/$8.99 Can
PRISONER OF MY DESIRE	75627-7/$6.99 US/$8.99 Can
ONCE A PRINCESS	75625-0/$6.99 US/$8.99 Can
WARRIOR'S WOMAN	75301-4/$6.99 US/$8.99 Can
MAN OF MY DREAMS	75626-9/$6.99 US/$8.99 Can
SURRENDER MY LOVE	76256-0/$6.50 US/$7.50 Can
YOU BELONG TO ME	76258-7/$6.99 US/$8.99 Can
UNTIL FOREVER	76259-5/$6.50 US/$8.50 Can
LOVE ME FOREVER	72570-3/$6.99 US/$8.99 Can
SAY YOU LOVE ME	72571-1/$6.99 US/$8.99 Can

Coming Soon in Hardcover
ALL I NEED IS YOU